SWAN BOATS AT FOUR

SWAN BOATS AT FOUR

A NOVEL

GEORGE V. HIGGINS

A JOHN MACRAE BOOK

HENRY HOLT AND COMPANY
NEW YORK

Henry Holt and Company, Inc.
Publishers since 1866
115 West 18th Street
New York, New York 10011

Henry Holt® is a registered trademark of Henry Holt and
Company, Inc.

Library of Congress Cataloging-in-Publication Data

Higgins, George V.
    Swan boats at four: a novel / George V. Higgins—1st ed.
        p.   cm.
    "A John Macrae book."
    I. Title.
    PS3558.I356S93   1995
    813'.54—dc20   94-40985
                                    CIP

ISBN 0-8050-3077-8

Henry Holt books are available for special
promotions and premiums. For details contact:
Director, Special Markets.

First Edition—1995

Designed by Helene Wald Berinsky

Printed in the United States of America
All first editions are printed on acid-free paper.∞

10 9 8 7 6 5 4 3 2 1

SWAN BOATS
AT FOUR

David Carroll's hour-nap before the directors' meeting on the wet gray evening of the third Thursday in March had lasted almost ninety minutes. Frances, knowing he needed it, had not awakened him. As he went out the door, half a hastily assembled roast beef sandwich in his right hand and his trench coat over his left arm, he promised he'd explain the entire situation to her when he got back that night. But the directors, feeling cornered as he did, wrangled late about strategies that would not work, and by the time that he returned she had been in bed for over an hour, and was sound asleep. He had told her the next night.

"It's very simple, Fran," he said in the long blue early evening gentling the cocktail hour in mid-springtime in the sunporch of the house on Pilot Hill. "It's what I've tried to tell you about so many times before. The long and the short of it is that this guy's out to get me, and also take down along with me all the businessmen and homeowners we've got that he can lay his hands on. And *his* boss wants to help him do it. And his *boss's* boss's egging him on—they've *all* got their tails in the same crack. After what happened in the Southwest when Charlie Keating, then the Texans, went to Washington and leased themselves some senators to scuttle audits for them. Treasury got blown out, may be a hundred forty billion. And they got blamed for it. They're a posse now. They've got blood in their eyes. So as a result they're taking it out on people like us, poor bastards we are. We're trophy-heads for them, to prove to the whole world that the FDIC *is* on the *job*. Hurrah, hurrah; we can all sleep better tonight. Unless you happen to be one of the human sacrifices they've selected. Unless yours's one of the fresh scalps they plan to take, show around and demonstrate they've finally shaped up.

"The problem is that *my* bank, and *my* customers, and I, we've all been selected for these unsolicited honors they're conferring. So the net result is that this little toad Gary Bettancourt and his boss're gonna be the best thing that's ever happened to the local economy since the Blizzard of Seventy-eight and Hurricane Bob put together. A pair-oared human disaster."

He swirled his vodka martini so that the ice chimed in the double-old-fashioned glass, and took a good measure of it. "I know how these people work, keep in mind, and if I hadn't known myself what this bastard's got in mind, before Rocky Veltri called this afternoon, 'd seen them plotting my demise over lunch at The Falls, well, damned straight I sure would now."

"Father Veltri was sure who they were?" she said.

"His favorite waitress told him," he said. "Jeanette, I guess it is?"

"Oh yeah," she said, "she's the tiny one. I know her. I almost always seem to get one of her tables, and I always sort of wish I dared to ask for someone else. She makes me feel, I don't know, *uneasy.* Acts like a puppy that had to go so bad she couldn't help herself, made another mistake on her cruel mistress's best oriental . . . and her mean mistress is me. Now she knows as soon's I catch her, I'm gonna roll up the morning newspaper and hit her with it again. When she comes to your table, she cowers, almost. She cringes. And I've never snapped at her once."

"Yeah, I guess that's the one," he said. "She said the white guy that came in first was somebody name of Bettancourt, because after he'd been there awhile, obviously waiting for somebody else to come, there was a phone-page for him that he evidently missed, but she heard it and that's how she got his name. And then when they'd finished eating—lobster salads, naturally, three Heinekens apiece; can't have our hardworking federal employees feeling faint out in the field for lack of solid nourishment—the black guy used his Master-Card. It was made out to Clyde Ramsey, and that's how he signed his name. She told Rocky what their names were, so that's how he knew. That's why he was sure."

"You know this boss, then, do you?" she said. "From before, I mean?"

"Well, I never actually met him when I was at Treasury, no," he said. "Don't believe I ever saw the guy, in fact; he was *with* the FDIC, but out in the Denver office, and just on his way up, back then. But he'd already gained a certain fame—an eminence, you know? Not quite a legend in his own time, but if you moved in any banking circles, or you were in regulation, well, it was pretty hard to do it very long without hearing about him. There were quite a lot of people who really resented him, and since they get around—promotions, job-transfers, conventions and so forth—what they had to say tended to get around too. He became sort of a universal symbol, inside that part of government, at least, of precisely what you hope will never, *never* happen, when you do exactly what the statutes and the court decisions tell you's what you'd *better do*, chum, when minorities apply for jobs or promotions're at stake.

"So, yeah, I know who Clyde Ramsey is, and how he made his mark and got to run the Boston office. At least, that is, how most white guys that I've had any contact with, how *they* think he's gotten so far on so little gas. And I mean to tell you, there's a real consensus on this—how it is that Clyde Ramsey'd climbed so far, so fast, in this fairly demanding life.

" 'He *looks* good, and he looks good in what today's become by far the very best way that a man in management *could* look good, if he wanted a sure shot to succeed—that's how he does it. He's made it big in this life the same way that some eighteen-year-old, dimwitted-but-shrewd agile bimbo with no singing voice at all but a nice little body and no shame at all, either, becomes an international celebrity and makes ten million bucks a year in TV and rock and roll. Instead of getting picked up and arrested, either chucked into jail or checked into an asylum, as anyone else'd be if *they* showed up in public with no real clothes on at all, grabbing at their crotch.

" 'Clyde played football for Syracuse. He was a running back either just before or just after the Jimmy Brown–Ernie Davis era. And after he got drafted, he played for an Army team, the Berlin Bears, someone said. He wasn't in the Brown-Davis league, no, not good enough for the pros. Didn't have enough moves. Maybe wasn't mean enough. But he must've *looked* the part, I guess, because by God, he does today. He *looks* like a million bucks, even with his clothes still on. If you stood Harry Belafonte up next to Clyde and asked the ladies what they think, they would say that Harry is the one who should have the plastic surgery—and maybe then he might look almost as good as Clyde looks now, without the operation. And also, to go with that, Clyde is a real charmer. Clyde is dazzling, in fact. By the time he gets through with you, his first visit to your ranch, there's not a bird in the tree, a dog on the meat-wagon or a dry eye in the house.

" 'It's not until you get to know him, expect him to do his job, that you find out what's inside that great big handsome head: next to nothin', that's what—that's what's in this statesman's head. The only thing that gorgeous Clyde knows—and someone has to've clued him in on it, too; he's never been bright enough to figure it out on his own—is that when he gets a job, or he gets promoted to a better one, the first thing and the last thing that he has to do is: as little as he can. The same thing, in fact, that's in his big lion's head, which of course is next to nothin', and plenty of it, too.

" 'All he has to do, and therefore all he's ever done, is make nice to the underlings, give them everything they want before they even know they want it, and then pat them on the back and hope to God that they're smart, smart enough to do their jobs. Not just smarter than he is; that's not enough; I know five dogs, can make that claim and back it up, real easy, too—but they could not audit banks. No, Clyde's people have to be smart enough to do their jobs, not only without any *interference* from him, but also without any *aid* from him. And as long as he doesn't try to interfere with them—and believe me, he never does; he must wear out a hundred rubber stamps in the average year—if they can meet that standard of relaxed mediocrity, then Clyde will be okay. And so far, I guess, they have. If anybody's fallen short, they got away with it.

" 'Clyde's sort of like the stupid skunk in the old fable, see? The fox is very smart, children, and knows a lot of things, but the fox can still get caught and killed if the dogs can run him down. The skunk is very stupid and he only knows one thing, but as any dog who's caught one found out, when he chased him down real quick, that skunk ain't gonna die: What the skunk knows is *important.* Clyde's like the skunk. The only thing he knows is that no one dares to touch him, because he can raise a stink, scream "racist bastards" on TV and slap a lawsuit on them. They are scared to *death* of that. So therefore unless they're forced to interfere with him, they leave him strictly alone. And once he made it clear to them, a long time ago, that if they'd just promote him, he'd never make a wave, well, they acted just like hostages. Which of course is what they are, you come right down to it: they are hostages to Clyde: they began to love their captor. As long as they've got Clyde out front, and they meet Clyde's price, they don't need to get another one, maybe some bomb-throwin' troublemaker who'd give them a real hard time, Mau-Mau them to death. So they massage the guy. Just like Clyde knew they would. Clyde may not know very much, but what he knows is important too.' "

She frowned. "Well then, how could this have all happened, that he got the Boston job? If everybody knew all this, years and years ago—it wasn't some kind of secret or something—then why'd they bring him back here from out West and make him the boss here? Couldn't someone've put a stop to it?"

"How?" he said. "Guy was just as black when he put his bid in for the opening as he'd been when he'd joined up, only now he had about twenty years of seniority to boot. On paper he was the dream nominee, man with two decades of federal experience in bank examining, steady record of promotions; you could've read a newspaper in the glow of his annual performance reports. 'Jeez, how the hell can you beat *that?*' Of course all the papers'd been filled out either by the people that he worked for, scared to disparage him, or people *they* worked for, who knew the same thing his direct supervisors knew, not that they liked it any better—so what was in those great reports was nothing more than all their old recycled crap.

"But so what? They weren't about to disown it, contradict themselves now, after all of these years, and admit that they'd caved in to quotas with him, put up that long with incompetence. No, the stuff is pure crap, but it's *there;* it exists. It's like a traffic island that serves no purpose whatsoever, and anyone can see it. So what? They've still gotta go around it, or tear the oil pans off the undercarriage of their cars. Clyde's *reality.* He's *there.* How does Washington turn him down? He's eminently qualified—I doubt any other person, white, black, striped or pinto; male or female, undecided; disabled or discouraged—applying at the same time, could've matched his résumé. The boss man at FDIC would've found out at firsthand what a really rotten time Jesus Christ had on Good Friday, if he'd turned Clyde Ramsey down. He would've had at least ten reverends, and a hundred 'activists,' standing on the sidewalk outside of Treasury at three in the afternoon, singing hymns and rousing rabbles, out to crucify him that same night, on national TV.

" 'A man with his experience, the kind of splendid applicant we very seldom see, our State salaries are so low, and he didn't get the job? This decision is outrageous. How can this ever be explained, if not by blatant racism? This is a modern lynching we've got here. Heat the tar and pluck the chickens; rip the top rail off the fence: Tonight the commissioner is going for a *ride.* One way, and out of town.' And the commissioner knows this will happen, of course—he isn't a real stupid man. Doesn't need to see it take place. Therefore Ramsey gets the plum job he wants.

"Now," David said, "there's communication between the regional offices. They *do* all have telephones, you know. So when Ramsey got to his new posting, his new people here were ready and waiting. They knew just what to expect, how this guy'd operate, because the Denver folks'd told them: 'Just another pretty face. He'll never fear his bosses, but he'll be afraid of *you.*' And it turned out to be . . . *true,* as Dickie the weatherboy says.

"Once they confirmed that for themselves," he said, "his new subordinates became extremely arrogant. Now when they're out dealing with the world, it's always your turn to curtsey, never their turn to bow. Because you can't complain. Who're you going to bitch to? You go over Clyde's head, the commissioner'll buck-slip Clyde's boss to look into it and see if your beef's justified. He'll nod and say 'Yessir' and so forth, and then do absolutely nothing of the sort, because he will know what is needed: just pretend he did look into it, nothing more than that, and then tell the commissioner there's no basis for your gripe.

"So, you might as well've bitched directly to Clyde. Are you gonna do that? Bitch to Clyde? Got to if you're gonna holler—he's the only choice you've got; those overbearing little squirts all report to him. He'll agree with every word you say. And then he will do nothing. Because *he's* afraid of *them.* So, go ahead, pull out all the stops, say anything you want, to any one of Clyde's people who gets on your nerves. You'll be lucky if he doesn't laugh in your face. Clyde's afraid of *him.* Clyde is *their* hostage. They can do what *they* want; Clyde's not gonna say a word.

"This guy Gary Bettancourt, all right? He knows what he's got: raw power, in his hands. And he knows what he can do with it: *any*thing he likes. Because his boss is stupid, and afraid to disapprove. Ramsey's got *his* bosses over the Civil Rights Act barrel? Well, turnabout's fair-play all around. The people who work under him have got *him* over their sawhorses. His whole life is in their hands. They're like the rover-backs on his old football defensive units. They can go anywhere they want, and then do whatever suits them when they get there. Completely independent contractors: that is what they are. Whoever thought the life of a humble bank examiner would be so glamorous? Oughta have a business card with a chess piece knight printed on it: 'Modem Bettancourt, Boston. This laptop for hire.'

"He sits there across the desk from me and it's all over his face; you can see it in his eyes. Here he is, a little clerk, but with a hangman's warrant that's made out in blank to 'Bearer.' The guy at the dinner party, with the bad haircut and the suit that doesn't fit. One who always looks at you and shakes his head in sorrow, the week after you finally got the Rolls-Royce Corniche of your dreams—a quarter-million bucks, whatever the damned thing costs—and says: 'Jeez, I wished you would've told me you wanted one of those. They can't *give* those pigs away. They're *desperate* for buyers. The only Rolls that's sellin' these days is the Bentley Continental. Know the one I mean? The two-door coupe there's the only one that's sellin' anything. The Corniche? Heck, *it* isn't movin' at all. Wished you'd called me up. I know a guy who put you in one, easy, eighty thousand dollars less, on that pieceah junk, 'thout breakin' a sweat. Shouldah given me a call.'

"In other words: the kind of guy you'd like to kill. He's sort of like a bounty hunter, 'cept he doesn't need a commission: just strings up anyone he picks and collects a bonus for it. I'm his current choice. He sits across from me, at forty, fifty grand a year, about ten years older'n I was when I first made deputy, quite a long time ago, and I am what he sees now, not much older'n he is, making six times or so, most likely, what *he* makes, plus profit sharing and stock options on top of that. And then when I retire, a pension that'll be at least four times what he can hope for.

"Naturally he hates my guts. I *did* all that to him. He looks at me, thinks to himself: 'You shouldn't've done that to me, you dirty rotten bastard. You've done better'n I have? I'm gonna fix your ass for that. See how you like it when I'm through, if you're such hot shit then.' I'm what he envies—'So why him, not me?' But he can't admit that to himself, so what he calls it, 'stead of that, is 'strict enforcement of the law.' "

"That isn't fair," she said. "He made his own choice, didn't he? No one made him do it. If he'd wanted to take chances, he could've been a banker, done what you did, after all—given up a lifetime job with the government, traded our security for the chance to make it big. So what if it turned out well? So what if we were lucky? What should that be to him? Would he've felt sorry for us, if the gamble went sour, if you'd lost your bet? Quit that nice job you had with Treasury and then lost your shirt and pants? Somehow I doubt it. So where does he come off here, then, resenting you because you bet a long shot and you won?"

"Fairness's got nothing to do with it," David said. "It'd be a contradiction in terms if it did. He's a government employee. That concept's not in his job description." He closed his eyes and rubbed the lids with his middle fingers. When he reopened them, he said:

"Ahhh, pollen's already bad this year. And it's not even really spring yet, except on the calendar."

"Eight on a scale of ten," she said absently, setting the table for two. "So the weatherman said last night, anyway, it was going to be today. It's the trees right now, I guess. Then the grass pollen comes in, but later."

He raised the vodka martini to his mouth and took a pull. He shook his head. "You can see it," he said wonderingly. "He comes into my office—what he does is barge right in, completely unannounced, hoping, I suppose, to catch me frantically at work on my clandestine set of books—with silly question after question: 'Sorry to bother you again, Dave, but can you clear this up for me?' I'm 'Dave' when he doesn't understand something, but still thinks it might be bank fraud, and wants to lull me into confessing. But when we're being formal—which means: when *he* is—then he's stern, and I'm 'Mister Carroll.' When he's got one of those pop-in questions. It's always something perfectly innocent, or at least I think it is, and I tell him what we did, and what our reasons were. Perfectly good reasons, too, any businessman would understand. But therefore quite beyond Mister Bettancourt's ability to grasp, because he's never *been* a businessman; he's been on the government tit his whole goddamned life.

"Imaginary conversation that I've had with him a hundred times: 'Ever meet a payroll, Gary?' 'Absolutely not—all my life I've *been* on one, the payroll that was *being* met.'"

"It's not going to help to get yourself all riled up, you know," she said practically.

"Oh, nuts," he said, "of course I know. But I just can't stand knowing someone's getting set to screw me, absolutely destroy me, for no good reason whatsoever. Especially when I can *see* it coming, watch him getting ready to do it, and there's not a thing in this whole world that I can do to stop him. I hate it, that's all: I just *hate* it.

" 'This Goodall loan,' he said today. 'You renegotiated the terms of his line of credit. You recommended raising his limit, first from half a million to three-quarters of a million, and then, not too long after that, from three-quarters to a million. And the underwriting people, the security committee, and then the executive board approved. I'm assume that they didn't do this *ex post facto*, of course, just ratify what you had done, after you had done it? They had full disclosure, did they? In advance I assume? Agreed with your decision? *Before* you acted on it?'

" 'Well for Christ sake,' I said, 'of course they approved.' I said to him: 'Look. Ted Goodall does a lot of business with the State from time to time, State Public Works Department. Towns and counties, too. Until recently it's never been what you'd call a major item on his balance sheet. Just something he'd take on now and then, keep his shop-people busy during a slow retail season.

" 'Well, as you may also know'—little light sarcasm there, totally lost on him, went right over his fool head—'the last few years've been one slow season after another. The construction industry's been way down, and the building contractors, heavy and light construction, both, historically've been some of his best and most regular customers, new and secondhand sales and service both. He's the biggest Ford truck dealer in this part of the world. Almost sixty people working for him.

" 'Good many of 'em're skilled mechanics, and those guys're hard to find. They're his bread and butter, really—any fool can sell a truck, and any fool can buy one, but not any fool can fix one, or keep it running right. So if the fool who sells the truck doesn't have a good smart mechanic in his shop who can fix it when it breaks, hold the downtime to a minimum—or even better, service it well enough that it doesn't break at all—pretty soon the fool who bought it goes to see *another* dealer, who has *got* a good mechanic, and then when that old truck wears out, buys his next new truck from him.

" 'So Ted's people are his secret weapon, in a very competitive market, and he wants to keep them that way, working for him. *On* his payroll, working, not laid off and maybe wandering off to other jobs with owners who've got slightly deeper pockets and can ride this damned thing out, jobs that when Ted wants them back, they won't want to leave. So, only natural that he'd bid on State fleet replacements, maintenance, so on and so forth, with the private sector down the way it's been. Keep the place in operation while he waits for better days to come.

" 'Two summers ago, State decided it'd be cheaper in the long run if they had Ted's people overhaul the snowplows and the mounting-gear and so forth, 'n it would be if they wasted everybody's time trying to get all the work done at the State garage. Part of this privatizing program the unions hate so much. But the State garage was already swamped, and I guess its work isn't much good anyway, at least so everyone says. So they gave Ted a contract, nothing going to make him rich, but a substantial job that he was damned glad to have—saved him having to lay off about twenty people, which he didn't really want to do. They'd been with him a long time, which meant of course that they weren't young—they'd've had trouble, finding other work to do. New permanent jobs can be hard to get, when you're only eight or ten years away from collecting a pension.

" 'The trouble was that after he'd done the job, completed it on time, the State as usual saw no reason to meet *its* obligations, in a timely fashion. Instead of paying up within thirty days, or even sixty, like his private customers do, they stalled him and stalled him and stalled him. So, well, what could he do? His payroll didn't take a breather while he waited for the State. His people had their obligations, obligations of their own, food to buy and rent to pay, mortgages they n had to meet, and of course had to pay their taxes too, mustn't leave that out. Just because the State takes its own sweet time paying you, that doesn't mean you can take *your* own sweet time, paying what you owe the State. Uh-uh, nothing doing—can't have that shit going on.

" 'So Ted came to me the first time and asked me whether it'd be all right if he used some of his line of credit to meet his payroll, instead of reserving it strictly for new inventory, outlined the situation in detail, and I on my own motion said that it would be okay, and go ahead and do it.'

" 'Ahh,' Bettancourt says to me, like I've just confessed to being Jack the Ripper, 'so then the board did *not* approve the first increase in advance. *You* decided, on your own, without *notice* to the board, and it was only *afterwards* you got around to telling them. *Then* they said: "What's done is done," and ratified your action—not that they had much choice, since what was done *was* done. But that's exactly what I was asking you: if you'd told them first. And you inferred you did.'

" 'Look,' I said, 'I didn't imply *any*thing. You're the one, did the inferring. I said the board approved both times, when Ted Goodall asked me to *increase* his credit limit. I was trying to give you some background to the situation he was in, long *before* he came around and asked me for the first increase. To help you understand a little better what it was that prompted me, and then the board, to give him those increases later: we knew the fix that he was in, and because he'd told us, that made him a better risk. *But:* Using the old limit to meet payroll instead of buying trucks—that was not an *increase*. That was just Ted being candid with me. With us. What he was doing with the dough, *before* he went and did it. And it *wasn't* unsecured. The trucks he hadn't sold: they were still in his possession. The collateral was still there, and its book value *exceeded* the limit of his credit line. That was a performing loan, regardless of what he was spending the money on. So, *that* time I said yes on my own. I told the executive committee the next time we got together. They had no objection to it at all, what I'd done, allowing Ted to use part of a secured line for payroll, under the circumstances. It made good sense to them. And at the next meeting of the full board of directors, we told them, *on the record*, what it was that we'd done—*pending their approval,* 'cause it was still revocable; we hadn't actually loaned out any more money— and they unanimously voted, *unanimously voted,* to endorse the move. And that is in the minutes of that meeting, as you would know, you'd looked at them.'

" 'Yes, but that *next* meeting, Mister Carroll,' he said, like a bossy first-grade teacher, 'the first time you *raised* the limit, was held almost a month after you did it. And not for a minor sum, either. A quarter-million dollars in a bank the size of this one to a company that size in that condition: that's a very big decision—or ought to be, at least. And then, not two years later, his position'd gotten worse, and you, instead of shutting him off, calling his outstanding loans— as most prudent people I know, at least, almost certainly would have done—you did just the opposite, took the risk, sent good money after bad: *you* did it *again.*'

" 'Well,' I said, 'you've got to remember that by then things'd started getting really sour in the economy around here, and as you know it wasn't until fairly recently that it even started to improve. So yeah, I think it was about a year, maybe year and a half later, Ted came to me again and said he really hated asking me, knowing how tough it was for everyone in business and we must need all the loan capital we could lay our hands on to bail out other people in the same fix he was in. But the State still hadn't paid him all it owed him—they were disputing some charge, purely to delay some more— and he wondered if he possibly could get us to agree to raise his limit, all the higher margin to be unsecured.

" 'Well, that one I didn't feel like I should tackle on my own, so I said: "Ted, you just sit tight, give me a day or two, and I'll confer with my committee and get their thinking on this." And then I called an emergency meeting of the executive committee, and they agreed with me, that we should do it. Ted's never been so much as seven days late in meeting his payments, even though his cash flow's been so low for all this time. He's always made the minimum, and if it meant dipping into his own capital, well, that was what he did. Deeper'n he probably really should've, from the point of view of safety, best interests of his family're concerned, or ever would've gone, as far as goes, if he'd've had a choice, and we thought that, since he'd done that, well, we saw that as another mark in his favor.

" 'So we had a telephone conference meeting of the full board. It was on pretty short notice; people away on business and so forth; nothing you can do about that. But we had all our ducks in a row on the phone, and that's always worked in the past. Well, I guess Sam Fairwood'd had to go out of town, one of his Masonic investitures or something that it seems like he's always going off to, and when we placed the call we couldn't find him, but since he'd already voted in favor on the executive committee, I counted him as an aye, and all in all I guess the count was ten in favor, two opposed, and three just voting "present." Not wanting to seem like they were saying that they didn't think Ted'd be good for the higher limit, if he had to use it, but at the same time not wanting it to be on the record that they'd voted to up *his* ceiling. So that then later on, if they felt they had to turn down somebody else who might want the same sort of thing but they didn't think oughta have it, that customer might say to them: "Well then, okay, I see your point. But then how come Ted Goodall got it?" And they'd be able to say then: "Well, I wasn't in favor of that. But the others outvoted me." So that was the way it happened. What it was.' And I told Bettancourt that, that's what I told the guy.

"Now you look at that proposition," he said to her, "and I would think if you're a moderately rational person, some experience in the banking business, and Ted Goodall was your customer, you would say: 'Well now, this is good. This is a thing that's good for Ted, and good for his employees, all of whom pay taxes too, and a good many of whom do their banking business with us, and they'll keep on doing those things if they're not thrown on unemployment with no work for them to do. And a good thing for the bank, too, since Ted's been a reliable, steady customer of ours for a good many years now. Got a million-dollar line of credit for his floor-plan financing, cars and trucks that he displays in his showroom and he uses for his demonstrators. Good business for Ted that way, pay our rates and not Fomoco's, 'til he sells the damned things, and good business for the bank as well: Ted's been renting money from us since John Moses started the bank up, and in bad times just as much as in the good, Ted's loans've always been current. He's always paid off the dollar on the dollar that he owed. That's a performing loan.

" 'That's the message that we want to send out to the community about our bank: that we *value* our good customers, and when they've gone the extra mile with us, over the course of several years, well, when the shoe's on the other foot, we'll go the extra mile with them. That was the right thing to do, and you went by the book when you did it.' Yeah, that's what you would've said, if I'd told you or any other realistic businessman what I said to Bettancourt. But that isn't what he is.

"He's, like I say, a damned clerk. Sort of turned up his nose and *sniffed,* when I'd finished, like he'd just smelled cat piss or something. Shook his head. 'Yeah,' he said, 'well, I dunno about that, Mister Carroll. I have to say it looks to me as though there's a serious question whether you didn't pretty clearly fail to exercise full due-diligence and good judgment here, think things all of the way through, dealing with this friend of yours.

" 'What bothers me the most, I suppose, is that you don't seem to me to've explored the alternatives, alternatives such as at least taking his receivables as collateral. Or looking to the possibility of pledging some of his family-trust property to secure the new limit. His residences or something. Instead of just, well, "caving in to him," "going down on your knees to him," would be the way I'd put it— because that's really what it looks like—and extending what amounted to a new loan, unsecured, *of half a million dollars.* On top of the half-million, secured, that you already knew from your ap-praisal of the market and the regional economy he couldn't possi-bly've come up with, that he couldn't've paid off, if you'd called in his loan. You knew, and you knew very well, as did your executive committee and your full board as well, that the only reason Mister Goodall was not, *is not,* legally insolvent, current assets insufficient to meet his current liabilities, was and is because you people, when you first saw that he was getting into trouble, *knowing* that he couldn't pay up, didn't ask then, *and still haven't asked now,* asked him to pay what he *owes.'*

"Or, in other words," Carroll said, "what he was saying to me was that because we could've thrown a good man into bankruptcy and raised God only knows how many kinds of pure unshirted hell in this community as a result, we should've gone and done it to him. Just gone and ruined him. Hanged him by the neck. Just because we *could.* That's what it amounted to. That was all it was.

" 'I have to say, Mister Carroll,' the little bastard said, 'this partic-ular transaction, and it's by no means the only one, worries me a lot. It smacks to me of favoritism, if not downright cronyism, and that, as I'm sure you're well aware from your long career at Treasury, is how many an officer of many a failed bank the size of this one, started his institution down the long, sad, slippery slope—to complete *ruin*. People who care too much, too deeply, about whether everybody likes them, should not be in this business, Mister Carroll. They should not be bankers. They should be running pet stores, selling love in the form of happy puppies to happy children, all of whom will always love them back.' "

"That son of a bitch," Frances said. "He said that to you? He actually said that to you?"

"Uh-huh," David said, "he said that to me, and he just loved doing it, too. Scolding the guy who made him feel small, just by having more talent.

" 'I think it's my duty to warn you here now,' he said, 'that if I find a pattern of this kind of thing, well, you know, I'm going to be pretty disturbed. And as it is, I'm going to have to flag this Goodall loan in my report, and it may very well turn out to be that it'll be one that my superiors'll end up telling me we have to classify.' "

He raised his voice into a simpering falsetto. " '*Mmmmm,* this may be one they'll end up telling me we have to *classify.*' " He resumed his normal conversational voice. "Goddamned little prick. As if he really expects me to believe that shit, that his *superiors*'re the ones that'll decide which loans're classified, when he knows I know, just as well as he does—if not better, actually—that *any* loan he recommends for classification *will* get classified, and no loan he *doesn't,* will, and then adding insult to injury by smugly suggesting that'll happen because his *superiors,* meaning asshole Clyde, do business the way I used to, down at Treasury. The creepy little bastard.

"Sure, I trusted my people in the field, when I was down there. If I wasn't going to trust them, if I didn't trust their judgment, then why the hell'd I hired them anyway, sent them out to size up situations and tell me as the deputy comp what the comptroller ought to do? So I could overrule their recommendations, as much as tell them I knew more about the situation that I'd sent them out to investigate'n *they* did? *After* they'd investigated? Take about fifteen minutes for word of *that* to get around in the Department, nationwide, you started doing that. Morale'd be lower'n a snake's ass in less time'n it'd take to eat a half a vending-machine, cream cheese–on–datenut bread sandwich at your desk, wash it down with a can of iced tea.

"But that didn't mean that I just took the reports from my people and okayed them, before I'd so much as read them. Which is what Clyde Ramsey does. I went over every single one of them, asked questions, called up people on the ground in the places where we'd been, and then I called the people who'd written the reports, or had them come down to Washington, made sure they were right, and that I did agree with them.

"And anyway: If he's down here to conduct an examination of our books and business methods, what the hell's he doing making his decisions on classification before he's even bothered to review the minutes of directors' meetings? You don't suppose he came in with a quota to fill, do you now? Jumped right off to his conclusions? Nah, couldn't be anything like that. That just wouldn't be *fair*. Bullshit." He finished the martini in one gulp and got up from his chair.

"Are you going where I think you're going?" she said.

"Yes, I am," he said, "and when I get there I'm going to do what you think I'm going to do, and then I'm going to come back out here and drink it. You can even watch me do it if you want. Because I don't give a rat's ass, all right? Not one good rat's ass do I give. That little bastard's gonna fix it so I have to call Ted Goodall's loan, and the little bastard's *right:* Ted can't pay it all now. Which will mean that either he finds another bank or some private angel someplace— and not many of *them*'ve been spotted around here in recent years— to give him a second mortgage on his home or his business, or both. Which he won't be able to, if he's asking a bank, because he'll have to tell them what he wants it for. And when he tells them that, they will know that what's happened is that in effect I've been ordered, by Gary Bettancourt, that little human turd, either to collect the loan or to close Ted's business down. That his grandfather started back in nineteen twenty-six, his father carried on after the war, and Ted came back from Vietnam and took over when his dad retired. And because no other banker in his right mind'll want Gary coming in to make his life miserable, because Gary found out that his bank refinanced one of our 'troubled loans,' they won't give Ted the dough. So Gary will get what he was after all along: We'll have to foreclose, and then Ted won't have any choice: he'll go out of business.

"When the little bastard's done that, wrecked a solid local business, he will also've thrown all Ted's people out of work, in the midst of what sure looks to me like a recession with a powerful ambition to become a real depression, a grand accomplishment, on their behalf as well, will Gary Bettancourt've made.

"Oh, and mustn't leave this out, just to finish the job off: At the same time he will've in addition put a hunk of damned good prime commercial real estate on the forced-sale market, at a time when the best that you can hope for's not a buyer at a fair price but some bottom-feeder who'll grab it up as distress merchandise, fifteen cents on the dollar. The town won't collect any more real-estate taxes on it while it's idle, and when it changes hands, like I say, at a stinking lousy price, the tax bill will go down accordingly, as will therefore what is paid. And Ted Goodall will still be ruined. Because of Gary Bettancourt. By the time he gets through, and all the results're in, what Gary Bettancourt will've done for Bradbury, Mass., 'll rank right up there just behind what Mrs. O'Leary's cow did for Chicago, and that was long before the lively ball, then, a very long time ago. And if he does that enough times here, to enough good people, pretty soon the bank's reserves to pay bad loans, and our unencumbered assets, will drop below the minimums. And then he'll seize the bank."

He sighed. "And then they'll feel great. Gary Bettancourt and his nitwit boss'll have their names in the newspaper, maybe even on TV, cracking down on sloppy banking practices, all that great good stuff. And Gary's *boss's* boss's pal, our great commissioner, down there in Washington, will appear with several fanfares to announce his full-scale—never half-scale, always full-scale—probe of banking in Massa-chusetts, two days after that. They'll all have all they can do not to grin and dance around. When the lights go off and the reporters go away, they'll be just as damned pleased with themselves as they can be, and go off to the next killing-ground like playful children to recess. Out to play with other people's lives, just because it's so much *fun. Jeezuss,* is this a great country or what?"

"You're drinking too much, you know, David," she said. "You've been drinking too much for some time. I'm getting so that I'm really worried about you. So's Gene Veltri, too, and Saul, good many of your friends, in fact. They're all very concerned about you. You're driving yourself far too hard, they all say, and I agree with them, too. 'What your husband needs is a rest. A good long vacation, just sit in the sun, if that's all he's up to, or go off for a month on his million-aire's yacht—best thing in the world for the guy,' that is what Sam Fairwood said. 'You'd better talk him into it, too, Fran,' he said to me, 'and no matter if he doesn't want to, you'd still better pull it off. 'Cause if you don't, then what you'll end up doing is talking me into speaking, delivering the eulogy at the memorial service. And *I* don't want to do that.'

"They're exactly right, David. You know it yourself," she said. "How long has it been since you invoked Summer Rules, David? Have you got any idea? Do you even remember them now? The Real Summer Rules, that you made up in high school, or college, whenever it was, before I ever met you, I know, and followed every year afterwards? No matter where you happened to be, or what else you'd been doing?

" 'In summer priorities get rearranged. The summer is mental-health time. In summer, smart people go out on their boats, and that's how you know they are smart. If they weren't smart, they'd stay home, and they'd get into trouble. That's why God gave us boats in the first place: to help us stay out of trouble—'cept for what we get into on the boats. It's people not going out on their boats—that's why we start getting so much crime and unrest in the cities, soon as the weather gets warm. The people who live in the cities all stay home and sweat in their tenements, and *naturally* they get all pissed off. Pretty soon one of them takes a swing at another one, and then it won't be very long before somebody starts shooting. If they'd all just do the sensible thing, go out on their boats like they should, put their lives in peril of the sea, they wouldn't be anywhere near so damned grouchy, and we'd all be that much happier. Plus think what we'd save on police. We could spend all that dough on the Coast Guard.'

"Well, when was it you decided, David, that you'd stop being smart? And why wasn't I even consulted? I thought the Rules were a great idea. It was summer when I met you, you know, and having no desire to get a husband who'd kill himself with too much, having had a father who worked himself right into an early grave, I took a look at you and thought: 'Well now, what have we here? A man with brains enough to know that there's more to life than work? He's got *that* all figured out? This could be worth a closer look.' I took that closer look, and I liked what I saw, well enough to marry it.

"I don't like what I'm seeing now, a defeated man who's drinking too much, and's forgotten his own Summer Rules. You had to hitch rides to go sailing back then. When you had the helm, the summer we met, you were some fat rich guy's chauffeur, and I couldn't come if he had lots of guests. Or if his snotty daughter was visiting, looking over the crop for a new husband to replace the one she'd just shucked. Younger or older, no matter. But now look at you: Our own gorgeous boat, you would've killed for it then, and what do you do with it, huh? You don't do anything with it, to speak of—it just sits on the mooring all summer. Oh, now and then we go out for a sunset sail, and once or twice on weekends, if it doesn't happen to rain, and you aren't completely exhausted. Do you realize it's been over two years since we took an overnight trip—spent even one night, much less a whole week, sailing our beautiful boat? Has that even registered on you, David? That's not obeying the Summer Rules. What that is is ignoring them."

He frowned. "Frances," he said wearily, "as you know, better'n anyone else, I've been under a lot of pressure here all at once—much more'n I ever expected, when I signed up for the job. Banking deregulation, regional takeovers, banks going into receivership, people going to jail; big banks coming onto what used to be our sacred turf, where before they could never get approval, routinely crossing state lines for capital steroid-scale buildups, to make them invincible when they become hostile and start making stock-tenders, as they most certainly will—all of those things, and then the economy, too, all of it happened at once."

He shook his head and looked miserable. "It's like one of those scientific demolitions you see now and then on TV: they pack the explosives into the building so that when the charge goes off, all the bricks and everything just crash in and down on themselves. The banking business we're in now is in buildings like those, some of them rigged to implode, and every day I'm scared to death I'm gonna see the TV-remote vans pull up in front of my operation, with the satellite dishes in place. That's when I'll know it's the weekend it happens, and my bank's the building that's rigged.

"Because it's gonna happen, no doubt of that. This business's too overheated right now to continue indefinitely. All I can hope is that it's not my building but some other poor bastard's, a rival's. And that's why I'm working so hard, to make sure as I can: that when the dust settles, our competition has just disappeared, gone out of business, but our little bank is still standing. Then we can get on with our lives.

"You know what I've had to contend with. None of it's been something I could put off; it's been one brushfire right after another. And if I don't put those fires out when they start, sooner or later one of them's gonna become a wildfire and spread, take my bank down along with it. You know what'll happen to Bradbury Bank, if one of those billion-dollar Boston behemoths swaggers in here, swallows some local bank whole? They'll have eighteen-wheelers trucking in automatic-teller machines, erecting freestanding mall-buildings overnight to keep them out of the rain, and we'll be dead dogs in the road.

"Those ATMs, do you realize what they cost? Twenty-six thousand apiece. We took a million-dollar hit for the thirty-eight we've still got and the other four that got hijacked and destroyed by those three guys with the tanker-winch on the big tow truck in Swansea. You think we could match what a big bank could come in here and do, put one of those things on every corner, and grind us down into fine powder?

"We could not. And pretty soon our customers'd start to notice how much more convenient it'd be if they had their checking accounts and their savings accounts, and their credit cards and car loans at that big other bank. Maybe even refinance their home mortgages, if the Gorilla Bank's rates were lower—as of course they would be. Their rates always are, during the grand-opening sales they run when they invade. That's the way they operate. They soften up the local opposition the best way that there is, by undermining customer loyalty that's taken years to build. They'd deny it, of course, indignantly, but what they'd do would be their very best to put us out of business, so they could then raise their rates with complete impunity, as they've done everywhere else they've been able to get in, and the devil of it is, it always works. They lowball the local bankers right out onto the street. And you know what'd happen then? They'd get away with it. They'd win. They always do.

"So now, on top of all of that, just to keep me occupied, I've got this goddamned little prick, doing his *best* to pull the plug on me, telling me that at the very least what he's going to do is classify some of our loans and then put that in the papers, and on TV, of course, get the people frightened, start them wondering if their deposits with us're secure. Asking when they come in, or they see you on the street: 'Is my money still safe here, Mister Carroll? Are you really sure of that, I'm not taking any risk?' How the *hell* can I play Summer Rules?"

"You can do it by taking stock of what you're doing to yourself," she said, "and coming to the right conclusion: that you can't keep doing it any longer. If there's nothing you can do about it then there's nothing you can do, and worrying won't help. Keep it up and you're gonna get sick."

He stared at her. Then he turned around and went into the house. After a while she heard the fresh ice dropping into the glass. The blue twilight was changing from deep blue into nightfall. Frances looked at the sky and nodded. "Good evening, Polaris," she said to herself, "you at least make me feel a little better. Still on your assigned station, standing your proper watch. We'll sail ourselves out of this mess yet."

2

In the glassed-in sunporch of the house on the hill in the gray late morning of the third Friday in March, feeling weary far too early in the day, Frances set down a cup of tea on the white wicker table next to her chair and in a desultory fashion began sorting through the mail. She already knew from the quick shuffle she had given it on her way in from the mailbox that it included no personal letters for her or her husband, as it seldom had in recent years. This disappointed her, even though she knew it really shouldn't. If David actually got any personal, purely social letters anymore—which she tended to doubt, knowing he and his friends relied on convention encounters and personal footnotes piggybacked onto business calls and letters—they would have come from people he knew in banking or one of his organizations, and have been sent to him at the bank. His friends (meaning, their secretaries) most likely didn't even have his home address or phone number in their Rolodexes.

She understood that her children's generation preferred electronic mail when they found themselves in situations unsuitable for voice communication, disdaining the resort to "snail mail." "And I also suspect," she had written two days before to her old friend Kitty Barber, by herself now, four years after Sam's stunning death—one soft blue Tuesday evening in June around 7:15 he had taken his red Jaguar XJS convertible from the lot near the office on K Street, where he had made a lot of money every year as a tidily ethical banking-industry lobbyist, and driven to the Jefferson Memorial. He had parked where he could see the statue, put the top of the car down, and then shot himself in the head; and no one who knew him knew why—in her now-too-large-and-costly home in Reston, Virginia, "that if I took the time and trouble to poll all the other people that we've both known for years, I'd find to my astonishment that a lot of them feel the same way now, too, and have learned how to use those machines themselves, taken one of those courses or something, and moved into the century of Right Now. But I've thought about that and I still don't know; all I know is I know I don't think so."

She would not hear from Kitty for ten days or so, at least; Kitty'd immersed herself in National District Hadassah activities about six months after Sam's death, scarcely leaving herself one free day a week, and so even though she was all by herself she did not have as much time as Frances did, to write letters.

"I'm used to the way that real letters *feel*, the pleasure of opening them, usually recognizing the return address so that I know even before the envelope's open who made me this nice little gift, for no reason at all, except that they wanted to. The sudden real bad news we've always gotten from someone who called up on the phone, but the letters I've always gotten—ever since I've gotten old enough to learn to read and write them—almost always've brought me good news. And I think they're better quality, too, our old-fashioned kind of letters—the way that we *make* them, spending time and care on them, time we have to set aside in advance, instead of just sitting down at some machine and dashing off whatever comes into your head, or sending some foolish greeting card that costs two dollars or so. I know those two or three days, or maybe a week, that I spend thinking about what you've written to me, they give me the time to get my thinking straight—what it is that I want to say to you. As though between the time I got your letter, and the time that I sat down to answer it, I'd been thinking on and off about what you wrote to me, and what I ought to say in response. And also: what I must be sure to include, in the way of news I've heard or thoughts I've had, since I last wrote to you. And then, when I'm sure I know, then I sit down and write it, not as a chore that I've been putting off, no, but instead as something I've looked forward to doing, ever since I got your letter, but not until I was sure I was ready. So's to be sure that I'd get it done right. And your letters, the same way: they compliment me, every one of them does. That you took the time to write them; that's a very nice and generous thing that you do.

"Of course I also know—and it makes me sad to know it—that another reason why I crave communication so much these days is because of the way it's all, all kinds of it, seemed to've dried up since we moved up here—and that's really a while ago now. We haven't made any new friends in those years and we've lost track of—or just plain lost—a lot of friends we had. It's not just because we're sure no one that we've met in the years we've been here would be anyone we'd like to have as friends; we're not sure of that at all. No, or that the people who live in this part of the world have been too distant, unpleasant or mean. I'm sure they're as friendly as anyone we knew, those days when we lived down near you. It's our own fault, really, all our own fault, that we haven't acquired any new pals in this area. It's because we've just kept ourselves too busy for that, or've managed to wear ourselves out all the time, to have the time to do what we did when we were all living down there, with you and Sam and all the guys, back when we were all young together.

"The whole bunch of you, Sam up on the Hill, meeting with David first at Treasury, and then coming up with Tony and Murray and Zeke, and all of those other people that we just sort of hung out with back then: we had so much damned *fun* in those days. Now we don't know where most of them went—*I* don't know, anyway. And no one's come along to replace them. So we don't do that anymore, get together and just have some fun. We don't ever seem to get to know the people that David meets in connection with his business, not really as real human beings, because we don't really take the time to make the effort that might've turned people that we've met, at meetings or dinners, into close personal friends, or even just into social ones, acquaintances, you know? And probably because most of them have spent most of their lives here, so they have old friends all around them, they haven't taken the time or made the effort either. So what's happened is that nothing's happened, as it usually does when nobody takes the initiative, makes the effort, to *make* anything happen, and the effect is we're all by ourselves. Or that's the way I feel, at least. We meet them from time to time, run into them as a matter of course at the convention dinners, and at the service clubs, or I see them in the course of the little community work I get roped into (which is of course mostly for the sake of advancing David's career), and we make our usual, oh-so-charming, superficial conversation, ordinary small talk. And then we don't so much as think of each other again, much less *see,* or even *call,* one another again, until the time comes for the next occasion, whatever organization happens to hold it.

"The thought occurs to me that most of those people probably think as a result, after all the years we've been here and how few new real friends we've made, how standoffish and cold the pair of *us* are, and I suppose they have a perfect right to, if they do. And at least as far as I'm concerned, it does look a lot like that.

"But that isn't what it really is. We really aren't like that. It's loneliness; that's what it is. What we are is lonely. Together without friends. Isolated, or at least that's how I feel—David may not feel it, being so damned busy and all. The spontaneous potlucks; the wonderful restaurant blowouts, as Sam always used to call them, at Cantina d'Italia, Joseph hovering over us, 'First we catchah da feesh, then we broilah da feesh, with justah *leedle,* nev-air too much, of the oil and the lemon and spice.' Or Lion d'Or or Jean-Pierre, or some other place that we really couldn't afford, back then, when there was some big occasion. The nights when we had no occasion at all, and even less money, but got together anyway and went out for movies and pizza and cheap red jug wine. Or just sat around in somebody's backyard, swatting bugs, drinking beer and kidding each other about who'd picked all the cashews out of the mixed nuts. And talking politics. Always talking politics, talking, talking, talking. The subject that never ends, and never goes away. But now it seems to have, for me. I don't even know which party all of David's acquaintances and their wives belong to, although I doubt many of them're Socialists—and more or less assume that most of them're Republicans. Isn't that something? The people that we know best here, or ought to know at least, after over sixteen years in the place—I don't know how they went by so fast; I never even noticed—we know so little about that it doesn't even occur to me to try to discuss politics with them. As though that would be an intrusion, and my question, or something I might say, would offend them.

"I really miss those days and nights of the interminable talking. I miss all of the simple things now, that I guess I took for granted back then. It's like I've suddenly discovered that I'm all alone in the world, when I know very well I am not. Someone's taken the fun away, stolen it out of the world, while I wasn't looking or something, wasn't paying attention. Does this mean the Beach Boys were right when they warned us, and now this's the day, the day's come? Or was that Jan and Dean I'm thinking of? Did the day come that they predicted, that Daddy really went and took that lovely little T-bird away, and I didn't even notice?

"It sure feels like that happened, that or something else that I never thought would happen. And the saddest part of it is that it's all but dried up the best part of the fun, I mean, the fun between David and me. And *we* were the ones who you always said—a little bit enviously, I thought sometimes myself—seemed to have so much fun by ourselves. Well, you were completely right of course, even though you *were* envious—I *could* tell—but it was still okay: you and Sam did the same thing yourselves, and for no good reason at all, I envied *you* two a little.

"All right, yes, I know what you must be saying here: 'What's going on here? What is the matter with her? At least David's still alive. If there's breath in the man there's still hope. She's just up to her nose in self-pity.' And then write me a note telling me to shape up, and get a good grip on myself.

"Well, you're probably right. I *am* feeling a little lower than usual today. Sorry for myself, I suppose. The weather we get here can do that to you. But doggone it, we *did*: we used to have such good times, back before he became *the* man in charge here, and I miss those good old days now, I sure do. It's really been a long time now since we've really done anything, just packed our bags and gone off by ourselves, taken two or three deep breaths and put business aside for a while. I know that the poor man's so terribly worried, all the uproar in banking going on around him up here, and of course it's made him obsessed to the point where he can't think of anything else. He's always been focused like that. But at the same time it can't be good for him —it can't help but shorten his life, and he's drinking more than he should, too.

"It isn't right. Something must've gone wrong. This is not what we bargained for, not at all. We've got more money now than we've ever had, or had any right to hope for. The tuitions're over; we've got our lovely boat—God must've smiled on us, we're doing so well. Only now we don't have any time, and we almost never use the boat. And I suppose that's what's really got me frightened. If we don't simply *take* some time for ourselves, pretty soon, David won't have any at all left that we can take, because all of his will've run out.

"I tell you, Kitty, if I'd known back then, if I'd had any idea, of just what 'this wonderful new challenge' that everyone we knew just rejoiced about with us, what it was really going to entail, I would have fought it, down to my last breath. I think what it's doing is killing the man, gradually wearing him down to the point where he just won't have anything left. It never really registered on me, until Sam died, I guess, that it was in fact really possible for that to happen, for a big job to kill the man in it.

"My parents always said it, and I heard their friends agree with them, but the concept of it, the reality of it, that never really set in until we came here, until we'd been here awhile, and John Moses finally retired—that a man's job really could, and would, kill him. If he let it. Or a woman, I suppose, in the same kind of situation—if women get into them now, and react to them the same way. Wouldn't that be something, if that turned out to have been what'd been going on? We'd have real equality then, wouldn't we? 'You've got a right to the kind of a job that'll kill you now, dearie, just like it would a man. And if you don't get it, well, you can go to court. Equal deaths for equal work.' What wonderful fine progress we've all been making here.

"Well, I'll stop whining now, having done far too much as it is. I just wish I could think of something I could do that would get him away for a while. I know my good husband fairly well, after all these years, and I know there still must be, somewhere inside him, hidden way down deep, the happy, cocky kid I married—the one just full of hell. I've got to stop feeling sorry for myself here and think of a way to smoke out that kid again, so we can go and play."

Idly she took a sip of tea, put her reading glasses on and went to the day's mail. There were no bills today for him to take upstairs to the study after dinner and pay electronically with a bar code scanner-pencil hitched up to a telephone set, claiming to relax from the long day's business business by doing personal business at home—that was one small piece of good news, at least. There was one of those "Have You Seen Me?" missing-child-picture occupant cards advertising a service or product that they wouldn't buy or use—she knew that without turning it over—and there were alumni fund-begging letters from Yale for him, and another from William & Mary (that would be hers). She would leave them out for him to look at when he came home, and he would say as he did every year, that he could not understand why any fundraiser with a functioning brain would come seeking contributions before the recipients had had time to incur the incipient wounds of April 15, Tax Day, let alone time to let them scab over and heal.

Then there was a glossy slick maroon six-by-nine-inch window-envelope with a certain heft to it, the contents addressed to both of them, the upper lefthand corner return address in gilt consisting of a coat of arms above the legend in gilt script, *Hayden Lines*, with a Manhattan address. "Now what the hell can this be?" she muttered to herself. "Some other damned throwaway thing, that cost someone four bucks to make?" But she opened it and began to read the gold-embossed Hayden Lines letterhead inside.

"Dear Mr. and Mrs. Carroll," it started, but she'd been around for a while and she recognized personalized computer-set letters, so even after she read the next lines she remained on her guard, "you will think this is another one of those 'personalized' letters that we all get in bunches these days. Bear with me, please, it is not. This is a genuine personal letter, sent to you by someone that you used to know, who was your guest, because when I was making up this list (I was told to be selective), your name came into my mind for the first time in too many years, and I thought: 'Well, it must be a sign.' As Claudia knows, I never overlook signs. I think you'll agree I was right doing that, if you'll bear with me a bit longer here.

"You're old enough now—now don't take offense here, please; this is a compliment—so you know that Jay Silverheels was Tonto, and Clayton Moore was the Lone Ranger, and many times, every day, you still return to the days of yesteryear. No, not to those days when the masked man and his faithful Indian companion rode the plains of the old Wild West; not to the days when somewhere west of Laramie there was a girl who loved the blend of the wild and the tame (and also the Jordan Playboy, the car they just made for a while), or the nights Cab Calloway played at the Cotton Club and Benny Goodman at Carnegie Hall; but to the days when the genuine people still met under the clock at the Biltmore; still ordered Beefeater martinis; still fully believed, and were right to believe, that the ultimate automobile was not any Rolls-Royce at all, but a red Cadillac convertible, with white leather seats—and all those people were *right*. All of the stuff that you were 'too young for,' when it was clearly the best stuff there was, the top-of-the-line (and you knew it, no matter what anyone said)—*that was the very best stuff*. And then when you finally got to be old enough for it, the best stuff was no longer around. Well, okay, some of it still is.

"I've got you now, haven't I? You bet I have; you know what I'm talking about. Eugene Ormandy conducted the Philadelphia Orchestra, and you wished that you could go. The Dorsey Brothers still had their band, and when they weren't playing the Rainbow Room, they were on tour, and came to the Parker House Roof. Vaughn Monroe sang "Ghost Riders" at The Meadows, and Benny Goodman brought his band to the Totem Pole Ballroom. Count Basie was around, and so was Duke Ellington.

"People smoked cigarettes with casual aplomb, and nobody minded, lighting up with their Dunhills or Ronsons, and when it rained, they wore their trench coats, not thinking about World War I and why the epaulets were useful (to secure the gas mask musette bags) or because they kept the rain off, but because those coats—like slingback pumps, single-strand pearl necklaces and dark blue suits by Coco Chanel—had *style*. The watches that all of you coveted most were either those small elegant rectangular ones with the black Roman numeral dials that Jacques Cartier designed and made—the French government's gift to the AEF tank-drivers liberating Paris during World War I—or one of those clunky old Hamiltons, and many of you wear them today. Write your checks with Parker pens, using Parker's Quink. When you feel a little flush you take the Orient Express, and when you get to Paris you can still stay at the Crillon if you like. But when you go to the West Coast, you don't take the Twentieth Century Limited to Chicago and change there for the Super Chief to L.A., or the Sunset Limited to New Orleans for Mardi Gras, because you can't—they're gone. And when you've gone to Europe (as you have—you see? I know you; what we can't learn from credit card records isn't really worth knowing), well, you've flown, because the days of the great North Atlantic liners, the all-horns-blowing, confettied-luxury and streamered-ceremony of arriving in New York—aboard *Normandie* or *Caronia, Queen Mary, Queen Elizabeth* or *France* (now in cruise service as *Norway*) have become a part of yesteryear, so that today but one still soldiers on: the *Queen Elizabeth II*.

"Until this May, when she'll be alone no more. The *USS America* will return to service this spring, fresh from the yards of East German Lloyd at Hamburg, where in closely veiled secrecy she's been undergoing rejuvenation, repair and refurbishment for the past three years, better than she was before, faster and more luxurious now than she was for her farewell voyage when she was retired, still holder of the Blue Riband for the fastest crossing, thirty-six years ago.

"Mr. and Mrs. Carroll, you belong on the passenger manifest for that crossing. You should be joining us May 6 for *America*'s return to the North Atlantic run, Southampton to New York. *America* has been reborn, and she shines again.

"Please join us. We at Hayden Lines are obviously earmarking these invitations for such people as yourselves, 1,800 people whom we hope will sail *America* again. You may meet some old friends you just haven't happened to run into before. And we're offering an enticement on this inaugural sailing: One of you sails free. When regular sailings begin in early June, the price for Senator Class will be $5,125 per person. But for this inaugural return, both of you can sail with us for $4,900, airfare to England included.

"Please write or call and say that you accept, say you'll come with us for what we promise will be the vacation of a lifetime. I'll be there waiting for you in Southampton, when that day comes, to welcome you aboard. I'm Melissa Murray. You'll remember me."

Indeed I do, you little tramp, Frances thought, sucking in her breath at the woman's sheer audacity, her own ennui now forgotten. You were lucky to get out of here without having your swanlike neck wrung, you little harlot.

"Please do give me a call. Or have your travel agent do it, either way you'd like. We're going to have a great time on this voyage, come next month. We want you to be with us. We hope to hear from you."

Frances put the letter down on the table next to her and reflected for a while. At last she concluded, as she would later write to Kitty, enigmatically, without any elaboration: "I've decided that the day has not yet come when I'm not as good as some 30-year-old is when it comes to keeping a man. Or that if I'm not, the hell with it; maybe I don't want him."

Then she picked the letter up again and got up from her chair. She went upstairs into the study, taking her wallet from her handbag resting on the umbrella stand on the first floor in the hallway, opening it as she climbed the steps. She sat down at the broad rolltop desk and picked up the telephone, at the same time removing her American Express card from her wallet. She had it in front of her when her call was answered by a young woman. "Yes," she said, "Melissa Murray, if you would." And when she was informed that "Miz Murray" was "away from her desk," said: "Fran Carroll calling. To take her up on her kind offer. Tell her: Yeah, I'll go for that."

When he got home in the twilight, bedraggled, with two and a half hours to himself before the monthly meeting of the board of directors, sure to run past 11:00, she first allowed him to make himself a drink, arrange himself in his chair and take what he clearly thought was a healing swallow. Then she handed him the letter, let him read it and think for a moment. Then she told him what she'd done. She said nothing about Melissa Murray.

He frowned. "David," she said, "you have *got* to have a vacation. You have got to stop killing yourself. And the only way you're going to do it is to get out of Bradbury for a while, even if it's only ten days. Physically remove yourself from this quiet little town on the river. Take yourself away from our nice home in that town. Because as long as you hang around here like this, day after day, week after week, month after month and year after year, patting yourself on the back when you actually, God-almighty, take a Saturday *and* Sunday off, you're going to continue to do it.

"This is the perfect chance," she said. "It's the chance of a lifetime, in fact. It's something I'll enjoy and it's something you'll enjoy, if you'll only let yourself. And it's also less than half-price. So don't tell me we don't have the money. We can find the money. If we had the money to trade up to *Traveler,* which we don't use half enough, we've *got* to have the money to take this great cruise from England."

"Oh, we've got the money," he said. The frown did not disappear.

"And you do need some vacation," she said.

His face cleared; he closed his eyes and put his head back. "Oh indeed I do," he said. "Bettancourt left this afternoon, making no written or oral threats of dire events to be happening soon, but clearly plotting more mischief. Still, at least he's out of my pubic hair for the immediate future, and I do have his oral statement to me to share with the board tonight: 'I have to go over my papers, of course, but until then, go on as before.'" He snickered. "'After which I'll hang you for not reforming, before my report, along with everything else, after I gave you fair warning.' He didn't actually say that, of course, but he might as well've, the prick.

"But at least for a while, things will seem as though they've gotten back to normal, which of course means that all of us who've been on tenterhooks for the past three weeks are now of course decompressing like a bunch of scuba divers who got reckless, and the bends. But I'm in a receptive mood, tonight, yeah. I could use a break. You caught me at a right time."

"Then why the scowl?" she said.

"Give me a little time, all right?" he said. "I've been living in a war zone. Now I've got a cease-fire and R-and-R combined? Too much for me to grasp, all in one short day."

3

Frances and David late in the morning of Thursday the sixth of May arrived by motorcoach from London with thirty-two other passengers at the great gray shed on the quay of the passenger-ship terminal at Southampton, England, each concealing disappointment, each silently hoping that the voyage home would make up to the other for the letdown their three days in London had been. "I don't know exactly what magical cure I'd expected the city to work on David in only three days," Fran would write to Kitty, "but whatever it was, he was immune to it. I made him take me to Scott's for lunch, and we went to a revival of *Oklahoma!*, and our last night there the concierge managed to get us dinner reservations at Rules on Maiden Lane—*very* hard to do. But nothing seemed to work. Oh, David made an effort to be cheerful, for my sake, but when he'd packed up his worries in his old kit bag, he'd carried that bag along with us. His mind hadn't flown to England with us—it'd stayed home, at the bank. The distance prevented him from actually trying to *do* anything about the situation that was on his mind all the time, but that was all, and it wasn't enough. All I could hope was that he hadn't noticed the fact that I was forcing my cheerfulness too, and that the boat—and as you know he's always loved boats, from small boats all the way up—would be big enough and different enough to get his mind off his troubles for a while. Well, she's certainly big, but that was still asking a lot."

The twelve-deck *America*, 875 feet long overall and 105 feet on the beam (like the *QE2*, about as close to Panamax—110 feet, the width of the locks of the Panama Canal—as civil naval architects hopeful of future large-vessel commissions permit their designs to approach; broader ships must steam all the long, slow and thus expensive way around the tip of South America at Cape Horn to pass between the great oceans), except for her sharply raked maroon prow, lay all hidden, tied up alongside the maw of an outsized urban barn.

The baggage handlers in gray uniforms had emptied the motorcoach luggage bins before the Carrolls were off the bus. A man in a maroon blazer crested with crossed American flags and in gold script below them *Hayden Lines,* stood at the bottom of the steps, gravely accepting each passenger's thick maroon plastic packet, stenciled *Hayden Lines*—the Carrolls' pair was stamped below that *2* in gold—and offering instructions in a voice so modulated that those still on the steps could not hear what he said to those standing with him on the pavement.

When the Carrolls reached him he smiled without displaying any teeth and inspected their packets quickly. "Right," he said, handing them back. "Now if you'll just proceed right through there, and then up the electric stairs, you'll find yourselves well taken care of on your way aboard the ship. And please do not be concerned about where your bags've disappeared to; this is not an airline that we're running here, you know, and they will reappear as if by magic in your cabin—probably already have. Trust you've had a lovely time on your stay with us; do come see us again. And do have a lovely crossing, home to your America—lovely country you have there—on *America.*"

"Okay," Frances said, nodding, as they followed the others to the escalator and then started up, "I think I can handle this—at least so far I can. I've got it down. When you fly to England on your trip, you get treated like an intruder on the airline. If the worst you get's a snarl from the dumb gestapos at security, and the guy who lets you board the plane lets you off with nothing more insulting than a rough grunt, you should count your lucky stars. But when you go home by ship from England, at least the first person greeting you is actually polite. Imagine that: a polite travel-person in a uniform. I thought there must've been a bounty put on them some years ago; that they'd become extinct. All shot on sight when seen."

"It does cost a little more, though," he said. "To do it this way, I mean."

She snickered. "Look, David," she said, "just because you're a small-town banker"—that was not an affectionate dig; it was his term for himself—"doesn't mean you always have to act like one, set a good example for the borrowers, when you're three thousand miles from home and they don't know what we've spent."

"No, they don't," he said. "Hell, I didn't myself, until *after* it'd all been spent. But *since* they don't, they're sure it was a whole lot more. Whole lot more than a whole lot."

They emerged slightly disoriented from the passageway into a corridor leading to the center entry of a completely enclosed, circular, cherry-paneled salon–reading room–lobby with a semicircular bar directly across the room ahead of them. There were wide doors on both flanks of the bar; they opened on corridors on the left (leading aft to the starboard side of the ship; the Carrolls and the other passengers in the salon had entered on Two Deck and were facing aft, toward the stern; port and starboard on a vessel are designated by looking forward, toward the bow) and right (leading aft to port). At each of those two doors there were two male stewards in maroon vests, white shirts with French cuffs and black twill trousers.

The stewards had clipboards with thick lists. They glanced at the Carrolls' packets, and then flipped through the papers. The one on their right murmured, "Yes, Mister and Mrs. Carroll. Cabin Forty-one-eleven-aitch, welcome to *America*," and directed them to starboard. There two young women in the same kind of uniform stood, accepting the passengers' packets there and then departing with them down the corridor. As one departed, another returned, so that as the Carrolls made their way toward the doors, the line was moving smoothly. The center of the room was taken up by a circle of three maroon leather curved sofas surrounding a low cherry table where frowning people filled out buff-colored forms with cheap white ballpoint pens. "What're they doing?" Frances said, nodding toward them.

Off to the port bow a young woman with honey-colored hair stood a step or two off the lounge in a companionway, unobtrusively scanning the file of passengers to starboard. When the Carrolls had passed her position, without looking back she raised her left hand and beckoned. An elegant man in a blue blazer and gray flannels, about sixty-five, with a faultlessly trimmed gray mane and military mustache, stepped out of the companionway and stood at her left shoulder. "Over there," she said, her voice chapel-hushed, "good-looking guy in the blazer, woman in the blue Chanel suit. Just about at the middle of the lounge sofa over there, maybe eight couples this side of the companionway. Those're the Carrolls—see them now?"

The man also kept his voice low. "Woman with the good henna

job? Guy looks like he used to be in pretty decent shape, 'fore he stopped working out not too long ago?"

She nodded, smiling. "You got 'em," she said.

"Not a bad-lookin' dame at all, not for a woman her age," he said. "Your horny banker gets maybe too playful with you again, starts neglecting her, there might be a little more in this for me than just the usual money. Not that we both don't like the money, of course, but still, if the spirit's still willin', and the body's still able, too . . ."

She chuckled and elbowed him gently in the stomach. "Don't get your hopes up, or anything else," she said. "Don't even dream of that happening. Because it won't. David may be a roamer, or he used to be anyway, but Frances's straight-arrow, married to the core. She doesn't like it when he runs around on her, does not like it at all, but she still keeps her vows. You'll get the captain into bed before you'll jump her bones."

"Ahh," he said, "not even for revenge? Tit for tat, so to speak?"

"Nope," she said, "never happen. The gander hurts her, gettin' his saucies; but she still won't go in for that stuff."

"Pity." He sighed, and when she turned to look skeptically at him, smiled and said: "Yes, well, okay—that still leaves the lovely money, and we all do like that stuff."

"Don't we, though?" she said. Then she turned and poked him in the ribs. "Git along with ye now, lad," she said, "and step lively. Don't want them to see you cahooting with me. Gregor's got the matter well in hand upstairs. Let him get his careful work done, set up the scene, before you go on the stage."

"Filling out embarkation papers they should've filled out at home, like we did," David said. The eight people in line ahead of them came to a stop just as they reached the end of the line. The couple at the head of it, two young men, seemed to be having some problem that required the attention of both of the young women, soon joined by a third and fourth, returning. In the resulting huddle the shorter of the two young men used much wrist action to present earnestly whatever the problem was, and then discuss it with the stewards. The taller of the two men interrupted twice, crying: "Harold, I can't do it. I can never get through this. You know how nervous I always get, how confrontation affects me. We'll just have to get off of this great bloody boat, and that is all there is to it." The shorter of them each time patted him gently and shushed him, saying: "Jeremy, Jeremy, I know. I'll take care of it. It'll be all right." One of the passengers in line began to fuss and fidget, muttering "Oh come on, for God's sake, willya? Get this over with," intending to be heard. At last one of the four stewards took over the entire matter, breaking up the huddle and escorting the two young men back to the male stewards at the salon entrance. Then the line began to move again, each pair of passengers handing the maroon packet to one of the two stewards flanking the entry to the starboard corridor, being escorted off to their cabins.

"I didn't fill out any papers like that at home," she said. "All I filled out was the one for the table-seating preference. And remembering that ghastly couple from the Caribbean that year—what were their names again?"

"Dick and Jane," he said promptly. "She called him *Rich*-ard, so it wouldn't occur to you to ask them who was taking care of Fluff and Spot at home, while they were off horsing around in Virgin Gorda. *Trilled* him *Rich*-ard, really, like she was the soprano summoning the tenor to her boudoir. God, what an awful woman."

"She really was," Frances said, as the line moved along. "If it hadn't've been for designer names and fashionable resorts, and famous restaurants in Rome, Paris and New York, she wouldn't've had anything to talk about at all, in that sawtooth voice of hers. God, she was obnoxious. But then again of course, she really had to've been, didn't she. For us to remember her for this long. What is it now— fifteen, sixteen years?"

"Must be at least that," he said.

"So," she said, "recalling those two beauties, and thinking how much they could do to ruin this whole trip, if they got seated with us, I asked for a banquette for just the two of us. But that's all I ever sent in."

"Yeah," he said. "Well, one of many nights when I got home late—after a very long day that I'd promised you it wouldn't be; long after you'd gone to bed—I just wanted to have a drink and relax. So while I was having it, I just sort of picked up the literature that they sent us with the tickets, which I hadn't read. And after I'd read it, I did what they were asking. Filled out the forms, I mean, and sent them back the next day. That's at least theoretically where they get their working passenger-manifest. Then what they do when you actually get on is look at the papers you've got with you, which theoretically ought to match two names on the working manifest exactly, but very often don't, because those passengers didn't send in their forms. So they have to sit down like naughty third-graders now, and get all of their homework done, before they can go to their rooms."

"Detention," she said.

"Exactly," he said. "But the people in charge of the boat don't have any choice in the matter: It's international law. They have to carry the list—and report to their offices ashore—the final manifest that the purser makes up from the first and the second ones, both, that tells them who actually got on board, and who issued their passports where, and all that sort of thing. So that they know their lovely vessel hasn't all of a sudden become a floating refuge for all kinds of international fugitives fleeing jurisdictions, and punishments for their crimes." He paused. "And also of course," he said thoughtfully, "so if she sinks they'll be able to say who got drowned."

"You're such a *good* boy," she said. "And the rest we just won't think about."

"Yeah," he said, "I've *always* been good."

The steward led them down a birch-paneled corridor carpeted in maroon and decorated with watercolors of the great liners of the past. The woman unlocked the door to Cabin 4111H and stood aside, smiling, to allow them to enter.

Ahead of them there were two large double-glazed toggle-bolted, dogged-down scuttles over a mirror lighted at each end by fluorescent bulbs enclosed in Art Deco chromed fixtures. Below that there was a leather-grained Formica counter. At the stern end there was a ten-inch TV set playing an endless loop of introductory matter about the ship. There was a swiveling, tilting, tan leather armchair at each end of the counter. Next to them there were two double beds covered in maroon brocade and separated by a night table that held a call-director telephone, lighted overhead by fluorescent tubes in a dark wooden sconce. There was another night table next to the inboard bed.

"The bath," the steward said in an identifiably English accent, opening the door to the head, " 's just in here. The shower's flexibly hosed," she said, demonstrating, "detachable if you'd like to use it for a nice hot tub. The phone is Inmarsat-equipped, International Marine Satellite, which means that you can use it to call anywhere in the world, any time you want, just as you would at home. All you need's the country code and the area. The buttons on it we think are self-explanatory, but if you have any problem just punch nine, and either I will be across the way on duty or else James or Nicholas will.

And one of us will come right down to help you with the telephone or any other little thing you need to get sorted out. But generally in the daytime I'm here. My name is Doreen.

"There's a refrigerator in the closet here," she said, sliding the door open. "As you see, your luggage has preceded you and we've taken the liberty of hanging up your garment bags. And here you see a bottle, nicely chilled, of Chassagne Montrachet, compliments of Hayden Lines. On this re-maiden voyage." She looked at her watch. "Yes," she said, "I think that does it. Luncheon will be served starting in about thirty minutes. I shall fetch you some ice now, and if there's anything else that you might need, please don't hesitate to ring me."

"Excuse me," Frances said.

"Yes, ma'am?" the steward said.

"The wine is chilled, you said, I think?" Frances said.

"Yes, ma'am," the steward said, "the wine's completely chilled."

"Good," Frances said, nodding again, "then hold off on the ice until after we've had lunch. We've both been up since before dawn, and we'd like not to be disturbed."

The steward did not quite repress a smirk. "Very good, ma'am," she said. "I'll hang out the privacy sign as I leave." She made a little curtsey before exiting.

"That was pretty bold," he said. "Even for a 're-maiden journey.' Finally, what the world's always needed: retroactive virginity."

"Well," she said, "I figure if they give out homework, and enforce detention too, it stands to reason, doesn't it, that there's a naptime too?"

"Yeah," he said, "but I don't think that's what Doreen thought you meant, at all."

"She was right: it wasn't," Frances said. "So shut up and count your blessings. No more talking here."

4

The Senator Grill was three levels up, on the quarterdeck, the elevator from Three Deck rising onto a semicircular foyer finished in gold leaf and furnished with a gilt fan-table on three fluted legs holding a large spray of spring-flowering pink, blue and white stock. Up two steps the Carrolls were greeted by two men wearing black sack coats, white shirts with winged, pinned collars, black waistcoats, oxford-gray striped ties and oxford-gray striped trousers. They presided on a raised landing, a doorway filled with sunlight behind them. The taller of them, in his late fifties, wearing silver-wire-framed eyeglasses, stood gravely hospitable next to a desk made from a cabinet minister's cherrywood dispatch box mounted on a square fluted standard, his right wrist resting on an open folio. The other, in his early fifties and attentively merrier, smiled, bowed and said: "Welcome aboard. Your name and cabin, please?"

David gave the information. The taller man located their names near the top of the folio and checked them off, for all the world like a punctilious schoolmaster assembling an entering class of God-only-knew what potential rambunctiousness, boisterousness and worrisome heartaches as well. Then he breathed deeply, looked up and smiled at them, as though wistfully hoping against contrary premonition that the day would never come when he would have to interrupt a joyous meal to deliver dreadfully bad news from home, not to anyone.

"Welcome aboard *America*, Mister and Mrs. Carroll, and to the Senator Grill. My name is Gregor," he said, as earnestly as though he had not already recited the very same speech to everyone else who had arrived before them. He nodded toward the shorter man. "William and I are here to do our very best to make sure this is the most memorable and luxurious voyage you have ever had. An Atlantic crossing you will always remember as your very best of all, no matter how many you've made. Or if this is your maiden crossing, one that you will recall always with such pleasure as to make many more with us. If at any time, *anything,* however minor, seems to you to have fallen short of your highest expectations, please let us know what you'd hoped for, and we will do our very best to make your dreams come true." To the other man he said, "Table forty-two," and William, turning to go through the bright doorway behind him, took one step down and said, "If you'd please follow me . . ."

Tables accommodating four and six were lined up next to the long triple-glazed ports giving out on the upper story and the roof of the terminal. Banquettes up one step from the ports completed the first level. On the second level, up two steps, enclosed within two sets of highly polished brass rails cast to resemble braided dock-lines: more tables for four and six overlooked the first level; banquettes for two—one occupied by the two young men whose problems at boarding had stalled the line of passengers waiting to be escorted to their cabins—and four were lined up along the second step. Two more steps up, another gleaming railing enclosed a third row of tables; abreast on the same level were arrayed still more banquettes.

The banquettes and the chairs were upholstered in maroon crushed velvet. The thick carpeting was navy blue. The tablecloths were thick white linen, set with heavy sterling silver tableware and crystal glassware, and at the places still unoccupied there were white service plates rimmed in maroon and gold, enameled with the Hayden Lines crest. At the center of each table was a compact bouquet of yellow, blue and white spring flowers.

The bulkhead to the left was decorated with a rose-turning-indigo mural of the Manhattan skyline at twilight, just as the skyscraper lights come on, seen from south of the Battery tip looking northwest. The Statue of Liberty loomed against the horizon, off to the left; it was the view those aboard a ship catch rounding the island in the brief blue hour just before full darkness falls. The mural on the wall far forward to their right depicted the Donald McKay clipper-ship *Flying Cloud* under full sail with a following sea, her wake boiling white, a rocky headland off to port, under a threatening, dark cumulonimbus-clouded sky shot through with icy columns of diamond-white sunlight.

William, either having judged that they had had sufficient time to take in their new surroundings or having gotten a sign from Gregor that he had new charges waiting, coughed discreetly once and increased the pace, ushering them down to the first level, turning left to lead them forward along the row of tall ports.

Turning slightly, William directed them to their right, having led them to the last window table to starboard. Frances cleared her throat and said, "Excuse me?"

"Madame?" William said.

"In the papers that came with the tickets," she said, "they asked what seating arrangements we wanted, and I specifically asked for a banquette for two. So that we would be by ourselves. Those two young men up there—we saw them when we first got on the ship just a little while ago, and *they* seem to have gotten one."

William looked repentant. "I know it," he said. "But I must be candid with you. The number of banquettes for two is very limited, as you can see if you look around. And the unfortunate fact of the matter is that company policy is to assign them preferentially to any repeat-customers of Hayden Lines who may request them. And to *them* in descending order according to the number of voyages taken. We get a list from the computer that we have to follow when we set the tables up. We simply have no choice. Those two men, and any other couples that you see being seated at banquettes: they must be repeat passengers, Frequent Sailors, if you will. Or so our computers think, at least—not saying mistakes are never made, because they are. Then, if there are any still open, to people traveling for the first time on a Hayden ship.

"Apparently the computers didn't recognize your name as a Hayden guest of long standing, so your request went to the bottom of the list. By the time we reached it, the couples banquettes were all gone. I'm truly sorry for this, ma'am, but we really had no choice other than to assign you to a table for four. Still, this is really quite a nice one, as I'm sure you'll agree, and the view is really better than it is from higher up."

"It's not the view that concerns me," Frances said, "it's who's going to be sharing the view with us. When we were on vacation in the Caribbean some years ago we had the terrible bad luck to spend a week in a small hotel with a perfectly obnoxious couple—well, obnoxious *woman*, really; he may've been just as unpleasant himself, but she never gave him a chance to show it—who did nothing but screech about how much money she spent on her *clothes*, and her *jewelry*, and her purebred *doggies*, and her purebred *children*, and her *Jag-u-ar*—most likely that was purebred too. Every mealtime. At the pool. On the beach. In the nightclub. Night and day and day and night—her mouth was going all the time. And it was just perfectly awful. We almost went out of our minds. We've never forgotten it. And that's why I asked to sit by ourselves. In case she or one of her sisters, or someone who acts like she did, happens to be on this boat."

William smiled. "I know exactly what you mean, madame," he said. "And I can assure you that we have another policy as well on Hayden Lines, which is to reassign any passengers who find they're incompatible—even merely bored—with those at the same table with them."

"Yes," she said, "and then every time after that when you run into the people you asked to be changed away from—and yes, I know, it's a very big boat, but it's something that's still bound to happen, something you just can't avoid, unless you stay in your room—you're going to get these dirty looks thrown at you, like: 'Oh look, dear—here's those people who think they're too good for us. Gee, what stinkers they are.'"

"I can't argue that," William said. "I've been at this line of work for a good many years—not on *this* ship, of course, but on other vessels much like it—and that's happened on my watches more than once. But there is another alternative: Let me remind you, lunch and dinner in the Senator Grill aren't divided into early and late seatings, as those in the Congressional Dining Room and the Delegates' Room meals are. You can come in any time that you like, as long as it's within the two hours at least that we're serving each meal. So if you find you'd rather not spend any more time than's absolutely necessary with the person we've put you with, but you don't feel strongly enough about it to wish to make a complete change, well, all you have to do is tell us, and we'll be glad to keep an eye on him, your table companion, I mean. And then when he's close to finishing, call your cabin and tell you, so that—purely by chance, of course—you can always seem to be arriving for your meal, whichever it happens to be, just as he's finishing his. Or, if he's one of those people who prefers to eat later in the servings, finishing yours just as he comes in. And in that way, no hard feelings."

He paused. "But," he said, "knowing Mister Rutledge as I have, for a good many years, I doubt very much that when you meet him, you'll find him to be a problem. No one I've ever known, seated with him and his late wife, ever's found him to be one. And I've put him with a lot of people, some of them quite fussy, in the course of several years. Just the opposite, in fact. If I'm any judge of people, and I like to think I am, my guess is that you'll find yourselves, rather than scheduling around him, doing quite the opposite, and actively coordinating your mealtimes with his. He's really quite a delightful man, Mister Rutledge is, or at least *I* think he is. A thoroughly delightful man."

She sighed. "We'll have to give it a shot then, I guess," she said.

He smiled, pulling out the chair facing the view for her. "Richard will be your service captain; he'll be right with you."

After he had gone away, Frances sighed and looked around. "They really must've . . . ," she said, "it must have cost an awful lot of money to make all of this gorgeous stuff around us happen, if this boat's been retired for almost forty years."

The service captain, a tall rangy light-skinned black with a mustache and painstakingly groomed hair, arrived and introduced himself in an accent that still retained some of its West Indian music. "It's a pleasure to welcome you aboard *America*, Mister and Mrs. Carroll," he said. "I'm instructed by Miss Murray to inquire whether we may serve you some champagne, with the compliments of Hayden Lines."

"They claim they've spent thirty-eight million," David said, after he had accepted Richard's offer, "about seventeen million more'n it cost to build her in the first place, back in nineteen fifty-four. They chose to do it because their survey estimates were that it'd cost at least ninety million to build a brand-new one as good."

"My god," she said. "Is it safe, you think?"

He grinned. "If I didn't, my sweet," he said, "I can assure you we would not be on her. Sure, it's safe enough, or at least as safe as any other brawny ship designed and constructed in the first place for the North Atlantic run and still in service now. You can generally figure that a boat that's in this service, running on this route, regardless of what it is or when or where it was built, has been kept up and then upgraded as much as it should be. To the maximum. Stinting's not an option on the North Atlantic run. You do it and you'll find out fast: Something bad will happen. The people who neglect their boat are going to lose their money even if it doesn't sink, and they aren't fond of that at all. And they will know they've lost their money, taken their ship out of service, long before disaster at sea gets a chance to happen. Because their US Coast Guard certification of seaworthiness and their Lloyd's certificates as well will not be renewed. You just try to fill a boat, with other people's cargo or with other people's people, when that hull can't be insured or certified seaworthy. Lloyd's may be in trouble these days, trouble of its own, from betting against too many big disasters that happened after all. But not as much damn personal financial trouble as any shipowner whose boat can't get a Lloyd's, so he can't get insured.

"No, unretiring this old boat was not skimping on safety; it was saving on construction and durable materials that both cost a lot more now. The money saved was all in building the hull and the superstructure of the thing, the shell, the basic boat. That itself's still nineteen fifty-four, but everything that's in it's nineteen nineties state-of-the-art. She's completely repowered: ten three-hundred-eighty-ton diesel-electric engines, generating twelve thousand volts per engine, close to forty knots at flank-speed. Which they never expect to use; get the luxury passengers across in three days, when you've had them drooling all their lives after five nights of high-seas hijinks and pampering, you won't see them returning soon. In the old days, before the planes came, speed was a real selling point. But not anymore. Now if speed was what mattered to the passengers, they wouldn't've gotten on the boat. Hayden won't really know for sure until they've made several crossings in this big seagoing diesel hot rod, but depending on head winds and head seas and so forth, even under the most adverse conditions six or eight engines running at any given time should give them all the speed they either need or want.

"The idea's efficiency and fuel economy. Slow-turning engines use less oil than high-speed. And it's also a matter of propulsion redundancy: rotating a six-to-eight-engine maximum workload among ten, so that each one of them's constantly getting regular service while the boat still stays underway. Under *moneymaking* way. If they can keep it steaming while they keep it in repair, or manage to keep it up so they don't need major repairs between long-term over-hauls, then they won't have any downtime—this expensive machine sitting idle at a pier, no passengers on board and no money being made, while they work people day and night, three shifts every working day, triple-overtime on weekends, bringing tired engines all the way back up to snuff."

The sommelier, a somewhat stout young woman with pageboy-length straight dirty-blonde hair, wearing a black Eisenhower jacket and gray striped shirt, a tasting cup on a chain around her neck, came to the table with a bottle of Charles Krug Brut champagne and four crystal flutes. She served both of them, leaving a flute empty at each of the vacant places, took one step back and said: "Will you be interested in seeing a wine list, sir?"

The elegant man in a blazer and gray flannels who had watched them boarding from the port-bow lounge companionway, approaching from behind her under William's guidance, said: "Yes, indeed, the wine list by all means. And don't hesitate a moment before filling my glass. We have some celebrating to do." He bowed to Frances and extended his hand to David. "Burton Rutledge," he said.

5

They had a four-course lunch, beginning with beluga caviar, continuing with asparagus with hollandaise sauce and lobster Newburg over wild rice, concluding with a compote of fresh berries with Cointreau, all of it washed down first with the rest of the champagne, raised in toasts as the hawsers were cast off, and then by a bottle and a half of a fine Chassagne Montrachet. The deep horn resonated and the great ship backed down slowly and smoothly from her berth, nudged by four tugs, two at the bow and two amidships, turning deliberately until she faced the English Channel, choppy and whitecapped beyond St. Catherines Point.

"Thank you," Rutledge said as they began, acknowledging Frances's expression of sympathy at the recent death of his wife. "We were together for so short a time, just a few years, but somehow that seems to make it even more difficult for me to bear. I've sometimes wondered, since she died, if perhaps subconsciously that wasn't the explanation for my failure to marry until late in life. Certainly it was no clear-cut, conscious *decision* that I made, exactly—not to do so, I mean. It was something all of my friends did at one time or another in their lives, some for better, some very much for worse, but something I just didn't do. Not that I didn't *like* women, not at all—quite the opposite in fact. I had a number of extended friendships with women, but they were confoundedly chaste. Perfectly nice girls they were, too nice by half, if you asked me, but entirely suitable as prospective wives. I simply didn't have an urge to make a wife out of any one of them. And one didn't have *affairs* back then when I was young, not in a small town, at least; not if one entertained any hopes of being considered respectable enough to be retained as a family lawyer, and represent the local bank. Had to wait 'til you were safely married, and older, to indulge a bit on the side. And you certainly didn't just move in with each other, as perfectly respectable widows and widowers in Barlow quite commonly do today, without the slightest sign of secular disapproval—that I can see, at least. The clergy don't really approve, even today, I suppose, but they keep it to themselves. They have these blinders that they put on when approaching something that they're not supposed to sanction, even if it's something that really does upset them, but also something that they know damned well they can't do a thing about. So therefore they don't really wish to see it.

"So anyway, in those days it was more or less expected, unless you were common riffraff, that when you were in town you would be at the very least painfully discreet, and that when you felt you simply had to be *in*discreet, every so often, you'd have the common decency to do it out of town. Take a room at the Parker House. Take the train to New York. Rent a cottage at Dennisport in August and misbehave yourself on old Cape Cod—or Provincetown, I suppose, if you happened to be queer, but no one even *mentioned* that kind of misconduct then, back when I was a young single man—to your heart's content. But not in Barlow, please—Barlow had moral *standards,* even if you couldn't meet them, and no one really thought you could. Or even should, as far as that goes. But you did have to pretend: hypocrisy was not an option; it was mandatory.

"So, since I wasn't married," Rutledge said, "and I was a normal healthy lad, that was what I did. I lived up to expectations: I was a hypocrite. And everyone admired me and said: 'What a fine young man.' And because I was a fine young man—not because I was a fine young *lawyer,* although in fact I entertained every intention of meriting that credential too; painfully, *excruciatingly,* meticulous about my clients' interests. Most of them, you see, at least in the beginning, were my late father's former clients, trusting me enough to leave their legal business to me, and I was very conscious of that fact: that I had him to live up to. His cherished reputation was in my hands now, and I took it very seriously indeed. I wrote their wills and deeds for them, and their mortgages as well, although I was doing those for the Barlow Cooperative Bank, another of my father's long-standing accounts that passed without interruption into my hands when he died in the fullness of his years. Not as lucrative a client as the Barlow Trust Company, one of those ferociously competitive and hugely profitable commercial banks—"

"I run one of those 'ferociously competitive commercial banks,' "

David said mildly. "Pilot Hill Bank and Trust, down there next door to New Bedford?"

"Well, we certainly seem to have put our foot right into it, there now, haven't we though?" Rutledge said, shifting in his chair. "My, my, yes indeed, I should say so. I have heard of Pilot Hill, though. Three of my friends're keen sailors, and they keep their boats down there. Claim it's well worth the drive. But I do hope I haven't offended you."

"Oh, for heaven's sake, no, of course not," David said, "I'm just sorry I can't say that you're right on the money with your description, but I can't say our bank's 'hugely profitable' just now, not with the economy in the tailspin it's been in, and our poor customers getting squeezed in it just like everybody else. But I have hopes, I must admit—I do have hopes of that, too."

"Well, I wish you all the luck in the world in that enterprise," Rutledge said, with some fervor. "Sometime in late eighty-nine I gradually found myself getting a new kind of business, one that I sincerely wished I didn't have, as much as I always liked fees: Chapter Seven and Chapter Eleven reorganizations, clients whose businesses'd been humming right along. And then gradually, over time, things began to slow down. They commenced to find themselves having trouble meeting bills on time; having difficulty collecting from good customers who always before'd paid promptly; laying people off. And then finally: with no choice open to them but to go in and beg the court for time enough to see if they could get themselves and their business back on an even keel. It's been rough. I know. Rough on all of us.

"But anyway, I thank you for the thickness of your skin. And the Barlow Cooperative was nothing to be sneezed at, either, in case I may've left that impression. A nice steady source of cash, for not too much demanding work. A six-mile trip to Dedham once a week, sometimes only every two, but generally every Thursday; a light workout with the heavy volumes doing the title searches for the week in the Register of Deeds office in the morning. Then a leisurely lunch at Mary Hackett's with Bobby Clyde from the D.A.'s office. Keeping an eye on the criminal side, what the judges were doing, in case one of my clients got busted for Driving Under or some other embarrassing thing. And so back to my office, as Samuel Pepys might've said, my honest retainer honestly earned. Justified in the sight of the Lord.

"It was not a bad life at all," he said, cutting the asparagus stalks precisely after carefully making sure that every last millimeter of them had been touched with hollandaise. "It wasn't a particularly *exciting* one, I grant you, but after what I saw in my two years in Korea during the so-called Conflict—looked a helluva lot like a regular war to us amateurs in the tanks, but the powers-that-be then said: 'No, it's a Conflict, a Police Action'; distinction without a difference if you ask me—that wasn't really a drawback. I was all by myself. Both my mother and father'd died mercifully, *quickly,* within four months of each other, he in his late sixties, she at seventy-three. I'd been their only child. I was in the same eight-room house that I'd grown up in, practicing law at the same desk that my father'd used in his practice. I'm not sure the law's ever been the 'seamless web' our scholars say it is, but my life up 'til then sure had been. The only difference between where I was then and where I'd been as a little boy was that I'd gotten bigger and I'd been left alone. That was it. And the hell of it was, I liked it."

"You don't practice law anymore?" Frances said. "Did you take an early retirement?"

He contorted his face ruefully. "Well," he said, "you *could* put it that way, I guess, if you liked: call it 'an early retirement.' But I didn't exactly choose it; it was more or less thrust upon me."

"I didn't mean to seem to pry," Frances said. "But was it a medical reason?"

"Frances, for God's sake," David said. "How can you not *seem* to be prying when prying's exactly what you're doing?"

Rutledge laughed. "It's all right," he said. "I don't mind at all. There *was* a health issue involved. The man who attacked me professionally was deranged. Clinically, psychotically. He'd become obsessed with the idea that I'd cheated him out of some money. People who knew both of us, and'd heard what he'd said about me, well, several of them came to me privately and said they truly believed Amy and I might be in real physical danger if I continued to defend myself against him. As I had been doing until then, and had had every intention of continuing to do. Amy and I talked it over. We had plenty of money, enough to do whatever we liked, anywhere in the world that we wanted. She'd had a cramped adult life before her marriage to Eldred, which'd ended tragically soon, and I'd worked for all of mine, nearly forty years if you counted the war—as you can be damned sure I did. What was the point of resisting this madman, and taking the chance that he'd kill us? Put all we had in hazard like that? No, the more sensible thing, the *rational* thing, was to appear to concede his point and resign from the practice, sell it to somebody else. So that was what we did." He exhaled heavily. "And much too soon afterwards, only a few fleeting years, *she* died. My father once said of my mother that the only mean thing she ever did to him was: 'She died on me.' I could say that of my Amy."

"Oh, you poor *man*," Frances said. "That's just a heartbreaking story."

He brightened up a little. "Oh, I think I'll probably live," he said. "But I'll do it as a nomad—I know I can't do it in Barlow. Too many memories there."

He swirled his wine. "I don't know whether you folks've ever been there," he said. "Been *through* it, I suppose'd be more likely. Isn't much reason to stop, now. Used to be, back in the old days, back when the inn served some other purpose'n just another cheap barroom with two-day-old sandwiches in Saran Wrap, and the mailcoaches went through every day. But that was a century ago." David shook his head, and Frances said she didn't believe they'd ever been there.

"It's not a *big* town," Rutledge said, "but it's a very *pretty* town. Just west of Dedham, north of Route One-oh-nine. Between four and five thousand people. The outskirts're farms, or used to be farms. They're too nicely kept to be working farms now; wouldn't have time enough to get the crops in, tend them and then harvest them, all the time it takes keeping up the white board fences and the stables, showcase-way they are. Those old farms now're to real farms as Bentleys are to automobiles: they still technically belong in the farm category—haven't been developed, so they're still taxed, when they're taxed at all, which is only if they haven't been put into conservation banks, 'forever wild,' as 'agricultural land'—but they're not the sort of farms, working farms, real people have in mind when they use the word. That's where the horse-lovers live. A horse-lover being, in my estimation, someone who loves another horse. But I didn't say that to my horse-loving clients, several of whom looked like horses themselves. No use in upsetting them needlessly, not when they were paying my bills. But when I asked them some question that called upon them to give me a number, I half-expected they were gonna whicker at me, and snort, and then stomp out the answer on the floor with a hoof, expect me to give them a carrot or apple, cube of sugar, for performing so well.

"The center of town," he said, emptying his tureen of lobster Newburg, spooning the last of the sauce from it, "is basically unprepossessing. Oh, there are some big houses, not saying there aren't, but they're not especially grand. Two have the tall white columns holding up the front porches, verandahs, I guess I should call them. But the columns're made of wood, and the houses are too, made of wood, not of brick, or fieldstone or something. The rest of the houses, even the big ones, are either Colonial or Federal. Very few ranchhouses in Barlow. Can't think of a one, in fact, offhand.

"They're attractive old places. Those that aren't white're gray, or yellow, maybe an ivory one scattered in here and there. They have this wonderful dignity about them, what I like to call *bearing*, if mere buildings can have that. My own, the one I got from my parents, wasn't one of those, of course—Nineteenth-Century Nondescript was what I called it, what used to be called a 'farm cottage.' Nice wide porch on the front and one side, white with green trim and blinds, swing hanging from chains in the roof. Sometimes in summer I'd take my clients out there, a little business *al fresco*. Pitcher of lemonade on the table, maple trees to give you some shade. And the whole general effect of coming through town, or traveling down my own street: it was all so comfortable to me. Take a walk in the evening— the sprinklers'd be going, people're proud of their lawns. At least for me, well, when I was still there, and doing that sort of thing, and I'd see something like *Our Town*, I'd think: 'That might just as well be set here.'

"It's a classic New England small town, Barlow is, a place on the earth with perspective. Where you can gather your wits. I liked the *pace* of the place, the way you can live your life there, if you've got brains enough just to do it, ignore what the world says to do."

"You really miss it a lot, don't you?" Frances said.

Rutledge nodded once. "I really do," he said, "I do. I had nothing like the glamour and excitement of the world I live in now, and don't let me mislead you here—I like the life I lead. But I also liked the life I had, and if I'd never had to leave it, I don't think I ever would've. I knew then where I fitted in—I knew where I belonged."

Leaving St. Catherines Point to port, the *America* swung her broad turn to starboard into the English Channel. Wake was no longer the concern it had been in the harbor anchorage at Southampton. There was a power surge more felt than heard deep in the hull, and she seemed to gather herself under it; if the whitecaps on the four-foot seas, kicked up by a twenty-knot westerly wind almost head-on the bow, had not been visible from the broad port-lights, none of the passengers would have suspected the conditions existed.

"But there you are," Rutledge said. "The first thing that you have to learn in a town like Barlow, especially if you've spent most of your life there and've gotten so you just take things for granted, is that your complacency's misplaced. And in all those years I'd lived there, I'd never learned that. 'There it is. It's always been there. There yesterday and there tomorrow; it'll always be there.' Or 'he' or 'she': the people, too, the ones you've always known, 've always been in the same place. It could be a person. Until one day one of them dies, or if it's a building something goes wrong in the wiring, and what was there in wind and weather, solid for a hundred years, burns down flat to the cellar-hole.

"Then maybe it might register on you, that what's always been there, *hasn't always been there*, and the day will come when it's not there anymore. Maybe not during your lifetime. Maybe not during other lives-in-being, as we like to say in the law, to distinguish them from the vast majority: lives-no-longer-in-being that faithfully turn out a hundred percent to cast the tie-breaking votes in the crucial elections. In Boston and Chicago they vote Democrat; and on old Cape Cod, Republican. But some day, sooner or later, what's always been there will no longer be there, just like someday you won't be there either.

"This is an unwelcome thought, and most of us manage, one way or another, to have it as seldom as possible. When I solemnly succeeded—and I *was* solemn, I assure you, very solemn indeed, much more so than I am today, when I'm old enough to be—to complete ownership and management of my father's practice, inherited it, if you like, it remained for me pretty much as it had been for him. Only superficially changed now and then by the reluctant defections and departures of a few inconsequential clients I could easily spare. Their nephews—and in recent years, nieces—had graduated from law school and passed the bar, and even though *their* fathers'd delivered their small patronage to *my* father, they really didn't have much choice. But they always felt bad about it, and I took that as a tribute to my skill. Their acknowledgment that as far as they were concerned, nothing'd really changed much except now they had a lawyer in the family, and they hoped I'd understand. As of course I did; I'd known them a long time, long before my father died.

"He'd been semiretired for the last six or eight years of our so-called 'partnership.' It wasn't that he was ailing. There wasn't a thing wrong with him, then. It was just that he figured the day'd come when he'd depart from this world, and after a lifetime of doing steady, hard work on the surface of this planet, he deserved to devote as many of his days remaining on it as he could to playing golf on the green grass, before he went under it. And then, after playing, having cold beers and club sandwiches, and playing bridge with his pals in the clubhouse. I'm sure he also had it in his mind that if the clients got used to dealing mostly with me, when he was still hale and hearty, they'd have less trouble dealing with me when he was neither no more. My father was one shrewd cookie.

"But whatever the reason, that's what he did. He played golf with a passion, as much as he could, whenever the rains didn't fall. In the warm weather he did it from home in Massachusetts, and in the cold weather he did it out of a small house he rented every year in Sarasota. That was where the Red Sox had spring training in those days, so a lot of his pals, and my mother's chums, too, went down there at the same time. He went to the spring training games, played golf and bridge, and he drank, and she sat by the pool, played canasta and drank: they both had a very good time. So, long before he went to his reward, I'd been the one that you'd see in the office, the one who'd done most of the work. And most of the clients knew this. So of course it'd been an easy transition, from taking his guidance to mine, because for some years his wisdom'd been mine, and they knew this, and generally mine'd worked well. So why not continue, along the same line? That's what I thought, at the time, accounted for their loyalty.

"Now I'm no longer so sure. Now I'm more inclined to think it was static inertia that accounted for it. That by leaving their legal business in the same place, geographically speaking, where it'd always been, the clients enabled themselves to avoid confronting the fact that the man who'd always been there to handle it wasn't there anymore. That he was in fact dead. They didn't wish to think about that, and so they *didn't*—think about it. They just left their business in my hands and went along as before. So for them, nothing'd changed.

"Looking back on it now, I suppose that, in a manner of speaking, the tale of my life's been a tale of two clients. If it hadn't've been for Eldred and Amy I doubt I would've left home again, once I'd gotten back from the war."

6

"Eldred Motley was born a rich man," Rutledge said, digging into his Cointreau-flavored compote of fruit. "My father'd handled his father's business, but his father was not the one that made the money. His father, Eldred's father—he'd been born a rich man himself. *Making* the money: that was his *grand*father's genius. He did it right after the Civil War, apparently so fast it'd take your breath away. Went from Shabby-genteel to More-money'n-God at perfectly breathtaking speed. I was never too clear on exactly how he'd managed it. I know he invested early on in something that made thrilling amounts of cold cash. Must've, because so far as anybody knew he didn't borrow any money to speak of to put into it—few hundred dollars, I guess, on his farm; wasn't worth much more in those days—and he didn't have much of his own. But whether it was railroads or textiles; copper mines, spice trade, the tea trade, or what-all—I must confess I don't know—I think we can assume it was shady. This was long before there were laws against monopolies, monopsynies, trusts and all those conveniences that came in so handy then if you were really greedy and were out to get rich quick. And also well before the income tax came along and made the simple matter of becoming filthy rich so much harder and more time-consuming. Most of the great fortunes assembled in those days lacked somewhat for the odor of sanctity. I know of no reason to believe that Eldred's ancestor was any more scrupulous or any less predatory than his contemporaries.

"Eldred lived in the family mansion, one of the two great-columned homes that grace our little town. It's a deceptively compact structure, from the front, outside. Yellow with white trim, nice rolling lawns. Looks like it might consist of ten or twelve rooms. But there's another wing out in the back, hidden by the elms and oaks, quite out of sight from the road. That mansion has thirty rooms. The back wing has the children's romping room, the billiard room and the servants' quarters, the scullery and the laundry room, and in the basement of it, a real live bowling alley. Eldred complained to me once about the bowling alley. He said he didn't object to his ancestors' including indoor leisure facilities when they built the house, quite the contrary, but he wished their idea of leisure'd been squash instead of bowling: 'Nixon bowls in the White House, for God's sake—that sums it all up right there: Bowling's so déclassé.'

"The thing's a royal *bitch* to heat, as you might imagine. Eldred used to suffer fits of fiscal responsibility from time to time, and when he was in one of them he'd close off the back wing in the winter, only heating it to about fifty degrees or so to keep the pipes from freezing, needing and having no servants himself, except for a once-a-week cleaning lady, and thus cutting down on the overhead. Eldred was thrifty like that, in his own extravagant way: He scattered dollars around like confetti, when they were for something he wanted, something that interested him—'something that's useful to me.' But when it came to something like coal, heating oil, whatever was used in the house, he threw nickels around like they were manhole-covers; *then* he was tighter'n Pullman-car windows.

"The price of that frugality, though, was that it deprived him of access to the annex of his library, the old drying-room where the laundry, the sheets and pillowcases, longjohns and so forth, was hung on lines to dry. Well, no further need for such spatial extravagance once washers and dryers were invented, and he was in there all by himself. So he'd converted it to something he *could* use: an addition to his library space. He'd had it shelved. And that was where he kept all the books that he'd culled from his main library as being the least frequently used. In order to make room for the new books he was constantly bringing home all the time. 'But,' he told me the trouble was, 'in the winter the old ones are all out of easy reach, if I need them for reference or something. As I invariably do need them, soon as I've culled them out and transferred them to the annex as being infrequently used, I generally find within a few days that I really need one of them again, and so there I am, buttoning my sweater, freezing my ass off in the annex, trying frantically to find a book I haven't needed to look at for years, and now need to refer to right off. It's all very frustrating, like the phone being silent all day until you sit down on the toilet, and then it goes off like a bomb. Makes me wonder if I'm losing my grip.'

"Eldred bought hundreds of books every year. The main library was two stories high, with a catwalk 'round the perimeter shelves halfway up the wall, and three or four of those pincer-type things on oak poles, to fetch and replace the books on the upper shelves up too high even for Eldred—he was six-four or -five—to reach."

"He must've been quite the scholar," Frances said.

"He was quite the everything," Rutledge said. "Never having any need for a job, he never held one. I don't think he ever so much as even applied for one. I know for a fact of three 'invitations to serve' in salaried positions that he received and declined. Very *modest* salaries to be sure, created in the expectation that they'd be paid to someone in Eldred's position who didn't really need to get any salary at all. More like honoraria, really. And therefore, predictably, all of those jobs were quite out of the question for acceptance by most of the people who might really've liked to've held them. Jobs with great prestige are wonderful things to have, but no one yet's figured out how to eat that stuff, prestige, and until somebody does, nobody who actually has to make a living from his work can hold them. Or her work, of course. But Eldred declined them, just the same. Graciously, to be sure, but still declined them.

"Not that any sort of misguided altruism to the best of my knowledge was ever involved in this. None of the ostentatious 'I've-got-plenty-of-money-and-I'm-not-going-to-take-a-job-away-from-somebody-who-really-needs-one' pompous claptrap that you get from lazy rich kids so shallow and lazy that no one'd hire them to mow lawns, if they were destitute, starving, in rags, because they'd surely cut their feet off in the blades. No, nothing like that at all. These were real, existing, genuine jobs, for which Eldred would've been eminently suited. Very modestly compensated, as I've said, to be sure, but still—actual jobs, tendered in good faith by administrators and boards of directors who genuinely and correctly believed that Eldred would be an excellent choice to do what they needed to have done.

"As in fact he would've been, too. There was a curatorship of the New England collection at a museum near Boston. There was the executive directorship of a maritime museum on the Cape that some people even richer than Eldred was were thinking of starting up, though more as a seasonal tourist attraction than anything else. And he was hotly pursued by one of the area universities to become a tenured professor offering a seminar in New England regional history. These were not watch-fob, make-believe, merely ornamental titles. They were not fabricated and offered to him in order to part him from some of his wealth by means of flattery. That wasn't necessary. He was inveterately generous to causes that he deemed worthy; no soft soap was necessary to get him to contribute if he thought that your cause was just, and no amount of it would be enough to wheedle money out of him if he didn't. He was very sure of himself. He was not to be tempted out of the way he lived his life, and to anyone who knew him, as I did, it was fairly easy to see why.

"The big bugaboo of the rich that I've known has been idleness," Rutledge said. "I'm not a religious man, but as far as those rumors about the devil finding work for idle hands are concerned, well, I'm inclined to think there's more than a grain of truth to them. The majority of the relatively few rich people that I've come to know in my time haven't been your jet-setting, much-married, art-collecting, high-profile, well-known-for-being-well-known idiots that you see either half-dressed or badly dressed in *People* magazine. These are people of substance who also *have* substance. Character. I know it's a lot easier to have character and principles when you've got a lot of money, but it's also a lot easier *not* to have character, and to do *without* principles, when you've got plenty of dough. But the people I've known who've had money've had it in their families for generations. Their parents learned from their grandparents how to handle it, and handed the training on down.

"Their first rule is, *Never flaunt it.* I'm convinced this is where they get their reputation—which most of them also completely deserve, but for other reasons entirely—for being extremely cheap. Skinflint-cheap. Four-or-five-days'-service-out-of-a-clean-shirt cheap. I don't know whether it was the Syndicalist bombings or the Sacco-Vanzetti case, or the Bolshevik threat, or what the devil it was, but *something* or other happened in America before the start of the Depression that made them very wary of vulgar display. Gun-shy, you might say. And it isn't modesty that motivates them; they're not being self-effacing when they refuse to show off. No, they do not lack for ego. One of the Irish members of the Massachusetts Senate nicely provided a slogan for the last campaign of a Wasp aristocrat for public office, and all his earlier campaigns that'd gone before it: ' "Vote for Elliot," ' he said. ' "He's better than you are." '

"And that is what they really think. When they refrain from showboating it's because secretly they fear that if they call attention to their wealth, sooner or later someone will come around and try to take it away from them. By main force if necessary. And they don't want that to happen, because they think a lot of their wealth. They *guard* it; they *cherish* it; they *nurture* it, as though it had been one of their offspring, their very own flesh and blood—in the hope and reasonable expectation that it will be around to comfort them in their old and feeble age. It's really almost touching, when you think about it, their parental, tender solicitude for the well-being of their money. It really *is* a personal thing; they don't invade principle, ever, unless they're truly desperate, for the same reason that they resist ordering up invasive medical procedures when one of them has some affliction: When they speak of the *corpus* of an estate, they speak of a living thing. Their reverence at time of death is not for the cadaver of the man or woman who left the property, the money; it's for the *wealth* that the decedent preserved and increased during a long and fruitful lifetime, so that it would endure and flourish after him, and approach eternity.

"When the opposite's happened, and there's been a *smaller* corpus remaining at the end of the decedent's life term as its comptroller and guardian, the reason in the end has always been that the decedent was an unprincipled fellow of bad character who literally dissipated the family wealth. He gambled. Or he drank. Or he used drugs. And it's nearly always one of the males who completely lays waste to the family's assets. The women go off the beam, too, to be sure, but when they get silly over golf pros and needy artists, dazzled by undiscovered musical geniuses or swept off their feet by Argentinian polo players, they generally retain enough of a grip on their wits to restrain themselves a little. They only shower their protégés with tokens of affection they can purchase from income. They don't sell off the bonds and utilities stocks, the city blocks and the oil leases that their male counterparts do, thrashing in the throes of their passions.

"Eldred, to my knowledge, never appeared to be subject to such fits. It was true that he never held a job, but he didn't *need* a job, to keep himself in *occupation,* as he called it. What Eldred had was *interests.* Not hobbies. Not mere avocations, no: *interests.* They made up his career. Subjects he pursued as seriously and sedulously as he would've attended to his duties on the job, if he'd had one, which of course was the reason why he had no time for one.

"I'm quite sure that I never knew about the entire spectrum of those interests, all of the subjects that attracted his attention over the years and prompted him to apply his historian's training—he was a Dartmouth graduate—and methods to mastering them. He often bubbled over with information he'd obtained about whatever'd engaged his attention, but it was spontaneous, and lively—he never, *ever*, bragged. He was always cognizant of the fact that his fully funded freedom to delve very deeply into whatever interested him was not something that most of the people whom he knew had ever enjoyed or ever would, being under lifetime sentences of having to spend their days making a living. He was also alert to a possibility that I've had to keep in mind myself: that spending so much time by himself, absorbed quite enjoyably by his own pursuits and persuasions but having neither the opportunity nor occasion for conversation, carried with it a concomitant risk that when he did find himself with companionship he'd promptly bore anyone he encountered to tears with his latest discoveries and insights. As he said to me: 'I still do it, of course, I'm so glad to meet a good listener. But I do my best not to, and if I should ever do it to you, I hope and pray you'll tell me so.'

"I never had occasion to tell him that," Rutledge said. "Well, that isn't entirely correct: I did have a couple of occasions when I was on the brink of telling him he was putting me to sleep. Once when he got completely carried away and was waxing on at great length about the evolution of ecclesiastical architecture since the completion of the cathedral at Chartres. And once again when he'd been immersing himself in the history of transportation by means of the steam engine, and liked to have driven me nuts talking about the Pennsylvania K-Sixteen locomotive, and I don't know what else. But I didn't, slap him down. I couldn't bear to, really. Eldred was a solemn man by nature, and when he became thoroughly engaged by his subject, he naturally wanted to share it. With people that he cared about, whom he believed cared about him. You rebuff such offerings at your peril. You can hurt people badly that way. And knowing this, having had people do it to me, I couldn't bring myself to do it to him. I did think the world of the man.

"And he obviously had such a good *time* when he was doing it. He became animated. He was normally quite pale, but when he, well, *warmed to his subject*, his face became flushed and his eyes really sparkled, and it was best to stand back a good foot or two from him—his discourses could be moist.

"And he was truly accomplished, he really was. When he took a given field as the subject of one of his interests, he not only explored it thoroughly but wisely. When he emerged from a period of study—and several of them comprehended two or three years—he was well-grounded in whatever his subject had been. He understood the complexities of the topic and the theories and hypotheses that explained them, and could converse on equal terms, at least as far as I could tell, with people who had mastered the field as professionals. A friend we had in common—Eldred taught me never to refer to such a person as a *mutual* friend; he said that was a friend who was always trying to sell you more insurance—was a professional auctioneer. I'm not sure there is such a thing as an amateur auctioneer, but if there is, he wasn't. This man—Harold Ford's his name; he's now retired, lives down on the Cape, in an Acorn-built A-frame house, filled with Danish Modern furniture; says if he ever sees another goddamned antique in his life he's going to vomit all over it. Spends most of his time playing golf. Made his living appraising and liquidating dead rich people's estates, which is how I first met him. Hired him as an appraiser in my work, settling estates. Spent his entire life traveling around New England, plus New York State, Pennsylvania and New Jersey. He had to know what he was doing. Because, as he said, if he started the bidding off at too low a figure, the sharks in the crowd'd've had his clothes off and him naked onstage in a minute.

"Harold Ford told me Eldred Motley knew at least as much about Persian rugs, and Early American furniture, and nineteenth-century carriages as he did. He said: 'If I had a question in my own mind about something in one of those categories, or pewter or china, as far as that goes—you could throw that stuff in with the rest—I'd call Eldred Motley and have him look at it, and pay him the going rate for it.' Harold Ford had no reason to lie. Eldred Motley was an accomplished man."

He sighed as he finished his fruit and his wine, and then he glanced at his watch. "Yes," he said, "I see that I've done it: the very thing that Eldred urged me not to let *him* do. Completely monopolized the luncheon conversation. We'll be leaving the Channel limit marker to port pretty soon, and the Eddystone Light off to starboard. As many times as I've taken this trip, although not in this boat, I've gotten set in my ways. I lie down for my nap before Wolf Rock at Falmouth, and sleep 'til we get to Bishop Rock in the Isles of Scilly, and change course for the Great Circle crossing. I do hope I haven't bored you."

"Not at all," David said, "not at all."

Rutledge stood up. He slapped his hands down on the tablecloth. "At dinner," he said, "you must pay me back. I do deserve it, I know. You must tell me about your good selves. I promise to behave myself."

ell before Rutledge had stood up from the table, Frances had begun to worry what they could safely tell him about themselves. Without stirring up what she'd describe to Kitty as "the trolls under our own private bridge, sleeping for over eight years." And she could expect scant assistance from David. For a man so doggedly vigilant at work to identify and avoid unnecessary risk, he was remarkably inattentive to it in the conduct of his personal life. "He thinks I'm a silly worrywart, 'wringing your hands about all kinds of dire public personal disgraces, none of which're ever going to happen. They don't put people in the stocks anymore, or banish them from the colony, when they get caught being naughty nowadays. They make fun of them, razz them, and make up jokes about them, but unless they're clergymen or they bother little children, it seldom does much harm now to their careers.' He may be partly right. But he takes it too far, just blithely disregards the embarrassment and shame that might happen to us, and that frustrates me. And scares me."

"Because Mister Rutledge is not the kind of man to let go, you know," she told David on the way to the grille elevator. "He isn't going to just drop it and forget about it. He's not the type who does that. He knows he's monopolized the conversation so far, and he knows he's not supposed to do that. Even though he really can't help himself when he gets a couple captives who'll have to listen to him. So he tries to make up for it two ways: by making sure that the stories he tells them about himself are good ones—"

"Regardless of whether they happen to be actually true," David murmured.

"What?" she said, pushing the elevator button and turning to face him. "You think he's *lying* to us?"

"I think it's a definite possibility," he said.

"Why would he be doing that?" she said. "What good would that do him?"

"I don't know," David said. "I don't know what he might be up to, or even if he's up to something at all." The elevator arrived and she preceded him into it. She turned and faced him, frowning, as the door closed behind him. "It's too soon to tell that," he said, "just what his objective might be. But it's not too soon at all to tell he's a silky old rogue with a polished delivery—he's been at this a very long time, and he's worked hard on his lines. People seldom do that, get that skilled at anything, unless they have a reason, and a very good one, too."

"Like what?" she said scornfully. "What could that be? What could we have, he'd want?"

The elevator door opened behind him and after glancing out into the vacant passageway he backed out into it. "Well, I can't be sure, of course, on a couple hours' exposure, but generally what con men want that work their charms on people, well, it's usually money."

"He's *got* plenty of money," she said. "You heard him say that to us."

"Uh-huh," he said, "I did. That's usually part of the routine, and the first part, too. If he can convince us he's got plenty of his own, then there's no way that we'd suspect he might be after ours."

"Oh, for heaven's sake," she said, starting down the passageway to Cabin 4111H. "Don't be a banker all the time. You're supposed to be on vacation."

"Okay," he said, "so I'm too cynical. But I've got to see a lot more of this bird before I'm convinced he's a sweet-singing robin, not some dive-bombing falcon." They reached the midships elevator and he touched her on her right elbow. "I'm going up to the NavStation," he said. "Play with the toys for big boys."

She turned and leaned and kissed him lightly. "Have fun, pal," she said. "Myself, I think I'll nap and take a bath. Meet me back here at cocktail time?"

"Five or so," he said, and pushed the call button as he watched her walk away.

"You see, I never told him," she'd written to Kitty back in March, after he agreed to make the voyage. "I never actually came right out and told him that I knew he'd had his little fling with Melissa. It was the only way that I could stay with him but keep a semblance of my pride. Either I'd keep still or leave him (I could've killed him, of course, but that would've meant jail, and jail's never appealed to me). So after some reflection I decided that I'm far too old and out of shape to go back to work now, and besides, I've got him all broken in. I haven't got the patience or the time to train another one of those unruly critters, not in what I deserve to enjoy as my comfortable middle age.

"So I suppose in a way I'm playing a very dangerous game now, dangling the bait right in front of him again, almost daring him to do it all to me again. Why, I wonder, why do this? Morbid curiosity? Or have I become so confident, since he's stayed with me all these years, that he'll never stray again, I have to find out if I'm wrong? I must say I don't know."

It was late afternoon when David saw Melissa Murray again. He handled it clumsily. In the quiet room on Signal Deck he had been as mellow and contented as a monk illuminating a manuscript. All alone with several other silent middle-aged-to-elderly men (two of them—one a squirrel-nimble ectomorph in a too smartly cut, very fitted, yellow-and-brown-houndstooth jacket that raised anew the question of how Savile Row had acquired and then contrived to keep its good name; the other a mesomorph, deliberate and economical of motion, in a vast white sweater acquired in some superbly conditioned, muscular yesteryear long past—did murmur to each other, but not very often, and then very quietly) in the monastery hush of the Passengers' Privilege Navigation Stations high on the top deck, just abaft the beam.

David had been using a clear plastic overlay and a washable green-ink rollerball to plot a GPS-informed running fix on the protected surface of the US Defense Mapping Agency North Atlantic (Western Portion) Chart spread before him. He pondered magisterially in a commander's gray-leather armchair bucket seat that Bull Halsey would have deemed acceptable for going in harm's way, hyperconscious of himself, moving as though he had been posing for photographs. The chart lay open on a luxuriously spacious, correctly angled teak surface, firm and smooth and steady, the main working table at the center of the desk in the alcove designated PassNavStation 3. Latitude-longitude readouts, updated every five seconds from the ship's Global Positioning Satellite receivers using signals from eight of twenty-four multibillion-dollar titanium birds in geostationary orbit 24,000 miles above the earth were silently and tidily repeated on the screen just above the table, flanked by a small green-on-gray radar-sweeper screen, a dial delivering steady digital readings from the gyrocompasses, and knot, depth and distance meters, all of them relaying information from the ship's official navigation station just aft of the bridge.

When he finished his calculations he would have charted his own course for the ship, a Great Circle route of approximately 45 degrees north beginning at Bishop Rock—007 degrees west, and an estimated time of arrival at the radio beacon (RBn on the chart) at Sable Island, off Nova Scotia, 44 degrees west, 60 degrees north. In the next two days he would log the distance made good over ground, reckon in the weather information, and from all of that project an estimated time of arrival at the radio beacon 40 nautical miles south of Nantucket, 41 degrees north, 070 degrees west.

When he began his calculations, the gauges told him that *America* was heading east into a 16-to-20-knot northeast wind with seas of 4 to 6 feet, at 28 knots made good, toward the edge of Little Sole Bank, the eastern edge of the North Atlantic where the depth increases from slightly over 115 feet to over 800—and thus the precise instant when he would order (in his mind) the next change of course to RBn 44 degrees north, 070 degrees west, south of Cape Sable. Therefore his brain on vacation was as thoroughly engaged as it would have been at his desk back at the bank, but relaxed, conducting this completely different business he was doing only for himself, because he wanted to.

It was the only way that he had ever been able to enjoy himself, even under Summer Rules. He could put aside the intellectual activity and variety of work only for leisure that involved continuous, varied mental activity. He required a steady supply of fresh problems to be solved and new puzzles to be worked out; otherwise he was bored and in loud, profane misery, until he could manage to escape. At his desk in the NavStation, he had what he needed.

Once he had initially become resigned to the ocean-crossing, back in April (submitting reluctantly to the indisputable fact that indeed he truly was exhausted, and that his health would break down if he continued to refuse to take time off), his habitual practice had kicked in. He had begun idly to browse the literature of the great liners, to find out what he was getting into. He had been hooked almost at once, as usually happened once his attention had been captured, becoming increasingly excited by what he learned. The more data he acquired, the more he wished to have.

The literature had spoken glowingly in praise of the unidentified designing-genius who had somehow retrofitted the Station into the ship during *America*'s emergence from the mothballed slumber in which she had spent more than thirty years: "Shoehorning it in by the simple and expeditious means of lopping about 180 square feet off the formerly palatial kennels on Signal Deck (the nice doggies'll never miss it), this unsung wizard, whoever he was, made a lovely little indoor playground for the incorrigibly serious amateur mariner.

"He knew his man, as the British put it: the person who's never been aboard a boat, any boat of any size, when he didn't want the con, or wish in his own mind to tell the helmsman how to steer. All the possible instrument readouts, at your individual station; workmanlike parallel rules and dividers, etc., provided by Hayden Lines, or bring your own tools if you like. Two blissfully undisturbed hours a day all your own if you so choose, reserved and guaranteed for any deadheading skipper who wants to spend some of his passage-time completely absorbed in the only deskwork that a genuine old salt of any vintage ever loves, each day of the voyage if you like. Reservable by sign-up, first-come to be first-served. Mugs of great coffee served, too, at this transatlantic Station, as strong and hot as you make it on your own boat. A wonderful Real-Adult Activity Room, in short, the best we've ever seen shipboard."

So when he had been at it for close to an hour, she had been able to sneak up on him without any trouble at all, and when she said softly: "Mister Carroll, I presume," he was mortified to realize instantly he'd been adolescently startled. In another instant he knew the reason: There was a new wintry throatiness in the timbre of her voice; it had to be deliberate. She'd installed it since he'd known her. She was the kind of woman who had decided early that she wanted it to be there, and had put it there on purpose, probably defensively. Most likely she decided that she needed something like it right after first her own body had astounded her, unprepared, at menarche. And then after she'd discovered how puberty changed not only how males treated her but how she looked at males—learning what she could from him; he doubted it was much, except that if she played her cards right, or even if she didn't, she could have older men, on call like taxicabs—all the difference that it made. The temperature of that voice was intended to convey her invariable wry amusement at any unfamiliar situation in which she might ever after find herself, so that at least she would have time enough to size it up before she made some new dumb mistake, and would never again be perceived by anyone, principally herself, as being at a loss, taken by stunning surprise. So she would have systems too. She would always have already seen it all, whatever it might turn out to be, especially if she had never seen any such damned thing before in her whole life.

"You do indeed," was all he said, keeping his voice low as well. He glanced around the Station; the other skippers gave no sign that they had been disturbed. She was no more than thirty now, and after fourteen years or so of sexual awareness, eight since he'd helped her to pursue it, had a fully practiced understanding of what advantages she could gain from the shape of her body, her aquamarine eyes, the elaborately tousled style she chose for her honey-blonde hair and the way she had her clothes tailored. If Frances had been there—he was not sorry she was not—she would have been able to provide a more accurate appraisal than he could of what this beautiful young woman's gray wool blazer and skirt had cost, plus an accurate divination of what its unseen labels said (and its tailoring declared), but from the fine hand of the fabric and his years of paying clothing bills for the three well-dressed women in his family, he could calculate with fair confidence that if she'd paid full price for it she'd had about enough left from five hundred dollars afterwards to buy a small bunch of violets from the sidewalk vendor who would have had his cart at curbside right outside the Fifth Avenue main entrance of the store, plus perhaps one truffle from the chocolatier in the lobby of the hotel just up the block.

But then he recalled that he'd met her because her college work required her to live temporarily near Boston and her financial situation obliged her to stay with friends, and revised his judgment: That edged memory would have stayed sharp in her mind; her wardrobe would be impeccable, certainly, but it would have been assembled at outlets and discount stores, always at bargain prices.

"Melissa," she said, "remember me? I'm so glad you came." She displayed in her smile an array of teeth that he had never noticed before, when most of the time he spent in her presence he had been thinking about getting her clothes off or how rewarding it had been when he had gotten her to remove them the previous time. That smile represented either faultless dental heredity or a fortune in orthodontia. She extended her right hand. "I didn't mean to startle you"—So she'd caught that, had she? he thought. Sure, of course she would have; no point in first seeking and then gaining an advantage if you're not going to seize it. No, it would not be responsible anymore to play high-stakes poker with this child—"but I thought I'd better turn myself in, before you came and hunted me down. I'm the one who got you into this."

"Ahh," he said inartfully, "so you *are* the same one in fact. How many years has it been?"

"Eight," she said promptly, "exactly eight years. But you see, I didn't forget you."

"Wait 'til you get to be my age," he said, wondering how on earth he had mustered the courage to go after her when she was still a college undergraduate and he was a small-town bank officer circling his fiftieth birthday like a winded boxer in the ring with a dangerous opponent, recklessly trying to recapture a youth he'd never captured in the first place, and marveling that she had allowed him to do it, when she could have humiliated him; at the time unaware that the entire idea had been hers in the first place, to seduce her teacher's father in her teacher's mother's house, just to see if she could do it. Another area of field research she was doing on her way to womanhood. "You won't be able to remember whether something happened eight *minutes* ago, let alone eight *years* ago."

She laughed. It was a splendid, confidential laugh, not to be shared with strangers without express permission, and it was as practiced as a virtuoso's Symphony Hall piano recital, every note in perfect pitch. As though reading his mind she lifted her left hand to her hair and moved one strand a trace, showing him that while there was a good sapphire-and-diamond ring on the third finger, there was no wedding band. This woman she had become had gotten into a bad habit: the switch was always On; she seduced reflexively, automatically, when she could not imaginably have seduction in mind. She shook her head. "No, no," she said, "I doubt that. You were pretty lively when I first met you, when Claudia first brought me to your house. At least I thought you were."

She paused to allow him to volley, but he didn't know what to say. She went on, "And I doubt you're that elderly yet. But I'm *so* glad that you and Frances took me up on the offer. The bosses told me to get people I liked, who might come back and see us again. To favor the people who deserve favoritism, but don't always get it. 'The ones who get all wet when the rich're soaked, the people who give and don't get. They're the ones that we want on the boat. We will *appreciate* them, and they'll appreciate us in return.' By which I think they meant: 'Our stock will appreciate, and therefore so will our options.' But don't say I said that because I can't be sure. I can't be certain of that."

"I see," he said, swiveling back and forth through about perhaps fifteen degrees and rubbing his chin with the thumb and forefinger of his right hand, listening to her with part of his mind at work on the question of her motive for seeking him out, why she had gone to this effort.

"But even so," she said, "a lot of the people I wrote couldn't come, for one reason or other. I think the economy had a lot to do with it, myself."

"Death and illness, too, for that matter," he said slyly, to knock her a little off balance, draw her attention to the fact that this was not going to be her game to play all by herself, with her rules. "Given the average age of your clients, at least the ones I've seen so far, those factors could enter in too."

"Oh yes," she said, completely unflustered, "no question about that at all. But there'd be other factors, too, other than that; simply being tired of liners, wanting a train vacation this time, Orient Express perhaps, now that they've added a train in the Far East; or an African safari, a trip to the South Pole; or chartering a big crewed yacht, cruising the Med or something. Our guests tend to be fairly demanding people, used to getting their own way, and if the itinerary doesn't suit them *precisely*, or the destination's unappealing, something along that line, well, they simply will not hear of it. We can bury them under the literature, offer them all kinds of deals, and it will have no effect at all: they'll have none of us.

"But those were still my orders: To find the people who'd be likeliest to come, and then to give them first crack. Find out how they'd react. And then after we'd sort of polled all of our previous passengers, go into the second phase: Write back to those who'd said they'd come and ask them to invite two more friends, friends of theirs, and if they got another couple, well, they'd *all* go then, half-price. Friends who'd never sailed with us, but who our senior analysts figured'd be a group of people who'd try something new with us, that maybe *their* friends'd already done. Well, not really the same thing, in this case, but still, the same *kind* of thing, there being very few people left now who'd actually crossed on the *America* in her first incarnation, unless their parents'd taken them when they were children, and not very many did or do that; children get bored on big boats, unless they're the Caribbean ships, with lots of islands to visit.

"After all, she was only in service six years the first time, before the big jets made her overpriced in most people's eyes, and obsolete to boot, and that put her right out of business. Twenty-six crossings a year in those days, thirteen in each direction, same as the *QE-Two* makes now, except the first year there were just twenty-two. If every one of those sailings was full, at most a little over two hundred and twenty-five thousand crossed on her, all of those decades ago. But all of those sailings most certainly were *not* full. We did well if we averaged fifteen hundred, eighty-three percent occupancy, over the course of a season, and that was only when we filled her to the rafters on the six high-season crossings, in July and August. We only managed that twice, as best I could figure out now. That was why her first life was so short; she was really obsolescent before she got her bottom wet. It was really over well before it started, years before they admitted it. The last years she was nowhere near full occupancy, which was why they *were* the last years: Hayden Lines was bleeding money. That's why they threw in the sponge.

"But still, just assume that we did do that, average eighty-three percent for every trip all of those years. Of course a lot of those two hundred thousand–plus people've died, become ill, or infirm, or grown away from what they did when they were young. Now they do different things, things they've learned to like to do; well, there's only so much money, unless you're very rich, and even if you're very rich, there's only so much time."

She smiled and shrugged. "So we have to develop new markets," she said, "if we're going to make this thing work. We have no choice in the matter. Don't try to sell transportation these days, unless you're tanking crude or stacking silent containers of freight. Don't even try to compete with the Concorde, or Virgin Atlantic. Sell excitement, ambience, an unforgettable experience. Compete with the luxury trains. Compete with the exotic photography tours. Compete with the big-game safaris. The *America*'s no longer a slow, antiquated means of getting your body and baggage to England, without the nuisance of jet lag; what she is, is a five-day luxury vacation, an experience like none that you've had—and still without the nuisance of jet lag.

"That's how we have to sell her, how we have to proceed now.

Renewing existing friendships; building new ones on top of them. Selling gracious living to a generation of people who've lived their entire lives in a hurry. You know something? I bet it works. I think they'll go for it."

He decided she was trying to tell him something in addition to the topics mentioned. But she had encoded the message, perhaps to delay his understanding of it until after she had left him. "And those new friends," he said, "since they move in the same circles as the established ones, should not only be likely to be able to scrape up the money to do it, but most likely by this time made sufficiently envious by the high-rolling world-travelers' years of bragging so as to be pretty much sold at the start."

"Exactly," she said.

"Especially if you cut the tariff in half," he said.

She grinned. "Uh-huh," she said, "exactly. Again. Getting other people to do our demographics for us. Cuts down on the marketing overhead."

"And not only that but your salesmanship, too," he said. "Pitching their own friends to join them. Much more efficient'n buying up lists of people with gold credit cards. Who promptly take your glossy mailings, curse, and feed them into the fire."

"Without even reading them," she said merrily. "You're exactly right. But then of course you'd have to know it, of course you'd know these things. Banking now's very competitive, isn't it? Christmas Clubs just aren't enough. What you need now are the credit card accounts; the cash machines; the telephone banking, all night and all day; the computer-banking and the endless hours. You bankers aren't dealing in *money,* nowadays, anymore; nothing as dead-dull as that. What you are doing is marketing, *marketing.* Selling your service is what you do now, you and your competition. You don't sell interest rates anymore; in fact, considering what the rates are now on savings deposits, you probably hope the customers don't even notice them."

He laughed briefly. "Well," he said, "that depends on what kind of customer. We trumpet the low mortgage-interest rates, hoping to attract new borrower business at seven to eight percent, creeping up, but we tend to be quiet on the savings interest: what we hope is that the depositors won't ask."

"So," she said, having decided to pretend she had joined forces with a new henchman, "services are what you sell. And that's what I just said. The same's we have to do."

Yes. So she had done that. Melissa Murray had taken the trouble to tap some current data-profile of him somewhere and knew how he spent his life, along with, of course, his money. That was one thing she was telling him, without saying much about it, one partial explanation of why it was that she had contrived this meeting: to let him know she still knew him well, without having seen him in years. But that was still not the only message she was sending, not even the principal one; that one he had not yet decoded.

And even that small disclosure, the part he understood so far, raised a larger question: why she had done that, gone to all that trouble and worked up a profile on him. She certainly did not go to such lengths for all passengers, however promising they might appear as future Hayden repeat-customers, cash cows of the fleet. The only—partial—explanation was that she'd assigned the project to herself. And the only reason he could think of that would have prompted her to do that was so preposterous that he dismissed it out of hand.

He thought of the story told by the bank's lawyer, Sam Fairwood, of the only day in the first year of law school that he'd ever enjoyed. "It was the day that we tackled the case of that winsome defendant best beloved of the law, and the doctrine of frolic and detour. If the servant was about his master's business, merely *detouring* from the main road to feed the master's horse and to take sustenance for himself, when he injured the plaintiff on the narrow byway by running over him with the cart, well, that was the sort of interruption that the master should've foreseen, normal for such a trip, and the master was therefore liable for the damages resulting.

"*But,* if the servant had left the main road on some errand of his own, bent on some personal wickedness, when the plaintiff's injury happened—and of course we were at liberty to guess what tavern-mischief he'd most likely had on his mind, as we immediately and lewdly did—then the master could not be held in damages. He would have had no proper business reason to foresee that in the normal course of commerce a dutiful and diligent servant would interrupt his work to go carousing and wenching in a den of low repute, during regular business hours, nor any feasible means to prevent him from doing so, once he'd set out on his own. The master would not therefore in such a case be liable, for the servant had been off upon a *frolic* of his own. For the damages of which the poor rundown plaintiff of course would have no earthly reason whatever to sue the reckless and negligent servant, though to be sure he might have, if he wished—servants had no money to pay such damages." And that was what this young woman had been on, when she'd punched up computer codes after business had closed down, and drawn his profile on a disk: no business of Hayden Lines; a frolic of her own.

"And even all that still isn't enough," he said, "all of that damned marketing that we do these days, instead of just guarding the money, the function that we were designed for. Sometimes I think all we accomplish by our endless bright-eyed efforts to massage the people Out There into giving us their business is confusion of the public. Look how we bombard them. Read a morning paper. Watch the TV news at night. What you will get from us, and you'll get a lot of it, is an unrelenting din about how much we want your business and how good we'll be to you. We *little* banks run little ads; we feature little people. People who have obviously never been on television, and never should be, either, or third-rate actors in pretty good suits wearing neckties by themselves in their studies at eleven o'clock at night, just in case clients should drop in, pretending to be homey kind of aw-shucks folks who shouldn't be on the TV, hem and haw, uh-huh, and those actors shouldn't either, because they flat-out *stink* and don't look like home-folks at all. While the big banks run the big ads, big broad-shouldered ads, tough stuff: 'We can take the burden off you of that thirty million dollars that your crazy Uncle Murray left you by mistake in his last will. We can fix it so you never have to leave your fireside armchair, let alone your cozy nest, to set up your new subsidiary plants in Addis Ababa and Macao. That's what we can do for you, if you're man enough.'

"What we all do with all that stuff is engender great confusion. We convince people that we will take their money worries off their hands, at last, forevermore. They'll never have to worry about money again, and always have enough—although we sure-God don't say *that*; we leave that to their eager interpolation. And then after they do it, if all that doesn't happen—they *don't* have plenty of money—well, my goodness, of course we deny it, that we had any part in making them think that: 'My god, how they *do* imagine'—because we'll take care of it. For a reasonable fee of course. Which they then somehow get the impression we wouldn't even *think* of charging them, let alone take it out of their checking accounts. And which they don't find reasonable at all when they find it debited on their monthly statements. That's when they decide we're all a bunch of crooks, crooks who've deceived them, to get their money from them. And that's when we see our reputations sinking fast, getting down close to the lawyers'."

She smiled, satisfied she'd made an ally, enlisted a supporter, in what cause yet he did not know. She patted his left forearm. "I've really got to run," she said. "Attend to the performing artists and make sure we're still afloat. But I *did* want to see you again. I wrote to Claudia and told her I'd invited you and that you'd—well, that Fran'd accepted. But I haven't heard back from my teacher. Maybe she isn't speaking to me anymore."

She paused again, but he did not say anything, and then she said: "Well, do you know? Do you know if she isn't?"

"I don't," he said. "She always was a lousy correspondent, though. When she was first at Chapel Hill it was all we could do to get her to call home once a week, much less write letters to us. So if she isn't answering her mail from you these days, well, things haven't changed that much, I guess."

"You don't think it's because she's mad at me, then," Melissa said. "That she knows what went on between us."

"I don't know," he said, "I never mentioned it to her, but I don't know what her mother may've said. I don't know anymore what anyone knows, or whether that's why they're mad. Since what we had ended and you went away, I've thought about it a lot, and I guess I've decided that what happened, happened, and I'm not a bit sorry it did. I had one hell of a damned good time, and if it hadn't ever happened I would've missed something that I'm very glad I didn't. And that's all that there is to that."

"Yes," she said, reappraising him. She became brisk. "Well then," she said, "so much for that. Do have lots of fun while you're aboard with us. Don't miss the casino—the slots, roulette and baccarat, and the crap-tables, of course. And don't overlook the big bingo tournament, either: Usually on our other ships it's a carry-over game; so if no one wins today's big jackpot, it's added to tomorrow's. But this being a special trip, we're making it a progressive game, too: a thousand-dollar big prize today, and no matter whether anyone wins it, at least two thousand tomorrow, three thousand the third day, and so forth, so on our last day at sea there'll be a jackpot of at least five thousand dollars—maybe even fifteen thousand, if no one's won by then. And the concerts, and the nightclub, and the cabaret—there really is so much to do, just so much to do."

"And so little time," he said. "Just so damned little time."

8

At dinner, black-tie, Rutledge marveled nostalgically about the effect that the Wampanoag Club had had on Eldred Motley. "I think it truly was an aspect unique in his life. It was *external;* it was *durable;* and it was *regular.* He had no religious affiliation; said he'd never felt the need for any, even as a child, when his mother'd forced him to attend Presbyterian services, or as a young adult, when chapel was compulsory at school. He belonged to no social clubs in Boston; though his father had been a stalwart of Tavern and Somerset, Eldred was uninterested and never bothered to join. He did keep nonresident membership at Brooks in London and Century in New York, convenient for his annual visits, but the lodging or dining services they offered were the only ones he used. So the Wampanoag was the only outside association, involving other people, that he ever chose, or kept. At least during the time that I knew him, which was most of his adult life. The only one that *regularly, frequently,* got him out of his reflections, his house and Barlow, into the great world.

"I think that until Amy came along, that quiet, stuffy club may have saved his sanity. It certainly extended his life. It's fine for a man to be studious, as Eldred certainly was, and you do need your solitude for that; it's pretty hard to be studious when there's a crowd around all the time. But it isn't good for a man if his studies turn him into a recluse, and it would not've been good for Eldred if the solo work he did so much had done that to him. The Wampanoag Club protected him in that respect, and an important one it was. Because nothing else that I'm aware of, except his books and his music and his other private interests, ever completely occupied an hour of Eldred's time. Until it dawned on him that Amy might actually *love* him, and would probably marry him in any case, since even though she was eleven years younger than he was, time runs out sooner for women. Even if they do then go on to outlive most men. After which he thought of little else, other than of pleasing her. But I get ahead of myself here.

"The Wampanoag's in the Back Bay of Boston. Terrible nuisance to get to from Barlow. Even more of a terrible nuisance to get home *from*. We have no public transportation to speak of, you see, just a perfunctory bus or two a day, so if you decided you wanted to go to the club, you really had to go by car. And then of course, unless you had dinner there—which very few members did then or do now; the food's perfectly acceptable, ordinary New England fare, but there's so few others in the room with you, you'd just rattle around—you could look forward to spending your evening in rush-hour traffic. It was a pain in the neck to get to and from, at least from our end of the world, and it hasn't changed much to this day."

He said it was a narrow three-story brownstone building—neither Frances nor David recalled ever having noticed it, or even hearing of it—three doors east of the intersection of Commonwealth Avenue and Beacon Street on the northerly side of Kenmore Square. It was hemmed in and overshadowed on the west by the broad-turreted brick triplex housing above ground the six viewing suites and offices (the four embalming rooms, refrigerated vaults, casket showrooms and loading docks surrounded the freight elevator shaft and boiler room in the basement) of the Bancroft & Sons funeral home. On the east it was crowded by a residential brownstone duplex owned by a fraternity and occupied by engineering students at Boston University. Each weekend they morosely consumed large quantities of beer while loudly lamenting the unjustifiable demands of their curriculum and their shortage of sexual companions, blaming each for their woes with the other.

The club, Rutledge told them, had been founded in 1946 by a group of wealthy amateur historians—most of them much like Eldred in disposition but then much older than he, over sixty or close to it— to house the Wampanoag Foundation. They had formed it and obtained a charter from the Commonwealth "as an eleemosynary charitable institution, for the purpose of fostering and encouraging scholarly studies of New England regional history of all types, including but not limited to: anthropology; sociology; indigenous species of fauna and flora; geology; topography; and cartography; and such other disciplines as may from time to time appear; to advance the true scholarly and common understanding, appreciation and conservation of the region, by the establishment and regular presentation and award of such scholarships, fellowships, honoraria and prizes as may be appropriate to that purpose; and as well by the provision of a central gathering place for the founding officers and members, and such other persons of like purposes and interests who may wish to join with them, by obtaining title to, and thenceforward maintaining, in good upkeep and repair, a central headquarters in Boston, affording to the founding officers and such other members and their guests as may from time to time join with them: offices and meeting-rooms, a lecture-forum space, reception area, dining rooms, modest sleeping accommodations for males, and a library and repository, the latter to receive, safeguard, make available and maintain, whether by donation, bequest, acquisition or outright purchase, such books, manuscripts, journals, diaries, records, artifacts, and other such memorabilia as may from time to time become available and of lasting interest to scholars and historians of the New England region."

Rutledge explained how he had become able without noticeable effort to recite the material "not really verbatim, but almost." He did so between spoons of a western beef broth with vegetables, alternated with draughts of a '78 Château Beychevelle. "There was a dreadful lot of work that desperately needed doing in that club when Eldred brought me into it—that was a big part of the reason that he'd brought me into it, as he later admitted. And if he and I were going to overcome the resistance of the mossbacks to those crucial repairs and improvements—that we felt we had to do or the old place'd fall down; it hadn't been kept up or been attended to for years: the Old Boys didn't want their dues going up, you know—well, both of us really had to know that charter, know it right down to the ground. So that when we sprang something on the Old Guard, and they'd harrumph and start voicing objections—we were 'exceeding the charter'—we'd be able to quote it right back to them, verbatim. Or at least come a lot closer to doing it than they could. And we'd rush them right along, too: never let them have the time to go and look it up. So that enabled us to ram a lot of things through."

The charter preamble stated that the founders—there were thirty-eight of them, all men, each at the time of relatively comfortable means, and that seemed to them at the time like a workable quorum—had "associated themselves for this purpose," as opposed to the preexisting associations that all but eleven of them had previously formed with two or more other clubs, for boating, golf, riding and business-venues in and about Boston, "in the first instance in order to gather and preserve intact their individual and private collections of such materials for the use and instruction of students and scholars of the New England region, in perpetuity." Its deliberate draftsman (also a founder: Lyman Bolster, of MacManus, Wyman & Bolster, with offices at Three Park Street, Boston) thought that a more than sufficiently civil way of expressing the grim founders' shared determination to thwart not only what he liked to call "the grabby resurrectionists" of the estates division of the Commonwealth's Department of Revenue but also the disrespectfully mercenary plans of their own heirs-presumptive, several of whom had inadvertently (or even recklessly: in three jaw-clenching instances, prized troves of valuable possessions had been disparaged and dismissed with such wounding phrases as "all that old junk," or "that bunch of crap down in the cellar") made it clear that sales of each of the collections in complete sets or as small lots and individual pieces—at the best prices *immediately* obtainable, which meant that they would not be high—could be confidently expected to follow swiftly after the interment of each of the volunteer guardians, in his inevitable turn.

Rutledge said he had joined the Wampanoag in the fall of 1978, his eighth year as a member of the Board of Directors of First Suffolk Safety Deposit. "On Eldred's nomination, in both instances," Rutledge said, "but of course with my prior agreement to serve. I myself knew the man well by then. My father'd been his lawyer before me; he'd always spoken highly of Eldred, and on my own, succeeding Dad, I'd encountered no reason whatever to think he'd been taken in. Eldred did not live an adventurous life, but that in itself was a recommendation why the bank needed him on the board. 'And that's why the bank also needs you,' Eldred said, this being to me.

"So, I'd agreed to serve, partly for the same reason that Eldred'd agreed to take his dad's place on the board. FS-SD is primarily a custodial bank, a conservator of assets, and the most important quality an executive or director can have is not aggressiveness, as it is in the commercial trust companies—and also among the more active savings banks, credit unions and so forth, as far as that goes. No, the most important quality that anyone can bring to FS-SD is an inveterate habit of prudence, careful good judgment. Almost a Hippocratic-oath kind of good judgment: First do no harm. Don't agree to any risk in the administration of what your client has entrusted to you. If there is the remotest chance that the action you have in mind might result in a depletion of his assets, *you must not take that action.* Even if the safer action you *do* take will not bring really very much appreciation.

"As a major stockholder in the bank," he said, "Eldred was obliged to divulge—but only to us, not to the public at large; this was a simpler time, when men were presumed to act in good will until a grand jury indicted them—all of his outside interests. He told me that as a client, but then he'd had to, of course, for me to advise him properly. But he also told me later that I'd given him the kind of management he wanted for his money—'And a damned good thing for me, too; in all likelihood I'd be broke today without you'; that was what he said to me. And so he knew from working with me the sort of money management I'd afford to others. I don't think he'd mind me telling you that now.

"Because he was not by any means invariably prudent himself, where his own money was concerned." Motley, then still a bachelor, while his father was alive, had acquired at most a desultory fraction of the regional archivist's zeal that prompted the old man to subscribe ten thousand dollars to the initial capital fund of the club, and in the years thereafter before his peaceful death in 1966, at the age of eighty-eight, to reduce the family's capital even further now and then by gifts of between one thousand and twenty-five hundred dollars. "But Eldred confessed that he'd kept those gifts up, after his father'd died.

" 'My best guess is,' Eldred told me," Rutledge said, seeming to be merely musing over his fillet of beef Wellington, " 'my best guess'd be that all in all the old boy'—this'd be Eldred's father—'dumped a cool fifty grand or so into that club for kindly fossils, before he became history himself, back in sixty-six, and in the course of pleasing Dad—by becoming a loyal member over forty years ago—I must've sunk another twenty, in addition to the dues, into it myself.' He paused. 'In fact,' he said to me, 'you'd better make that thirty, now that I think about it.' "

*R*utledge lapsed into silence. He had gotten lost in his own mind and gone back twenty years before. By themselves as usual, he and Motley were sitting in the dimness of the Café Sonata, the old small waiter having vanished, talking over sharply chilled Gibsons served straight-up, the pearl onions gleaming palely at the bottoms of their glasses. They were at a small square table with a low brass lamp.

Rutledge remembered it had had a white paper shade dyed richly tan by the smoke of cigarettes of many years that had risen through it from the small black plastic ashtray at the lamp-base. From some other room a deck and amplifier faintly played Rudolf Serkin eight-track tapes of Beethoven piano works, also as usual.

"The café," Rutledge said to the Carrolls, catching himself in his reverie and willing himself out of it, "was in the cellar of a small residential hotel for refined ladies and gentlemen. I never saw a re-fined gentleman either coming out or going in, but I did see many of the ladies, much given to white lace at the collars of dresses of black, blue or deep purple silk; one gathered that *refined* chiefly meant *el-derly* and *alone*. One of them, portly old Queen Victoria type, gave tarot readings, filling her days and evenings, ten to twelve, two to four, seven to eight. Mondays, Wednesdays and Fridays. Eldred'd got-ten to know her from the café, over the years, and he'd never fail to flirt with her. Well, pretend to flirt with her, really. It was a whole routine that they had. She was as old as Great Blue Hill. 'Suppose your schedule's still far too full to work me in for a reading some-time,' which of course he had no desire for at all, as she of course very well knew, 'and perhaps a kind cup of tea.'

" 'Oh, my, yes, as always, chockablock-full,' she'd always say; it never varied. 'I do book an occasional Tuesday session, to accommo-date a steady but seasonal customer just back from wintering in West Palm. But I'm getting a little along in my years now. I have to re-member to rest.'

"Another one of the hotel ladies," Rutledge told the Carrolls, "—you understand that I got all of this from Eldred—kept busy augmenting her small trust-income and Social Security checks with about twenty-one thousand dollars a year in cash and personal checks. Apparently neither she nor her tax accountant, one of her longtime customers, saw any need to upset the IRS needlessly by suddenly commencing to report her earnings, and then paying taxes on them. 'Especially after having failed to do so since about'—this was Eldred's calculation—'nineteen fifty-four. She does it by tying "Dorothy's Best Custom" trout- and salmon-flies. Her work is uni-versally accounted by her dozens of satisfied clients—my father was an ardent fisherman, and he was among them. Another one's a prominent New York tax lawyer, formerly commissioner of the IRS. Themselves lured by words of mouth whispered confidentially, invariably by solicitous and treasured relatives or old comrades, bucking them up after a dejecting day of fruitless fishing. That does happen, you get skunked, even when you're a guest at some of the best lodges in the world. Near the banks of famous streams and lakes in New York, Vermont, New Hampshire, Maine, Nova Scotia, Newfoundland, Iceland, Greenland, Ireland, Scotland and Norway. And they'd all been assured, on those gloomy nights, that her lures were "without any question, not only by far the most expensive but the best damned trout-flies you can get on this whole earth." As I suppose they may have been. But as much as I know it disappointed him, I just never liked fishing that much. Any of the outdoor sports, I guess. I couldn't help that, of course, and I'm sure he must've known that. But I've regretted it all of my life.'

"The residential hotel where the Café Sonata was, was on Fairfield Street, in the Back Bay," Rutledge told the Carrolls. "It's gone condo now, and the Sonata went out of business years and years ago. Not enough ambience, I suppose, along with a great many other things it had going against it—proprietress growing old and so forth, way most of us seem to do. When you sat at a window table, as we invariably did after one of the board meetings at the bank, you looked up and out through the lower sash of whichever one of the eight windows you'd drawn; it didn't matter in the slightest which one. They were set deeply into the easterly wall, thick cement. Offered views from underground of discarded cigarette packs, matchbooks, candy wrappers and dead leaves blown into the cement drywells sunk into the sidewalk, and from the upper sashes the calves of pedestrians' legs and the wheels of cars parked along the curb.

" 'Not too scenic,' as Eldred put it," Rutledge said, "the first time that he took me there. 'But I don't come here for the view, and you sure can't beat the convenience.' Eldred'd proposed me, when the FS-SB decided to 'broaden our scope.' Whatever the hell that was supposed to mean. I think it meant someone'd died. From the Sonata it was only a short walk around the corner and then half a block down on Commonwealth toward Exeter Street to the bay-windowed, three-story, twelve-room brickfront where Eldred had his apartment. 'For the odd stroke of good luck, you know, which surprisingly enough still does happen. But nowhere near as often, I find, and then with much older women. But there are compensations. As Ben Franklin said, they're so grateful, you know? And I'm more grateful myself. Ever so much better than renting a room, you know, most awkward business that is, and handier to Symphony, except when that plumber's trying to play Mozart. About which he hasn't a clue. It was a black day for us when Leinsdorf left town. And to the Museum, when they have some special show on.'

"We dined at the Sonata once a month, at least," Rutledge said, conformably to their post–directors'/executive-board-meeting bargain, made six years before that when Motley had returned to service on the bank board after a six-week convalescence from his first heart attack. It had been a severe one, resulting from arterial blockages that would later require him to undergo triple-bypass surgery, as soon as he was judged able to bear it, in the following summer, in 1979. Saving Motley the bother of hailing a cab that would cost him four-forty (a four-dollar fare plus a forty-cent tip that he would have meticulously readied before leaving for the bank) for a ride back to the first-floor two-bedroom pied-à-terre on Commonwealth Avenue that the Motleys had owned since the turn of the century. In what he called his declining years, Eldred before onset of his heart trouble had prepared for the day's activities by situating himself for them either in Barlow or Boston, as might be called for, the night before. On board-meeting nights in Boston, he segregated four one-dollar bills in his left-front pants pocket and a quarter, nickel and dime in his righthand vest-pocket for the trip back to an empty flat and a cold dinner by himself. After the surgery Rutledge had ignored Motley's initial mild-but-pleased demurrer and put the considerable detour into his normal evening route from the State Street financial district to his own home—the simplest way was via the Central Artery to the Massachusetts Turnpike, and then onto 128—to furnish Motley his ride to his home-away-from-home. Motley, seeing his firm resolution, had then gratefully accepted. " 'But only on condition I stand dinner. Also drinks.' "

It had worked out very well, over the remaining years. The café offered eleven other tables, but the longtime clientele, unrefreshed by much new blood, had grown old, learning to prefer early dinners and bedtimes. Usually by eight or so no more than two of them were occupied. The middle-aged thin, silent man who had served them for several years seemed to be the only waiter on the premises. They could discuss any subject they chose, business or personal, regardless of its confidential nature and importance, or its public and complete triviality, a luxury they lacked at the bank and seldom enjoyed after other evening meetings with other people, away from it.

"Doesn't seem to make a lot of sense, in retrospect, I suppose," Rutledge said that night aboard *America,* pouring more truffled Madeira sauce over his beef, "that we kept on throwing money into it like that, when we knew it was on the skids. But it wasn't really an investment for us, something we did for the club; it was something we did for each other.

"It wasn't that neither of us gave it any thought," Rutledge said. "I put that question to him myself. 'Then why do it?' was what I said. 'If it's moribund'—as it clearly was—'then why the hell not let it die? If you know it's going under, I mean.'

" 'Oh, buying time, I guess,' he said to me, 'just buying the old wreck some time. Good ideas're worth preserving, at least for as long as you can, no matter if demand dies out. And let's be realistic here: I won't be doing it for that much longer anyway. I'm about at the same age now that my father and most of his friends were, back in forty-six, when the bunch of them got together and started the damned thing. Only four of them're left now, and old Ab Bohannon can't hold out that much longer, not at a hundred and one—although, give the old geezer his due, people've been saying that for a good many years now, ever since old Ab turned ninety. "Old Ab can't last much longer." But he's still kickin' around. Still startin' his luncheon off with his martini, I notice. Then havin' another one. Gettin' his palate prepared. And still one of our customers, too, our customers at the bank, still just as sharp as a tack.'

" 'Of course most of the original Wampanoagers—call them that 'cause they're members of the club, not the tribe—were, as I'm sure you aren't all that surprised to hear, customers of our bank, and their descendants are today. One way or the other, either as co-trustees with us, or as birdbrained, scatterbrained beneficiaries of spendthrift trusts that we administer. Because just as their ancestors figured they wouldn't be able to, see to their own interests, I mean, sure as shootin' it turned out: they can't. They cannot control themselves, can't control themselves at all. No more brains'n a dog's got feathers. Without us they'd go broke in a year. Those trusts were a damned good idea.'

" 'As was the club. *It* was a good idea back then, too, for the Originals to start it up, because there *was* a bunch of them had that interest in common. But now there aren't that many, not any more. They didn't breed much, those founders; not a real fecund bunch at all. Spent too much of their time digging up arrowheads, I s'pose, studying dusty old deeds. Must've exhausted themselves, made 'em too tired for romance. Although having met a lot of their wives, I'd have to say if I'd been forced to choose, nap alone would've looked pretty good. And those kids they did manage to breed, not very many bred true—not that many scholars among 'em. Or else they sired girls, strong brawny lassies, and the boys were the runts of their litters. Not bright enough to be much use to anyone, least of all to themselves. Not a really robust tribe at all.' "

Motley had exhaled and speared a roasted potato. "He said: 'I'm one of the few current members with a late founder even in the family, let alone a direct descendant of one. And the other members, the majority, few as they are, too, aren't what you'd call promising stock for the club's rejuvenation. Rather pallid lot. Oh, nice enough *people,* mind you, not a thing wrong with them there, but those who aren't widows, or widowers, coming into it or just sticking with it out of habit, mostly for the genteel social side, a nice convenient refuge to while away the idle hours drinking tea, a late-afternoon sherry, just getting around to reading the morning papers. The ones that really *use* the place for what it was meant to be, they're all short-timers, nonresidents.

" 'And even if they claim they're permanent, they're not even really convinced themselves. They're faculty at prep schools and small colleges, state schools all around New England, doing their obscure research for their obscure papers, that no one'll ever read, finally finishing up dissertations, after many sluggish years; all of them at least still trying to believe that when their work is done and published they'll be *inundated* with fancy offers that'll whisk them right out of here. They're mistaken, of course. They won't be.'

"He was right," Rutledge said to the Carrolls. "Mostly because of Amy. When she was still alive, I got roped into serving on about a dozen of those confounded search committees, seems like, between being on the boards at Fessenden and New Prep, and Worcester and Mount Ida, looking for new deans and so forth, headmasters at the schools, and we just got *bombarded* with their applications. Heck, from what the chancellors tell me, personnel directors too, we're still inundated with them every day, even when we're not looking. They're out there all the time, always looking to move on to a better time and place, where their dreams will all come true.

"I don't mean they're stupid, or that they're unqualified to teach. Don't mean that at all. What I mean is that there're just so *many* of them, and they all look just the same. The ones that really stick out, well, them we have to go and get, and boy, they're hard to sway. And damned expensive, too.

"Now I also see the outlines of the projects that our guest-scholars are working on at the Wampanoag, and the résumés that they submit. And those records tell me that the people who submit them to us're not in the select group, the ones committees go out looking *for*. These're the ones that're always volunteering, every time they smell an opening . . . And they never stand a chance.

"And that's the reaction that they'll get from the rest of the great uncaring world, if they ever do get finished—as a hell of a lot of them won't and don't, just sort of peter out, stop showing up, after vacations or something—dead silence. Or a form letter. No real reaction at all. Nothing really ever happens to them, either way. They don't actually get hired—they're lucky if they get an interview. But they don't actually get turned down either. Because nobody likes to do that. Make it official, I mean. Write a letter to someone that says: 'Sorry, Bub, you're just not good enough.' That's a pretty hard thing to do. There *isn't* any nice way to do it, and believe me, I know. Firsthand. I've had to do it in my time, now and then, and I haven't liked it a bit. I've *done* it, oh yes, I've bitten the bullet, swallowed the bitter draught down. But I didn't *like* doing it, one single bit, and if someone else who's supposed to do it somehow never gets around to it—well, I can't say I blame him too much.

"Still, must be tough on those scholars, or whatever you want to call 'em. Must get kind of discouraging, I guess, never knowing for sure, on any given day, whether you've still got a chance. Until the day finally comes, when it's been so long since you've heard anything, you know without picking up the phone what the answer is. Naturally you get down in the dumps; wouldn't be all that surprising.

"But anyway, when they finally do throw in the towel, that's often the last we hear of them. They give us back silence for the silence they got, for all the work they did here. Not even a letter of thanks for the time they spent with us, the fishcakes and baked beans that we fed them, all the weak tea and bad coffee they drank. Same farewell to us as the one all of their hard work is always going to bring them: resounding silence. They must know that, too, I guess. Probably always have.

"But by and large, my guess would be, they're secretly relieved. They *like* it here in Boston, Cambridge, Concord and so forth, being a real part of the scenery of the place. Just bit-players in the background, and they know it, too. But even though they know they're not good enough to be dominant figures at all, if they ever had to choose between being rather, well, unimportant, obscure spring peepers in their little puddle of this grand swamp, or locally famous great-horned bullfrogs roaring in a backwater somewhere else, I'd bet you they'd prefer to remain firmly seated on the small lilypads they've found here, thank you very much, and add their feeble croakings to the general Boston chorus.

"But it'd be kind of humiliating, you know? To come right out and admit it. If they were forced to do that. So they'd just as soon not be asked, and that's another thing that we do for them: We never ask how it all turned out, all that hard, dreary work they did with us. Whether it got published. Whether anybody cared. Another considerable kindness. Maybe *that's* why they just vanish, come to think of it—they don't know we'd never ask, and they're afraid we might, so therefore to be on the safe side they just disappear.

"Not that there's anything wrong with that, with what they're doing, either. That kind of harmless fantasy was the sort of thing the founders had in mind when they started the place. They maybe didn't think of it that way, but all the same, they shared it, one way or another, imagining themselves to be these brilliant amateurs of scholarship who at some future date—that somehow never got much closer—would *astound* the world of intellects with the work of genius that they'd produced, complete unknowns.

" 'The trouble is,' he told me," Rutledge said, at last dealing with his salad of garden greens with spring onions and radishes, vinaigrette on the side, " 'that from the club's standpoint there's nothing beneficial in those fantasies, either, not over the long pull, at least. The people who use the club for research now aren't the kind of people who established it. Not at all. Purebred amateurs, in the strict sense of the word; people who did what they did purely for the love of it, *and could afford to do it:* that was what the founders were, really.

" 'Not that they were extravagant, not by any means. Their philanthropy was real, but it was also pure—purely incidental. They didn't set up the foundation so the poor struggling scholars would have a warm place to study and a plain, filling lunch that'd stick to their ribs—no indeed, they didn't do that. They set up the foundation because the attorneys among them said that'd be by far the cheapest way to amuse themselves with the work that they wanted to do, while preserving the work that they'd done. The charitable, educational, nonprofit aspect of it was simply the only way to make what they put into their hobby deductible. Purely a hardheaded, practical decision they made, going that route to cut down the overhead by paying it with pre-, and not post-, tax dollars. Making their hobby-expenses deductible, best overhead that there is.

" 'But what we've got now, thanks to that shrewd tax-planning, are the apprentice, practicing drudges, who really ought to have baths, and the journeymen scholars who ought to get haircuts, and should have their clothes at least aired-out as well, if not professionally cleaned.' "

David laughed. Rutledge bowed to the applause and continued. That was a part of their unspoken bargain, along with the wines and the dinners (never mentioned by either, of course): Rutledge would accept the *carte des vins* at lunch and dinner, and order as he liked. "He knows more about it than I do," David said to her. And then he had spoken to Gregory, instructing him to bill Rutledge and him alternately, regardless of what was ordered. They understood that the conversations had been carefully composed in the other evenings he spent alone, with no one to listen.

"Randomly wandering glassy-eyed through the stacks like hired apparitions. They haven't got the means it takes to run a private Athenaeum-thing like the Wampanoag Club. They pay the nominal dues we require—full- or family-membership, associate, friend, whatever—and the visiting scholars, using our archives and so forth, who also want to eat and stay with us, make the very nominal contributions, that we really *have* to charge, to defray their board and room costs, those few that do need rooms—the meals are very cheap. But *every*one has to pay something; the days of fellowships, stipends and honoraria—even free rides—are long past, I'm sorry to say.

"None of this makes a bit of difference to the people who visit the club. Regardless of what category they pay in, dues or fees, or how much it is, none of that matters at all. They don't *consider* the sum to be nominal, not in the slightest. Those who don't openly resent paying have to be dunned, repeatedly, or waylaid and reminded that they owe us money, when they show up after their cards've expired. And then actually grumble as they dig their purses out. Well, they may be knuckling under but they still begrudge the money; don't kid yourself about that.

"They genuinely don't think the charges're justified. No charge for them possibly could be. And therefore when they *have* paid it, whatever charge they must, well, that's *all* that they're going to pay, no chance of anything more. The basic minimum. No sustaining memberships. No patrons or founders' clubs. They look at it like buying a ticket to the ballgame . . . well, probably not a ballgame, come to think of it; wouldn't be their cup of tea. Say, a concert, a recital or a play. They pay the going, asking price, the admission charge, but since they get no faculty- or student-discount like the kind they know about, are *accustomed to receiving,* and think that they *deserve,* they not only resent it—they think therefore that pittance is the *full* price, the actual, true, intrinsic value of what they're buying, and that should be enough.

"More than enough, in fact. If any other funding's necessary—they'd be willing to concede, purely for the sake of argument, that it possibly might be—well, given their vaguely Marxist hangovers they're firmly convinced it should *not* be expected from *them.* Aren't we aware that in the just society, each takes according to his need—or in their case, their worthiness, and they're all of them *very* worthy, as they're only too eager to admit? That each pays according to his or her means? Well, they don't *have* any means, as they see it, and even if they did, it would make no difference at all. They are simply not the kind of people who make *gifts* to worthy causes; they *are* the worthy causes.

"Eldred told me that. He said: 'Everything they tell you is based on the provision that you fully understand that premise: they are always rightly on the take, entitled to be on the take, and should never have to pay. They'd have to say, if we ever should ask them, that as far as they're concerned they can't really see why we seem to think it costs so much to run the thing, but they'll take us at our word: it does, and we do need it. *But,* we should either get it from endowment—which of course we *can't,* because that wasn't much to start with, and it's long since depleted now—or else raise the annual dues. In other words: Get it from somebody else. Preferably somebody who's dead and can't spend the stuff anyway; and if there isn't a dead person handy, then from somebody who's so old and decrepit he wouldn't get any fun out of it if he did go and waste it on himself, so that he'll never miss it. And if there aren't any dotty old invalids out there, to be euchred out of their life's savings, then charge everyone *else* who uses the place, but nowhere near as much, lots more money than we're charging *them.* But always: "Someone else will pick up the check." Theme song of their generation: "Put it on *their* credit card; I left my checkbook at home."

" 'And that's another thing we can't do, because if we did, we'd lose even more dues-paying members than we're losing now each year, just through normal attrition. The members who've stayed on because of family-tradition, purely sentimental reasons: if we raised the price too high they'd just have to draw the line. "How much can we spend on this Chinese ancestor-worship of ours, after all? We'll have to draw the line somewhere." And the newer members, those sullen, dusty, ghostly scholars: well, no matter what they say they think, or what they tell themselves, they *can't* afford, really, to pay their share of what it costs to run the place. And so they quite reasonably won't, if we ask them for it.' " Rutledge drank some of the Bordeaux. " 'If we do,' he said, and he was right, 'they'll just get mad, and that'll be the last we'll see of them.'

" 'And you'll—the club, I mean—be worse off than before,' I said to him.

" 'That's about the size of it,' Eldred said. I remember that he sighed. 'My father used to bring me here,' he said, 'brought me here for dinner after Symphony, or to Dini's for lunch, before. We saw Maurice Tobin in here one night, when he was governor, and Edwin O'Connor several times before *The Last Hurrah* came out. Arthur Fiedler used to come in, when he could corral someone else to pay, and Danny Kaye would have a meal here, when he had a show in town. My father introduced me to Fred Allen in this place, and one night when we came in, Bob and Ray were here. Bob Elliott and Ray Goulding—he knew them from way, way back, and they did two of their routines for us and about six other people, right here in this room. Pulled Philippa right out of the kitchen, along with whoever else was working here back then, a Wally Ballou skit and then the second one was a Mary Backstage thing: "Mary Backstage, Noble Wife."

" 'Now my father's long gone and so're most of them, not all of them yet, but it's not hard to see what the trend is—Dini's is going, I hear. I don't know, really, if any even slightly famous local characters've even been seen in here for many, many years. If they've dropped in, *I* haven't noticed or seen them. My eyes must be giving out too. Or how long it'll be until Philippa comes out of the kitchen some night and tells me it's her last one, that she's closing down for good. The good years my father knew, and the good things he loved to do, those are the years that have gone by, and the things've gone by too, along with them.'

"Then he thought for a little while—waited, really, as though he was thinking about something, and wanted to be sure he'd gotten it right—and then he picked up his glass, like this." Rutledge picked up his glass and stared over the wine at them, and said: " 'I know all this,' he said, holding up the glass and looking at the drink. 'I know very well that the time for things goes by, and always has. It wasn't Cole Porter's idea; he wasn't the first one who noticed, anymore'n I'll be the last one. And there's not a thing that anyone in this wide world can do to make the things that go by, summers or Christmases, or lives, last any longer than they do. Or do to bring them back, after they've gone away. But still, you know? You have to try. You have to do at least that much, to try to make them last, as long as possible.' "

"For whom, if you know they've gone by, and most of the people've gone with them? Or for what, if that's not the right question," David said, as gently as he could. "Who or what're you doing this for?"

Rutledge set the glass down and folded his hands on the table. "That's what I said to Eldred that night," he said. " 'Oh, I don't know,' he said. 'Various things. Ancestor-worship, as I just said. Filial piety, maybe. Honoring the Lares and Penates, our family household gods. That could be one of the reasons.'

" 'But your father's *dead*,' I said. 'I don't mean to question what your beliefs are, but 'til now I've sort of assumed that, well, that you weren't too religious, and if that was wrong, well, I'm sorry.' "

Rutledge made a dismissive flicking gesture with the tips of the fingers of his right hand. "That was what he did then," he said, "when I asked him that. He said: 'Do I think that he's up there, watching?' he said. 'Looking on and being proud, pointing me out to his old pals that he knew when he was here, on their way to the biweekly meeting of the executive board, First Celestial Safety Deposit? Admiring my devoted work at my studies and the bank, using the skills that he taught me? And my generous gifts to the club, carrying on his quest for historical truth? Nudging his good friend, Johnny, Johnny Cangelosi—Dad always got the best cuts of meat when he went to Johnny's store in the old Quincy Market, when it was still the real Quincy Market, not the multimillion-dollar-a-year tourist attraction that it is today. "Hey, Johnny," he's saying to him—they always kidded each other; he approved all of Johnny's loans—"your kid's doin' good, you say? Good for him and good for you: that is what I say. And over there, see over there? 'Atsa *my* boy, there, and he's doing just fine too. Just like I always wanted. We brought those kids up *right*." Is that what you think I think?'

"He laughed at me," Rutledge said. " 'Put your mind at ease; I do not. I have not lost *all* my buttons. But do I think that those four surviving founders are looking on from right down here, where they are today, although it may not be for long, dozing in the reading room, having their fish chowder, enjoying their nonvintage ports of modest price, and shouting at each other to hold normal conversations, from transcontinental distances of three or four feet off? You bet your life I do. They see me, my father's son, being loyal to his purpose at the club just as I've been at the bank, and that pleases them. They don't see many of their own doing that in either place. I know they appreciate it. It makes them feel better, allows them to think, if they like: Here is the proper continuity of life. Someone who *knows*, is here among us. Someone who will carry on.

" 'I represent the institutional memory of their lives. I arrived while they were still vigorous, and by the looks of things I'll be around at least a little while after the last of them have gone, making sure that when it's my turn to join them, someone who remembers *me* will therefore remember them. Not who they were, as individual people, but *as* they were collectively: what they stood for; what they did; the code that they obeyed. So, the things that they've valued during their time will endure after they've gone.

" 'So: yes, to that extent, in some small way I guess I do: Hope that sort of makes up to my father for the fact I never had a son. To grow up as his grandson. To carry on when I am gone, and further honor him. Evens things out, as much as I can, for not having given him that. He had high hopes for it—as most fathers do, I guess, although never having been one, I wouldn't really know. But yes, in some odd-angled way, I guess, I'm doing it for him.'

"We'd both ordered *boeuf Bourguignon* that night," Rutledge said. "I can see it as clearly as if it'd been brought to me today. They cooked and served it at the Sonata in individual portions, in brown casserole boats accompanied by plates heaped with flat noodles. The café offered wines in magnum bottles. They labeled and stored unfinished bottles for frequent customers. I remember the silent waiter, that night as always, wrapping the neck of the bottle with a large white napkin. Removing the cork and sniffing it to ascertain that the second half of the '67 Château Palmer remained potable, and then solemnly pouring the claret, first into Eldred's glass, deferring to his status as senior customer and host, and then into mine. And when he had wiped the neck of the bottle with the napkin, he set it on the broad flat sill of the window at the table, and disappeared again.

"We raised our glasses, nodded, and drank a silent toast, to some damned thing or another. As we always did. And then I surrendered and said: 'Tell me something, Eldred, if you'd be good enough: just what does membership entail, in the Wampanoag Club? Is it like being born-again, like Mister Carter says he is, and joining some new church? So you have to go to meetin', seems like every blessed night, and can't talk about a single thing in this whole world, 'cept you got right with *Jesus,* and therefore so should everyone else?'

"He laughed at me again and said: 'No, no, not like that at all.'

" 'Not like the difference between having fun and just staying a regular old drunk, instead of getting uppity and trying to get classy, becoming an alcoholic—so you have to go to meetings all the time?'

" 'Nope,' Motley said, 'no resemblance to AA at all. Although I do have to say in point of fact that now and then I have thought that one or two of our membership stalwarts might give some consideration to affiliation with that particular association. Abner Bohannon, for example: Abner's an eminent old toper. To my own personal knowledge, while he was en route to his great seniority, he was an elderly old toper of impressive capacity, and before that he was a middle-aged old toper of formidable intake. According to my father, Ab was well-known as a collegiate old toper in their Dartmouth days together, and never to my father's knowledge ever missed a beat, not one single day, of taking on his full ration, going on through middle age. My father in fact told me a good many times, "Ab'll never die. Why should he bother? He's got no reason to move on, nothing to be gained. He's been embalming himself every day since he was weaned at the age of five, and if there's anything to this heredity stuff, his mother probably saw to it that her milk that suckled him was pretty well-spiked too." For a long time now it's looked to me like Dad was probably right.

" '*But,* and this's the important thing, from Ab's point of view, while he's drinking at the club, every day so far's I know, he goes there because he *wants* to, not because he has to go. He could drink somewhere else, if he liked; he could even drink at home. Attendance is not taken, at the Wampanoag Club.'

" '*So,* if someone were to join, but then almost never went there,' I said," Rutledge said, " 'the other members wouldn't get, well, all *put out* with him. I guess. "Take offense" or "be annoyed," would be what I mean to say.'

"And indeed they were not," Rutledge said. " 'Absolutely not,' Eldred said. 'In fact, the new member wouldn't even have to *visit* the club before he joined, or ever go there afterwards. All he'd have to do is fill out a form, get two sponsors and write out a check. In due course—meaning, perhaps not by return mail, but at least as soon as his check cleared—he'd hear from his principal sponsor that he'd been promptly admitted, and welcomed, and here was his membership card. Who'd ever know if he never showed up? So few ever visit the place. And most of them, when they do, don't even come into the club. They're using their parking privilege, which may be the real reason that they get and keep their memberships in the first place: it's so *convenient* for the ballgame.

" 'It reminds me more than a little, in fact, of that most peculiar society in the Sherlock Holmes case of "The Red-Headed League," the club with two members, the first of them seen only once by the second, the day he landed the job of copying the encyclopedia. So few are the visitors now, if you tripped an antipersonnel mine in the place almost any afternoon or early evening, you'd certainly do some most regrettable property damage—we *do* have to keep the place in the best shape we possibly can, you see, since we may have to sell it at any time if we don't raise some cash pretty soon. So property damage *would* vex us; you'd have to make good on that. You'd be posted for sure 'til you did. And you might also fetch a meek scholar or two a nasty shrapnel wound, but we have so many of them, we could easily spare one or two. Otherwise, no real damage.

" '*So*, unless the member, old or recent, decides to commit a genuine atrocity—something along the lines of those forbidden by the Geneva conventions—we're in no position to chivvy him. In the first place, we're so chronically strapped for cash that we'd probably think twice before we'd dare to do so much as even *chide* a paid-up member who'd been convicted, say, of molesting trusting wee little tots, and was about to go to jail for a long spell, let alone *chastise* one for confining his club activities to aloofly sending in nonrubberized checks while yet remaining standoffish.'

" 'And, if I may ask,' I said," Rutledge said, having made his way through his dinner, " 'how large would those checks generally be?' He was a good man, Eldred was. He frowned. He kept his eyes focused on his plate and chewed for a moment or two until he answered. 'Well,' he said, having thought about it and swallowed, 'the initiation fee's thirty-five hundred dollars—which is actually pretty low, not really enough, as private-equity clubs go, the members each owning a share of the assets, the building and so forth, you see, not enough to keep the place running—but still a good deal more than the younger generation's accustomed to laying out to join the privately owned, for-profit clubs they usually tie up with these days.'

" 'And the annual dues?' I said. Eldred still did not lift his gaze. 'Eight hundred,' he said, 'this year, that is. Next year, I'm afraid, it'll be nine. Have to be, no way around it. Plus any bar bills the member incurs. Anything of that sort in addition.' "

"Forty-three hundred dollars," Carroll said.

Rutledge nodded, continuing to chew, his eyes still fixed on his plate. " 'If you'd scout up another sponsor for me,' I said, 'I'd apply for a membership, Eldred.'

"The frown deepened. The chewing stopped. Eldred swallowed again and lifted his gaze. He cleared his throat. When he tried to speak his voice was still somewhat clotted, so that he had to shake his head irritably, cough, and take a drink of wine. 'I, ah,' Eldred said, 'I hope you don't feel like, well, you've been'—his voice trailing down—'*pressured* in this at all. I wouldn't want to think that, that that might be how you might feel.'

" 'I didn't feel "pressured," in any way, Eldred,' I said. 'I interpreted what you were saying as what one good friend who could really use a favor would say to another good friend who would do it if he possibly could, but whose circumstances might not allow him to do so.

" 'As it is, my father with the assistance of much canny advice shrewdly managed things so that though he *did* die, far too early, I've always had more than I've really had, or ever will have, any need of. Believe me, Eldred, I can afford this. So while I'm inclined to side with you, that he's not up there, looking down, he did take damned good care of me, while he *was* down, not just looking, here. And you helped him to do that.'

" 'Now and then,' Eldred said, 'now and then. At least I rather hope I did, anyway. That was what I meant to do.'

"So that was what Eldred was like," Rutledge said. "And he was who Amy first married."

9

"The Nevilles lived in the big three-story ivory Colonial overlooking the Common. If you're coming into Barlow from the east, it's the first big house you see. And a big majestic old barn it is, too, built in the late eighteenth century by the town's namesake, Roger Barlow. He owned the mill at the falls. That mill did all right by him, too. He must've been one rich fella. He owned most of the land in the town. Have to, if you want to name it after yourself, or if you're too modest then after you're dead someone else thinks the decision's so obvious they do it for you. Most of the land that went with the house'd been sold off, as you'd expect, by the time Henry got his hands on it—it'd been in his family before that, of course; his mother'd left it to him—over the course of nearly two hundred years. But quite a lot still went with it, when Amy inherited it from him. Little over twenty acres, according to surveyors for the people who bought it when I settled Henry's estate. Not much for Texas or Kansas, maybe, but a lot for our part of the world.

"Piece of land that desirable—and that *size*—in a town like Barlow, well, it attracts the tax assessors like salt licks draw deer. And judges' salaries back then being what they are today—and what they've always been in Massachusetts: disgraceful, pathetic, the short route to the poorhouse; we expect you to eat the prestige, and exchange it for shelter and warmth—Judge Neville had money troubles. I know from my father that he got so sick of it, so damned tired of always wondering how'd he pay the next bill for insurance or whatever it happened to be, that he sometimes thought of selling off the acreage and getting off the bench. And then if he couldn't make a go of it in private practice, after being so many years away from it, well, he figured he and Amy could live off the profit from the land sale—plus what they wouldn't be out every year anymore, paying much lower real-estate taxes—for the rest of his life."

David had invited Rutledge to join them for an after-dinner drink in the Senator Club, to her mild displeasure. She would not have objected to a nightcap much later, after spending two or three relatively nonalcoholic hours in the casino—or even better, watching the French art film in the theater, with no drinks at all. So he had managed to duck it again, as he had when it had played first in the multiplex theater in New Bedford, and then again when it had played an extended run in the shabby little theater in Bradbury. As she would write to Kitty, she was "willing to concede the extension proved nothing about the film's excellence." The Bradbury theater was "a stripped-down operation principally attracting geezers still believing that conversations ought not to be conducted in the audience during movies, and that unfinished soft drinks shouldn't be dumped on the floor. But I guess we're an endangered species. There don't seem to be very many of us. If a given movie attracts at least eight people every night for a week, it's certain to be Held Over."

She knew at once he'd spotted the listing in *America's Daily Log*, slipped under their cabin door that afternoon, and, as she wrote to Kitty, "curses, used it to foil me again. He'll never actually come right out and just refuse to see that film with me—that's another thing that annoys me: When I say that's what one of them is, he says: 'Oh, you mean it's a *movie?*' He can be a maddening man.

"I sometimes do think, though, when he's done something like that, that he does seem to have coarsened a little in the years since we were young. Back in those days we went to see films like *Hiroshima, Mon Amour,* and *L'Avventura,* and *La Dolce Vita,* and he was docile enough. But now? No way, he won't go. None of the women (I was going to say 'ladies,' but I stopped myself in time; once you start thinking in those terms about women only slightly older than you are, you're definitely getting up there) that I've met in the years we've been in Bradbury have had much response to make to any light conversations I've attempted to raise on the subject. I don't think they really knew, or even cared to know, to tell the truth, what on earth I was talking about. So there's no help for me there. And I *hate* going to the movies by myself. Claudia used to go to them with me (I think she was humoring Mom), but of course now she's down at Chapel Hill. So now except when she and Walter and the boys come over here for a week to visit us, after they've spent August at his parents' place on the Vineyard—the week after Labor Day the fall semester gets underway in earnest at the university and they both have to go back; they both like the island better than they like it here, not that I blame them; there's ever so much more to do—I have no one to go with me. And then it's not only touch-and-go whether one of the theaters will be showing one of the films I want to see; it's also whether we really want to spend that much of the little time we get to spend with each other these days sitting silently cooped up in the dark at the movies. So the upshot of the whole thing is that usually I don't get to see anywhere near the number of films that interest me. I don't mind telling you, Kitty, there're times when that pisses me off.

"In my cooler moods, though, I suppose the explanation more likely is that David's just got so much more on his mind at work these days than he did when he was at Treasury, that when he actually *gets* a little time he thinks he can afford to spend just relaxing, he doesn't want to spend it doing anything that might require him to think. Time off for him these days, well, he wants it to be time *off*. The trouble is that all too often these days that means he pours his relaxation from a bottle into a glass."

But as the three of them sat at the table next to the wide port— she facing it, watching the dark ocean stream by narrowly in the white beam of the ship's lights, the two men facing each other; the pianist delivering a lavish performance of "Begin the Beguine," in the center of the lounge behind her; on the four-couple dance-floor one elderly couple expertly showing off, all by themselves, ignored by the rest in the room—Rutledge was nursing his Calvados. That surprised her, since she'd seen how greedily he had tucked into the wines at lunch and dinner, making good on his word to hold his own on that score. She was also reassured: When drinking with others, David tended to pace his consumption to theirs, and after nearly half an hour he still had nearly a third of his first Warre's late-bottled vintage port before him.

" 'That'd still leave her the house,' Henry Neville told Dad, 'and after I'm gone, she could sell that for another fair piece of change. Won't *need* so much room, all by herself as she'll be of course when that happens; be a burden to her, in fact. Not that I'm in any damned *hurry* for it to happen, of course.' But the Judge was guilty of doing something that all lawyers, especially judges, are supposed to always remember not to do. We're taught it from the beginning: Never assume anything. He was *assuming* Amy would be by herself, and expected to be, after he went to his reward. When, as far as I know, she'd never conceded that point—and *if* she had, she went back on her word when he did, just as fast as she could.

"But it was only natural he would do that, make that assumption. So did everybody else who couldn't read her mind, as no one I ever met could—and there was a heck of a lot more going on in there than anyone assumed. It was a lot different, too, what was going on in there. Not at all what you would've thought, to've seen her all devoted and demure, the prim maiden lady attending to her dear father. 'Get herself a little place and teach her music lessons.'

"Amy was very accomplished at the piano. She also taught voice and two or three of the reed instruments as well, although in her later years, by the time we were married, she'd pretty much given up the other things, the clarinet and oboe and saxophone, and stuck to piano. There wasn't much call for them then. Seemed as though what the kids who didn't want to play piano wanted to play was the electric guitar, and she had no patience for that. Rock and roll. 'Maybe land a job teaching school right in town here. Wouldn't pay her much, of course, those positions never do, but then it wouldn't have to. That's my one consolation, when you come right down to it: After I'm gone and she's all by herself, when I'm not around to look out for her and take care of her, Amy'll still be all right. She'll still be well taken-care-of.'

"When Amy, of course, was the one doing the taking care of, and he was the one being cared *for*. But Henry always talked like that, as if he was down in the dumps about something. Feeling sorry for himself. People he knew, like my father, well, after a while they got used to it. Not that they had a whole lot of choice: it happened a lot with the Judge. 'Only thing, really, you *can* do,' Dad used to say, 'let the poor man talk it out. And that can take a long time, a whole evening, because when Henry gets down in the dumps, he *really* gets down in the dumps.' He'd get to feeling real low.

"I think it'd probably've been fair to say—and most likely would've *been* said anyway, fair or not, if someone in his position went downhill that way today, way that people've gotten so now— that Henry was losing his mind. If he'd been around in recent years and sitting on the bench, you know what'd be in the papers, what everyone'd be saying: that he was clinically depressed and ought to retire. 'And if he won't step down, well then, throw the bum out. Not fit to be meddling around in the lives of parents and children, the way a judge has to, when he's sitting on the probate side.' As though what judges do in the civil and criminal sessions's got no effect at all on the lives of parents and children—which unless I'm mistaken is three words for one, which is *people,* most of whom've had parents, and many of whom have had children.

"We're all so *damned* critical now, so all-fired damned certain we're right. Have to impose our views on others, regardless of what they may think. But back then in the fifties and sixties, well, you hear a lot now about how people mistreated minorities then, and didn't treat women right. All the men acted like Ralph Kramden, stomping around, blustering all the time about these great ideas they had that somehow never seemed to turn out right; and all the women just sat back and took it, like Alice. Bullies and martyrs.

"Well, it wasn't like that. Most people didn't act like that then, or generally didn't, not that *I* saw, at least. Not that there weren't some faults in the way things were then, when if you possibly could, you overlooked a man's faults, or his weakness, turned a blind eye to it, as long as you could. Of course there were some times when things went wrong, something went wrong because of it. But usually everybody muddled through pretty well. The other judges and the people in the clerk's office saw to it the tough cases got routed to somebody else, and when a case that everyone thought was simple at the beginning turned out to be pretty complicated, well, the other judges sort of made it their business to keep abreast of it, and mention it from time to time to the man who was handling it, encourage him to talk about it, and then give him some fairly forceful advice about what he ought to do with it. And all the time the calendar was working its magic, and pretty soon mandatory-retirement age did the rest. Mopped it up. Nobody's feelings got hurt.

"People were more *circumspect,* then, about individuals, I mean. And there *were* individuals back then, not members of *groups* like today, every damned one of which it seems like's got some kind of beef or another, so they should get special treatment and privileges, which usually means a better crack at a cushy job than a white man can get, and a whole lot of government money. Back then as long as a person could function, *did* function, was still showing up on the job, and you knew he was doing his best, well, most people felt he deserved a fair chance to get things worked out for himself, and they'd cut him some slack while he tried.

"People don't think that way anymore. Now they say: 'No, that's not the way to do it. There were a lot of abuses back then.' I think they imagine a lot of them, though I suppose some damage must've been done, by people who stayed in power too long, after they'd lost control of themselves. But what I myself think is that people were kinder, not so damned ready—hell, *eager*—to judge, when somebody else had some bad trouble, knocked him off his pins for a while. Almost as though now what people really *want* to see is someone go down, so then they can start kicking him. Right in the teeth. A couple of my young friends on the board at the Barlow Bank say I'm just getting old, and maybe they're right, but anyway, that's what I think.

"And as far as that went, if Henry was, well, disturbed, he had pretty good reasons to be. And since Barlow was a small town then, just as it is now, and since he'd been born and brought up there, in addition to spending the rest of his life there, just about everyone who lived there knew about those reasons, in detail. And, I suppose, made allowances for him. He never did any real injury or harm to anyone *I* ever heard about, either when he was still practicing law in the town, or after he went on the bench. And you can bet that I *would've* heard, too, just for that very reason: because it *was* such a small town, and his court was the one down the street. And as I say, I never did."

Rutledge hesitated. "I always liked Henry, myself. I suppose that was partly because my father always admired him, 'after all the poor man's been through.' But it was also because, as *I* got to know him, he struck me as courageous, even though he knew that could cost him something—as it *certainly* had—to face up to things like he did." He fell silent and looked melancholic.

"To be polite," she would later write Kitty, "and because he so obviously wanted either me or David to do it, offer him some reason to think that we were both glad he was with us, and more interested in what he was saying than we were in the piano music, not bored by an old man's garrulity, I said: 'What sort of things do you mean?' But in fact, I guess we both actually were more interested in his memories than the music. The piano player wasn't *bad;* just kind of, well, *normal.* The music was all right, nostalgic, but nostalgia's not all that it's cracked up to be, not when you get to be our age and really get eligible for it. We'd all heard it all before, many times, and quite a long time ago. The standard, right-out-of-the-fifties, grown-up, cocktail lounge repertoire: Cole Porter; Richard Rodgers; the old Gershwin songbook; 'Satin Doll'; 'Sophisticated Lady'; even a couple of the old tunes I heard played by Glen Gray and his Casa Loma Orchestra—'Mood Indigo,' stuff like that—at one of my proms in college. All of the songs we always heard at dances, and in the oh-so-In bars in Philadelphia and New York that we went to back then, when we still had to use fake IDs. Before the Platters and Elvis were acknowledged in polite adult society.

"Now that I think of it, in fact, the pianist looked like he might have been right out of that era himself, but now once again going strong. Like he'd been mothballed along with the boat. Or frozen and kept in cold storage, then thawed out again, just for our trip, after which he was probably going to shatter, just break into a million bits."

"Well, to start with," Rutledge said, "his daughter, Amy, was the oldest, and she just worshiped her father. But the apple of Henry's eye was always her brother, as though he'd never gotten over learning about the rule of male primogeniture in law school, and never intended to, either. That would've been William, which no one hardly ever called him. Or 'Will' or 'Billy,' either, because five minutes after you'd been formally introduced, he told you his friends all called him 'Rover,' and since he hoped you'd be his friend, he hoped you'd call him that, too. I never knew how he'd come up with that dog's name for a nickname, although like everybody else, that was what I always called him, even when he wasn't around. Amy's theory was that he'd lifted it out of his dad's boys' books about the Rover Boys, because that's what he was reading—he read all the time—when it first dawned on him that he'd always hated his real name. She said she thought he wanted to be Tom, the fun-loving Rover. Or maybe, I think it was Dick, the serious Rover. And there was another one too. His name I forget. She admitted she didn't have any real evidence; that was just her surmise. But anyway, if you mentioned him in a conversation, didn't matter whether you were younger or older, that was how you referred to him: 'Rover.' Usually without even his last name. Everyone knew who you meant.

"He was the kind of man—heck, he was the kind of little *boy*— who could make people do what he wanted. Well, more like: *Get* them to do what he wanted. Make them *want* to do what he wanted. Follow his wishes and carry them out, and be grateful that they had the chance. That he'd done them the favor of letting them know, so they could do exactly what was going to make him happiest.

"He was a *genuinely* charming young man. His charm wasn't the least bit counterfeit, the slightest bit forced, if you follow me. It was the real McCoy. My father used to say that Rover was a born politician. 'He has a gift. The only human adult males'—he said it really wasn't fair to ask any man, even a man like Rover, to charm another man the way that any halfway good-looking *woman* could do it, without even trying—'that I ever met who could've competed with Rover in the charm department were FDR, JFK, and Richard Cardinal Cushing. I didn't subscribe to any of their views. I was strongly opposed to all of them. But if you'd caught me within half an hour of the time I met any one of those guys for the first and only time I ever did, before I'd had time enough to come out of my swoon, get a grip on myself and recover my wits, I would've sounded for all the world like one of their disciples. Maybe even one of their *apostles*.

" 'But even while I was going under their spells, and then afterwards, while I was still under hypnosis, I was always aware, in the back of my mind, that I was getting the Treatment. Getting my back scratched, arching it in bliss; begging for more like a big, hairy, stupid, slobbering *dog*. Grateful for the attention. But still fully aware that whoever was doing it wasn't having anywhere near as much pure *fun* as I was; he wasn't having any fun at all. He was doing actual *work*. Work he was very good at, superbly good at, but still: actual work. Just like a lot, if not all, of other people who'd buttered me up, but weren't anywhere near as good at it, and failed: They all wanted something from me, that *something* almost always being money, and so for that reason, and that reason alone, they were making a real special effort. Exerting themselves, doing their best, to persuade me to give it to them.

" 'With Rover you just never thought that. The thought never entered your mind. Rover had an *effortless* charm; he didn't have to give any thought to doing it, and he didn't have to extend himself at all while he was doing it. Henry said to me one night, while Rover was still at Andover—this was a year or so before the Japs and Roosevelt combined to get us into the war—that he thought if the people who had sons and husbands Rover's age could only somehow come to their senses, *see* what they'd be risking with their patriotic cheap heroics, that someday Rover if he wanted to could sit in the US Senate. And I said to Henry that night, meaning just what I said, and no disrespect for the Senate: "Why on earth should he settle for that?" '

"Well," Rutledge said, as the pianist flicked on a CD-player next to his bench and in a Germanically guttural voice said into the microphone that he was "haffing a short break now, you know—vee do get a liddle time off," but that he'd "soon be beck." George Shearing's version of "Lullaby of Birdland" came up as he stepped off. "As we all know now, Henry's wishful thinking that night did not in fact come true. And Rover, true to form, I guess, enlisted out of Yale, with one year still left to go for his bachelor's in biology. If he'd stayed and finished, as he could have, he would've had a decent chance of a draft deferment—meaning, *almost* a safe-conduct pass out of all combat zones, and danger, as close as you could get—for another five years at least. All he had to do was carry out his plans to go to medical school. The military needed all the doctors they could get. They weren't in the habit of interfering with people intending to become docs; if he'd done that, they'd've left him strictly alone, planning to grab him as soon as he finished. But as things turned out, the war would've been *over* before he finished, and they probably never would've come after him.

"'At least he didn't sign up in the Ninety-Day-Wonder program,' Henry said to my dad. I guess the life-expectancy of new army second lieutenants was something like twelve minutes. 'At least he's gone in the navy. Not a safe-conduct pass, but they're not giving those out, and at least he'll have iron around him.'

"He didn't have iron around him, of course," Rutledge said. "What Rover had around him was steel, steel armor-plate, as thick as they could provide for the pilots of the Grumman Avengers without making the planes too heavy to fly. But it wasn't *all* around him—the canopy over him and his copilot was Plexiglas or some sort of thing like that. Not bulletproof at all. My father recalled it vividly, the sequence of events, better than I did. But then of course when they occurred, he was a good deal older. He grasped their significance at the time that they occurred.

"I didn't. I was fifteen years old, and like every other boy in that condition, I didn't have a lick of sense in me. If you want the truth of it, I really hoped the war'd last a little *longer*. For *me*. So that *I* could fight too, like Rover was doing, and perform many valorous deeds. Maybe even die gloriously, sacrificing my own life in order to prevent the slaughter of my gallant comrades. All of whom, of course, would be tearfully at the church for my funeral, rising as one to attest to my courage. Forgetting, as I did so, that I would not be present, except as a cadaver, to witness the heartbreaking spectacle. In other words, I was like every other young fool, in any age you'd care to name: Between your twelfth or fourteenth birthday, when those male hormones kick in, and maybe when you're twenty-five or thirty, when you begin to see the truth, you honestly believe that no harm can ever befall you. You're literally bulletproof, just like Rover and his copilot and his cockpit canopy were not. For some reason or another—stupidity's the likeliest explanation—that conviction in no way negates the possibility of your valiant death. But the explanation *you* prefer is that you're one of the immortals. *You're* going to get to hang around *after* you've died, so's to go to your own funeral. Like Huck Finn did: You'll be able to watch everybody grieving. Achilles, that's who you are, but without that little problem he had with his foot.

"That day engraved itself on my father's mind. It stayed with him all his life. So as long as his life lasted, more than thirty years, and he had to deal with Henry, it stayed with him. And therefore, even though they're both long dead, that day still also stays with me. His version of it, I mean. The people who were your friends and who were with you on days when important things happened—good important things or bad important things; doesn't make any difference at all—are friends it's especially hard to lose ever after the event. They've marked the passages of time with you, the ones that were so significant no one could overlook them, as most of us generally do our best to do, while the hours pass and the days fly by, and the years peel off the calendars.

"What those people are, are eyewitnesses, witnesses to your very life on this earth. People you can call upon to prove you didn't make it all up. You were really here. Were born. Grew tall. Went to school. Learned a trade. Worked at it, in good course. Took a mate. Had a child. Kept your place in the long caravan while you were waiting for the summons to join the even longer one, the one that travels in the silent halls of death. Human validation to support your claim that you were alive and on this earth, in important times. And that you were important *in* them, because you were affected, and you are a witness too.

"On Easter in nineteen forty-five, it was April first that year, we'd invited Henry, Emily and Amy to come back to our house with us after services, for dinner. Not that the dinner was entirely on us, not by any means; it was a joint enterprise. I don't mean to exaggerate the effect that the war had on our food supplies—we had just as much trouble getting tires and gasoline as anybody else, and did our share of griping about it. Meat wasn't plentiful. But it was adequate, enough, considering the sacrifices others had to make. Still, by getting together like that for dinner, we could have a nicer dinner. More or less pool our resources—our ration coupons, I mean. And that way end up with a much better table than either of our families could've managed to've set by ourselves.

"Besides, Emily hadn't been well. My mother's invitation to have dinner at our house was in part to spare the poor thing from what for most women—and for *her*, as far as that goes, before Rover went away—would've been the ordinary holiday chore of cooking a big dinner for her little family. In those days the term they used for what seemed to be wrong with her was *nervous exhaustion*, as I recall it. But nobody ever seemed to be too clear on what it *meant*. Except that whoever had it hadn't had a *nervous breakdown* yet, but looked to be a likely candidate for one in the not-too-distant future.

"My father never forgot that day," Rutledge said. "Not as long as he lived. 'Emily was pale; tremulous; very thin; easily startled; a little unsteady on her pins even when she didn't have a drop of sherry in her—although from hints Henry let slip I gathered that most days she generally did. Maybe more than one. "It's the war, and Rover," he'd say, if you let him, and by that I mean if you mentioned anything remotely related to how Emily looked or acted, you were letting him. "She's been distraught like this ever since she found out that he'd gone and enlisted. Sometimes when I come home early I'll find her in the sewing room, crying her eyes out: 'I know he's been killed today. I just know it. I felt a cold wind go over me here, and I knew it was Death passing. Gloating. Death's taken him.' When as we later find out, he's in fact been perfectly fine. It's been terribly hard on her. It weighs on her mind like a heavy stone, weighs on it every day. She simply isn't herself."

" 'But that Easter Sunday she seemed to be in better spirits than we'd seen her in a while. Not really what you could call *happy*, but still, in better form. So we were all encouraged by that, fussed over her a lot. And I suppose that in turn made her feel better than she'd felt before. We all could feel it, or at least we thought we could: The war was finally winding down. Most likely the reason we all thought it, were so sure that we could sense the end coming, was nothing more than sheer fatigue. Weariness. Because by then it'd gone on *so* long. It seemed like it'd been going on most of our lives by then. Although of course it hadn't. But so many families like ours, or people we knew very well, had lost so very much, young men and women dear to us, we never would or could forget, and I suppose subconsciously we simply felt we couldn't take it for much longer. Therefore it simply *had* to end.

" 'So we had a hope that we quite willingly—perhaps even deliberately—mistook for a premonition, and didn't question it: That it *was* about to end. We were going to win it. We were going to win it *soon*. All our sacrifices hadn't been in vain. And Rover, the war's hostage closest to us, had been fine so far; he'd be coming home. His mother'd smile again, and birds would sing, and there'd be sunlight in the land.

" 'He'd been flying off the carrier *Lexington,* for more than three long years. He'd won the Navy Cross. He didn't have a scratch on him. Surely he must be charmed in battle, as he was charming in life. He was going to come back home to us, his family and friends. And what we all were certain would be a *brilliant* career.

" 'That Easter Sunday while we celebrated cautiously, half a world away—which we did not know—the battle for Okinawa'd begun. We later learned that initially it had gone perplexingly well. The Japanese general, Ushijima, 'd followed the commands of his superiors to the letter. "Defense in depth," they called it. Meaning: "Backtrack inland from an invading force with superior naval firepower, to a point beyond its range, and when the enemy has followed you there, *Banzai.* Attack, attack, attack."

" 'But in the course of that deceptive lull—perhaps during the very time when we were beginning to feel so much better; Henry never did find out precisely what time it had been over Okinawa that Sunday, and therefore here in Barlow, when his whole world came apart—three Japanese Zeroes came out of the sun and started shooting at Rover's plane. He was on a useless low-level bombing run, over a beach where the enemy wasn't. But the enemy *was* in the sun above and behind him, and one of them got him. Blew him right out of the sky.

" 'And when *she* got the news—the confirmation that what she'd known all along was going to happen now really *had* happened— Emily was blown out of her own sky here, too. Not all that far behind him. Nothing dramatic, of course. Drama wasn't her style. She just subsided into constant, quiet tears for a while, and then with the iron will that long-term melancholy so often conceals so well, starved herself to death. It only took her a little less than a year. No one really tried to interfere. Amy didn't try at all. "There was no point," she said. "Mother's life was over." Henry made a few feeble attempts, but his heart wasn't in it; the hopelessness of the victim doesn't improve the rescuer's effort in what he knows to be a lost cause from the beginning.

" 'In fact I think in a way that Henry might've actually envied her a little. She'd seen enough of the show. She didn't like it, and she was going home now, before it got over with. His case was different. He had to stay. If Rover'd had to go—and Henry for all his disapproval could understand that; it was his obligation—then Henry had to stay. That was his obligation. Whereas in her case it was so plainly God's will, and her own, that Emily should now be departing. There wouldn't've been any point in objecting, trying to talk her out of it. That was just the way that things were, and trying to make them be different would've amounted to swimming against the damned tide.

" 'Henry survived, as did Amy, if you can call what Henry did *surviving*. Myself, what I'd call it was *pining*. He never got over what'd happened to them. It was like what happens to the edge of a good tool, an ax or a hatchet, when you bang it hard, at a bad angle, against a rock or another, harder piece of steel. Or it's been through a white-hot fire. No matter what you do and no matter how hard you try, you can never restore that good edge. The temper's gone, and once it's gone, you'll never bring it back.'

"God having a perverse sense of humor, Henry didn't die until the spring of seventy-eight. Passed away in his sleep. When he didn't come down in the morning, Amy went up to knock on his door, and he was dead in his bed. Thirty-three years after Rover was killed. Thirty-two after his wife. Eighty years old, himself; Rover'd been twenty-two. Amy came to my office, after the funeral and so forth, and we set about settling the estate. What her plans were and how best to achieve them. I got the shock of my life, up to then. But she was only just getting started."

"You still don't like him," Frances said close to midnight, after Rutledge had looked at his watch and said: "Bless my ears and whiskers, I must be off to bed," and they had gone for a stroll. "You think he's a very bad man." They sat on red leather, barrel-backed chairs in the dark-paneled Library Bar, demis of decaf espresso and glasses of port on the mahogany table between them. They had been up to Sports Deck and had gone out to stand under the overhang of the superstructure and look back out over the stern to the wake roiling white briefly in the light that spilled from the ship, but after a few minutes the backdraft of the night wind of the North Atlantic in early May had gone from bracing to chilling, and they had retreated inside. Glenn Gould's first book of recordings from Bach's Well-tempered Clavier played softly but insistently in the background.

"Oh, I *like* him well enough," David said. "And if you could make a judgment you could trust, on the basis of two meals' observation, maybe totaling four hours at the outside, mine would be that I don't think he's a bad man at all—if it's skill that we're talking about. I think he's a *very* good man. What bothers me is that I don't know what it is that he's very good *at*. Is he just naturally and habitually good, as I know you believe he is? Or does he have to make an effort to be very good, in order to get things from people? As most people who are good to me have to be, and so I think he probably is. I'm a banker. I've got habits too, and one of them is deep mistrust. I don't trust people who do great amounts of work to get into my good graces, unless and until I know what it is they hope to get. That usually turns out to be the bank's money, which I am in the last analysis the man in charge of lending, and so therefore what I want to know then is how likely the bank is to get that money *back*, after I lend it to them. Old dogs and their old tricks, Frances; I may not be able to learn many new ones, but I never forget the old ones."

"Oh, I know that," she said.

"So, where in my experience do I fit in Mister Rutledge, who says he found it more expedient to give up his license to practice law than he did to fight a crazy man who threatened to kill him, Rutledge says, because he's insane and thinks that Rutledge swindled him? How's that again? This guy's running around making death threats, which can get you certified against your will, 'constitutes a danger to himself or others,' into the nuthouse for a very thorough inspection. And here's Rutledge, a lawyer, totally innocent of any wrongdoing at all, or so he's telling us, and instead of calling the cops and having the madman picked up, he chucks it all, to travel the world, and help the poor crazy as well.

"I've got trouble with that song, and the dance bothers me some too. This is not the sort of story I'd expect to hear from the lips of a truthful, rich, handsome, elderly widower, sailing all seven seas by himself, bereft of his late-in-life bride. This strikes me, for now, as the sort of story I'd hear from a sleek brown sea otter, a beautiful seagoing weasel who's spotted *my* fish, and now plans to take it from *me*. So, what concerns me is why he's making all this effort to be so very good at working us. What does he want from us? Well, you already know what I think it is."

"*Cherchez l'argent*—yes, I know." She said it wearily. "But how would he know that we've got any money?"

"Well, for one thing, we're here," David said. "You don't get where we are without money."

She yawned and finished her drink. "I give up," she said, "I give up." She stood up. "I think I'll go back to the cabin. Take your time—I don't mean to rush you."

"I'm not hurrying, darling," he said. "I'll be down in a while. By and by."

10

*R*utledge said: "She told me that 'the hardest times were the mink years. Oh, I shouldn't say this; I know that. I've known for *years* how *pathetic,* and how *trivial,* and oh, *gosh,* just so awful and demeaning this was all going to sound, when and if I ever did say it. But it's no good trying to deny it; I've wanted to say it a good many times, for a good many years. But that wouldn't've done, not at all. It might've gotten back to Dad. It would've hurt him terribly. He would've blamed himself—when of course the fault was all mine; it'd always been entirely my choice. I didn't know it would be the minks, not specifically, but I did know that something very much like minks would hurt when it started to happen—when friends of mine reached the stage in life where they could start enjoying the world with their husbands. "Savoring the world," as one of them put it to me grandly once. "Arthur and I've been savoring the planet." She sounded like a grand fool when she said it, but then Rose'd always been a bit of a fool. My mistake was that I'd under*esti*mated the hurt, the sharp pain of being excluded. It was *much* greater than I'd expected. So, I'd made a mistake. But back then I couldn't admit it.

" 'Now I can. Now it doesn't matter. Now I'm finally saying it. Exposing myself for the *mean, envious, little* person I've tried so hard never to be, ever since Rover got killed. The hardest times to bear began about sixteen or seventeen years ago, and went on for—I guess—three or four: when all my friends from college, most of them anyway, all seemed to be getting their minks.

" 'Not when they got engaged to handsome men, or even ordinary-looking men, and I wasn't even getting asked to go out on dates.

Although I'm sure that if you'd asked them—those that'd thought about it, anyway—most of them would've said they assumed that's when it was, when it was hardest for me.

" 'It was like I had leprosy. Men were initially attracted—quite a few of them, too. But then they just shied away from me. Even though I knew I wasn't ugly. No beauty queen, to be sure, but not one of those poor women whose friends all tried desperately to fix her up with blind dates with their boyfriends' friends, and all they had to work with was what a great personality she had. And then, after they'd fail, as they'd secretly sort of hoped they would, get to pretend oleaginously, just ever so *smarmily,* to poor misshapen Nancy that they just couldn't *understand* why it was they all'd had such rotten luck trying to get her a lousy date. Never ever saying what they of course knew very well they had no need to say: that no one, including Nancy, could get a date for Nancy because Nancy was a *dog.* Women are really so mean.

" 'It wasn't that hard for me when they got married, either, and asked me to be a bridesmaid. And I said of course I would, and I was flattered to be asked. Because they were my friends, and remain so to this day. Or would remain, if I ever saw them, I guess. But anyway, that meant I had to go and buy a dress and shoes I knew I'd never wear again. And then at the rehearsal dinner and the next day at the wedding, every single time, I'd flirt shamelessly with one of the groom's men and have too much to drink, so I'd have that for an excuse and feel a little better later about having let him feel me up. "Well, yes, he did paw me, and I didn't push him away, make any protest when he did it. I have to admit I might've had a bit too much to drink." A little appetizer? What my friend Julia who's a TV-news producer calls "a little tease at ten, you know? 'Well-known politician seen with socialite in compromising position. We'll have tape at eleven.' So they'll stay *tuned* 'til eleven, when your local news comes on." After he'd copped his feel and groped me good, he'd leave with my phone number. And I'd be so pleased with myself; I'd think, "Greater things're in store." But they weren't. It didn't matter which one the *he* was that I'd misbehaved with: none of them ever did call.

" 'Now, the he obviously didn't "lose" that number because I'd been frigid with him, or made the opposite mistake of giving him all he wanted on his very first try, either, so he'd had me and I was old news—time to find a new challenge—there wasn't really any point in coming back to me for more. The reason that he always misplaced the number—and all of them did it, too, every single one of them, every single damned time—was because some kindly friend who knew us both had tipped him off to the truth.

"'Maybe I'd done it myself. Without meaning to, of course, but you know how it is after you've gotten into the whiskey sours. Started the ball rolling downhill on top of myself by carelessly giving him some hint I didn't mean to let slip about how my father was old and fragile, and alone in the world except for me, alone in the world. And I lived at home and took care of him still, and that's what I'd always do. Because he was totally dependent on me, and I couldn't possibly leave him.

"'And *that* was why, at twenty-six, or twenty-seven or twenty-nine—maybe even thirty-one; I think that was the last time—I never got called, was still unattached, and most likely to remain so. I didn't even have the ordinary opportunities to meet ordinary men that women who have jobs meet on the job every day—I didn't *have* such a job. So I never really got to know any men; no man stayed around long enough for either of us to get to know what the other one was like.

"'It was tough to take, knowing that. It wasn't because I was "a bad-lookin' broad," as one tipsy gentleman tactfully assured me one wedding evening I really was not—never saw *him* again, either—or because I was really a dyke. There *were,* I'm sure, just as many lezzies around all over the place then as there are today, but they didn't generally go around hand in hand, broadcasting their tastes, declaiming their superiority and demanding professional preference because of what they liked to do in bed, calling people who objected "sexist, bigoted pigs." Not in places this far from the Seine, in those prim little days long ago; the closets were much bigger then. More comfortable, too, I should think, judging by all their complaints, than the Great World outside is for them today. So the men had to be on their guard. But I didn't really think that I gave any signals to that effect, certainly not when I was allowing them to knead my breasts like bread dough, and moaning. Didn't intend to, anyway; no, quite the opposite message.

"'My situation—my predicament, I guess you could call it—was much simpler than that. It was because I was living at home and keeping a big house for my daddy, and it was a full-time job, even though he wasn't sick yet. And it didn't take a crystal ball for any man to see that that's what I'd be doing 'til the day my daddy died. And that was in fact exactly what I did do, wasn't it. *Exactly* what I did, a damned blueprint for it, just as young Lochinvar could've predicted back then, and as he did predict, in every incarnation.

" 'And given that prediction, there wasn't any point at all in going after me, was there? How could you hope to compete with my daddy for me, if I was that devoted to him? And more to the point: Why would you even bother? You wouldn't've. You would've said to yourself: "In my Father's house there are many *maidens,* easier to woo, and just as eager to *be* wooed."

" 'So, if you were a nice, young, eligible, heterosexual fella—we had the other kind of *men* back then too, of course, but it was much the same thing then as it was with the ladies who liked ladies: did their best to keep still about it. Very few back then did any flaunting. But if you were the conventional sort, and you were old enough and settled-down enough to think it was time that you acquired a good wife, or at least a good steady woman, so you really went into the market; well, if I was the first thing you found—you stumbled over me and you thought you might be smitten—as soon you'd had time enough to find out a little more, you backed right away again. You did. You did your hunting and gathering elsewhere. And sooner or later it paid off for you. You found your Special Someone. Someone to take out for dinners and drinks; to plays and to concerts; to poetry readings. Maybe even on long-weekend trips. And then in the natural course of events—the natural course was much longer then—to bed on a regular basis, before or after each one of those outings. Maybe even at last to the altar. And both of you felt much better for it. You knew you were fortunate people. There was no room for me in that *both.*

" 'So, since no eligible, rational man—which was the kind I preferred, just the basic long-wearing model, no fancy accessories needed—wanted any part of that, had any long-term sexual interest in a woman chained to her father like I was, I was not a hot item. And after a while I not only *knew* it; I knew it was not going to *change.* Until after another event, which I of course could not plan for, and had to pretend that I dreaded. What I didn't know was how long my dear—and he *was* dear, very dear to me—old father was going to take to get where he was finally going to go. And that's no slur on his memory, either—it's where we're all going to, too. Most of *us* don't know our own schedules either. But that was the hard and the fast of it, the rule that I'd come under: No decent, rational, eligible man was going to have any matrimonial interest in me until my daddy was dead.

" 'Well, it took him a while, didn't it?' she said to me," Rutledge said. " 'It took him a *hell* of a while. And while he was doing it, my friends I knew at Beaver Country Day School, and then later on at Smith, they were making their orderly progresses through their well-arranged lives. They were having their children; having their affairs; having their nasty divorces when their husbands began to bore them or vice versa. And in more than a couple of cases, having their troubles with booze, or too many pills; in two cases large helpings of both. Which in one of those cases no one's supposed to know about, and everybody does, led to the last of the problems: a little trouble with death, maybe not accidental. Or they were coming late in life to grips with the discovery that they'd really rather have sex with another woman than any man who ever lived, including Robert Redford.

" 'But they were also going to Europe, the Caribbean in the winter; to the theater, and the opera; and to their lovely summer homes overlooking the dunes of the Cape, and off in the near distance, the ocean. In later years they were even briskly resuming careers they'd interrupted to have children.

" 'In college I'd planned on having one of those myself: a real career, doing work that interested me. I took it for granted, of course, more or less *assumed,* that at some point I'd get married, maybe to some gentle colleague. But I'd still go on with my career. And if it turned out that I had to suspend it at some later point to have a child—maybe two or even three children, for that matter—well, that was done all the time. It didn't rule out a career.

" 'But those other things, besides the career, they weren't something I thought you could plan for. Marriage and children would be something that *happened,* or didn't. Probably at precisely the wrong time, when they did, but what use was there in fretting about it? Most people's lives were untidy. Most people's lives that I'd seen. When something happened that fouled up your plans, well then, it did: You'd accept it. Gracefully. "Of course we'd wanted to have at least one child, although not quite at this time. But then, this is life. What happens to you while you're planning your future." Ever so nice, don't you think? So *grown-up;* so darned *mature.*

" '*My* career was supposed to've been in college teaching. I'd majored in French art history. I was close to the end of my Master's year at Columbia the Easter that Rover got killed. If it hadn't've been for that, and also for that bastard Hitler, the next year I would've gone to the Sorbonne. But as a result of Rover's death, and then my mother's, well, that career of mine'd never really gotten off the ground. So I have nothing to resume now that my father's finally dead.

" 'Cooking meals; keeping house; balancing the checkbook—Daddy hated that chore, too, so of course I dutifully took it on as soon as Mother became ill—serving every Friday night as Daddy's partner at the Streeters, old friends of his, but *very* old for me, as a steady diet, nice though they always were; Mister Streeter (I could never bring myself to call him "Jack," as he said I should) really made *excellent* stingers, so the evenings did tend to drift by, in a pleasant warm/cool liquid haze—"for a hand or two of bridge": Only if you count doing those things for thirty-three years as a career have I had a real one, all too completely without interruption. "But that isn't the way that I count." "Well, that doesn't matter at all, dear. That's not an option for you."

" 'And it wasn't, either. Until a week ago. Until then here I was, just the same—only older—as I'd been in nineteen forty-six. Sitting in Barlow, with Dad. But I've thought about this since he died, and—it surprises me to find I have to say this—I guess I was mostly content.

" 'I suppose it was partly because there's a major selfish satisfaction that you get from nobly, and *publicly, unselfishly,* sacrificing your life to serve someone else. A girl I knew at Beaver went into a convent after she finished at Regis. Became a Madame of the Sacred Heart, I believe it was. Taught American literature at Newton College of the Sacred Heart, which doesn't exist anymore—Boston College bought it up when Sacred Heart went under, at the same time as a lot of other single-sex, convent schools for girls; moved its law school into some of its buildings and turned the rest into dorms. Very pretty girl, too, Christine was; she didn't do it because she lacked for suitors. None of us could figure out what on earth had possessed her to do it; she'd never *seemed* that devout. Heck, she'd never really *seemed* to be that Catholic. It must've been because she decided that was what she really wanted to do.

" 'I ran into her one afternoon, maybe fifteen years ago, having ice cream at the Brigham's that used to be there near the Star Market in the mall at Chestnut Hill. She was with another nun, I forget what her name was, and I was by myself. So she invited me to join them. I didn't really want to. Dad was retired by then, home underfoot most days. A major part of what he did with those days was keep constant tabs on me. I was the only person he really had to talk to. And talk to me he did, hollering at me from the study, where he was reading. Hunting me down in *my* study, where I'd be having a moment's peace listening to Schubert while I was sorting through the mail— that was not permitted me. Tracking me out into the garden, even, where I'd taken refuge among the tomato plants or roses, to confirm his opinion that we were indeed having a very nice day. Taking me for one of his interminable damned "spins" in the car, when what I wanted was a nap. Reading aloud to me from the *Transcript*. On and on and on. If I hadn't screwed up the courage to put my foot down and say *No*, he would've driven me to the doctor for my annual checkups, too, as he volunteered to do. As though he was afraid if he let me go by myself, I might take to my heels and not come back. So maybe he did sense something, suspected how sometimes I got *so* impatient with him. He needn't've worried. I was afraid of what he might do, if he found himself *by* himself; go into a blue funk or something, and never come out of it again. Why did he think I'd begun staying with him in the first place, if he thought what I really wanted to do was run away? I didn't dare leave him alone.

" 'So one of the best parts of escaping from him and the house for the rare afternoon when he had an appointment outside the house—they didn't come along that often; I was dismayed the day he announced he wasn't going to Rotary anymore. It was only one after- noon a week, and the meetings were short, no more than an hour. But he said he was sick of those people. "All they ever want to talk about is sports, and how well their sons're all doing." But I didn't say anything; he still went to the regular luncheon meetings of the retired judges, and now and then to some bar association meeting. So they'd never been very frequent, anyway, and never as long as I would've liked, my cherished respites from him, and now one was being taken away from me. The few I had left I almost hoarded, like a furtive child hoards her Halloween candy. They furnished something I needed. It irked me to see one of them slip away into the grasp of this middle-aged nun I'd just happened to know as a girl.

" 'She was stealing the voluptuous solitude that I had on those afternoons alone among many people. Just luxuriating in *being* alone, and silent, by myself. Nobody talking to me, and expecting me to reply. I really didn't *want* to join Chris and her friend, but I did it. I couldn't think of a polite excuse fast enough to turn her down. And so although it'd been years and years since I'd seen her, I didn't want to be rude, so I said yes, and sat down.

" 'Before I'd gotten halfway through my coffee and brownie with vanilla ice cream, I regretted not having been rude. She was so damned *sanctimonious*. So *pleased* with herself, for being so humble. So *patronizing* toward the rest of the world—and her sidekick was the same way—for not being willing to make the same sacrifice of their lives for Jesus as they in their holiness had. It was disgusting, enough to make you throw up. I invented a reason why I had to run and grabbed all of our checks—their protest was mild, implying it was usual, strictly pro forma, and maybe exposing the motive for the invitation in the first place, when I'd thought about it—got out of the place and went home.

" 'Dad was already home when I got there, and I tell you, the sound of that voice was music. It was *ceaseless*, and *loud*—he'd gotten hard of hearing, so he raised his voice until the volume sounded normal in his ears, and like a shout to everybody else. It was like the waves pounding on the rocks along the coast of Maine. But at least I *liked* the person it was coming from. I may've given up an interesting life, one that I'd really wanted, to take care of him, but I was getting something too, while I did it. While he was occupying my days the same way our soldiers occupied Germany, he was also sparing me the necessity that most other adults have to face, some of them every day, as soon as they get to work: compulsory association, in close quarters, with people who make them grit their teeth, people whom they simply cannot *stand*.

" 'I'd never had a real worry in the world, and that was on account of him. I'd worried about my brother, sure, and unfortunately my forebodings had been right. And then I'd worried about my mother, and once more, I was right, doggone it. But I'd never had to worry about *me*, what would happen to *me*. Ever since I'd first come into the great world, Dad—and of course, Mother—'d shielded me from it. Made it as nice for me as they possibly could. I'd had shelter. I'd had food, whatever I liked best. As long as it was good for me, of course, or if I'd already finished all the stuff that was nourishing and good, and this was a treat I'd earned. I was nicely dressed and made to feel as though I was a treasured little girl. I never once found myself in a situation like some of my classmates did at Beaver, where they were afraid they might have to drop out of school because one of their fathers'd suddenly died and there might not be enough money. When I was at Smith, I didn't have to worry about tuition. Even though Dad'd become a judge by then, and he certainly *did* have to worry—and as I know now, he sure did. But without a word to me. If the German armies'd only stayed home, I *would've* done my

/ 115

grad work abroad, even though they really couldn't've afforded it. I wanted to. That was enough. The money would have been found.

" 'But they would've had to look for it, real hard. That judgeship was a luxury. The only thing that you could really say in favor of it was that it was secure. You were there for life. You couldn't get laid off, and the business would go on—no fear of shutting down the Commonwealth. And a pension came with it. I think that was the major reason he took it, even though it paid so poorly. The Depression'd thrown a scare into him, as it had a lot of people. "I saw a lot of lawyers starve," he said. "Go right out of business. People who'd been in practice a long time, too, very capable men. Didn't matter. When their clients went bust, why, they went broke too. Had to close their offices and try to find work as accountants. Anything, to eat."

" 'My mother'd brought some money into the marriage, from her family, but it wasn't all that much. I think Beaver for me and Milton Academy for Rover pretty much ate it all up. And it wasn't replenished by deaths on her side. As I guess was common when it came time for her parents to divide up their estate—most of which was the family home-heat business. It was a big one, too: Campbell Oil, in Cleveland, back where she came from—she'd gotten a pittance from them. According to what the will said, they just assumed that she was amply taken care of with my father's income. But there was an undertone of spite in the decision. Resentment. She'd chosen to stay here when she'd finished at Smith, hadn't she? Married out here, lived out here, and didn't get back to see them that much. She must be doing all right on her own. So when they died, my grandparents, Mother's brothers got the business, the lock, the stock and the barrel. Families're funny organizations. Not always paternalistic, not by any means.

" 'But as I say, we were comfortable when I was growing up. As much as I pitied myself in these years I've spent at home taking care of Dad—and I did, extravagantly—for missing out on my grand career that of course I might never've had, I was never under the impression that the academic life would've been an endless cycle of song, a medley of extemporanea. I knew very well, from a few professors I'd gotten to know well enough to talk to, that pride of place was the rule rather than the exception among faculty members, no matter where they were teaching. That the competition *for* the places was nasty and brutish, and that when the battle ended, the wounded were usually shot. I was giving up something for Daddy, but Daddy was sparing me that.

" 'I suppose that was why none of the *stuff*, the trappings of upper-middle-class life that I didn't have, and saw my school-friends all having—really relishing, you know? In their spacious lives—that none of that ever really *bothered* me. *Impinged* on me, you know? Except those three or four years that I mentioned, when they all started getting their minks. I was really quite startled when I realized that in fact I did covet those new coats.

" 'I've never been particularly materialistic. At least *I* don't think I have, though I'd most likely be among the very last to know. I've been complimented on my appearance now and then, somewhat more frequently when I was younger than I am today, at fifty-six, as you'd expect, but still from time to time even now. My mother reared me to take an interest in style, but not an *unseemly* interest.

" ' "I'm not teaching you how to dress *fashionably*, dear," she would say. "I think any woman who tries to do that takes an enormous risk of making herself look perfectly ridiculous, because unless you get it exactly right, you have it entirely wrong. And people will see at once what you've attempted to do, and failed at, and laugh at you in your foolish vanity for trying to do it. No, the art to acquire, dear, is the art of dressing *correctly*. Dress *carefully*, so that your clothes never draw attention to you, for *any* reason, any reason at all. Clothing obviously self-consciously selected—revealing too much; concealing too much; garish or dowdy or unkempt: no matter; all of that is to be avoided. What you must have are simply the clothes that anyone of good taste would choose, for whatever it is that you're doing.

" ' "You do *know*, after all, what you're going to be doing, before you actually do it. As you would not choose overalls as your ensemble for a formal ball, so it would be *eeee*qually grotesque to wear a formal gown for digging in the garden. Your clothing should invariably be of absolutely no matter. Simply have and wear the clothing appropriate for the activity you have in mind. You should be perfectly fine. Oh, and one more thing: Pay absolutely no attention to what men say, about whatever you're wearing. They know nothing about style; unless they're designers themselves, they have no need to know. If they have a clean shirt and creased trousers, and their shoes are not scuffed, and they know how to tie a necktie and they own a clean blue blazer, unrumpled, with no dandruff on the shoulders, well then, they're perfectly fine for almost any occasion."

" 'And so out of habit I've continued to do what she taught me back then. She also trained me to have my hair done twice a month, and so I've got that habit, too. But when I've kept my fortnightly appointments, it's been because I was convinced very early in my life that just as all men—personified at first of course by Dad, and then later on, by Rover—had to have their hair cut every week, to look presentable, so all women, personified by Mother, had to have theirs attended to only half as often. Although of course it did take us roughly twice as long, and cost about three times as much, but it was part of the job of being presentable, always.

" 'When I've bought clothes, I've bought *good* clothes, designs that I think will last, from dressmakers who've made good garments I've bought before, that have lasted a good long time. Not because I like to shop, although I don't hate it, either; it's just a thing I have to do, like getting my regular haircut. So it's one of the things that I always *have* done. Quite conscientiously, too.

" 'But *now*,' she said to me that day, and I thought then and continue to think to this very day this was the most extraordinary thing I have ever had a client say to me, in all my years of practice, up 'til then and up 'til now, 'now that Dad is dead I will have some things to do.

" 'I am not a virgin,' she said, very matter-of-fact. 'If I've given that impression, it was without meaning to. If you've taken anything I've said to mean that, contrary to my intention, please dismiss it.'

"I was quite taken aback. I hadn't taken that impression, or its opposite, either. The sexual history of my clients had never been a matter of concern to me, except insofar as it bore upon their particular cases—divorces, for example, when adultery was alleged, or the real reason behind the injured spouse's vengefully extreme settlement demands. I told her the truth: 'I really hadn't given any thought to the matter,' I said.

"She decided, I think, to believe me. 'Yes,' she said, 'well, very well then. I just think if I expect you to advise me properly, and successfully, to accomplish what I want to, you'd better know exactly what sort of a person you're dealing with.'

" 'I'm always more comfortable when I do,' I said. Although if pressed I would've had to admit that only those divorce cases I've mentioned—there'd been only two of them in nearly a quarter of a century of practice—had prompted or necessitated my elicitation of such information. Then there was one involving a most unfortunate encounter that my client, a respected businessman, had been accused of having with a male prostitute, resulting in the arrest of both of them for sodomy. And the fourth had been a will-contest in which the children of the first marriage had attempted to seize the second wife's bequest under the decedent's will—and a very generous one it was—on the grounds that unknown to her poor incapacitated husband, she had taken a lover during the three years he had been infirm. 'But he *did* know,' she said. 'He told me to do it. He even told me *who* I ought to go with. He thought very highly of Jim. It wasn't just that Clarence approved: It was all *his* idea.' She prevailed in the action, on that argument. I wondered then and I've often wondered since then if that really was the truth. Not the affair, that was surely the truth, but whose idea it had really been.

" 'Yes,' she said, 'I should think so. Well, at any rate, the fact of the matter is that in college I had a classmate named Eleanor. We were never that close. I never knew her that well, or wished to, and I have no reason to believe that she felt any differently about me. I don't mean there was any bad blood between us. When we encountered each other at college we were civil enough, as you have to be when you live in a small community like that, and in the thirty-five years since then when we've happened to meet, we've always been cordial enough. Like the weather on a warm sunny day in May's cordial, after a very rough winter: indiscriminately pleasant to everyone present; absolutely nothing personal's involved.

" 'My mother since God only knows when—well before I was born—had been a member of the Museum of Fine Arts, a modest enough expenditure for a lady of increasingly limited means, in a very good cause that I of course came to appreciate greatly once I'd commenced my studies. I wouldn't be a bit surprised if our many trips to the place hadn't had a little to do with the direction that my interests took, too, when I began to have interests. And so when I reached the age where her membership no longer covered me, I talked her into giving me one of my own. It wasn't a very hard job.

" 'I faithfully preserved the connection over the years, while I was taking care of Dad. I suppose at first it enabled me to buck myself up with the falsehood that by means of the lectures and special exhibits I was still at least "keeping up" with the latest news from the French art-world. Against the day when I'd go back to it all, as I knew very well I would not. During the first ten or fifteen years of it, Dad was still on the bench. He was conscientious about his work, so that kept him occupied most of the day, until the late afternoon. I was free to go into town, visit the Gardner as well, meet friends for lunch—I did have some of those—and I did it. It was only the semblance of a valid life I was making out of what was really a housekeeper's job, a

Potemkin village of a life in the arts, but it enabled me to keep my sanity, I guess, and that was no negligible thing.

" 'I ran into Eleanor at one of those much-ballyhooed luncheon-celebrations of one thing or another that everyone promptly forgets as soon as it's over with and the funds for it all've been raised. At least until the next tax-time, and then after the deduction's taken, forevermore, thank you so much. Neither of us made any great to-do about seeing each other again. It was more a matter of "Oh, there you are. How nice to see you. Everything going quite well?" Eleanor hadn't cared enough about me, back in school, to think about my prospects in life, any more than I had about hers, so now that she knew for sure my life'd turned out dreary, she didn't care enough to gloat. If she even listened while I politely described it, in response to her polite question. I did listen to her account of her own, but not because I was particularly concerned about Eleanor: My own days were so dull that I was avid for details about the lives that other, *real*, people lived. However commonplace and pedestrian they might seem to those who led them, they were surely more exciting than mine.

" 'Eleanor's, to tell the truth, did not really seem so, at least not at first. She had had no children. I gathered from her expression that this had not been by choice. I had the impression she was trying to convey to me, without actually saying it, that this was not because she had been impregnable; that it was all his fault. I didn't press the matter, since it didn't interest me.

" 'A favorite aunt had left her some real estate up in Newbury-port from an aunt some years before that. Some residential property, I gathered, several large old houses that the aunt'd bought up over the years as they'd come onto the market, usually in quite bad shape. Then she'd had them gutted and rewired—new furnaces put in, all that sort of thing—and then cut them up into apartments. So when the aunt died the whole business had fallen on Eleanor.

" 'It really sounded quite interesting to me,' Amy said to me," Rutledge said. " 'But Eleanor didn't see it that way at all. "There we are out there in Sudbury—where Carl insists that he's staying, it was his father's house—and there's all that property way up there in Newburyport. My land, it's over fifty miles away, by the time that I get through driving around. And it seems as though there's not a single day goes by that I don't get some kind of call from a tenant with a problem, or my manager, Eugene, telling me there's no help for it and that something else went wrong, and I'll just have to drive on up there and say what I want to do. I hired Eugene and I pay him a goodly sum, along with his place rent-free, to be the superintendent and deal with those things for me. But it seems as though unless it's small, and very obvious—whether to have the lawn mowed, or shovel off the walks in the wintertime—it's too much for him to handle. I must come up and approve. I'm up there two or three times a week. It was one thing for Julia, she was right there on the scene, but I'm twenty-five or thirty miles or so away and it's a different thing for me."

" 'That's always the way, isn't it?' Amy said. 'I'm not saying I envied Eleanor the chore of keeping track of property that far away, but if my family'd had some within ten miles of Barlow, I would've welcomed having the responsibility for it. It would've given me something to do. Everybody else's problems look so attractive, next to your own. If only we could all just swap.

" 'But anyway, that was our first reunion, that day at the museum, if you could put it that way,' Amy said to me. 'Eleanor's and mine. And it began to seem as though we'd formed a better bond, a much better bond, on nothing more than the fact that we'd recognized each other after all those years since college, and had now therefore somehow become the sort of friends we'd never been before. We did not become *close* friends; we were never close. But when we saw each other at some fund-raising event, we gravitated toward each other, two vaguely unhappy women who'd spent four years together in the long-ago without much noticing each other, but were reassured to see each other, still alive and kicking, so long afterwards. Nothing more than having shared survival, really; not much, but still—more than we had in common with the other people there. And after some few years of this, white wine and sympathy, I finally met Carl.' "

Rutledge finished his third Calvados and idly shot his left coatsleeve to expose his watch. "My god," he said, "will you look at that? It's damned near one in the morning. Although since the clocks get set back an hour every night 'til we get home, it's really only midnight. I've kept you two nice people up all night." He stood up at once and bowed to Frances. He nodded to David, who was looking noticeably drowsy. "I do apologize. See you at breakfast, my good friends," he said. "But not too early, and perhaps not too bright. Be of the best possible cheer: I'm incoherent at breakfast. I won't bore you again until noon."

11

After breakfast (a western omelette, two eggs over easy with ham, while Rutledge soldiered in determined silence through three slices of French toast and a side order of bacon, each of them beginning with honeydew melon and taking a Danish pastry to top off the meal) on the second day at sea, Frances went to a lecture on bridge in the Madison Room on the Upper Deck. David went back to the PassNavStation on Signal Deck to get the satellite data for his entry in the ship's daily mileage pool, from noon to noon (despite the fact that they had not left Southampton until nearly 1300 hours on the first day). He was rather puzzled there would be such a mileage tote offered on a vessel supplying any passenger who desired it with all the information he would need—the relevant charts and running GPS fixes, accurate to within 100 meters even if the US Defense Department happened to be dithering the normal accuracy up from 30 meters—to chart the ship's progress up to the moment of 1045 hours when the two-dollar betting closed. One minute of latitude or longitude (there are sixty in a degree) equals one nautical mile, 6,080.2 feet, 1.15 statute miles.

At 10:17—1017 hours on the naval-time clocks of the PassNavStation, now retarded one hour from the Greenwich mean (or universal) time on which the ship had sailed, David relinquished his place and took the elevator down to Boat Deck (where the white lifeboats were suspended from massive davits, canvas-covered against the weather, simultaneously offering strollers and joggers on the outdoor promenade reassurance of constant preparedness and strong reminder of the omnipresent danger to be survived) and the Cruise Staff Center. He placed his bet, 634.8 nautical miles, based on his expectation that the *America* between 1045 hours and 1200 hours would maintain the average speed of 27.6 knots she had made good over the ground during the 21.25 hours he had had available to use in his calculations.

Then, feeling at somewhat of a loss, halfway absently deciding to go out on deck for a breath of fresh air (maybe, if it was pleasant, even a virtuous walk of a mile or two—five or ten laps—to work off the calories he'd already had in only three heavy meals), he turned out of the companionway into the portside interior passageway and headed forward. He was initially mildly annoyed to find each of the first three companionway doors—heavy steel hatchways three steps up from the indoor walkway, each equipped with six thick bolts, one at top and bottom, two on each side—dogged down. There, on a narrow chain hanging across the fourth one farthest forward, he saw a black plastic signboard with two lines of white block-letters that read: "OUTDOOR PROMENADE CLOSED—SEVERE HEADWINDS."

All of the private smug delight he had relished in the exercise of his initiate's navigational skills at PassNavStation 3 evaporated. Chiefly he was humiliated by his heedlessness of the instrument readings he'd just finished taking. He was ruefully grateful that at least he had not gone down to lunch and tried to talk Frances and Rutledge into joining him for an outdoor stroll, but also partly chagrined that he had not made an unsuccessful effort to do exactly that: the process of persuading them might have required him to pause long enough to add *America*'s nearly 28-knot speed to the velocity of the nor'-nor'east fresh breeze averaging 18 knots she was bucking on the port bow, and to figure out that the combined apparent wind on the outdoor deck—nearly 53 mph, when converted from nautical to statute measurement—would equal a Force 9–Strong Gale rating on the Beaufort scale, a steady wind high enough even after partial deflection by the vessel's cladding superstructure to knock a grown man off his feet. Of course the officer of the watch would have ordered the hatchways secured, lest some terminally stupid, hopelessly ignorant, or simply fatally inattentive fool among the passengers or serving staff unwarily venture out, almost certainly to be slammed bodily into a davit stanchion, getting badly hurt, or blown ass-over-teakettle overboard almost at once.

Feeling sheepish, he reversed direction, walking counterclockwise back around the enclosed inner corridor toward the stern, emerging aft of the stairwell into a wide indoor promenade leading to three levels of small shops at the stern, the upper of them on the same level; the middle halfway down, also overlooking the Gallery Atrium;

the lower shops on the same level as the Atrium floor, on the Quarter Deck below. Ahead of him a two-tiered double escalator, rising over a large pool bordered by water lilies and framed by tall fountains, conveyed passengers between the Atrium floor and the two upper levels of shops. Opposite him, across the Atrium airspace, was the open inner promenade serving the starboard side.

He rested his forearms on the railing, gradually becoming luxuriously aware that he had no obligation to go anywhere or do anything, except exactly what he pleased, until he returned to the Grill at noon to meet Frances and Rutledge for another two-hour lunch. He grinned at the spaciousness of it, having nothing at all to do. Below and opposite him, on the starboard side, a low gilded railing separated the Gallery space from ivory-leather lounge chairs and low glass-topped tables forming reading and conversational groupings on both sides of the corridor, daylighted by wide ports; he leaned over the railing to peer down and verify that the same sort of accommodations were offered on the portside Quarter Deck below him.

Inside the railing, tables accommodating two, four and six people were arranged around the polished wooden dance floor of the Atrium itself. Around them were compact, cushioned, wicker-backed barrel-chairs, sparsely occupied by an odd combination of a small group of restlessly loud young people in their middle teens, all elbows and lurching lunges, and, in the places that afforded the best view of any activity on the dance floor, a much larger number—close to a hundred of them—of lethargic people of retirement age or older, most of them women, indolently but completely occupied with their own perfunctory conversations, expertly killing time and conserving energy until something good happened, pretty much ignoring what was going on before them.

David understood their point of view. Between the forward edge of the dance floor and the foot of the cramped, unlighted, unoccupied bandstand—crowded with a drum-set, a double-keyboard synthesizer mounted on a trestle, four large speaker sets, straight chairs and music stands; David made a mental note to avoid the neighborhood at night, when the band that used them went to work—a sweaty, fairly recently young man with unnaturally glossy black hair, costumed as Elvis Presley in a Las Vegas jumpsuit of white satin with gold sequins and enormously flared pants, the top open to his navel on his nascent paunch, stood in a spotlight and repeatedly tumbled three large dice in a chromium-plated, hourglass-shaped wire cage, on a dark-green-baize-draped small table next to him. Each time the dice rattled to rest he hailed the occasion joyfully, flourishing a handheld microphone rigged to a small but booming amplifier and with many whoops and hollers using it first to remind "all you racing fans out there" that the holders of each ticket "on the winning steed will win at least twenty dollars, guaranteed, if that bangtail comes in." Then he used the sound system to instruct two full-breasted and long-legged young women in red and blue satin push-up teddies cut low on top and high down low, teetering on high heels, which of six numbered plywood-profile painted horses to move how many lengths along the green-baize runner laid on the polished dance-floor, according to the numbers on the dice.

Each of the young women was careful each time to place her left hand on her left knee and bend entirely from the waist, using her free right hand to pluck the designated toy horse up daintily by its mane and move it along the floor, so that her buttocks were presented high and round and firm to those behind her and her breasts ballooned abundantly before those in front of her, affording the more nostalgic of the few old men betting on the races at least generous glimpses of bounties long since left far out of reach. The palomino Number 4 horse, its painted jockey silked in white with a diagonal green stripe, came up four times in two revolutions of the cage as David stood there, pulling three lengths ahead of its nearest competitor, with four more lengths to go. The counterfeit Elvis managed to rouse a little weak, halfhearted cheering by the more obliging elders, corrupted by sarcastic near-jeering from the teenagers.

David straightened up, understanding why the bogus Elvis sweated so, resolving to inquire of Melissa, if he encountered her again, whether she counted this among the many delightful things to do aboard *America*. He would ask her whether there were also Grange meetings offered, for those whose hearts might be too weak to stand too much excitement. Having no wish to descend from on high via the Stairway-to-Paradise escalator into the antic near-despondency of the Elvis in the Gallery, he retraced his steps forward toward the portside stairwell he had used to come down from Signal Deck, and met Melissa emerging from it.

Today's outfit was a café-au-lait version of the gray suit she had worn on the first day. The rest of the package remained deliciously the same, and the smile if anything was higher voltage. She came up to him and took his left arm in both hands. "Good morning, David," she said, in that voice that had aged like fine wine. "Are you all by yourself?"

"Well, yeah," he said, his voice coagulating as he discovered suddenly what it was that he wanted to do with the time when he'd nothing to do. He had to clear his throat. "As a matter of fact, I seem to be that. Completely without adult supervision." He looked at his watch; it read 11:20.

"I don't go on duty 'til two," she said, lowering her gaze and feigning shyness. Then she looked up at him. "Join me for a coffee?" she said. "No one will see us, you know; I have a small suite to myself. Crew having sex with the passengers, gigolos for unescorted ladies: well, you know, it's a liner tradition."

*R*utledge was good company but he surely did relish his wine. Frances, nursing a manhattan she had ordered without really wanting one but thinking vaguely that it seemed an appropriate way of behaving with appropriate recklessness on a transatlantic crossing, began to think as he poured his third glass of Sancerre that he would surely fall asleep without having any lunch if he didn't eat something soon.

"Look, Burt," she said, "it's not that I don't appreciate your keeping me company like this, but it is twenty past and you really shouldn't wait any longer to order your lunch. If he finally gets here and you're finished, well, too bad for him. He knew what time we all said we'd meet, and that's when he should've been here. There's no reason to wait any longer."

"Oh, I don't mind waiting," Rutledge said. "One of the reasons I continue to book crossings and cruises for my vacations is that I'm guaranteed to have company at meals. Usually delightful company, too, although I have had a few stinkers and had to beg the stewards to rescue me. Amy's been gone two years now, and by now you'd think I'd've gotten used to it: eating by myself again. After all, I did it for nineteen years, after my mother died in nineteen seventy, and I'd done it quite a lot before that, too—when my father was still alive and they lived in Florida. But I guess it must be I'm still not—used to the fact that she's gone. Maybe it's all right not to have any company at meals unless you've been in a situation where you got used to having company at meals. Then when you don't, it's not all right anymore. It really bothers you. Or at least it bothers me. It's amazing how fast it happens to you, how quickly you just start taking it for granted that when it's dinnertime the other person will be there. We were only together just the three years; that was all I had with Amy. But it feels as though she was with me my whole life; that's how big her absence is. Now I truly hate to eat alone. So unless you really mind, I'd much prefer to wait until your husband comes."

"You may get very hungry," she said. "You may not get fed at all. They only serve the lunch 'til two, isn't that what someone said?"

"You could of course order without him," Rutledge said. "Or does he have to be here?"

"Oh, I suppose I could do that," she said. "But that would be spending my nice little grievance without really getting anything for it. Just making him feel put-upon. No, I'd rather save his guilt-pangs for when I want to do something he doesn't. But you should really go ahead."

"Well," Rutledge said, giving it some thought, "but surely he'll be here before too much longer. After all, he has to eat too. And didn't he say what he was going to do, bet on the day's mileage tote, had to play it by ten forty-five? What could be keeping him now?"

Frances sighed. "Oh, any number of things, I'm afraid. David works very hard, *far* too hard lately. And he loves the sea and being on boats that sail on it. He knows a lot about it too, the sea and ships and so forth; he never wearies of it. That's why, when he decided it was time for him to leave his previous job—"

"I don't mean to pry," Rutledge said. "Is it all right to ask what he did? Most bankers I know've always been bankers, ever since they got out of school. I gather your husband did something else, and that he was pretty good at it, or he wouldn't've gotten the job he has now. The one you say he works too hard at. Which most bankers I know take care not to do—afraid they'll get winded or something."

"Oh, no, you're not prying," she said. "He was Deputy Comptroller of the Currency. In the Treasury Department. It was a very responsible job, and you're right—he was good at it. But the reason he took it was precisely that: If you did it well for a number of years, then you could pretty much go anywhere you liked, in the private banking sector, and get a much better job than you otherwise could have if you'd come into it cold.

"David's not from a long line of bankers, you see. His father was a small-town lawyer down in East Greenwich, Rhode Island, and he did very well at it, too. David's grandad was a lawyer. He was one of the men who founded the firm that David's father was in. For a very long time it was not only the town's largest, but for all practical purposes, the town's *only*, big law firm. The Carrolls had a comfortable life.

"And David loved growing up there. It's really a beautiful, beautiful town, and it's right on the water, you know? So that's where he always wanted to live, and therefore where he wanted to work, ultimately. Not in Washington, though we were happy there. But that was always an interim thing; he always planned to come back. It didn't necessarily have to be to East Greenwich, although I'm sure if there'd been an opening there he would've snapped it right up. But any real good banking job in southern New England, if possible right on the shore. If not—within ten miles of the coast. Well now, that would suit him just fine. And Bradbury fitted that bill."

"I should think it would've been a lot easier for him if he'd just become a lawyer," Rutledge said.

"Yes, it would've," she said. "But he didn't want to *be* a lawyer. His two brothers did, and they run the firm now, and it's still doing very well for them. Just as happy as two fat pigs in mud. But David wanted no part of it. Banking was his choice in life."

"Most lawyers I know, including myself, know quite a good many bankers," Rutledge said. "Couldn't his dad've done something?"

"He could have, of course," she said, "but David wouldn't let him. He said he was making it all on his own, or else he wasn't going to make it. He's very much his own man, an individual."

"Yes," Rutledge said, drawing it out, "an admirable attitude in a young man, I suppose, though since my father built the practice from the ground up, and I accepted it happily, I certainly can't claim to've had it. And I do think it can be carried to an extreme."

"Burt," she said, "that's exactly it: If it's something that David wants to do, something that absorbs him, and it can be carried to an extreme, he will carry it there. That's the way he is, about everything he does. Banking just happens to be the thing he likes to do that makes our living for us."

"You make it sound as though it were almost a *calling* of sorts," Rutledge said. "The kind of thing that clergymen and poets're always claiming that they're answering in their careers. Much more elevated than mere *jobs*, you know."

"You know," she said, "I agree with you. I am doing that, making it sound like a calling. But where David's concerned, that's what it is. What he was put on this earth to do. I know it sounds odd, to say a man's passionate about *banking*, but that's actually what he is. And that's the way he *always* is, about anything that truly interests him. Whether it's the banking business, or sailing, or whatever it is that gets hold of him. He just gets so *involved*, in up to his eyebrows, with everything that he does.

"Just before we planned this trip, the federal bank examiners were at the bank, just the regular audit, and he was all but *beside* himself. He was *convinced* they were out to make him look bad, by classifying the loans of some of his best customers—I was going to say 'best customers he knows,' but of course all the good customers he has automatically become his best customers and people that he knows, and then becomes attached to. The businesses that they pledged and mortgaged a few years ago as collateral for loans—their accounts receivable, and their buildings, land and so forth—just aren't worth as much in the recession as they were before. And so the bank's security that was there when the loan was made, it just isn't there today. And the examiners *still* may do it—their decision wasn't final when we left—unless the economy improves, which would mean that David then would have no choice but to call their loans.

"They can't pay those loans. They're not in default; their installments're all up to date. As David says he keeps on saying to this bank examiner: 'These are *current* loans. *Performing.* But it's like he can't hear me; he goes deaf when I say that.' It just about drives him nuts. 'They're meeting their obligations, they are doing that, and very faithfully. But they can't pay the loans in full; they just don't have the cash. Do we want to ruin them? Is *that* what we want to do, *really* want to do? Put their employees, all those people, out of work in this town? Start a domino effect that'll make them lose their homes? What *sense* does this make?'

"But the examiner won't listen. And if that's what he and his bosses decide they're going to do—classify those loans—when we get home David'll have to do things that will throw these customers, these friends of his, into bankruptcy. He won't want to; it'll kill him and they'll know it, but he won't have any choice. And when he auctions off their land, their buildings and equipment—their homes if they mortgaged those—the prices that he'll get on the distress sales won't pay the loans in full, of course, because there's that recession. The one that hurt their businesses in the first place, reduced the value of their collateral and started this black snowball rolling."

She shook her head. "I don't know what he'll do. I don't think that he knows either. If the auction prices aren't enough—the loans won't be paid off in full. That will mean the bank's reserves won't be in required proportion to its liabilities, so the Feds will seize the bank." She shuddered. "They're bastards, of course, just like he says, and stupid. They do a lot of damage and they don't seem to even care. But there's nothing David can do about it, and he knows it. But gee, he takes it all so *hard*."

"Well," Rutledge said, "but under the circumstances that you describe, I really can't say I blame him. More bankers should be like he is. This country would be a better place."

"Yes," she said, "I know that. If all the bankers like David could hang onto their sanity while they were being like him. I'm not really sure that *he* can. He's managed it so far, but at a cost. The damned bank's become his whole life. This trip was not his idea. I *made* him come on this trip. I'm really worried about him. The two things he loves to do don't go together very well, working too hard and loving the water, unless your line of work's in the maritime. Banking isn't that kind of work. So the result for David has been that the only one of the two, what, occupations in his life that he's spent any real time on in the past two years has been the one in the bank. The man is close to exhaustion."

She chewed on her lower lip. "So far this trip hasn't been any-where near what I'd hoped it would be, not for him. He certainly hasn't relaxed much. He had a quarrel with the concierge at the Connaught, a perfectly nice, polite young man in a wonderfully se-rene hotel, because he hadn't been able to get tickets to the play David wanted to see. He told David, very reasonably, that everybody else wanted to see the show too, and it was sold out for the next two months. The only way he was going to be able to get tickets was if he went to a scalper.

"David flew completely off the handle. His face got all red and there he was, his voice raised in this quiet, small lobby, saying: 'Sure I can, pay a scalper double, and I'd bet a dollar the scalper's your brother-in-law.' I was just mortified, all those people standing around, openmouthed, staring at us. I had to pull him away.

"He was *convinced* all the taxi-drivers were taking the long way around just to cheat us. 'The minute we open our mouths,' he said, 'they know we're American tourists. Don't know the short way around. They still hate all the Yanks, after we bailed them out in World War Two. They hate us *because* we bailed them out, when they couldn't do it themselves. Remember what they said about our soldiers? "The only three things wrong with Americans are: They're overpaid, oversexed, and over here." So because our soldiers went after their girls, and some of them had some success, they're still getting even with us.' His way of getting back at them was by deliberately—insultingly, really—undertipping. They yelled sarcastic thanks at us as they pulled away, and when one we'd picked up outside the hotel was back there the next day as we came out, he took off empty the minute he saw us. I didn't blame him a bit. And this is a man who all his life has routinely given even the laziest waitress twenty percent of the bill.

"No one we met there would believe me if I told them that he really isn't this way, the way that they saw him, a nasty American boor. Because of course, that's what they did see, and precisely what he'd been, as a guest in their country—as far as they were concerned he's a loudmouthed American lout. I'll be at my wits' end if things haven't miraculously improved by the time this boat gets to New York. I'm getting desperate. He pretends to relax, tries to have a good time, but none of it's for real. He's still wound-up tight as a watchspring. I tell you: I'd arrange almost anything if I thought it would work, to get him at peace with himself."

"Yes," Rutledge said. "Well, he's coming in now. I take it I shouldn't say anything?"

"Oh, you can scold him, if you like," she said, "for being so late. For keeping us waiting like this. I certainly plan to do that. But don't mention to him, please, what I just told you, about how he's working too hard. Lecturing him doesn't work, especially about that. He gets his back up the minute he hears it."

"Because he knows it's the truth?" Rutledge said.

"Yes," she said, as David approached, "and doesn't want it to be." Her watch read 12:33.

"Were you waiting to see if you'd won the mileage pool, dear?" she said very sweetly to him as he started to sit down.

He paused in the act of pulling out his chair and looked at her intently. "*I* know I'm late," he said. "I realize that. I was going to apologize, and explain, if you'd just let me sit down." To Rutledge he said: "I apologize to both of you," looking first at Burt and then back at her, "but I seem to've lost track of the time."

He sat down then and snapped the napkin open over onto his lap. "They've got everything a sailor could possibly want on this thing," he said. "Instruments, charts, videos of all the charts. After I worked the mileage out, well, my guess of it, I mean, I took a short walk around the Boat Deck—I would've liked it better if I could've gone outside, but the wind's too strong on the bow—and then I went into the ship's library there, two decks down on the Quarter, and what a collection they've got. Wonderful, what they've thought of."

"Well," Frances said, patting him on his right hand with her left as she picked up her menu with her right, "it's so nice you're having *such* a good time. And you were the one I had to convince, when you didn't even want to come." She looked up at Rutledge and smiled. "Isn't that always the way?"

12

"She told me—this'd be Amy," Rutledge said, digging efficiently into mignons of pork in a cream sauce containing sautéed pears and walnuts, pausing every so often for a pull of the '84 Chateauneuf du Pape he had tasted and pronounced "potable," "that she first encountered Carl at an MFA Members' Preview of some touring collection of bronzes." He smoothly made it seem as though he merely was resuming the monologue the lateness of the hour had interrupted in the lounge that morning; that no daggers had been drawn; and that he had been oblivious to Frances's imploring eyes.

" 'I want to say "Remingtons," ' she said, 'most likely because I'm not much interested in bronzes and the museum has a Remington or two, so I just fall back on that and say: Well, then that's what they must've been. But of course it doesn't matter. This would've been a few years back, seventy, seventy-one. Nixon was still president, taking a fearful beating about the war in Vietnam—the Watergate business hadn't really begun to boil yet. I thought he richly deserved it. Now don't get mad at me for saying that. I would've thought the same thing if he'd had us battling the legions of Satan; I'd become an unreconstructed pacifist the day we learned that Rover'd been shot down. It wouldn't've mattered to me who the president had been. I would've hated anyone who either got us into a situation where our young men were being maimed and killed, or only passively inherited the mess from someone else, but still failed to get them out.

" 'My father had the opposite reaction. His way of coping with Rover's death was to tell himself it'd been a noble sacrifice. And therefore any war our men were fighting had to be, by definition, just as noble as the cause that had cost him his son. It made no difference that we'd been sneak-attacked to start the war that Rover fought, and we not only hadn't been attacked in Vietnam, we were the invaders. If we were in it, it was just, and that was the end of that. He even went so far as to be convinced that Nixon him*self* was a victim of the war and red-eyed liberal hatreds. We had a truce on the subject in the house: We didn't mention it. It was the only way.' "

David beckoned the wine steward and ordered a carafe of the house white, to go with his fillet of halibut baked in a crust with warm balsamic dressing. Rutledge reminded him of their agreement about the wine list, but David shrugged it off and said since he and Frances were both having meat—she had ordered chicken poached in bouillon with a vegetable julienne—for their entrees, he was "out of the loop on this one" and would fend for himself.

" 'I was no more than mildly interested in Carl, and that was only because I'd been a little curious to see what sort of man my newly found old friend Eleanor'd gotten coupled to. It was kind of difficult for me, in fact, to imagine Eleanor coupling with any man, no matter how attractive, actually being naked in a bed with a naked man. Like imagining Queen Elizabeth without her handbag, the one she always has with her. Maybe she didn't have it in bed with her when she and Prince Philip were conceiving those preposterous princes and princesses, but I'd find that hard to believe. Well, the same sort of thing pertained to Eleanor: She was so *very* fastidious, and sex can be *quite* messy. Of course it was quite possible that in fact she'd never actually done it. They had no children, after all, and there are such things as companionate marriages, meant to fend off suspicion and keep up appearances, but without requiring any of that *common* copulation. One of those would've been perfectly compatible with the personality and behavior of the Eleanor I was only just getting to know, twenty-five years out of college.

" 'She'd told me Carl was a bond specialist with Oaken, Maynard and Beane. I'd never heard of the firm, but I gathered it did a lot of business underwriting such things, and selling stocks—the usual brokerage-house stuff. Dad and I hadn't been in a position to study up on such matters or need all that much information about investments; people who have no more money than they need to get by on enjoy a luxury of indolent ignorance the well-to-do cannot afford. While Eleanor didn't come right out and say it—she would never've been so vulgar—she did manage to make sure I also gathered that he made a good deal of money, and that he apparently did it without ever breaking a sweat. He seemed to spend a lot of time at his clubs, and not just having his business lunch or drinks after work, either: amateur theatricals at the Tavern, getting dressed up as the bear; various special events at the Somerset and the Saint Botolph; and, according to Eleanor, "going to every damned evening lecture the Athenaeum offers."

" 'So if it *was* a companionate marriage, it sounded to me as though Carl wasn't keeping his end of the bargain: keeping poor Eleanor company. He sounded to me like the kind of man who spent no more time at home than he absolutely had to, sleeping and washing and changing his clothes, and to be honest with you—although of course I didn't say it to Eleanor—therefore the kind of man who might very well have, in addition to all his club activities and a wife like Eleanor, a girlfriend on the side. To do the dirty deed that Eleanor found coarse. The girlfriend'd most likely be married herself, having developed her interest in other women's husbands after she'd begun to lose interest in her own. Or discovered that he'd taken an interest in his young secretary. But at the same time she'd be in no hurry to relinquish her security and reputation. Therefore she'd have the same kinds of things to lose that Carl'd have, if they were caught. And therefore she'd be just as careful as he'd be to make sure that they weren't. She'd be certain to be most discreet. So that was the cause of my mild curiosity: to see whether Carl in the flesh looked like the kind of man I'd envisioned him as being.' "

The steward delivered David's wine and poured a glass of it. David picked it up immediately and drank half of it.

" 'He did, and he did not,' she said," Rutledge said, sawing through sliced tomatoes with basil in a light vinaigrette. " 'A pen-and-ink drawing of Carl ought to be in every dictionary to illustrate the definition of *normal*. His height was normal, just under six feet. His weight was quite normal: one-sixty or so. His muscle tone: slack, as is normal, or at least was quite normal back then, for a man of his age and station. His normal suit a gray pinstripe from Brooks, a bit shiny in the seat; probably two or three years beyond the age when it should've been retired, would've been my guess. If you'd've said that to him he would've said: "What? Stuff and nonsense. Plenty of wear in it yet." Surely nothing *ab*normal there.

" 'What he said suggested to me that what went on inside his head was just as regular and normal as you would expect. His comments about the artwork being shown were exactly what a well-to-do businessman would say if he thought it would be good for business if he patronized the arts and therefore allowed his polite—*rich*—clients to extort donations from him to their favorite causes. Because if he didn't they'd take their trade elsewhere. Knew it because he'd had it drilled into him by his first superiors, when he was very young, and besides, it also kept his wife amused. Nothing more and nothing less. And so without intending to, by doing all of this he also made it very plain that he had had no idea at all exactly why all it should be. All this *ritual*. Why it *mattered* to people—who mattered to *him*—that he was always willing to subsidize daubs, and figures on horseback, and collections of old furniture—and the people who made, bought or took care of them—about which he cared not a fig.

" 'He obviously couldn't figure out the connection between his contributions of money and time—he was on two boards of directors of cultural institutions, appointed for his financial skills—and his best customers' delivery of their investment business to him. All he knew was that there *was* that connection, and that's why he did what he did.' "

David poured a second glass of white wine and drank deeply from it. He said, "Ahh," and topped it off after he set it down.

" 'You see them at every celebration of the arts, these perfectly nice, white, middle-aged males in dark suits—now and then, gussied up in black-tie—wondering what the devil they're doing there, amidst all this, well, all this *stuff*. Or if it's the ballet or the symphony, or some chamber ensemble, why it's necessary for them to get all dressed up and come out for the afternoon or the evening to hear music they don't like very much, when they could nap so much more comfortably in their old clothes at home. Without disturbing anyone if they snored. So far I'd had Carl dead to rights in my mind, precisely the way he'd turned out.' "

David refilled his wineglass, emptied it, and poured the last half-glass from the carafe. He put his elbows on the table and cupped his chin in his hands. He stared intently at Rutledge, as though finding it hard to get him in focus.

" 'But in one respect I'd been wrong. That was in the assumption that he had all those diversions that kept him away from home because at least one of them was a cover for the afternoon or evening a week—Wednesdays, *cinq à sept*?—that he spent in a room somewhere, with that married woman of his. Carl had a bond-salesman's eyes. He looked at me—I later learned, he looked at everyone—as though I'd been a balance sheet; before he committed himself to anything involving me or anyone else, he intended to find out if the books'd been cooked. He did that because, as I later found out, he *didn't* have the sexual friend that I'd imagined for him, and'd in fact never had one. But after considerable reflection he'd decided that a man of his mature years, sober habits and industriousness really was entitled to have a friendship with a woman who would do for him what was lacking in his life—what Eleanor would not do—and for whom in turn he would supply what was lacking in hers. So, not long before we met, he had concluded that the time had come for him to acquire such a friend, and for that vacancy he was appraising me.

" 'If I looked like a good prospect,' Amy said to me," Rutledge said, savoring an apple Calvados slice in caramel sauce, drinking cappuccino with it, " 'the reason was of course that I was. If I'd known the job was open I would've applied for it, although probably not in writing—I couldn't've come up with three references, for one thing, and neither of the two I had would've liked it if I'd mentioned them, after our mere one-night stands twenty or so years before that. But I was definitely interested in such an opening, if one in fact did exist. There I was, a perfectly healthy woman, in that respect fully as normal as Carl, forty-seven years old, bored most of the time and sexually deprived—*horny*, I believe the term is—and beyond childbearing years, which is more than young bimbos can say. Sex with me for him would be as close to an invisible affair as he could get—without becoming an angel.'

"Needless to say," Rutledge said, finishing the dessert and turning his full attention to the cappuccino, "I was completely at a loss as to how to deal with this. Men of my generation who had never been married to, or seriously involved with, a woman—I suppose now I should say 'another person,' since there seems to be so much of that stuff going on these days—found ourselves at a serious disadvantage whenever we were called upon to confront a woman who took the same blunt attitude toward, well, biological matters, that we were quite comfortable with taking when we were with other men. It was understood among us that there were certain matters that needed dealing with, on a regular basis. The regularity was individually variable, but the need was common. No harm in that at all, as we saw it at least. But deal with it away from home, so's to cause no talk, and what you did to ease yourself, well, you kept it to yourself. Except in the most general terms, when with other men. Not at all like it is now.

"So it was very different then when a woman talked that way. I had no idea *that* they did it, talked that way, I mean, as sheltered as I guess I'd been, and I did not know what to do. I have found in my career that when you don't know what to do, you'd better not do anything. You're too likely to be wrong. So I said nothing. That seemed to be sufficient. She nodded and went on.

" 'Carl—and we were in the midst of quite a lot of people now, sipping wine and making knowing comments about things they didn't understand, so there was some inhibition; most of our communication was by means of the eyes—said he was glad to meet me. Ellie'd talked a lot about me and I'd been good for her. He said she had "a cramped life," which I thought was interesting: an insight unexpected from a man as dull as he so obviously was. But still, healthy, nonetheless.

" 'I pushed him on it and he said, "I'm not much company for her. We have such different interests. Mine are mostly business. It still fascinates me. That's why I do it well. And when I'm finished for the day, well, then I have my friends, all in business too. Whose company she dreads, those few occasions every year when she really must appear with me, annual dinners and so forth.

" ' "And hers—her interests, I mean—well, about the only ones she really had until you came along were the properties she has there, up on the North Shore. She always *liked* this sort of thing, for relaxation, but unless she was going with someone, or meeting someone there, she very seldom went. Now she's out all the time, because she has you to depend on.

" ' "That's taken a big load off me. My off-duty pastimes don't appeal to her, and what she likes to do for fun, events that she goes to with you, do not appeal to me. It's really too bad all around, but we're bored with each other. I'm sure you've noticed that."

" 'I wasn't going to make it that easy for him,' she told me," Rutledge said. " 'I'd been burned too many times. I said, as coldly as I could: "Actually, no, I hadn't." He got all flustered and confused. He wasn't good at this, at being bold with women. Of course if he had been, he probably wouldn't've married Eleanor. He coughed, got red and coughed again.

" ' "I assume you won't tell her that," he said to me. "She knows it just as well as I do, and she feels it just as much, but I haven't said it to her, and I'd much rather that it didn't come from—"

" ' "Someone else," I said. "Don't worry. It won't." And that was the beginning of it. I asked him what it was he did. How he made his living. Pretended that my father and I'd been considering selling off the acreage and investing the money. Pure poppycock, of course, fiction I'd just made up, as he may very well have suspected, but any excuse would do to prolong our conversation, and he grabbed it with both hands.

" 'Said it might make very good sense. "Cut down on the property taxes, of course, save you some money right there. And since you're getting no real income whatever from the way you're using it now"—we'd been renting pasture rights for years to three or four of the neighbors who kept riding horses; brought in a few hundred dollars—"almost any investment that you made, really, would have to be an improvement. I'd give it some serious thought, if I were you, talk it over with your father. See if he doesn't agree that it'd make good sense to convert that idle land into money and put it to work for you."

" 'If anyone'd overheard us,' Amy said, 'and of course there were people all around us, so anyone who was there and wanted to could've eavesdropped on every word we spoke, they wouldn't've noticed a hair out of place. But who on earth would've wanted to do that? Most natural thing in the world: "Eleanor's husband's a broker. Amy's Eleanor's classmate from college; they've become very close. Amy doesn't have a husband to take care of her, and she's taking care of her father. Needs some investment advice. Of *course* Carl would do whatever he could to take some of the burden off her, make sure she got the proper advice." A perfectly innocuous discussion about selling land and investing money, assuring security, all of those things, that was really and also a well-mannered invitation and acceptance to an adulterous affair. And we were the only ones who knew, the only ones in a large, crowded room. It was like having a treehouse or something, back when you were a child: You had to know the password to get on the ladder; otherwise you were shut out. Childish? Perhaps. But children have fun. Grown-ups too often do not.

" ' "A moderately aggressive stance would be the approach that I'd recommend, in your position, I think. From what you tell me, your father's income's so far been at least adequate to cover the necessities. I've got a couple of retired judges among my customers, been doing business with them for years. I assume the pension for probate judges's the same as it is for federal court—you keep the same pay after retirement that you had the day you retired, and if it's been keeping you both warm and dry now, it'll do so when he's retired."

" 'I said I wasn't sure. "I'll look into that," he said. "First thing next week. Research a number of things, in fact, that might suit your needs very well. Because of course it's not the same thing as it would be if you were his wife and not his daughter, and he predeceased you. His wife would get a much more generous annuity, under his pension and Social Security, enough to keep her for life. But you, being so much younger, will almost certainly outlive whatever he leaves."

" 'I told him I had no Social Security of my own, never having held a real job. He said, "There you go. So that makes it imperative, then, that we get cracking on this right away. So that if something happens, as we all hope it won't, you won't find yourself high and dry. Why not talk to your father tonight or tomorrow and see how he feels about this?" I said Dad'd proposed it himself several times in the past, and that I'd fully agreed. But it just seemed as though we never got beyond the point of *agreeing* to do it, got around to actually *doing* something about it. Getting rid of the land and seeing if we then couldn't increase our income by investing what we got for it, so we wouldn't be so darned strapped for cash all the time. Getting along, but just barely. So there wouldn't be any problem with Dad; he'd do whatever I said.

" ' "Well, fine then," Carl said, in that brisk way that businessmen have of talking when they think they've made an unexpected sale and're feeling pleased with themselves—they're so good they can't *help* selling; even when they're just at a social occasion they didn't want to be at, purely as a matter of courtesy, they can't help closing a deal. "Why don't we say then, I think I'm free"—he took his appointment book out of his pocket and riffed through it fast— "yes, next Wednesday. Why don't we just say, pencil in here, next Wednesday, my office, 'bout five? And by then I'll have my stuff all ready for you, for you to look at, and we see where we go then, from here." I said that was all right by me. He nodded and wrote it down in the book, and then closed it and put it away.

" 'So it was all arranged then, as easy as that. I don't think Carl'd ever had so much fun in his life. It was as though he had to hold himself back from just breaking out in a giggle. I saw him the following Wednesday, in his office as we'd agreed. We started to put all the pieces in place, and as you know, later on, because you passed the papers and so forth, we sold off the acreage for a fair price and set it to working for us.' "

Rutledge finished his cappuccino and dropped his napkin on the table. "Excellent lunch, without any doubt. Truly an excellent lunch. Calls for a cigar, I should say. Believe I'll repair to the lounge."

David finished his iced coffee. He drank the last of the white wine. He lifted his napkin from his lap, and allowed it to drop to the floor. He gripped the edge of the table with his left hand while he fished around for the napkin with his right hand on the carpet, his head on its right side on the table. A busboy came and picked up the napkin, shook it out and handed it to him. "Thank you . . . very much," David said. He blotted his lips. He nodded. "Yes," he said after a while, "yes, I think so. I think that it's time for a nap, and I'll therefore ask you to excuse me. From cigars in the lounge." He bowed at Frances. "If that's okay with you, dear."

"Certainly, David," she said, getting up and stooping to give him a kiss on the cheek and muss his hair. "The sweetest of dreams to you, dear."

13

rances and Rutledge, en route to the starboard lounge on Upper Deck where he would have his cigar, at his suggestion detoured to the casino. He had assured her that their stay there would be short, but it turned out longer than he'd planned because it took him a while to lose ten dollars on the quarter slot machines. "It's a ritual I honor," he explained. "Amy allowed herself to lose ten dollars a day and no more. Woman with an iron will. As soon as that was gone, she was out of the casino. Some days she was gone in fifteen minutes and some days she was still playing when the cocktail hour came. When that happened we'd return to the casino after dinner and she'd go right back at it.

"She always quit at midnight, even if she'd had a run of luck all day and was up a couple or three hundred dollars. That was another one of her rules. 'Midnight or ten dollars: Whichever goes first, that's when you quit for the day.' She said enough was enough: 'Doesn't do to get too fond of this, you know. I've got no intention of turning into one of those sad women who fly out to Las Vegas every month or so to maintain their addiction, relax by listening to Buddy Hackett tell dirty jokes.' One time she won sixteen hundred dollars. Midnight came and she still quit. 'That's how winners stay winners, you know.' The next day she lost ten dollars in five minutes. She quit."

"Gambling makes me nervous," she said, when he had urged her to play. "It's supposed to be fun but it just makes me nervous, and I don't think that's fun."

"Suit yourself, my dear," he said, "but you're missing something. Initiation into the ranks of Those Who Know the Score." He was set back several times by small but clangorous jackpots of five, ten and twenty dollars, each time shaking his head grimly and telling the machine, "It's no use, trying to trick me. I know what the rules are, what the regulations say." He said to Frances, "Really shouldn't do that, I suppose. They say that's the first sign of Alzheimer's: When you start talking to machines—the garbage disposal and so forth. Having conversations with the toaster. You know it's really gotten serious when the machines start talking back."

She asked him why he played. "Well, there's two main reasons, I suppose. The first one, like I say, is that Amy always did it. Now she's not around to do it anymore, so I do it for her. Continuity. Have to have that. As Eldred said, the Lares and Penates, you know? The spirits of the departed still hovering around, taking a keen interest in us. So we have to honor their ways. So they'll know that they're fondly remembered.

"The second reason's the one she always gave, when someone asked *her* why she did it. 'You have to propitiate the gods of chance with a sacrifice of at least ten bucks. So they don't get miffed and not only decide to sink the boat but see to it that the crew takes all the lifeboats and abandons ship, leaving all the passengers on board. They can be dangerous creatures. And anyway, even if there may *be* no gods of chance—although we all know, of course, there are—it still doesn't do to take chances, now, does it.' She also said that unless you do that, drop your ten bucks every day, you haven't got a prayer of winning anything worth winning. 'That's the kind of life I had before I married Eldred: too afraid to gamble for fear that I might lose. And I'm here to tell you that's no kind of life to have.' " Timidly Frances had then begun to play.

"Not that any of that means the gods're going to make it easy for you after you've done that, obeyed their little rules. No, no chance of that. First they tempt you, tempt you hard, really try to fool you. Into thinking you can win, no matter what they do. They want to make sure you *believe;* that you're *sincere,* that you really understand that you can't win without them. And if you do win it's because, and *only* because, they have smiled on you. So they throw you these little bones and scraps of payoffs, to see if you'll quit winners, just quit and walk away and never play again. Because if you do that, then they know—they know they have got you good. Way down deep inside you, you're a sinner still. You still think you can *beat* them; take a little at a time, and they won't even notice. Think you're smarter than they are. Well, the joke's on you, my friend. These gods know all about these things, and they don't like insolence. They've been at it a long time, and this is all they do.

"They want to make it so that you'll come back tonight, and then tomorrow too, and you'll lose and you'll lose and you'll lose. Kidding yourself, playing quarters, never silver dollars, or doubling or tripling up, for the really big jackpots. And what you're doing when you do that, playing safe on these machines, is kidding yourself badly. Playing right into their hands. You can't play it safe and gamble at the same time. It's a contradiction in terms to believe you can do it; it cannot be done. And if you try to do it anyway, well, by the time you get off this boat in New York, they'll have taken you for a couple hundred bucks, at least, maybe three or four—that you dropped into these machines, hoping for more small change."

After half an hour she was up forty-eight dollars and said she thought she'd quit. "Just as you please," Rutledge said firmly, "but mark my words: If you do they'll get it all back, and lots more besides. You'll come back up here tomorrow thinking that perhaps you can win another forty-eight bucks, and you won't stop at losing ten. And that's when they'll have you. That's how they get everyone: they get them so fascinated that their judgment disappears. It's always been their way."

In the great lounge next to the atrium he was just as assured and informative about the shops on the Sports Deck above. "Amy could teach me all of this," he said, "because by the time we got together she'd learned it all from Eldred. She certainly hadn't learned it in her sheltered life before that, but she'd always been a good student; Eldred'd been *everywhere*, and trained her perfectly. We made three crossings on the *QE-Two*, at her insistence of course, and she passed all of it on to me.

"As a general rule they sell four kinds of things in those places on the promenades, no matter which boat you're on. The first kind is *most* of the things that you forgot to pack. But not all of them. If you forgot to pack aspirin, or toothpaste, or a tooth*brush*, they will have that. Mouthwash or foot-powder, denture-adhesive: things like that they may have or they may not. There isn't any rhyme or reason to it, what they have or they don't have. And what they do have will probably not be the brand you're used to, or one you'd ever buy at home, but something that will get you through the next four days or so. At exorbitant prices, of course, but what the hell choice do you have? You're not a good enough swimmer, 'd be my guess, that you could get off to go and get it somewhere else: Pay the price or go without.

"The second kind of thing they sell is the type of clothing that you probably do wear and could use; or your friends and relatives could. Sweatshirts, tee shirts, sweaters and scarves; polo shirts, windbreakers, that sort of thing. But very well-made, and very expensive, and all monogrammed with the ship's logo. Oh, and playing cards, placemats, coasters and glassware. I don't presume to advise you on this. You're totally on your own here. I don't like things with *my* monogram on them, let alone somebody else's. It's good-quality stuff, though, very good-quality stuff. Over*priced*, but good-quality stuff, and you won't see it elsewhere for less.

"The third kind of stuff that's for sale—or for rent—is what you didn't know you'd need, before you came on board. Or you plain forgot. If your husband left his cummerbund at home—if he still wears one of the damned things—well, he can buy one up there. Three times the money that he'd pay at home, but if he's got strong feelings about being seen in black-tie without his cummerbund on—which David obviously doesn't since he has that handsome weskit—this is the place where he'd look. If he'd forgotten the whole bloody suit, he could've rented one up here, or bought one, at triple the price ashore. Or you can rent yourself an evening gown. Right out of the fifties, I bet. In case you don't have three or four of your own, in your spare-bedroom closet back home. As Amy did but never brought in the few years we took these boats: She said it would be silly to pack them because 'I can't get into them anymore. And don't bother telling me to get new ones. I'm too old to dress up the mutton as lamb and show my turkey skin to the crowd.'

"The last kind of stuff that they sell in these places I have never managed to get straight. Why anyone buys it, I mean. Souvenirs of the country that you're going to. If you're an Englishman, or a European, you can buy statues of Miss Liberty, and trivets, and that stuff. Can if you're an American, too, but if you're an American you get off and take them home. You're a visitor, you buy 'em on board here and then cart 'em around the country they're souvenirs of, and then when your trip's over, carry them all back home. Good ballast, I suppose—heavy, though, I should think. And cheap watches and booze and perfume, and all of that junk: To carry around over here? And then see the very same kind of stuff in the duty-free shops at the airport when you go to get your flight home? The cigarettes, maybe, I could understand—if you're a smoker, at least, or you're visiting people who smoke. If they haven't been rounded up yet, and shot—for their own protection of course. Those things cost all get-out ashore at home now, all the secular preachers screaming how damned evil they are: Duty-free here on board'd make sense. Bring 'em in cheap and smoke 'em when you get home. Give cancer to all of your friends who smoke. But otherwise I don't know who on earth they expect to buy it. Still, people do: I've *seen* people buying the stuff."

Descending two levels to the Quarter Deck, they sat down at a small marble-topped table in the café overlooking the domed indoor/ outdoor pool at the stern, intending to have coffee, but the service bar was deserted in the late afternoon and no one came to serve them. The dome was closed; there was no one in the pool among the little whitecaps churned up by the ship's motion. "Lively little place, isn't it?" Rutledge said. "Very restful. I don't see any corpse on display yet, though. We must be too early for visiting hours."

"Maybe if we went inside," Frances said after a period of silence. "We could have coffee inside, maybe."

They found a table for two at the rail bordering the port side of the Gallery Atrium and settled down into the deep soft chairs with gratitude, Rutledge at last lighting his cigar.

The day outside was brilliant now, the wind scudding foam off the whitecaps on shining dark blue-green seas of four to six feet. Frances sat in distracted silence, sadness exposed on her face. Rutledge became mildly concerned. "Are you all right?" he said, leaning forward. Later, as she wrote to Kitty Barber, she would decide that had been the moment when she "first began to realize that I had to admit to myself what I knew—that nothing had finally ended after all, as I'd tried to talk myself into thinking. That once more something was not the way it should have been at all, or even the way I guess I'd just assumed that it would be, that it had to be. That instead something was horribly wrong again. And not only that I had to admit that it was, and I knew it, but I also had to tell it to somebody else. Or else I was just going to explode.

"I didn't really know this man Rutledge at all," she would write to Kitty. "We'd only met him the day before. He certainly *seemed* nice enough, and he'd been very open with us, telling us his whole long story. But I didn't know whether I could trust him to hear what was on my mind and then keep it to himself. We had three more days at sea, and if the wine he had loosened up his tongue, so that he let something slip and David found out I'd talked, there'd be an awful row. But in the condition that I was in, I didn't have much of a choice. Either I told somebody or else I kept it to myself and went nuts. And he was the only person I knew on the boat, except for David and his little tart."

"No," she said, exhaling as though she'd just finished a footrace, "no, I'm not all right at all. I'm the very opposite of *all right,* in fact. Although exactly what that would be I really don't know—*all wrong,* I suppose would be it."

"Can I help?" Rutledge said.

"I don't know," she said. "I don't know if anyone could, if I were at home now and could go see old friends; I don't even know if *they* could. Oh, they'd be glad to see me, and they'd cheer me up, and I'd feel better while I was with them. But sooner or later I'd have to go home. We all have to, sooner or later, don't we? Have to do that: sure we do. And when I did that, it would still be there, all around me like some kind of goddamned fog bank that slams down on you like a hammer, while you're out sailing on a perfect day, and leaves you alone and scared in the world—scared that in fact you're not really alone, there's a freighter bearing down on you at fifteen knots or so. Your little fiberglass boat isn't showing up on its radar screen, and its crew isn't blowing its horn. Or hearing the one that you're blowing."

"Seems to me then that you don't have much choice right now," Rutledge said. "If you've got something on your mind that you need to talk about, and you don't want to sell your house for the price of a helicopter ride back to England and the next Concorde home, so you can visit your friends, it's either tell me or stew in your own juice. I *am* a lawyer, you know. We're supposed to keep secret the secrets we're told, and most of us routinely do it. I won't tell your husband what you tell me, unless you tell me to do so. And I won't accidentally drop any hints that would allow a smart man, which he is, to figure out I knew something more about you than I've heard in the Grill at mealtimes."

A middle-aged male steward, apparently sensitized by experience to perceive suddenly volatile, shifting moods of passengers, approached cautiously with small maroon leather–bound menus. He asked whether they would like tea. Rutledge gravely accepted the menus, handing one of them to Frances.

"If you'd just give us a moment to look at these," Rutledge said.

"Certainly, sir," the steward said. "Shall I bring tea or coffee while you're deciding? We have quite an extensive selection . . ."

"I'll have cappuccino," Frances said.

"Sounds good," Rutledge said. "And why don't you have a

Sambuca to go with that, as well? I'm going to have one myself—but I'd like an espresso, please—and you look to me like you could use one." She nodded helplessly.

"Very good, sir," he said, writing and then bowing, "and perhaps a pastry, madame? Could I tempt you with dacquoise, maybe, or New York cheesecake with fresh fruit?"

"No," Frances said curtly, with enormous fatigue, "and I don't care for any little sandwiches and so forth, either. It's too soon after lunch for me, for that."

"Very good, madame," he said, outwardly unruffled, taking her menu from the table and turning to Rutledge. "And for you, sir?" he said.

"On second thought, yes," Rutledge said. "I'll hazard a slice of the dacquoise."

"The steward nodded and went away," she wrote to Kitty, "most likely planning to look for the ship's cat the instant the galley door shut behind him, in order to kick the hell out of it for what I'd just done to him, and there I was, all by myself with this *gentle*man I hardly knew, completely on my own. I was afraid I was going to cry. I know he could see tears in my eyes."

Rutledge put his left hand on Frances's right. "There *is* something badly the matter, of course," he said. "There must be, with you feeling like this. Would you like to go back to your stateroom, maybe, and just lie down for a while? I know when I travel it sometimes exhausts me—and I need an afternoon rest."

Frances shook her head. "I'm not overtired," she said, "not at all. I slept well last night, and all I did between that mammoth breakfast this morning and the four courses between the smoked salmon and chocolate rum mousse I had for lunch was listen to a man talk more nonsense about bridge than I've ever heard in my life—and I'm not even that good at bridge. After that I went back to our cabin and rested up for lunch, I guess you could call it, and listened to classical music. I read a *Town and Country* magazine I brought from home and thought about buying a Henri Bendel suit that I'd seen in Saks that really costs far too much money. David told me to go ahead and get it—he's always been that way: If I want it, I should get it. Pampered me outrageously. Never denied me a thing. But there are times when I'm convinced that I really want far too many things and should curb my appetites." She managed a small smile. "Try to build some character at long last, for a change.

"So," she said, regaining some of her normal equanimity in the confrontation of disagreeable but unalterable facts, "your natural question is: 'If that's what's happened to her so far on this lovely adventure, what on earth is she so gloomy about? What would it take to please her, anyway?' I'm right about that, am I not?"

"Well, yes, as a matter of fact," Rutledge said, as the steward delivered their orders.

"Yes," Frances said, nodding approval as the steward put a small pewter Revere bowl of sugar on the table, "I knew I was right. And if I didn't know the answer so well," she said, scooping half a teaspoon of sugar onto the frothed milk and shaved chocolate floating on the coffee, "I'd have the same question myself."

She stirred the mixture. "But I do know the answer, you see," she said, lifting the cup to her mouth and taking a sip. "Ooh, very hot still, I see." She set it back down in the saucer as the steward finished serving Rutledge's espresso, Sambuca and dessert pastry, baked layers of almond meringue filled with blackberry cream and then chilled. Frances appraised it. "You know," she said to the steward, "that does look rather good."

"Madame would like a slice?" he said.

"If you'd be so kind," she said, "now that I've snapped at you. Without any reason at all."

He bowed. "It was not a problem, madame," he said. "I took no offense. I'll have your sweet here directly."

When he had retreated out of earshot she said, "Yes, and when you present our check, bills including service, and we sign our cabin numbers, you will be very much surprised if you don't find an added tip for you. Fee for extra service, as it were, the service being disregard of passenger's gratuitous rudeness."

She sighed. "Not, of course, that I have any real need of the calories that this little self-indulgence will provide—would you believe that I ever was slim? Actually had a nice figure?" She snickered. "The right answer to that one's, 'Of course.' In case you were hesitating—but only because you weren't sure. Followed by, 'Of course you did, and you're not very far from it now.' Which is a lie, a blatant falsehood, but one that would make me feel good, and allow me to lie to myself. There's much to be said for kind little lies that make people who hear them feel better. I've always thought that at least. In fact I don't know what we'd all do without them, all those nice comforting lies." She paused as the steward returned with her dacquoise, put it down with the wish that she'd enjoy it, and disappeared once more. "I don't know what *I'd* do, at least. Facing reality, naked, defenseless—don't know as I'm up to that, after all of these years on the run."

"Well, of course I don't know you very well," Rutledge said, "but you strike me as fairly realistic. What causes you to think you might not be?"

Frances had used the edge of her fork to sever a major piece of the pastry and then the flat of it to convey the portion to her mouth. She thoughtfully finished chewing, working the question over in her mind as she broke up the creamed meringue. She swallowed, nodded, and had some cappuccino. Then she cleared her throat and said, "Yes. Well, even with the big things, it's always best to begin small.

"You asked me when we sat down a little while ago if I didn't want to go back to the stateroom and take myself a little rest," she said.

"Yes," Rutledge said, "but I certainly didn't mean any . . ."

". . . and I didn't take any, either," Frances said, "take any offense, I mean. It was a perfectly harmless, nice, thoughtful suggestion on your part. But, you see, that option isn't open to me. I don't have that choice to make, and the reason I don't, while you of course couldn't know it, is very painful to me.

"You remember after lunch," she said, "when you were telling us what you planned to do this afternoon, and I said that sounded good, and David said if it was all the same to us he'd rather go back to the stateroom and take himself a short siesta?"

"Yes," Rutledge said, looking puzzled. "But surely if he's still asleep there, and you went in very quietly, you wouldn't disturb him at all. You still could have a rest yourself."

"You don't understand what I'm saying," Frances said, "probably because I haven't finished saying it yet. This gets very complicated, and it's the first time I've tried saying it to anyone, really, except to my daughter Claudia one night long ago. So I'm not very good at talking about it yet. You'll have to be patient with me.

"You see, while I'm sure, without checking up, that David *did* go and play captain this morning—and maybe he went to the library, too, just as he told us at lunch—I believe after lunch that he went back to our stateroom to lie down for a nice nap. And I'm sure he did really need one. Because while I believe that he went to the navigation station, and may have gone to the library, I don't believe that's *all* he did this morning. Or that getting caught up in those activities was what made him late for lunch.

"All that foolishness with the napkin when he got up from the table, dropping it on the floor to make it look like he was tipsy, best-off lying down for a rest? That was what my drama coach, when I was at William and Mary, used to call 'stage business.' Extra action you'd throw in to make your lines more credible, something that the audience could see as well as hear. I've seen David many times before, over the course of the years, when he's been free to let himself go and unleashed himself in the wine list. It takes a lot more than he had at lunch today to make him high, high enough to need a nap. No, the reason that he wants a nap is because it's very common to want one after having intercourse, but David had to put his off after he got laid this morning; by the time he washed her perfume off—that's the way I caught him once; he had the other woman's scent on him; she uses a distinctive one, Shalimar as I recall, and I recognized it; he won't make that mistake again—and got his clothes back on, he was already late for lunch. He had no time for a snooze."

She told Rutledge about Melissa Murray's presence on the vessel and described how she had looked the last time Frances had seen her. "They knew each other years ago, and liked each other very well. Altogether too well, from my point of view at least. They must've met sometime this morning," she said. "Accident? Design? Accident on his part, perhaps, but long-term design on hers? She'd be capable of that. And working on the boat as she does, she would've had a quiet place where they could go and be alone. I don't have any doubt they were.

"So, while I don't doubt that he did go back to the cabin, or that he's napping there, I'm too angry at him now to take the chance he might wake up. With no one else around, as you were at lunch, I'd have no reason not to tell him what I think of him and his rotten behavior, and be damned blunt about it, too."

"Well," Rutledge said mildly, having finished his pastry and alternating sips of espresso and Sambuca, measuring his words out, "if you're sure that you're quite right, and you certainly seem to be; and you're very angry at him, and he's caused you to be sad; since he's given you good reason to denounce him face-to-face, tell him what you think of him—why not go down there and *do* it? Let the scoundrel have it good."

"In the first place, he'd deny it," she said. "He'd deny the accusation and put on his injured look."

"So what?" Rutledge said. "He's the one in the wrong. You'd feel better, venting things, and what if he was hurt? That's called punishment, I think, and it's meted out for crimes. He's committed an offense against you. You have got a grievance and a right to punish him, at least in this man's book."

"And after I got finished, and he went into that sulk, we'd still have three days at sea, alone except for you at meals. And those three days would not be fun. I know Gregor and William will change your table if you don't like your tablemates, but Gregor and William, good-hearted as they may be, are not in a position to change your bed-assignment, if you've decided you don't like the person who sleeps with you in it. That kind of stuff takes lawyers.

"So, now do you begin to see what I mean when I say 'complicated'? *He's* the bad boy in this thing, but *I'd* be the one whose trip would be spoiled—and as much as he needed it, I needed this trip a lot too. I know it's a paradox, but as angry as he makes me sometimes, I also worry about him. I've *been* worried about him, as I told you, for a while. What I'm sure he did this morning isn't something that I've just found out about, something that I haven't known about for a long time. If I brace him with it I'll've ruined his trip, that he desperately needed. And at the same I'll've forced him to make it clear, *again, remind* me, that as good as he's been to me, he's got this second gear that he shifts into now and then, where he doesn't care at all about any other human being but himself. Or how upset I get then, no matter what he buys me. And then *my* trip will be ruined."

"You've lost me," Rutledge said.

"I don't wonder," Frances said. "I lose myself as well. I've been in this maze for a long time, many years in fact, and as much as I dislike it, you'd still think by now at least that I'd know my way around. But even I still get lost sometimes and can't find my own way back.

"What I said a little while ago," she said, methodically dismantling the elaborate meringue structure of the dacquoise into manageable pieces and then making them disappear, one by one, "about how I used to have a nice tidy body? That wasn't vanity. Well, it wasn't *just* vanity; it was also the truth. When I was . . . well, until I was in my early thirties, I was a good-looking woman. I knew it myself, of course, but even if I hadn't known, enough people told me so—and not just men, either; three or four of the most ardent ones were women, the kind of females that played golf and tennis in a way that reminded you of the way men played, if you get my meaning. So that even though lesbianism back then wasn't really considered, what, a 'viable option,' as I gather it's presented now as, there was no doubt in my mind they were *different,* and they did *not* just want to be friends. So that even without the attention from men, I would've figured it out after a while, even if I'd started out completely oblivious to it myself. That I was one good-looking young woman.

"This did not upset me, not in the slightest," she said. "I very seldom found myself sitting around by myself on a Saturday night in college. Unless I'd given myself a good talking-to the previous Sunday night and laid down the law to myself—'Okay, no dates this weekend; the term paper's due, the exam's coming up, and you don't know beans about Wittgenstein's theories; it's time to get serious here'— well, I was out on the town. But unless I did that—and I did, now and then; I really wanted good grades—I had a good choice of escorts, with money to spend and places to go where there was always a party, and I really liked that a lot.

"My mother did her best to 'channel' this, was the way she put it. Make sure I didn't treat the parties and the good times as just fun and games, but as opportunities—to snare a husband—on no account to be wasted.

"Mother was a firm believer that while it was certainly all right, a good idea, for a girl to be choosy and so forth, there was also such a thing as just being too picky when it came to selecting a husband. She hammered that principle into me, starting when I was fourteen. 'Remember: You're not going to be perfect yourself when you grow up, a perfect wife to some man. God help you if you are; no one else'll be able to stand you. But therefore you can't expect to have a perfect husband. It just stands to reason, I think.'

"I used to think that didn't sound like much of a compliment for my father, and I think she realized that—I never heard her say it when he could've overheard it. But it did seem to have a certain amount of common sense to it, and after I'd heard it often enough, over the course of the years, I started to take it to heart. Maybe I took it *too* much to heart, settled for less than I should've, or took bigger risks than I had to.

"But anyway, when I married David, I was well aware that he had certain, well, let's call them *imperfections*. Some fairly serious character defects, in fact, if you'd wanted to write back then what one of my sons-in-law calls 'a worst-case scenario' of what could go wrong if I married this man, and would damage our life together. And what could be done—what I could do—to fix what went wrong if it did."

She sighed heavily and finished the cappuccino. "As it did," she said. "As of course it naturally did. As it always does. It doesn't matter if you know where the weak links are in your marriage: They're still in the chain. You can't get them out; and the world is going to haul on it, if you give the world enough time. And that's when your chain's going to break—right where you knew that it would."

She looked up and stared into Rutledge's face. Her face was animated, but her eyes were flat and dull. "I've never told anyone this before, Burt, not one single soul in the world. I don't think I'd even be telling you now if we were back home, on the land. Or even in England, some foreign country, but with our two feet on the ground. But this is different, a different world somehow; sort of a limbo-world, you know? Suspended in time, with different rules, and nobody knows or cares what you do because nobody knows who you are. How could they? They're all ghosts too."

She hesitated. She looked down and absently smoothed her skirt in her lap. "Yes," she said, clearing her throat again and turning her head to the right as she looked up, so that the gaze she returned to Rutledge's face came almost slyly from the corners of her eyes, "so this is a kind of permission. You see what I'm saying," she said.

"I'm not sure," Rutledge said, finishing the last of his cold espresso.

"Why, *folie à deux,*" Frances said. "That's what I'm talking about. It's a medical term, psychiatric, for two people who're separately utterly normal, but together have pathological delusions. There are times when I think that explains the whole thing, the arrangement that David and I seem to have had, when we started out in our life with each other. That he had a powerful urge to do things that I had equally powerful reasons not to want him to do. So that to make it work we both had to understand, from the very beginning, that the only way it would survive and leave us both intact at the end would be if I gave him no reason whatsoever that would allow him to do what he knew he was going to do. Because sooner or later I'd have no choice, and I would give him a reason. My delusion was that somehow I could go through an entire adult lifetime as his wife without ever, voluntarily or otherwise, issuing the license that he in his delusion felt he had to have, in order to do what he was going to do before our lifetime together was ended."

"This is all about sex, then?" Rutledge said.

"Mostly," Frances said. "A large part of it is. And a pretty *large* part of it, too. But then aren't most things that bother and torment us mortals—aren't most of them, just as Freud thought, mostly concerned about sex? But at the same time: Partly it isn't. Partly it's not sex. And that part's considerable too."

She hunched forward over the table, her brows furrowed over her eyes. She shook her head as though to shake her thoughts down into more compact collections. "What I was telling you, about my figure, and how I didn't mind that at all? Because it meant I had so much attention? All the men hanging around? Well, that was true: I didn't mind that at all. But I wouldn't let them. I knew the rules: As soon as you did that, you were through. They'd declare open season on you. And so I would not do that. But then David proposed to me, gave me the ring, and after that it was all right. That was the understanding back then, and that was how everyone played. So then I could put out for him.

"Everything was all right as long as that lasted, and it lasted for eleven years, thirteen really, but two were before we got married. It had not been easy for me, saying no to all those guys, and once it was all right to give in and do the thing, well, then I went right to town. And we had a very good time.

"But then a bad thing happened," she said, looking sorrowful, "a lot sooner than it's supposed to. Not that it's ever *supposed* to happen, supposed to happen at all. But when it does, to women at least around forty. When I got it, I was too young. I hadn't yet turned thirty-five."

"What was it?" Rutledge said.

"Oh, endometriosis," Frances said, waving her right hand dismissively. "It's not like it was cancer or something, although it might as well've been, I guess. For all of the good it did me. I began to have this terrible pain before I had my periods, and then it got worse. Really hideous pain, lots of blood, when it was going on. I had trouble going to the bathroom, blood in my urine, bad constipation, and when I made love with David, well, I was in agony, that's all. To the point where I just couldn't do it for him, no matter what might happen next. I had tissue from my uterus growing all over the place in my pelvis, places where it didn't belong, and the pain was excruciating. I just couldn't bear to have sex."

She nodded twice. "And that was what did it," she said. "That was the trigger. That was the permit he wanted. If I couldn't sleep with him, someone else would, and he'd leave me alone. I knew what he was doing. But I rationalized it. It hurt me so much to do it, and he needed it so much, that maybe this was the best way to go, until I got better and all. And I did get better. But he believed that that permit of his was irrevocable, don't you see? Once he had it he had it for life. I had minor surgery, took lots of drugs, had the whole damned thing corrected, and after a while I was fine, and we could go at it again. But David still kept his okay to wander. He'd stop using it, for the time being, unless and until he was really tempted. But he wasn't giving it up."

"Oh dear," Rutledge said, resignation in his voice. "That's really too bad for you, isn't it."

"Oh, I guess I asked for it," Frances said. "I knew what the rules were, going in. I'm just ashamed of myself for letting him do this to me." She paused. "She's the one who wrote the letter to us about taking this trip. Melissa wrote the damned letter. I knew she'd be on it with us. She told me she would be, before I signed us up. It isn't like this is a big surprise for me. I just figured that, well, since I'm all right now, David will leave her alone. Well, I seem to've been wrong. She wasn't the first one, not by any means, and she probably won't be the last. But she's his favorite dolly and I've often wondered why."

She shook her head. "Maybe because of the circumstances," she said wonderingly. "Maybe because when he first had her, he had her right in our bed. He had her right in the bed that we shared and *I* slept in. The bed that I slept in with him."

"The son of a bitch," Rutledge said.

"Now please don't say anything to him," she said. "Remember: You promised."

ntil Frances had cracked, however slightly, Rutledge had planned to attend a 3:00 P.M. illustrated lecture in the theater about the quality of recent vintages of the wines of Burgundy (the wines were still aging in casks—the lecture was entitled "Slumbering Giants"—causing Rutledge to suspect that the lecturer, one Jean-Claud Rameau, had purchased at favorable prices a piece of the action in each of the wines that he would recommend as best-buys in the wine-futures market). But when she had begun to teeter on the brink of going all to pieces, he had swiftly decided that his time would be better spent keeping an eye on her than in the theater being smoothly blandished by a minor-league confidence man. He had ordered two more coffees, suggesting that she take hers black, along with another Sambuca, and after a while the relief of having told him—having told anyone, he surmised, other than her friend Kitty, who at a distance and in writing could not be a firm shoulder to cry on—began to ease her mind. They sat without much conversation for close to forty minutes, and then she sniffled and looked at him and said, "Thank you very much. Does it happen to you often, that people whom you hardly know unload their woes on you? And ruin your vacations? If it does, I pity you."

"Oddly enough, it does," he said, "although only since I got tied up with Amy. But it hasn't ruined my vacations, not by any means. Heck, until Amy and I got together, I think I'd only had two of them, in the course of about thirty years. Neither of which I'd really enjoyed. I drove up to Boothbay Harbor once and stayed at a hotel. A very nice old hotel made of wood and painted white, with a broad veranda where the guests could sit on green Adirondack chairs, look at the ocean, think about Eternity, not that far off, for most of them, and wonder what the dinner special'd be: lobster, clams, and what? Perfectly lovely place, restful and serene. But I was by myself. Except for waiters and bartenders, not a soul talked to me, unless I spoke to them first.

"It took me about four or five years to recover from that—people that I knew kept saying to me, 'Damnit, Burt, you're working too hard. You should take a vacation.' Inculcating guilt, as good friends have a way of doing when they're addressing what they believe to be your own best interests: 'Guilt is *good* for you.' But after a while it all took its toll—I think I lost a tough case, too, which had more than a little to do with it—and this time, it was in September, I drove up to Quebec City and stayed at the Château Frontenac. Don't ask me why; someone must've told me I should. I've always been easily led. But anyway, the same thing happened—or else the same thing failed to happen—as had happened at Boothbay: I can't give you a good explanation for it, my irrational belief that total strangers for some reason or another should be friendlier and more outgoing than the people in Barlow and Boston, whom I've known all of my life, but apparently I do hold that opinion. Or used to, at least, anyway. And when they weren't, when they failed to meet my expectations for them, I was badly disappointed. So, after Quebec there weren't any more trips. I didn't have any fun on the first two, came home more depressed than I'd been when I went, and until I got together with Amy I didn't want any more.

"Still, except for those rather depressing brief trips, when I've been at home, at my work, people've always seemed to confide in me, felt quite comfortable doing it. And being a lawyer, I've welcomed that, as of course you would expect. I can't prove it, but I've always thought a good deal of the relatively modest amount of money that I've made, at least that I've been paid by new clients, I've made because people do feel at ease with me, comfortable telling me things. I'm grateful for that, although I must say I don't really know why it is."

"I think I do," she said. "It's because you listen to them, and when they get finished, don't call them damned fools when they have been."

"Frances," Rutledge said, "if we all start making a rule that from here on out we'll only listen to people who've never made fools of themselves, who's going to listen to us?"

That actually fetched a smile from her, which gave him a satisfying sense of accomplishment. She was enjoying herself again, he believed, and in a while she'd be all right. Tacitly cooperating in her own therapy, Frances delayed her return to Stateroom 4111H until shortly after five; by then she was quite sure that her eyes, by then dry, would remain so, and her manner would stay composed when she opened the door and saw David.

He wasn't there. That disconcerted her. She had rehearsed her behavior at their next encounter in her mind—not too stiff but aloof and dignified—and his unexpected absence forced postponement of her performance. When he returned, just before six, she was watching a black-and-white movie adapted from an Agatha Christie novel that she had never read. She had selected it from the *America*'s computerized film library, and while she watched it she was nursing a glass of white wine she had poured from the welcoming bottle. "*Hullo*," she said, somewhat tight. "Where in Hell've you been?"

He narrowed his eyes and inspected her. She was slouched in her slip in the overstuffed leather barrel-chair farthest from the TV on the vanity counter. Her right leg was cocked over the arm of the chair and there was a slackness about her.

He closed the cabin door and opened the closet door, hanging up his blazer. "They had a four-thirty lecture in the theater about stock market trends," he said. "I figured it'd be mostly hogwash, one of those 'on the one hand, this; on the other hand, that' jaw-exercise sessions with some bozo who wouldn't know much, but still more than his listeners did. And that's exactly what it turned out to be. But when I woke up, well, after all, I had nothing much else to do, so I did that instead of nothing. He was absolutely full of crap. 'Buy low, sell high': that'd sum it all up. But of course he was the one who was having the last laugh, on us: he's getting paid for his flatulent bullshit, and we jerks're the ones paying him."

He hunkered down and opened the refrigerator. It was empty. He nodded, shut the door and stood up. He frowned and hiked his trousers up. Then he went to the telephone between the two beds and pushed the nine button for Room Service. He waited for a moment and then said: "Yes, Nicholas, Mister Carroll in Four-one-one-one-aitch. We'd like a bottle of that splendid Chassagne Montrachet of yours, the vintage we had waiting here for us, when we came on board? Yes, yesterday, when we boarded the ship. And if that's all gone then we'll take whatever vintage you've got. Yes, and an ice-bucket, too, if you don't keep it chilled, and some fresh glasses as well." He put the telephone down.

"Won't that be pretty expensive?" she said.

"I assume so," he said. "We *are* on a boat here, a long way from land, and they know we don't want to get off. But then again, how often do we get into this fix? Out on a big boat like this? And when are we likely to be again?"

"Excuse me," she said, "I just thought when you did that, maybe that was your way of saying, telling me, you'd won the pool. The ship's mileage pool, I mean. Since you put so much work into it."

"Nope, I didn't," he said, making his way around the beds. "I was off by thirteen-point-three miles. I think what they did was alter our speed as soon as all the bets were in. Just to screw up all of us real sea dogs and give the dumb yokels a chance. I think the old fix was in."

"Sore loser," she said.

"Merely all of my life," he said, taking the other armchair and sitting down, crossing his legs. "And what did you do with *your* afternoon? Spend it watching *Cat on a Hot Tin Roof,* and punishing your liver in tribute to Tennessee Williams? Or something equally uplifting?"

"I spent most of it with Mister Rutledge," she said with the dignity she'd planned to show when she'd returned to the cabin. "We had coffee and cake in the promenade lounge, and talked of a great many things." She flipped her head, tossing her hair.

"How nice," he said.

"He's a very kind gentleman," she said slowly and distinctly. "He was *so* in love with his wife. He still doesn't believe that she's gone."

"Or at any rate, that's what he says," David said. "We don't know if she ever was."

"I don't know what you mean by that," she said, looking troubled. "I don't know at all what you mean when you say that."

There was a knock at the door. David pulled himself out of the chair and went to it. Outside, there was a compact, swarthy, sinister-looking man about five feet, four inches tall, his black hair cut short and plastered forward on his cratered scalp, disfigured by an old four-inch scar beginning near the top of his right ear and proceeding diagonally forward toward his temple, his teeth bared in what his obsequious tone of voice suggested was meant to be an ingratiating smile. He carried a silver tray with two stemmed glasses and a sweating silver ice-bucket containing a green wine bottle swathed in a large maroon linen napkin. He said, "Meester *Cah*-roll, please, yes?"

"Yes, Nicholas, do come right on in," David said, opening the cabin door wider as Frances, having muttered "*Shit!*" and jumped from her chair and fled in her stockinged feet across the cabin, went into the bathroom and shut the door behind her.

Nicholas set the tray on the top of the counter and asked whether David wished him to open the wine. "If you would, please, yes," David said, and Nicholas with swift economy of motion stripped the lead foil from the neck of the bottle and screwed the cork out neat and clean. "Beautiful," David said. Nicholas bowed and smiled slyly, putting his corkscrew away. "Practice," he said, "sir, that is the key, practice and practice and practice. Very much practice indeed." He produced a chit from inside his white jacket, along with a maroon ballpoint pen trimmed in gold and stenciled *America* on the barrel. David signed the chit and added a ten percent tip. "Thank you very much, sir, I'm sure," Nicholas said, bowing. "You are a true gentleman."

"As are you, Nicholas," David said, sweeping the cabin door open for him. He departed with tall dignity.

Frances emerged from the bathroom in one of the nubby white terrycloth robes provided with the cabin, her hair pinned up and her face showing displeasure. "You could at least've given me a *chance*," she said.

"*What?*" he said, pouring a glass of wine. "You were sitting right here when I made the call. You were here yesterday when Doreen told us that one of the three of them's always on duty, practically right across the hall. You want to loll around here like some off-duty whore in a second-rate crib, when you know someone's going to come in? Okay by me, if that's what you want. You're old enough now to decide."

She shouldered him aside and refilled her own glass. "What did you mean about Burt?" she said. "I think he's a very nice man." The TV set segued from Agatha Christie into a Hollywood musical.

"What did I mean *what*, about Burt?" he said.

"When I said he still didn't believe that his wife was gone, you said: 'Or so he says,' or something like that. What was it that you meant by that?"

"Oh, nothing particular," he said. "Just that he strikes me as a manipulator, and also a *very* quick study. He plays the part of the sleepy, easygoin', small-town hayseed lawyer—'Oh, jes' deeds 'n wills 'n instruments, and settlin' *ess*-tates: jes' a common country lawyer; that's 'bout all I am'—but he's thinking all the time. He sizes people up like an undertaker overstocked with odd-lot caskets: fifty-twos, all portly-short. Takes your pulse and gets everything else you've got on you, while you think he's just keeping the time. And I'll bet he's seldom been mistaken in a judgment that he's made."

"But his wife," she said.

"We don't know if she ever existed," he said. "There *are* people, you know, two-legged tramp steamers, live on these boats and travel the world. Spend their whole lives on big ships surviving on nothing but Willy Loman's shoeshine, a smile and their own brand of patter. Dream-weavers; this century's version of the old-time privateers. Hopping off one ship in Macao onto another one, bound for Trieste. From one place on to the next. People who know what Prometheus didn't, and never do have to touch actual earth. Make pretty good livings, sometimes cheating at cards or counting them at the black-jack tables, and proceed in comfort off what they can sweet-talk the real tourists out of. The credulous people, who pay for the rides, on the boat and the ones that they take from them. Con men, in other words. Swindlers."

"Burt's not one of those," she said. "Look how much he knows about Barlow. And how much he knows about Boston. He wouldn't know those things if he was a fake. Nobody'd go to such work."

"They would if that *was* their work," David said. "And how do we know he knows so much about Barlow? We've never been there, have we? Or what he knows about Boston is true? Have you ever heard of that Wampanoag Club? We've already told him we haven't. Have dinner at Café Sonata? It doesn't exist anymore. We couldn't go there if we tried. Did he resign from the bar, to save a poor deranged client? Or was he disbarred, for stealing the money? Or did he ever belong? How would we know if he made it all up? We've got no way to check up. We can't look it up where we are at the moment, twenty-four-hundred-feet-deep wet miles from home. This guy could be blowing smoke at us."

"Well, he might be exaggerating slightly when he talks about other things," she said, "but he isn't lying about her."

"If he were, my dear, you wouldn't know it," David said. "You wouldn't and neither would I." He sat down in the armchair again. "That's the way swindlers work, and the way that good ones prosper: by getting so good at slinging the bull that even smart people believe what they say—long enough to lie down to get skinned. This's only the second day out. If he's a crook he's still softening us up, still making us into old friends. If he's after our money he's at least one day away from the move to get his hands on it. He's obviously thought from the very beginning that you're a better prospect than I am, so he's concentrating on you. And he's telling you what he believes is what you'd like to hear. So you'll be sympathetic to him. Don't write him any checks, Frances, after he's been plying you with booze: That's my considered advice."

"Oh, for heaven's sake," she said.

"Okay," he said, "have it your way. I didn't say it was so. I merely said that it might be the case, and therefore you should keep it in mind. We don't know that this Amy ever existed, except as a ghost in his head that he trots out on special occasions like this, to amaze and delight the onlookers. Whenever he thinks it might work."

For a while she brooded, a frown on her face, and then she brightened up again. "Well," she said, "give you one thing at least: You didn't say what I thought you might say. About Mister Scheherazade."

"And what was that?" David said.

"Well, that he's a queer, of course," she said.

He got up and refilled his wineglass. "I didn't say he wasn't one, either," he said. "If he's what I think he might be, he'd probably be that when it suited his program to be it. He's no respecter of persons, I think. Whatever it takes to gain your confidence, that he is willing to do. That's why they're called 'con-men,' you know."

That evening in the Grille Lounge they had Kir Royales of Pol Roger champagne "profaned," as Rutledge said, with crème de cassis, and beluga caviar on toast points with dabs of sour cream and bits of chopped onion as hors d'oeuvres. Then they went in to dinner. Rutledge ordered grilled paillard of beef with Mornay sauce and both the Carrolls chose roasted rack of lamb. Rutledge selected a 1988 Volnay Burgundy, Clos des Ducs, which he declared to be "hard to find because it's good and there isn't much of it, coming as it does from a six-acre vineyard." He gave the *carte des vins* to David for his inspection; he saw the price per bottle was $140, nodded his assent without comment and put the wine list down. "When last we met you were telling us about Amy," David said. "I believe there was more to the story."

"Indeed there is, a good deal more," Rutledge said. "The first day she came to see me she had a further revelation. Amy well before the trend began believed in full disclosure. 'Carl's getting tired of me now,' she said. 'Perhaps that sentence was too long. It could be that Carl is simply getting tired. Of everything. It's only natural if he is.

We've had more than six years of our Wednesdays. Habit dulls the sharpest appetite, and I suppose—though I don't know—that as his career winds down, he thinks he should cut down. I don't know how much he pays for his share of that shabby studio apartment he and a couple of his partners keep to screw in at the old Hotel Touraine, but it's probably an expense he's resented twice every single month since he got into the deal. First when he wrote the check to cover his share of it, and then when he balanced his books at the end of the month. And's already decided that in the future he can do nicely without it, but doesn't know yet how to tell me.'

" 'You don't know that,' I said," Rutledge said. " 'Don't be too hard on him.' "

" 'I've been *sleeping* with the man for almost seven years,' she said. 'Don't sit there like a goddamned fool and tell me I don't *know* him. Of course I know him by now, and I know how he thinks. He thinks in arithmetical terms, mathematical terms. Which is dandy if he's handling your investments of the profits that you made from selling off your land, but not so agreeable at all when you can see him working around to telling you, you cost more than you're worth.'

"I said, 'No,' which seemed to be a reasonably safe response," Rutledge said. "And anyway it was the only one that quickly came to mind.

"She said, 'Yes.' Firmly, as though that settled it, and as far as I was concerned, if that was what she wanted then it did. 'So that's another chapter closed. Good fun while it lasted, indispensable in fact, but now it's over and done with, and I can't say I'm that upset.' Amy was an intensely *practical* woman.

" 'Now,' she said, 'what I want you to do as soon as you've gotten everything all straightened out with the estate, as far as that's concerned, paid the taxes and so forth'—I said I couldn't do that until I'd gotten an appraisal, but I doubted there'd be any; Henry hadn't been that well-to-do—'is start thinking about whether I should sell house and land and contents all at once, or auction off the contents separately. And the car, of course, as well. That Roadmaster may be almost thirty years old, but it's got low mileage, and Dad kept it immaculate. Unless I've been misinformed, there're people with real money who buy old cars like that. More's the fools they are.'

" 'But you'll have to have a car,' I said. 'How will you get around, if you don't have a car?'

" 'Eldred has four cars,' she said. 'I'm sure he'll let me use one of them, or if he wants to be a stinker, I can buy my own. A Ford Escort or something.'

"I said, 'I'm aware he has four cars.' As I was. Among Eldred's many interests were a fifty-nine navy-blue Cadillac convertible with white-leather seats, and a fifty-seven Thunderbird, black, with red-leather seats. He seldom drove either one. For one thing, as I've told you, Eldred didn't like to drive; he just liked collecting cars. But when he had to drive, in the winter he drove his dark green Range Rover. In the summer he went around in his red sixty-six Mustang convertible. He said he could handle having either one of those 'dinged up by the idiots who open their car doors against the sides of yours in supermarket parking lots,' which he couldn't do if they were damaging his truly valuable cars. 'But,' I said to Amy, 'I don't see what Eldred having those four cars has to do with you.'

" 'Why, it's very simple,' she said. 'I'm going to marry Eldred.' "

15

"It seemed to me as though she was taking rather a lot for granted," Rutledge said, reviewing the menu he had approved at lunch. "I asked her how she could be so sure that Eldred would cooperate in her design. I said that at least to me he seemed a bit beyond the age at which males are bewitched.

"She said that was 'nonsense. The older they are, the harder they fall. And anyway, that's another thing I learned from my mother: "If you want something badly enough, you'll find a way to make it happen. And if you don't, you won't. So if it doesn't, you have only yourself to blame. You didn't want it badly enough, so you didn't work hard enough for it, and that's the end of that." It makes good sense for Eldred and me to pool our resources, live in his house and sell mine. It makes no sense for each of us to stay where we are, using up twice as much fossil fuel as we have any real need to, maintaining two pieces of property, paying two real-estate tax bills.

" 'It's not as though I were a mendicant, in need of shelter and food. Carl can be a bore and he's gotten tired of me, but his financial advice was good. If Dad and I'd held on to that acreage instead of selling it when we did, we most likely could've gotten twice what we did when we sold it seven years ago. But by following Carl's invest-ment advice, I've more than doubled the price that we did get, and those stocks are still on the way up. If I sell the house now for what it should bring—I figure two hundred thousand, and that's a conserva-tive guess—and put that into a lifetime annuity, I'll be a woman of means, at long last, and that will be most satisfying. I've always wanted to be one.'

"I asked if she really knew him. She said, 'No, I don't. But I plan to.' " The steward returned to the table. Rutledge ordered dilled salmon, gazpacho, and broiled snapper. He asked for a bottle of Meursault. Frances ordered the salmon and roast leg of lamb. David said, "Salmon and osso buco," and ordered a Gevry Chambertin. Rutledge nodded approval. He said, "I asked her how she planned to do that, and she said: 'You're going to do it for me.'

"I admit that I laughed in her face. The whole idea was preposterous. Me as matchmaker? Honest to God. Never was a man more ill-suited to an office. I said, 'You have to be joking.'

"She said, 'Not a bit. I'm dead serious. You're going to throw us together. Just take care of that and then I'll do the rest. Trust me. I know what I'm doing.'

"I had no idea what she had in mind. She explained. 'I know about the business at the Wampanoag Club,' she said. 'And I think I can be of some help in this, all this historical building restoration stuff that's been driving you both nuts.' I said: 'How do you know about that?' She said: 'Eldred mentioned it to Daddy.'

"Ah, good," Rutledge said, as the steward brought the first course and the sommelier appeared with the wines. "What she asked seemed simple enough on its face, but it took a bit of scheming. She thought it was essential that Eldred believe she was at the club by spontaneous chance. So I waited until the next meeting of the FS-SD board, and then at the Sonata afterwards mentioned that I was coming back in the next day around noon. I said I wanted to check on the progress of the renovations at the club in cold daylight. I had to see a client in the morning, 'Henry Neville's daughter, Amy, about his estate, but that shouldn't take long, and then I'll be coming in-town. Care to join me for lunch?' He thought it was a fine idea.

"I recall it vividly," Rutledge said. "It was shortly after one on a Friday afternoon. I had brought Amy to the club with me. I'd turned Amy loose on the first floor, at her request, I might add, and'd gone up to the third floor to wait for Eldred. There was a bunch of those black-lacquered wooden armchairs decorated with a VE RI TAS seal around the long directors' table and I dragged one of them over to the window. There was a light rain falling. I noticed out of habit that the paint was peeling off the fire escape, one of those black steel things. I made a mental note to mention it to Steve Mayberry—he was the general manager. I sat down in the chair at the window. I had a panoramic view of the parking lot below."

Rutledge said there had been a battered blue Dempster Dumpster taking up two spaces at the northeasterly corner of the lot. The club financed 102 percent of the contract for its service and maintenance with the proceeds of two rental agreements that he had proposed to the other members of the board of directors to offer to the funeral home and the engineering fraternity. "My theory being that since we have to have some receptacle for our own trash and garbage anyway, the only realistic choice is between footing the entire bill ourselves—and taking a loss on it that we can ill afford, however small it might be—or kindly allowing our good neighbors to subsidize us. So that then maybe we could at least partly offset what we spend on the dumpster with what we take in from them. I thought we might even come close to breaking even, although we didn't want to get *too* greedy—they might decide to get their own. But I really thought we ought to at least try charging them for this convenient way of getting rid of their rubbish. Especially since we know damned well they'd use it anyway, *completely* at our expense, if we didn't. Especially the frat-boys; they'd've tossed their stuff into it at night, when we weren't around. They're up until all hours; we never would've caught them at it. So it seemed to me as though it might be worth considering."

Rutledge said that had been "the insinuating point of the oyster knife of gradual but radical reform" that he and Motley, wielding the new-member numerical advantage they had recruited for those very purposes, had inserted under the hard shell of the club's ossified management policies. The unwary older directors had not perceived that initial proposal for what it was: the inception of the process Rutledge had with considerable difficulty managed to plot with Motley: to ease them out of power as tactfully as possible but as mercilessly as necessary, by reason either of their parsimony or their penury. "It's your call, Eldred," he had said, "but you've got to make the choice. You say you want to save the club, so it will go on after you. Then you say you don't want to upset the old-timers."

"I'm one of them, Burt," Motley had said. "I'm closer to their age than yours. Of course I sympathize with them. I can't help that, you know."

"You may be one of them, Eldred," Rutledge had said, "but these guys ain't the Three Musketeers: You may be one-for-all with them, but they're not all-for-one with you, and that's for goddamned sure. Go through the books and then tell me what those guys and their fathers before them've contributed to the thing, while you and your father've been kicking in a cool eighty or a hundred thousand dollars. The whole bunch of them together, I bet, haven't equaled that."

"Well, probably not," Motley had said uncomfortably. "But most of them didn't have the means. And still don't, in fact. They weren't as well-off as we were. And I never had a family. That has an effect, too, on what a man can spare—you have to realize that."

"I'll go along with that," Rutledge had said. "I agree with you. And to show I really mean it, here's what I will do: You add up what each one of them, his family, has donated to the club, since, say, nineteen sixty. And then we'll both make our best educated guesses of what those families've been on the average worth, over those twenty years. And then we'll prorate those donations on a basis of comparable net worth. So that if what you've given comes to a hundred thousand, and that's five percent of your estate, then what they should've kicked in too, to demonstrate *their* devotion, will be five percent of theirs.

"Now make me a prediction, Eldred, just for the fun of it—I won't hold you to it: Just how many of these stalwarts—whose tender feelings you are *so* afraid to hurt—just how many of them do you think we're going to find've actually been doing that? Hell, 've done even half as much as what you've done and your father did before you, because you thought it was the right thing to do? All of them? Come on, you're a grown-up—you couldn't think that. Two-thirds of them? A bare majority? A quorum, even? You'll do well if you get that."

Motley had sighed and shaken his head. "I don't have to go over the books," he said. "I know pretty well right this minute, sitting right here, what they've given over the years. I hate to admit it, but what you're telling me I've known for at least ten years now. The biggest single voluntary gift that any one of them've made in that time has been five hundred bucks, at Christmas. And those were the few exceptions—most of them've responded to the annual appeals, shamelessly begging for at *least* that amount, with checks for a hundred bucks. And some of those've even bounced, which's been embarrassing, when we've had to go back and ask them if they'd correct their 'oversight.'

"When one of the old-timers's died off, and his family—if he's got any left; his executor, if he hasn't—at his request has put in the death notice, 'In lieu of flowers, donations may be made to the Wampanoag Club in his memory,' the largest one we've ever gotten from any surviving other member has been fifty dollars. And most of the few that've given anything at all've kicked in only five or ten bucks, I'm ashamed to say.

"No, you're absolutely right: Their mouths've always been very active where the club's been concerned, but their money's always been somewhere else, somewhere way out of town. My guess would be that most of them, one way or another, wind up giving more to the Channel Two Auction every year than they do to help the club. They spend a hell of a lot more time under the club's roof than they do watching 'Masterpiece Theater' and 'Live from the Met,' all of which their tax dollars also support, but they don't look at it that way. The way they see it, when they give to Channel Two, they get a ten-dollar tote bag or something, something they didn't have before that, but what they give to the club, beyond regular dues, is good money they've just thrown away. They don't get anything new and useful they can carry through Harvard Square."

"Well," Rutledge had said, "are you prepared to act on it now? Because if you aren't, then I can promise you: The club's going down with a thud, as soon as you're not around anymore. It won't outlast you by more'n two years. I'm with you, you know that, and with you all the way, and between us it can survive you. But if something isn't done to change things pretty soon, I'm telling you right now that once you're not around, I'm going to start packing my bags. I'm not going to hang around to subsidize a bunch of insolent freeloaders who brag all the time about how highly they respect their heritage, and value their traditions, but then see nothing wrong at all with refusing to cough up their actual share of what it costs to keep that heritage going. You can think what you like about them; what I think is that the truth isn't in them—and when I say that to you, you know, all I'm telling you is what you've told me, to honorably let me know what I'd be letting myself in for, if I did decide to join. It's time, Eldred, it's time. You've got to make the choice now."

"You know," Motley had said, "I wouldn't be a bit surprised if this wasn't really what I had in mind all along, but wouldn't even admit to myself—that the real reason why I maneuvered you into a position where you'd have to join the club was because I knew as soon as you got involved in it, you'd tell me what I guess I've lacked the courage to do myself, but've known just the same that someone was going to have to do, sooner or later. Or it would all disappear. Let's go to work. I'm mad at 'em myself now. Kick their tails off the board."

Complacent, the old-timers had peacefully gone along with the dumpster idea, liking the notion that one of them called "getting a fair price for our rubbish. That's the sort of thing all those Jew outfits do—pick up every cent they can. Should've thought of it years ago."

But as the newcomers proceeded, unseating one after another of the old guard from the board and instituting changes that those ousted did not like at all—conversion of the seldom-used "modest sleeping accommodations for males" into small conference rooms and office-hideaways for lease by executives and corporate officials engaged in projects, strategic planning or exploratory negotiations that they preferred not to disclose prematurely to their own professional colleagues; proposing a new bylaw declaring that applicants be considered, and all paid employees hired, without regard to race, religion, gender or country of national origin—they resentfully lumped the newcomers together as "the Rutledge group" or "the Motley collection," several bitterly disparaging them semipublicly at every opportunity, declaring them to be "in no uncertain terms why so many of us don't even go there anymore, a place our parents built before us, we've belonged to all our lives. That gang's just driven us out. Just a bunch of common, ordinary, money-grubbing limo-liberals with no more real interest in New England than they've got in Africa. Maybe not as much, in fact, you come right down to it, inviting damned niggers to join—no sense of history at all."

Satisfied that the new policies had restored the club and the foundation to a solid, firm financial footing, and confident that he would be promptly informed if things began to come unstuck again, Rutledge said that he had not kept track of its balance sheets since his five-year term as a director and member of the steering committee had ended several years before, two years after Motley had died in 1984. But in 1983 the "Rubbish Fund," as the account had become known, had produced its first annual net profit of $39.75, and at the club at least, Motley had been vocally prouder of that gain, and of Rutledge for perceiving the means to obtain it, than he had ever been of most of the thousands his father and he accumulated, managing their trusts at the bank.

Rutledge had angled his faded old garnet-enameled Mercedes diesel sedan into the space at the southwest corner, so that no one could park another car close enough to swing a door against it; there were six other cars in the lot. He had seated himself in the chair and looked out the window, folding his hands in his lap.

About five minutes later a gray-bearded man wearing a black baseball cap, a soiled and torn Kelly-green Boston Celtics satin warm-up jacket, fingerless gray gloves, baggy brown pants and brown shoes had pushed a heavily overloaded metal supermarket shopping-cart off Beacon Street up the slight incline into the parking lot and over to the dumpster, bending his back to put as much of his weight as possible behind it. The cart was filled with bulging green-plastic rubbish-bags knotted closed; an open one, about half full, was clipped to its front, and a fisherman's aluminum gaff-hook hung on a cord tied to a drapery clip next to it. Plastic spray-dispensing bottles with bright red, green and blue nozzles jiggled from the sides by their pistol-grip triggers.

The man was short, and heavy in the belly; his work was hard for him; when he had steered the cart to a stop against the dumpster he stopped and took several deep breaths, putting his hands on his hips, swelling his cheeks with air and then whooshing it out again. After that he shook himself in the rain, as a dignified but patiently long-suffering family dog might irritably shake out its fur after being startled by a mischievous child playing with a garden hose. Then he resettled his shoulders and turned to put both hands on the edge of the bin. He had to rise up on his toes to look over the cargo. Rutledge said his angle had prevented him from seeing exactly what was in the dumpster, but since as far as he knew it was still serviced on Tuesdays, he guessed it was probably about half full. He imagined the tableau that the man would have offered for an onlooker: "In Real-life Living Color: 'Kilroy was here.'"

The man had taken inventory carefully. Then he'd nodded, backed up one step to the cart without looking at it, and untied the bag from the front. He lifted it up over the edge of the bin and let it slide down inside the angled front. Then he reached back to the cart again, still not taking his eyes from the bin, like a stalker keeping his gaze fixed on his prey while readying his weapon, unclipped the gaff and hooked it over the edge of the dumpster. He'd stepped back again, hitched up his trousers, adjusted his genitals, advanced to the bin, repositioned his hands firmly on the edge, and with considerably more strength and agility than Rutledge had expected, managed to raise his torso high enough so that he was able to hoist his right foot and leg over the edge and then straddle it, swinging his left foot and leg up and over as he balanced himself, then using his buttocks as a fulcrum to swivel himself around before sliding down into the rubbish, slowing himself with his hands. He sank in over his knees, but with some difficulty he could still move around. He took the gaff in his right hand and what Rutledge assumed was his half-empty bag with his left and began moving purposefully toward the middle, turning his body and swinging the gaff vigorously every so often to one side and then the other.

"I assumed he was probably ripping open other plastic rubbish-bags," Rutledge said. "Then bending down, his shoulders working, evidently raking through the trash and picking up items he had uncovered."

Rutledge said he had been fascinated, so much so that he might have failed to notice the approach of Motley's Mustang on Beacon Street if Motley had not eased it to a stop at the entrance to the parking lot and lowered his window before turning in. "He wanted a good close look at the layout before he committed himself to anything," Rutledge said to the Carrolls while he worked on his main course. "Although I must say I can't for the life of me imagine what on earth he thought he was looking for. He'd been coming there for years. The Bancroft back lot beside the club's is clearly marked 'Funeral Parlor Loading Zone—No Parking Day Or Night.' And the frat-house doesn't have a lot, which is why the poor American students whose daddies can't afford to buy Boston condos for them, with underground garages, like Kyoto daddies can, are always sneaking their rattletrap jalopies into our lot late at night, or when there's a snowstorm ban on on-street parking. So the one that belongs to us really had to be the one that he was looking at, even if the sign in the back is kind of small, and hard to see from the street. We ought to do something about that, I suppose; we've been saying we ought to for years. But still, we do have a sign. And he couldn't've thought it was mined. Then I knew the reason for his hesitation: He'd never driven his own car there before; he'd walked, or he'd come by cab. But today after lunch he was going back to Barlow, so for that reason he'd come in his car.

"Anyway, I guess he was satisfied. Didn't see any sign anybody'd booby-trapped the place just for fun, to kill him, so he let off the brake and came in. Parked his car the same way I park my own: at an angle, so nobody else could get close. Took up two spaces, of course, inconsiderate, selfish bastard that he is, but being as I'm one myself, I couldn't fault him for that. He took a minute, reaching around behind the passenger seat for something I couldn't make out, and then he got out with it in his hand: an umbrella. A red-and-blue-striped umbrella, one of those pop-up jobbies you can put in your coat pocket—almost matched his tie. He didn't open it at first. He started to, but then he stopped. He just stood there with it in his hand, doing just what I'd been doing—except I was doing it indoors, nice and dry—before he'd driven into the lot. He was rubbernecking.

"He'd spotted the bum in the dumpster, rooting around in the trash like a pig snouting truffles or something, and Eldred'd led a sheltered life; I guess *he'd* never seen that done right in front of him before either, no more'n I had myself. *Read* about it, of course, sure; seen it on TV: all the sob-sister stories around Christmas, about how the homeless're all doing their food shopping in the restaurant garbage cans, fighting with the rats in the alleys—can't get away from them. But seeing it with your own eyes: That's a far different thing. Makes a much greater impression. This isn't something that some smart-ass, big-mouth, grandstanding activist's staged, like putting on *Macbeth* with trained performing dogs or something, to make the evening news. This is some poor bastard's *life*, going on right in front of your face. If he knew you were watching, most likely he wouldn't like the idea. Might fling a ripe fruit at your head. That's not the same thing as the TV news, dear; that's not the same thing at all.

"I looked at my watch. It was precisely one twenty-five, ten aristocratic, lord-of-the-manor, gamesmanship minutes Eldred'd already kept me and Amy waiting, and now because he'd been distracted by something, he's quite willing to keep us some more. It is possible that he tried to call me from home to warn me he was running late, but given the occasional forgetfulness of our faithful club retainers, getting on in years, the message never made it into my hands. But at any rate I hadn't gotten one, and even if I had, he still should've hurried in. But that was pure Eldred for you, self-centered Eldred Motley all the way. I valued his friendship, and he was a very good client, but he could be a trial to his friends, without ever meaning to be—a genuine pain in the neck.

"I really didn't mind that much, though, you know? I didn't have to be anywhere else, and I was having a pretty good time. I couldn't hear anything from where I was, of course, being three stories up, but I'd imagine, way that guy was working, digging around in that junk, there had to've been some sort of sound effects, too, down where Eldred was, on the ground. So there we are: The rain's coming down, not too hard, to be sure; I'm sitting upstairs in the club, nice and dry at the window, looking on; and there is poor Eldred, out there in the midst of it, standing there holding a folded umbrella, rain coming down on his head.

"I tell you, if the guy'd deliberately set out to *prove*, absolutely, exactly, what people've been saying about him behind his back ever since I can remember, he couldn't've staged it any better: If I'd've had my camera, I'd've taken a picture, had copies made, and sent one to everyone I knew who knew Eldred. 'Here it is, ladies and gentlemen, the proof we've been waiting for. It really is true, just as we thought; in fact it's even worse. Eldred not only hasn't got enough sense to come in out of the rain; he hasn't even got enough sense to open his umbrella when he's out in it and he's holding the damned thing in his hand.'

"Anyway," Rutledge said, "finally the news penetrated that his head was getting rained on. He confirmed this development by wiping his head with his right hand—which, from my seat on the third floor, probably a vantage point that he wouldn't think was fair, I had no trouble seeing had lost quite a lot of hair in the years that'd passed since I met him. His part had become very wide. The nerve endings in his fingertips agreed with those in his scalp; his head was indeed getting wet. He unfurled the umbrella and popped it open. Then he held it over his old bald head while he locked up his car, and started toward the back door.

"Meantime the old bum seemed to be just about finishing up. I still couldn't see exactly what it was that he was getting out of the rubbish, flailing away like a madman with his gaff, but his time between hacks was getting longer and longer, so I assumed he'd gone about as deep's he could, or cared or dared to. So, just as Eldred'd gotten about halfway between his car and the back door, the bum stood up and turned around: He was going back to where he'd gotten in, in order to get out. And that was the first he'd seen of Eldred. Eldred'd been watching *him* all along, glancing back every step or two at the old derelict, thrashing around in the dumpster, all the time he was crossing the lot, but this was the first the bum'd seen of Eldred, hadn't known he was on the same planet. So now the two of them're just stopped and standing where they are, stock-still, the bum knee-deep in the rubbish with his Celtics jacket on, and Eldred in his blue poplin suit, his blue shirt and his striped tie, standing in the parking lot under his umbrella. Staring at each other. As though one of them'd been a Martian and the other one an earthling—I don't know who would've been which—and not only'd neither one of them ever seen anything like the other one before, but'd never even dreamed that such a remarkable creature might exist.

"I was having a wonderful time for myself," Rutledge said. "It was absolutely comical, slapstick, baggy-pants comedy. A privilege to be present for it. The only things missing were subtitles: 'What the *hell*'re you?' 'Never mind *me*—what the hell're *you*? And what the *hell* do you think you're doing?' I'm telling you, it was exciting. And there was real suspense in this. This had all the makings of one of those baffling confrontations that you never see anything but the outcomes of on TV late at night, the EMTs lifting the body bag off of the sidewalk and onto the cart, and loading it into the van. One total stranger pulled a gun out on a busy street and shot another one, and no one can understand why.

"But this time there wasn't any gunplay. The bum came to grips with it first. He nodded his head a few times—like he was saying to himself: 'Well, takes all kinds, I guess'—and started wading toward the edge again. He's dragging his bag, which now seems to've gotten very heavy, result of all the work he's done, stomping around up to his crotch in other people's garbage, and now he's using his hook to help him pull himself along. I was beginning to see where he'd gotten that upper-body strength I'd been surprised to see he had—he'd come by it honest. He leaned over the edge and sort of soft-dropped the green bag to the ground, as gently as he could, but he hadn't tied it closed, so when it landed it came open at the top, and some of what was in it, the stuff he'd been collecting, spilled out onto the lot. Beer cans. Coke cans. Pepsi cans, all kinds of you-name-it cans, rolling around on the pavement.

"He'd gone into that dumpster for returnable containers, was what he'd done, and now what he was going to do with them was take them in and reclaim the deposits. I'd imagine he'd probably picked up between ten and twenty dollars' worth, all his hard and dirty work, but still, after all, thirty-five or forty bucks a day ain't too shabby, for walking-around money, right? Assuming of course that he could keep it up long enough to stay out every day, all day, filling that cart up again twice. With no taxes or withholding, no real overhead. No equipment investment on your part either, if you swipe the grocery cart that cost the guy who owns the store fifty, sixty bucks, as I assume such people do. That isn't really too bad pay, in a recession like it seemed like we'd been in since Carter became president. Kind of a tough job in the winter, snow and ice'd be a real problem, I'm sure, pushing that old cart around. And now and then I'd imagine you'd disturb a rat or two having dinner and they wouldn't want to share—might give you a nice little dose of bubonic plague just to put their point across. So, not a red-hot career choice, no, but still, until they give you enough welfare money to keep you well supplied with all the Sterno you can drink, or white port and muscatel if that's what your taste runs to, it's a helluva lot better'n going cold-turkey thirsty—far, far better'n that."

"The club throws away the returnable bottles?" Frances said, gasping, putting her left hand to her breast and pretending a fainting dismay. "My god, aren't you people environmentally conscious?"

"The club does *not* throw away its deposit bottles, I assure you," Rutledge said. "The club never did, though it seemed to. That was one of the first of the dozens of petty items I looked into, back when I was on the board and that very question came up. Because when you added up all the petty items together you could see them slowly but surely nickel-and-diming us down the toilet, putting the club right down into its grave: the death of a thousand cuts. 'How come we never see any credits from our suppliers for returning our empty bottles, but we keep on paying deposits? We pay the deposits, every delivery, but we never get anything back. Either these invoices should be showing credits, or else they shouldn't include more deposits. All we sell in this place is the beverage, not the bottle. What's going on with the bottles and cans? Are we throwing the damned things away? If so, then we cut that out, and we cut it out as of today.'

"Well, come to find out, we were not doing that, throwing our nickels away. No, what we were doing, without knowing we were doing it, was letting the help walk out with the empties at night, swiping a little spare change for themselves in addition to their paltry wages. I was all over them like a rash. I made it known that the next guy who did that, walked out with a case of Coke cans or Heineken bottles under his arm, he'd be cashiered on the spot and out on the street himself that same night with no job to come to in the morning. Just like he would've been if the bills from the provision company hadn't all of a sudden stopped showing us buying as many steaks, chops and roasts every three or four months as we were cooking and selling to our members and guests in the course of an average *year*. That seemed to've put a stop to *that*, the sirloin roasts sneaking out the back door of the kitchen at night, hiding under the coats of the help, so now I was after the empties? Well, they were used to me now. I was against all that petty-thievery stuff, and I'd hurt them if it didn't stop. Which it thereupon did. Well, most of it did, anyway, which is always the best you can hope for.

"So anyway, no, those were not our cans and bottles that the bum'd dug out of the trash. Those were cans and bottles mostly from the frat-house, I'd guess, and maybe a few from the funeral home, too—the night-help and embalming staff tossing out their lunch leavings, along with the odd ear or nose here and there, should one of them ever become detached by an errant straight razor, in the process of improving some plain old cadaver into a well-dressed dearly departed, freshly barbered and shaven, dearly beloved, no less.

"Seeing the bum finish up for the day, at least at that particular stop, seemed to make Eldred stop and think. About what I don't know to this day. He didn't move, just stayed in his tracks—I couldn't see his face now, him being under the umbrella and all—but he stood still for a minute and then he started up again and came in the back door of the club."

Rutledge said the man in the Celtics jacket had reversed the procedures he had followed to get into the dumpster and climbed out of it, almost gracefully letting himself down to a bent-knee-cushioned soft landing on the asphalt. He dusted his hands off and then stooped to pick up the six or seven cans and bottles that had fallen out of the bag, collecting them in the crook of his left arm until he got back to the bag and dropped them in again. Then, holding the top of the bag closed, he spun it expertly several times, twisting it so that he could knot it on itself. He put it on the rack under the basket of the cart, using his foot to jam it securely in place. Then he took the gaff from the edge of the dumpster and replaced it on the cart, this time hanging it from the handlebar at the rear. He removed the baseball cap and rumpled his gray hair until it stood up nearly straight, scratching his scalp as he did so. He took a cleaning-spray container with a bright blue top from the side of the cart and sprayed his head several times, rubbing whatever the liquid was into his hair and scalp. He put the container back on the cart. He smoothed his hair down from front to back with both hands and then put his cap back on. He shook himself again in the rain, resettled his genitals once more, took two or three deep breaths, clamped his hands on the cart, bent his back and slowly got the cart turned around and underway, back out to the street.

"I felt like applauding," Rutledge said. "I don't know what happened to that guy that left him with nothing better to do every day than spend it going through the barrels and the trash-bins and the wire baskets along the sidewalk—which I've also seen a good many times, but never really noticed, never really thought about, the bums doing, digging empties out of the garbage—and I don't know how he made his living before whatever it was happened. Whether he did a bad thing to himself, drank or drugged himself out of a job; if somebody did it to him, abolished his job and put him out of work; or if he cracked up once and couldn't function anymore doing what he did before, just another casualty of the partial system-meltdown that we've been going through these past few years. But whatever it was he was doing before he got clobbered, ruined his life by mistake or on purpose, did it all to himself, by himself, sometime or somewhere before it all happened he'd developed good work-habits, and if he ever gets another break in this life, I'll bet he'll make good use of it. If I had a doughnut shop, a truckers' greasy spoon, or a barroom, something like that, and I could use a guy who'd sweep out and maybe wash some dishes for me, I'd offer that poor bum a job, and make him a side-bet to go with it, no investment on his part; that inside of six weeks he'd be behind the counter, cleaned up and taking orders, with a decent place to live, and in a year he'd be the grill-man, but getting set as soon's he could work up the courage to give me notice he was leaving to become a manager at some better joint."

"But you don't," Frances said. "So, too bad for him, but he's still plumb out of luck."

"Yeah, I know," Rutledge said, at first taken aback, "talk is cheap. But that's what I would've done, if I could have."

"That doesn't increase the value of the talk, though," Frances said, slicing her lamb. "Not a particle."

16

He said he had sat back in the chair and waited. After a while he heard the old, slow, three-person elevator wheeze back into its mechanical life deep in its narrow shaft and begin the long, softly grinding ascent to the third floor. After what seemed like a long time he heard it stop at the doorway in the hall outside the directors' meeting room, the clashing sound of the inner, accordioned metal gate being opened and then the latch clicking in the oaken door onto the floor. He did not move. He heard soft padding footsteps outside and then a timid knock at the frame of the door. "Mister, ah, Rutledge?" It was said in an old and abraded low voice.

Rutledge said he had turned his head to his left without moving his torso, suggesting that he meant to look at the speaker, and would do so in good time, but hadn't yet quite gotten around to it. "Yes, Arthur?" he said.

"Well, I'm sorry to bother you, Mister Rutledge," the old voice said somewhat more firmly, "but Mister Motley's in the bar and he says he had an appointment to meet you here today. Do you have an appointment to meet this particular member?"

"It sounded like Arthur was telling me," Rutledge said to the Carrolls, "that if on second thought I didn't think I *wanted* to have an appointment to meet Eldred, he would find some way to get rid of him without his feelings being hurt in any way. Arthur didn't like hurt feelings. Arthur wanted everyone who came to his club—he's been dead for years now, but during his lifetime he always considered it *his*—to come in happy. Not boisterous, mind you; just in a pleasant good humor. And he wanted them to leave at least in as good condition as they were when they came in. If possible: even better. And if

Arthur knew the two of us had been in league to force the directors to modernize the club and upgrade the facilities, as he most likely did, he was certainly not going to give his knowledge away to me.

" 'I did agree to meet him, Arthur,' I said," Rutledge said, " 'and he did indeed have an appointment to meet me here today. At one-fifteen.' I looked at my watch, the same one I wear now"—he un-snapped the bracelet and handed it to David; it was a stainless steel Rolex Oyster Perpetual engraved on the back—"the initials are my grandfather's and my father's, my dad's graduation gift from him at Middlebury, Class of Twenty-nine." David looked at it idly and im-mediately gave it back. " 'It's now exactly one thirty-four, by my extremely reliable watch. So, if you'd be so good, Arthur, as to inform Mister Motley that I'm terribly sorry but I was called away to take a call up here just before he arrived, and so I'll have to ask him to be patient while I finish it, and then I'll come down to join him. Would you tell him that for me, please, Arthur?' "

There had been a short pause. Then the old voice said, "Cer-tainly, Mister Rutledge. I'll say you asked if he'd be kind enough to wait, and you'll be right down as soon as you've finished."

"No, Arthur, you will not," Rutledge had said firmly. "You will tell Mister Motley exactly what I told you to tell him, nothing more and nothing less. You will tell him I was called upstairs to take a call just before he arrived, and that I'll be down when I've finished it. No embellishments whatsoever, Arthur. No ruffles and flourishes; no bows and no curtsies; no nineteen-gun salutes. Is that clear to you, Arthur?"

"Yes, Mister Rutledge," the voice had said, the door shutting be-hind it as the padding footsteps resumed, the sound fading away from the doorway.

"I waited for exactly fourteen minutes," Rutledge said. "You see, I'd left Amy on the first floor when we had arrived, on the understanding that when Eldred arrived she would waylay him, and tell him I'd brought her with me to see him. In order for her to inspect the decor and give us her expert advice as an artist, or at least as an art connoisseur." So it had been 1:48 P.M. when Rutledge had stepped off the space- and fuel-wasting, ceremonially wide stair-case—"an asset to the club only because its formal-photo stage set appealed to young women and their parents renting facilities for weddings and receptions"—onto the landing of the second floor, turning left on the worn blue-bordered oriental runner carpeting the hall and then into the first doorway on the right, opening into the bar, the ivory-painted room crowded with beautifully framed third-rate nineteenth-century American landscape paintings, considered by many visitors to be the finest room in the club.

" 'They've all generally been pretty thirsty, of course, when they've paid us that compliment,' I told Amy the day we showed her around. 'They would've sworn to any lie we asked them to, if that'd been what it would take to get a stiff drink out of us.'

"Eldred told me later, after he'd found out the whole occasion had been rigged—when that was I've never been exactly sure; but he was not a stupid man, just a negligent one—that he'd found her sitting by herself at the center table of the five grouped at the bay windows at the front of the bar. They give a southwesterly view. He said she 'appeared to have been mesmerized by the traffic on Commonwealth Avenue, pretending to be waiting for you. She told me she'd told you she'd had business in town, and you said that you did too. That you'd offered her a ride, and that you'd promised her lunch. After you'd offered me lunch. And that you'd left her at the stairs, so you could make a call.'

"He said that she hadn't looked up when he'd entered the bar and paused to look for me. When I got down to the bar they were sitting in the bay window, oblivious to me and the rest of the world, engaged in their own conversation. Of course they'd known each other before, the way small-town people usually did then, but only in the most superficial way. So I thought I'd give them a little more time, since they seemed to be getting along so well on their own."

He said the bar had been unattended. Henry, a recent Filipino immigrant nearing fifty, had negotiated carefully after he had proven to be the most personable of five persons on the list supplied by the Boston Bartenders' School. Steve Mayberry had requested it six months before, when Henry's predecessor, the inveterately cheerful Desmond, had given his amiable notice, to the astonishment of his employers of more than twenty-three years. Using a diction and inflection they had not heard him use before, and exhibiting an extensive repertoire of mannerisms he had not previously shown to them, Desmond had explained that "my lover, Jay," never before mentioned to them, either by name or function, "and I've gone and bought a bed-and-*break*fast. We've been saving up for simply *years*, and now we've just up and *done* it. It's 'The Last Best Hope,' on the

Cape, down in Wellfleet, and we both hope you'll all come and see us, lots and lots of times. Once we get *settled,* I mean. We'll have to re*dec*orate and so forth, of course, put in a whole new mo-*teef.* And also we're going to re*name* it, Jay wants to, which will mean painting new signs and so forth. 'The Purple Catamount'—Jay being from Vermont, he's got a real *thing* for those *crea*-tures. It's right near the National Seashore, so *that's* a big natural attraction plus. And we do have *so many* friends, oh, *numerous* friends, scads of them, really, right nearby in Provincetown that we *know* that we can count on, to give us good word-of-*mouth.*"

To management's offer of what Henry had not known would have amounted to three-quarters of Desmond's salary, Henry had made a counteroffer. He proposed that he work a five-hour split shift—11:30 to 2:00 and 4:30 to 7:30—for what he clearly calculated would have been seventy-five percent of Desmond's pay.

"So, in a nutshell," Mayberry had said, ashamed of himself for concealing his personal repugnance for the task of screwing another working-stiff out of a fair wage in order to suck up to the cheap rich bastards just because they had a good grip on his own short hairs too, "what we get when we sum it all up is that this guy—who *I* at least think is the best of the lot; I held his audition, and I watched him work, and I know I can live with this guy—if we hire him, will be custom-tailored staffing. Instead of working Desmond's eight-hour day, eleven in the morning to seven-thirty every night, with the half-hour for lunch at two, for what we didn't actually tell him but certainly led him to believe would have been what we'd been paying Desmond, we'll hire him like you'd lease a car. Pay him for tending bar only during those hours when we need a bartender. Buy only as much bartending as we actually use. He'll take care of the people who drink before lunch; then he'll leave, and come back for the cocktail-hour crowd.

"In other words," Mayberry had said, "what it amounts to is that without knowing it, this guy's offering to do five-eighths of Desmond's work, sixty-two-and-a-half percent, for fifty percent of his pay."

"Fifty-six-and-a-quarter percent, actually," Rutledge had said.

"Okay," Mayberry said, deliberately not trying hard enough to hide his irritation, "fifty-six percent, then. That still means the club's up six percent on the deal before he mixes one single drink."

"And also means we were in fact overpaying Desmond, and've

been doing so for several years in fact. Just as I said the last time you raised the question of giving Desmond a raise," Rutledge had said, relentlessly. "And not, as you still insisted, that we weren't."

"Well, whatever," Mayberry said. "The point of it is, as I see it at least, this is a good deal for us, this proposal that Henry's made us. We already know we can get along all right without those other three hours of bartending work. At least I know we can, because as long as I've been here, I've never actually seen Desmond do much of anything during them except the same thing he did on his lunch-break— when it was perfectly all right because he wasn't *supposed* to be working during it: sit in the bar with the Sports Channel on and the *Racing Form* in front of him, updating his handicap files. But damned if I ever could say anything to him, because his work was always done. Glasses all washed and neatly polished. Garnishes just as they should be. Records in good shape, members' chits up-to-date: What the hell could I tell him to do, instead of sitting there doping the horses? I couldn't think of a damn thing.

"Except now I can, by God, you bet. I should've said: 'Hey, Desmond, while you're about it, pick a few ponies for me and the board. We could all use a sure thing ourselves.' Because I have to say I know that must be where all the cash came from, that he says he and Jay saved up their whole lives for their own little love-nest on the beach. They bet a bundle on some longshot, probably another gelding who'd whinnied in the tip himself, with some unsuspecting bookie, and then that darling horsie romped right home, jiggety-jiggety-jig. All that stuff about life-savings's a smokescreen for the tax-boys, and nothing more'n that. I just wish he'd given me a horse before he lit out of here; old Desmond is a real fox."

Rutledge said he had made another mental note to inform Mayberry that Henry appeared to have ducked out early from his first shift of the day. "It's not as though I mind Henry having his angle," he would say. "That's not what bothers me. Everybody in the place's got his own angle, or else his ancestors had one before him, because otherwise he wouldn't have the coin it takes to join, and then keep belonging to, a silly enterprise like this. The thing that I mind is that one angle is supposed to be all that any one man gets to play. Henry has some motive, some reason he does not see fit to tell us, for wanting to work that split shift. Very few of the people in his line of work, the hospitality business, regard split shifts with any kind of pleasure. They look at them as being at best a necessary evil, and almost none of them would ever willingly take one, if they were given a choice. There isn't enough time between the two stints to really get anything else done, or even go home for a nap, so the person who draws one of them feels all the time like he's getting half a day's pay for a day and a half on the job. So whatever it is that he does with the time, it's something that he likes to do.

"But none of that matters to us, so long as he does his job here. He told us that's what he wanted, and it looked like a good deal for us, so we said in effect: 'Okay, Henry, fine. What you do with your free time when you're not here is none of our business at all, so long as your wife doesn't mind, if you have one, or your husband if you're more like Desmond.' But now Henry's got to be told that he has to work here the *whole* of both those two shifts—no cutting corners at other angles to hold down a side-job at some other place."

He had gone behind the bar and taken a double-old-fashioned glass from the shelf, "the kind we generally used at the club in those days for serving niggardly portions of Bass ale on draft," sliding the door of the ice machine open and half-filling the glass with clinking cubes. With his back to the front windows he could not see what Motley and Amy were doing, but he could hear them talking in low voices, some urgency in their tone, "as though their subjects had been important." Still without looking up he had turned back to the working area under the bar and filled the glass with San Pellegrino water. He had disregarded the tongs and picked a wedge of lime out of the stainless steel container with his fingers. He heard her say, "*No, that won't do. That simply will not do at all.*" Then he dried his hands on the towel hanging from a fixture on the sink and on a small red-lined yellow pad next to the bar-rail wrote out a check for $1.50 and initialed it. As he picked up the drink and looked up he saw them studying him.

"I don't think they were sure whether they even recognized me," Rutledge said to the Carrolls that night. "They'd been that caught up in their discussion. It'd been quite a while, I guess, since they'd even seen each other, several years, as a matter of fact, and I really don't know whether they'd ever had anything more than desultory conversation before that. And of course over the years their appearances'd changed, just as my own'd changed, too. Eldred, in addition to losing a lot of his hair, had become considerably stouter. And I'm sure I've had that same stupid look on my face a good many times myself, too, when someone's come up to me at a meeting or convention, some such large group as that, in the middle of a conversation that's really interested me—lots of other people around that I'm not used to seeing on a day-to-day regular basis, but many of whom I'm fairly sure I must know, have met a few times, or ought to recognize, at least—whose names should be familiar enough to me so that they come right to my lips. But they don't. So I stand there like a ninny, looking for all the world, I'm sure, like I've just misplaced the laundry ticket from the place where I left my brain to be washed a week ago, so I don't have it with me now when I really need it, and I really wish I did.

"Eldred started to get up, you know? One of those little half-hearted movements that you make when you're not sure whether you should really do it but at the same time you're afraid not to do it— you're coming out of a daze. So you sort of compromise by hanging your hand out loose in front of you and letting it flop there, like it was something that you'd meant to put away where it belonged after you finished doing what you'd needed it for, but then the phone rang or something and you forgot to do it. So it won't look like you're trying to shake hands with the guy whose name you know as well as you know your own, but can't place because you've been off in a daze. Still, at the same time you want to leave it so it *will* look like of *course* you meant to shake hands with him all along, in case that *does* turn out to be what you'd should've been planning to do all along. Someone you know and ought to remember, but momentarily can't. Like I'll most likely be, or you'll be, if we meet again, but ashore, out of the context we met in here, not on a great bloody boat. So I won't think you've gotten simple since the last convention, so that you've started forgetting the names of important people like I know I am, because after all, I've been telling you so here myself.

"Except when we've had the joint rented out to some society of teachers or social workers or something that's needed a small place to meet, have a conference or throw a small celebration, at the club we seldom see strangers. So I took the lead in the matter. Gave Eldred the lawyer's best dignified greeting, the one we all practiced, our first *years* in practice, and always have on hand for good clients. Apologized abjectly for my tardiness. 'Simply had to take a call.' So they'll know right off we're all perfectly secure and have absolutely nothing to fear, no reproaches or nothin'. Because clients can *smell* negligence and guilty fear like *guard* dogs, and when they do, they *attack*. By hiring themselves different lawyers."

Rutledge said that Motley's hand was dry and cool to his shake; his brown eyes were clear and untroubled. " '*Burt,*' " he said to me. Whether it was because he'd figured out I'd set him up, or he'd been enjoying himself so much that thought'd never crossed his mind, I've never known. 'Sorry I was late. Just having one of those days like we all seem to have from time to time, I guess, when it doesn't seem to matter how you try to speed things up, or what you try to do, you're still gonna run late all day long.'

" 'I know the feeling,' I said. 'Frustrating as hell, isn't it? And then when you finally *do* get here, *I've* gotten myself tied up. So then *you* end up waiting for me. But the heck with it. I see you did manage to get yourself a drink, at least, before our courteous uniformed attendant skipped out on his duties a little early.' "

"I did," Motley had said, "a glass of Bass ale, and it tasted damned good, too, I can tell you."

"Good, good," Rutledge had said. "Mayberry's been telling me ever since you put me on the executive committee: We sell a surprising amount of that stuff—surprising at least to me. Our previous barkeep," he had said to Amy, "a fellow named Desmond—turned out to be quite the fairy, which came as a real shock to us; not that it would've made any difference far's his job here was concerned, because it wouldn't've, but still, it was kind of a shock—he told me that's why it's so popular here: 'It's popular because it's so popular,' he said. 'All beers and ales're like that. They're not like the good wines at all: they don't get better with age; they get worse. You have to sell them at a good steady clip, or your stock'll go stale. And if it does that then you won't sell any. Malt beverages taste a great deal better if they're fresh. They do not get better with age, especially when they're on draught. So, if you sell a lot, then you'll probably sell more, because word gets around fast among drinkers that your beer on draught is fresh. And if you don't sell much, pretty soon you will find that you're not selling any at all.' The Beer Paradox. Goes with Zeno's: you can never get where you're going, because it's always half the distance away from where you've gotten to so far—so you're always halfway there. But the hell with all this philosophy, huh? I assume you two haven't had lunch."

"*I* haven't," Motley had said. Amy had not said anything. He had patted his waist. "Although some'd probably say it wouldn't do me any harm at all, I did miss a meal or two, here and there."

"Well, if you do decide to do that, it can wait 'til tomorrow," Rutledge had said, taking Motley's upper right arm lightly with his left hand to turn him toward the door. To Amy he had said: "We're liable to find that we're all by ourselves in the dining room at this hour. Our members tend to eat early, large portions, quickly, like the early-supper sitting in a boardinghouse of hungry workingmen: get there first and get as much of it's you can, before it's all gone—and then clear out of sight. They seem to think it's vaguely sinful to linger over lunch. But that's all the better for us, when we've got something confidential to discuss."

"Absolutely," Motley had said, looking at Amy to make sure she understood. "Strictly between the three of us, yes."

"Well of course," Rutledge had said, as they reached the door and started down the hallway to the left toward the dining room on the other side of the great hall, also overlooking Commonwealth Avenue, "that's the real, hidden beauty of this place. It's a little bit like one of those Quiet Rooms that the telephone company built to test I-don't-know-what-the-hell-all—so quiet, I read somewhere, that if you stayed in one of them very long you felt like you were losing your mind, the quiet was that unnatural. Well, sort of the same thing with this building here, only our Quiet Room's our sanctuary from the entire world outside; we come in here to make sure we stay sane. Everything outside these walls stays outside, and everything inside stays inside. Nobody in that world's ever supposed to hear anything that's gone on in here, unless all the parties agree in advance. So anything said in this building stays here. No echoes outside of this place."

"No," Amy had said after a moment, as though she had been grateful for the time she had been allowed to think carefully about so complex a concept. "Well, I can see where it could be good, to have a secure place like this. If you needed to keep something quiet. I myself never knew it was here. Never even noticed it, let alone knew it was a private club or thought about who belonged to it—what they did here. It's surprising, the things that you never've noticed, when you've lived around a town for so long."

"Just how long's your family actually lived in Barlow?" Motley had said, turning to his right into the dining room.

"He said it as though he assumed that of course a Neville, the daughter of a *judge*, would understand that the Motleys, for heaven's sake, had never actually noticed her family was on the earth," Rutledge said. "I liked Eldred a lot, and we got along real well. But there was no getting 'round the fact that without even knowing he was really doing it, he could be an utter *shit*.

"She didn't actually *say* anything. She just stopped and stood there. There was no one else in the dining room. It was as though she'd unexpectedly and inexplicably found herself in surroundings that long ago had been familiar to her but she hadn't seen for years. One day they'd gone away and now here they were again."

The hardwood floor had gleamed around the tables, reflecting the soft gray daylight from the northerly windows up onto the window-less westerly wall; it was entirely taken up by a mural depicting a southeasterly view of a late afternoon at the duck pond in the Boston Public Garden, one swan boat entering from the left, emerging into slanting golden sunlight from the deep green shade under the broad footbridge, blue-green and airily delicate in the picture; the other, most of its passengers children with rosily whitish, indistinct features, partially shaded by the brims of ecru straw hats with dark blue bands and fluttering ribbons, having just made the turn around the island where fat mallards and black ducks dozed squatting down like fat matrons in their Elizabethan ruffs of feathers, complacently resting and digesting between regal paddles for handouts of peanuts and Cracker Jack. There was an engraved brass plaque centered on the chair rail under it.

" 'That mural's an original,' she said.

" 'That it is,' Eldred said. 'Well past its prime, of course, now. One of our projects rebuilding this place's going to be getting it cleaned. Fearfully expensive, or so some've said, but if that's what it costs, well, then it will cost that. It has some historical value. Done by the son of the man who built this house. Or rebuilt it into what it was when we got it, when he left it to us. Reminds me of a print we used to have in our dining room over the sideboard. Ours was in wintertime, though. At sunset, I think, kind of an orangey-dark sky. Women in fur hats and men with heavy coats on. Print my mother bought at the Museum of Fine Arts. She was always fond of it. I was partial to it myself. My father always hated it. Threw it out right after she died.'

" '*Boston Common at Twilight*,' Amy said. 'That *is* popular. Al-ways has been, since I can remember, and with very good reason, I think. Childe Hassam. Dead well over fifty years now, 'd be my guess, but he captured the city in that one. The guy who did this sad article here—*Swan Boats at Four in July*, he called it—was one of his stu-dents, copycats, whatever you want to call them, and not one of his better ones, either. What an ignominious end to come to: Not even a good counterfeiter. More like a cheap fake, I guess you might say, sorry excuse for a painter—according to most of the critics, at least, as capricious as they can be.

" 'But this is one time I agree with them. You take a close look at that thing and you see it; you begin to see what they mean. The ducks're all right. He was okay with ducks. Probably had the Audubon prints, or knew that everyone else did, and thought he'd better get that part at least right. But he fouled up the bridge good and proper. The real one's gray, and it's stone. Not green iron, tracery, really, the way he makes it look here. And real children never looked like that, didn't then and don't today. Someone painting the thing from real life—which he presumably did; he'd lived around here all his life—he should've known things like that. Known them and gotten them right. You can't paint your *mind's* impression of what the eye sees until your *eyes've* seen it right, and made a true impression, and you have registered it. If you don't do it you get everything wrong. This gentleman didn't do it.

" 'That's the whole secret of getting your life right, I'm convinced: always making sure you've got the right angle on whatever it is that concerns you, so you're always sure you're seeing it in what's the right light. The light that's right for you, I mean, for what you want to do.

" 'But not this guy. If he actually knew what he wanted to do, he got it completely screwed up. Even fouled up the title; the sky's not that color in July around here, not at four in the afternoon, at least— that color sky, that angle of the light: at that time of the day it's more late-September, early-October. A man who'd lived in Boston within half a mile or so of his subject—who'd supposedly paid some attention to becoming a painter and all—he should've had some notion of how things really *looked*. And how they changed in the light depending on the earth's angle to it, in the year. He might've missed it one year, if that was all he spent. But this guy'd missed it every year, and he'd been here all of them. He didn't get it right. Had no true eye at all, on the best day he ever had: a rank Impressionist imitator.

" 'But then, of course, he didn't *have* to be good, if his father owned the building. After all, it was the family home, wasn't it?' she said.

"Eldred was close to transfixed," Rutledge said, having made short work of the broiled red snapper and washed it down with Meursault. "He was absolutely enthralled. I'd been his lawyer for twenty-five years and I'd never seen him in that condition. He was accustomed to playing the sage, and here he'd just encountered someone who knew more about a subject than he did, her very first time in the building where he'd spent a good many days of his life. With all the time that he'd had for his *interests*? And she'd topped him without thinking twice: How could this possibly be? And even more, *she* was a *woman*. I don't think the possibility of such a thing happening had ever even crossed his mind before. He was completely captivated. He had to shake himself a bit before he could agree that indeed the painter's family had owned the wall he'd painted.

" 'And so,' she said, 'since his mother was convinced he was at least as good as Claude Monet, maybe even better, when it came time to commission an artist to do the mural for the family ballroom (hard to imagine that, now—families with their own ballrooms—but a lot of them did in those days) he had the real inside track. And he still lived here himself too, of course, lived his entire life in this place. But that didn't make him a Frederick Childe Hassam. It may've been his wall, but he was still a lousy painter.'

"Eldred made a feeble show of resistance," Rutledge said, as the busboy removed the dinner plates. " 'I always liked that kind of picture. The one that we had at home: Lots of times my father said we should get rid of it, you know? We should really take it down. "Oh, everyone's got one of those things," he'd say, "it's everywhere now. Wherever you go, I don't care where it is, you go anywhere and you see that. You go somewhere and there it is again, everywhere you go, always right square in front of you. I'm tired of it; sick of it, that's what it is. We've outgrown that old picture now's what we've done. We've gone beyond where we used to be. We should get something *different* for ourselves, something that not everyone else we know's got, too; you don't see every time you go out. We can afford it. We've *earned* something new, something brand-new of our own. Something that's real, *genuine*. That's more'n just something that both of us happened to like at the time, and that time was long ago now; something that's *distinctive*, too."

" 'That was what he would say. But I never agreed with him on it. I never felt like I wanted to do that, and not just with that nice picture, either. I always felt like, well, if you liked it the day that you bought it and paid for it, liked it then well enough to pay out your good money, and you've always been happy with it ever since, liked to look at it still, ever since? Well then, what I think is that the fact that it's gotten old shouldn't mean *anna*-thin', not if you still feel like you like it. Why just go and change something anyway, if you still like it all right? If you still think it's okay, and like seeing it when you're home? Just so you'll have something to do? There's nothing wrong with *familiar*, I think; I like what I liked years ago. Changing things, changing things, all of the time? Just for the sake of the changes? I don't think so now, I've never thought so, and I don't think that I ever will. That stuff never made any sense to me then and it doesn't make any sense to me now. Never made me no sense at all. I think we have to restore that painting. It's history. It belongs to us, and we're a historical club. We're the custodians of that mural. It was entrusted to us.'

"All she said was, 'Well, to each his own. But you'll be wasting your money. You ought to paint over that thing.' Eldred really looked stricken. I figured her campaign was dead."

17

*R*utledge laughed. "It all seemed to make such good sense. Instead of the club paying an enormous amount of money to repair a mural no one who belonged to it actually liked, Eldred and I were being urged by a person who knew something about such matters to simply *obliterate* it. With a six-dollar bucket of paint. So we brought it up with satisfaction at the next meeting of the executive board, expecting prompt agreement, and Ab Bohannon dashed our hopes. Simply dashed our hopes." Absently, without consulting them, he ordered crêpes suzette, coffee and a bottle of Barsac.

" 'Well, Eldred,' he said, 'the late Parker Bowser would applaud your point of view, and that of this woman you've mentioned, if he hadn't died himself back during World War Two. Because thanks to his father's foresight, or cussedness, whichever you want to call it, that picture that you're looking at is in fact a very valuable painting, must be worth close to a million by now, least as far as this club is concerned. Even though it's still no damned good at all, not as art, from an art connoisseur's point of view.' "

"Would someone have paid for it then, do you think?" David said. "Even though she'd said it was no good?"

Rutledge said, "No. They wouldn't if they could help themselves, no. But they might've if they didn't look out. Eldred and I might've bought ourselves a high-priced share of those miserable daubings, along with our other directors and members, without ever meaning to do so. But for our narrow escape."

He said, "There's a brass plaque there now, under the middle of that travesty. We put it there. It's to warn future directors, now that Abner Bohannon's passed on, and won't be around to save the next board that has to refurbish this place, and I may not be around either. Tells them what we found out just in time.

"It'd taken us a while to get enough cash together to start getting the old place spruced up. It was really in terrible shape. That was one of the first things that we thought of doing, after Amy spoke up, when we came to redoing that room: painting over that damned third-rate mural—she'd also used the word *eyesore*—instead of spending the very large amount it was going to cost to restore the thing to the lovely state it's in today.

"See, the mural'd been neglected too, along with everything else in the place, in the thirty years and more since the original members'd gotten together and bought it in fairly good shape, and pretty cheap, too, from Chauncey Bowser's estate, Chauncey having been the late painter's late father. But unlike the walls, which needed paint, and the woodwork, that needed varnish, and the ceilings, that needed whitening—all that sort of normal thing which was still going to cost real money—the restoration of that painting was going to be a truly *huge* expense, one we couldn't possibly ever see ourselves as being able to justify to the membership, never mind 'afford to undertake,' even if we could've sold them on the idea. Which we couldn't've, skinflints that they were. Even if the damned thing'd been *worth* restoring in the first place—which everyone who really knew anything about the subject said it certainly was not.

" 'Early Twentieth-century American graffiti,' was what one young authority said, totally supporting Amy. One of those art history majors not long out of Sarah Lawrence but very assured in his judgments, as only insufferable young curators can be. 'Just one more thing we clumsy Americans don't do very well, and really shouldn't do at all.' So the hell with it, that was our viewpoint. Give it three coats of flat-white to cover it up, and two coats of semigloss lager–pale gold to make it presentable again. And then hang something else over it.

"So anyway, there we were, springtime of seventy-eight it was, all pretty pleased with ourselves. Figured that we'd finally, after all those many years of really terrible neglect, gotten our plans made for renovation, all set to go full-speed-ahead with the thing, soon's summertime rolled 'round again. So the carpenters and painters could have the windows open, let the sawdust and the fumes out—and also because we certainly hadn't wanted to have the furnace and the entire heating system shut down for a complete overhaul, put in air-conditioning, in the wintertime, either; and *that* was long overdue, too. We decided that about the only thing we had left to do was call a general meeting of the membership, bring them all up-to-date on exactly what it was that the directors'd decided to do. Brief them on the contracts, tell them: which companies we'd chosen to do the work we needed done, for what we'd determined were the lowest good-faith bids from solid, reputable firms; what it all was going to cost us (more than we could afford, of course, but then they'd known that all along, that was the reason the work was so long overdue); how long it was going to take—all that sort of thing. Because it certainly couldn't help but affect them—rooms closed off; people hammering in the basement; power saws going; and then the paint fumes, like I said, all around them all summer long.

"The people we had there were very much set in their ways. Very traditional people, people not friendly to change or disruption, no matter how badly it's needed. The renovation was going to be hard for them, no matter what we did, more than hard enough for them. They were not going to like it, not one iota, while it was all going on. And this would be so if they *knew* in advance, exactly what to expect—why it was so necessary. If they *didn't* know, and it still happened, well then, all hell would surely break loose. They'd be *all* up in arms with us, then. They would've been forming up lynch mobs.

"So we called the meeting and laid out the plans. Made a clean breast of it all, you might say, left out nothing at all. How painful it was going to be, and so forth. There was a good deal of grumbling and griping—exactly the sort of stuff we'd expected: 'Why do we have to go through all of this now, spend all this money and make all this noise, just when my back's acting up?' Our members tended to be just a bit solipsistic now and then, so no big surprises in that. But then we came to the dining room work, and it was our turn to get rocked.

"One of the founding members, this was old Ab Bohannon— over a hundred and two he was then, but still around the place, seemed like to most of us, just about every day; still in command of his wits, and quite predictably not one bit delighted with me and Eldred, for any number of reasons—raised his hand and stood up. Stood up very carefully. It took him quite a while. He said, Well, he didn't think so.

"Said he wasn't sure he liked that idea much, of just painting over the mural. Old Ab reminded us he'd been around for a long time. He wasn't in any real hurry, getting around to the point. Probably thought if he was willing to spend some of whatever little time he had left for himself on telling us kids where to head in, we ought to have the common decency to appreciate the wisdom he was giving. Said he thought that painting over Parker's work'd probably end up costing the club a great deal more money'n we had any notion of spending on the whole project we'd laid out. 'Get the club here in a damned-fine legal mess here, that's what you'll do if you do that, and at my age I don't want to see that. Another damned lawsuit to fight comes along here, only ones getting rich and coming out of it with any money left'll be the goddamned lawyers, mark my words. Long's I've been around—and that's quite a long time, before most of your fathers were born—as far as I've seen, all those goddamned lawyers're the only ones ever make any money, people let one of those silly rows just get itself started, and then go right out of control. And I'll tell you, my young friends: If that should happen, it'll make these big repair-bills we're looking at here and that've got us all scared shitless, it'll make all them look like small change, is what it'll do. Piss halfway across 'em—the whole way, had the wind at your back, by the time you get through with that business.'

"Said he'd known Chauncey Bowser from the leather business, and those two went back a long way. Abner's business was importing top-grade hides, 'only the best,' from abroad: Africa, Cuba, South American countries. Chauncey's firm'd bought the hides from outfits like Abner's, then wholesaled them to most of the top shoe factories that were still going strong then, all over New England—and there were a lot of them, too, back in those days, first half of the century and more.

"Said Chauncey's two other sons'd been 'real businessmen, none of your goddamned-fool artists.' He'd set one of 'em up in his own business, shoe machinery, and the boy'd done real well, and the other one'd wanted to go west and buy a ranch, so he'd bankrolled that venture as well. And Richard'd done very well with his spread out there, just a few miles south of Tulsa, even before all the drilling rights turned out to be so valuable. The daughter he'd already been more'n fair to, he thought, given her and her husband not only their first home, very fine place out there in Wellesley Hills, but also left them the place the family'd always spent their summers, on the ocean up there on Crane's Beach. And her husband'd done pretty well, in his own right, so he thought that took care of that pair.

" 'So that meant the only one left for Chauncey to provide for— he'd taken care of his good wife with his own retirement trust—was the family artist, Parker, and Chauncey's opinion was that what the boy needed most was protection from himself. He said Parker was a good boy, and God knew he always meant well, but Parker was the sort of man that'd always be a boy, just a carefree boy, no matter how many cares he might have. Nothing in the world that anyone could do a thing about: he'd been born and he would die, go to his grave, a lifetime scatterbrain. "All he's ever wanted, and I blame his mother for this, is to spend all day at the museum, or traveling in Europe, going to museums there, or else by himself upstairs there, the back room on the third floor, painting all his pretty pictures. That she says are wonderful—and could be, for all I know." Chauncey told me that he thought if Parker ever got turned loose without someone to look after him—as it looked as though he was sure to be—the day came when Chauncey died, well, unless some steps were taken first, someone'd rob him blind. When you've got a boy who won't take care, even when he should, the only thing that you can do is make sure he gets no cares. Put someone else in charge of them; let him just do what he likes.

" 'So Chauncey took those steps,' or at least so Abner said, and left the place to Parker. 'But he tied it up real good.' Since Chauncey's lawyer was the same one who'd end up later on drawing up the charters for the club and the foundation—Lyman Bolster, this'd be, of MacManus, Wyman, Bolster—Abner said they'd all been clear what was involved when they first came in.

" 'We knew when we bought this place that there were some restrictions. Most of them don't matter to us anymore, I'd have to think, but if I'm not mistaken there's one that still applies. I don't think you can touch that mural, Parker's swan boat picture, on the ballroom wall. Except to keep it up. Preserve it; whatever they call it. I think you'll find that in the deed. An easement of some kind or something—covenant, maybe, that runs with the land? Something along that line. Think you'd better look it up, 'cause if I'm right and you can't touch it, and then you go and do it anyway, we could have a problem here.'

"Well, Ab was right," Rutledge said. "That was exactly what Chauncey'd done. He'd left a life-estate in the place, and only that, to his son. He'd fixed it so that Parker, regardless of what he did, couldn't ever spend his way totally broke and out on the street, with no roof of his own over his head, no matter how foolish he got. What he'd done was, he'd tied it up. Hell, he'd all but bound and gagged it, so that Parker couldn't sell it to anyone, give it away, or borrow cash on it either. And if he ever got married—which I guess wasn't likely, from some of the gossip I've heard about Parker, since then, but if for some reason or other he had—his wife couldn't unload it either, even if he tried to leave it to her, and then went and died before she did: Chauncey's will wouldn't let him do that. If there'd been a wife, a Mrs. Parker, and they had managed to have kids, I guess Chauncey figured the kids would've taken after their father. So he and Bolster'd locked it up so that if kids ever did come into the picture, *they* couldn't've pissed it away either. And then, when all of them were dead, either Parker by himself or his wife or his kids died, if he'd ever came by such connections, the place was to be sold and the money paid over to the Mother Church, First Church of Christ, Scientist, Boston. Without anyone then, or anyone thereafter, touching that sacred mural unless Parker himself said he could do it. Gave his permission. In writing.

"That was the only thing Chauncey'd left up to Parker to make a decision about with the place, if he wanted. And the late Parker hadn't ever wanted to do it, I guess—or if he did want to, he never got around to it, because there wasn't any evidence that he'd ever done it."

" 'What,' Amy said," Rutledge said, " 'would've happened if you'd done it? Painted over the mural, I mean? If you hadn't known that you couldn't do that, what could've happened to you? To the club, I mean, of course.'

" 'Oh, it would've happened to us personally, too, I assure you,' I said. 'Or at least the fallout from it would've. Just as Abner'd told us, Chauncey's will said that if anyone did "deface, alter or in any way change, obscure, or obliterate, or cause anyone else to do so, *Swan Boats at Four in July,* such person or persons shall be jointly and severally strictly liable in liquidated damages to the Mother Church, that is to say, the First Church of Christ, Scientist, Boston, in the amount of One hundred thousand dollars, plus interest, which shall have accrued on said sum at the maximum legal rate then applying, compounded since the date of the life-tenant's death." '

"In other words, if we'd painted over that damned picture in the summer of nineteen seventy-eight, we would've made the club, and ourselves individually, liable for a hundred thousand bucks, plus interest at, say, an average of seven percent per annum, compounded for thirty-four years. Mrs. Eddy would've known. She would've known right off. She would've said to herself: 'Right, those fools've gone and done it. They've finally gone and done it, like Chauncey and I always knew, knew some day they would. Painted over Parker's simply awful, *awful* mural. And now they're going to pay for their foolishness, and pay handsomely for it, too, I can tell you. Pay very handsomely for it.' She would've picked up that phone people've always said she's got right beside her in her mausoleum and rung up her lawyers right on the spot, demanding they get a certified check."

David, opening his menu, looked at Rutledge and blinked. "Off-hand," he said, "I can't even imagine how much that would've been."

"At the time, I couldn't either," Rutledge said. "And neither could my friend Eldred. But we knew it was more'n pocket-change, and we were both curious, so we looked it up—I don't mean we figured it out. The closest we could get to it on an interest table was what it would've been at seven percent, fixed-rate—though the rate of course *hadn't* stayed fixed at that or any other level either, over that long a time; jumped around like a flea on a griddle, in fact—for a term of thirty-*five* years, but we figured: What the hell, since we got saved by Ab's sharp memory, and we don't have to pay it, we'll call it thirty-five years. I don't recall the exact figure, but it came out to around a million and a half dollars. So we called in a flying-squad through the MFA, certified restorers of fine paintings, some such fool-thing or other like that, that people who're easily entertained actually go to school for years to learn. Paid them what was easily a king's ransom, far more money than the damned thing's really worth—about twenty-three grand, as I seem to recall—and counted ourselves lucky we weren't all in Chapter Eleven ourselves instead. And that was back then, over fifteen years ago. Have to be closer to four million–plus, by now. Interest really piles up, you compound it for that long, and the principal never declines."

"And the club would've had to pay, if you'd had it painted over," David said.

"The club would've been *liable* for it, I said," Rutledge said. "The club would not've had in fact to *pay* it, for the simple reason that it couldn't've. The club was approximately an inch and a half from going into receivership back then, and didn't have the money to pay *any*thing of any magnitude, beyond those major-repair bills. No matter what the new bill might've been for.

"It'd really all gone straight to Hell. The building'd been allowed to deteriorate so far for so long that nobody else ever wanted to rent it anymore, for outside functions, reunions, what-have-you, and so forth. And consequently there *was* no income to speak of, beyond membership dues, bar bills and meals revenues.

"You can't run a metropolitan club in a city like Boston on that narrow a revenue base these days. It simply cannot be done. You've got to keep it attractive enough so that outsiders'll want to rent it, and so that your members will use it, too, for their own private parties and special occasions. There's a real market there, and a lucrative one. Just to give you one example—and one I certainly never would've thought of, myself—for cocktail luncheons after funerals. Instead of the family having the undertaker or the clergyman announce at the cemetery that everyone's invited to come back 'to the late residence,' tuck into the dead man's victuals and wine cellar there, they have him invite everyone here. And then our people mix the drinks and cook the food, and do the cleanup afterwards, when all the mourners've gone home. All of the clubs, now, look for that business, and very aggressively, too. They say the big wedding receptions've more or less gone out of style, now, but death's still a strong growth industry. People still die all the time, dropping around us like flies. And look where we are here, right next door to a top funeral home, where all the best people get brought to be laid out when they've come to room temperature. I wouldn't suggest money hasn't changed hands, when an undertaker's steered us some of that business, but I know our manager; he wants to succeed; I sure wouldn't rule it out, either.

"Your whole purpose in all of this sort of thing is to get your members and your visitors to think of it as a real asset, a status-type luxury, you know? A privilege that belongs to *them*, they have proprietary access to—the riffraff cannot get in. Because members're somehow special—season's-tickets, inner-circle, friends-of-bigwigs *special.* Which usually translates into: *rich, successful,* and *influential,* even if they cleverly inherited all their money and've never personally done a damned thing in their whole lives that amounted to a pisshole in the snow. They're still, coincidentally enough, precisely the kind of people that you want to join your club. Because people who'll pay big money to buy status symbols seldom interfere with the people who produce them. As long as they remain convinced that what they've bought means that they're still superior, well, that's all they ever asked—they won't bother you at all.

"It was that sort of subtle, constant, stroking-thing that hadn't been done—not 'not much,' but not at all—when we took control of the club, not for about twenty years. So the club was broke, and getting broker. And that meant if the directors'd broken the covenant, we would've had to come up with the dough. Personally pay over to the Mother Church about three hundred eighty-three grand apiece, if all twelve of us could've done that out of our own personal funds.

"This caused us to swallow quite hard. Being neither millionaires, most of us, nor devoted Christian Scientists, so far as any of us knew, not that we'd ever asked, we had no real desire to more than halve the biggest of our fortunes to the advancement of current missions and money-bleeding TV stations then ongoing in Mrs. Eddy's name, however wholesome we were all prepared to grant they surely must have been.

"Oh, we could've fought it, of course, if we'd painted out the picture, and some unsuspected Scientist among us'd gone promptly running off to church to spill the beans—as there surely would've been one, and he surely would've done; you could've bet the ranch on that and never lost a wink of sleep. When the only thing that can possibly ruin you is an episode of bad luck unique in any century, depend on it: You'll surely have it.

"What could we've done? Well, we could've argued that that kind of covenant couldn't run with the land unless it was some kind of national landmark. Or that enforcing it would impose upon us an unconscionable burden that we should not be asked to bear; something along that line—sure, we could've done that. And it might've worked, too. The restriction, being very silly, and of importance solely to people now all dead, might very well not've stood up in court, if we had. My guess is it probably would not've.

"But what would the court fight've cost us? Old Ab was right about that, too. There's no entity on the face of the earth that fights longer and harder—and meaner, too; don't leave that out—at less cost to itself (since its true believers're doing the fighting, charging nothing or overhead only) than a church does, when money's involved. And I don't care which church it is, either. They're all the same when it comes to two subjects. They're against one and in favor of the other. And they get themselves all dug in to their positions, good and deep, armed to the teeth, overstocked with provisions, and there they will fight until Doomsday.

"One subject's sex and the other one's money; they think what they think and that's it. You can't have the first one; the second one's theirs; and they'll fight you to the death, anywhere, anytime, about either one—your choice and you pick it, if that's how you want it to be. Just like Churchill said the British were going to fight Hitler: on the beaches, in the fields; on the streets and in the houses; room-to-room and chair-to-chair, if it ever comes to that. They will make Churchill on the beaches, in the streets, look like a regular sissy: they will *never* give up. Sex or money, either one: they will *never* surrender. We would've gone broke in the long run ourselves, if we'd told them we weren't going to pay."

18

A couple hours after lunch on the third day, Frances sat at the desk in Cabin 4111H and began a letter to Kitty, "because if I wait until we've gotten home I'll forget too much of what's gone on." That was not the real reason; her motive for mailing it in the ship's small US post office (along with cheerful postcards to every other family member and to several casual friends) was to get the *America*'s cancellation mark. Two days later she would regret that decision to show off and wish she'd never mailed that letter, anywhere in the world.

"It's sort of funny. The captain gave a talk this morning I went to with Burt Rutledge, the nice man who shares our table and has been so kind and good to me (David thinks he's a con man, a crook, probably because he's so considerate of me there has to be something wrong with him, and of course as far as the captain's concerned, and the ship, David already Knows It All and didn't want to hear the talk. So he was going up to his chart room. His treehouse. I almost said: 'Yeah, *first*—first we eat our vegetables, showing self-control, and then we go for our dessert, yummy, yummy, yummy.' But I managed to hold my tongue). The skipper said the route we're taking's well south of the one that the *Titanic* was on, way back in 1912, which was reassuring news. He said the ice that we're avoiding—the same sort of mostly submerged floating iceberg the *Titanic* hit—froze at least two years ago, before it broke off and floated south. He said the US Coast Guard and Canadian Navy keep a constant and close eye with planes and ships on how far south the ice has drifted—it doesn't show up on ships' radar because it's just frozen water—and the navigators plan their courses to stay thirty to forty miles south of the southern edge of it. 'It makes the distance greater,' the captain said, 'and that increases fuel expense, but we at Hayden Lines believe it's worth the cost, that one *Titanic* was quite enough. We hope you'll all get to heaven, but we're all determined not to get you any nearer to your God on this voyage than we can possibly help.'

"After the captain said that, Burt whispered to me that he didn't know much about boats, but thanks to Amy he did know a thing or two about musical history. He said that the band on the *Titanic,* the night that it went down, was not playing 'Nearer My God to Thee,' as the legend has it, but 'Autumn,' from Vivaldi's *Four Seasons.* But Glazunov also wrote a piece about the changing year, called *Seasons,* and there was an 'Autumn' in that one, too. 'So which was it?' he said. 'I really don't know. Maybe the legend is right. Maybe it *was* the damned hymn.'

"This morning we passed the Point of No Return—which I guess I always thought was just a metaphor, for what I didn't know—thirty-five miles or so south of Greenland, about 1,645 miles from England and about the same distance from New York, bound for Cape Race, Newfoundland, and then south of Sable Island, off Nova Scotia. The captain took questions for about half an hour after he had spoken, and one woman got the microphone and asked: 'How deep is the ocean?' He got the strangest look on his face, and I just know what he wanted to say: 'How high is the sky?' But he controlled himself and didn't. Instead he told her that the bottom over the Great Sole Bank west of England drops off from about 350 feet to about 1,350, and that parts of the mid-Atlantic, about where we are now, are over 4,600 feet deep. 'But there are mounts and rises, and ridges and holes, just as there are peaks and valleys ashore, under the ocean of air, above the oceans of water, that constitutes earth's atmosphere. So whether you're ashore or afloat, the depth depends on where you happen to be at any given time. As long as we've got at least 50 feet of water under us, I'm fairly comfortable. Less'n that and I start to get nervous—don't want to have happen to *America* what happened to the QE2 back in '92, when she grounded off Martha's Vineyard, do we now? Many red faces off that sortie.'

"He said our next marker is the automated radio beacon south of Nantucket, where the Lightship used to be anchored, too far south of the island for us to see it. He said the head winds have diminished to about 18 knots; the current as always is about half a knot against us; and he's put on more power, so we're now making what on land would be 31.35 miles an hour. 'For a passenger ship this size, 97,000 tons, that is very fast indeed. Blazing speed, in fact.'

"I guess I've just never really thought about it before, the sheer immensity and power of the ocean that we've both flown so blithely over, back and forth, so many times, and that David and I've sailed on every summer since we met—not way out to sea, of course, but still on the same ocean. At least until recently, that is.

"I was a little afraid of boredom when we started out on this, so I brought three books with me. I haven't opened *one.* The literature they send is really right; there *is* a lot to do. Burt told us this morning at breakfast—Lord, but he does *eat*—grudgingly, he doesn't like to talk at breakfast, that he 'lost about eleven thousand dollars last night shooting craps.' Thankfully we haven't done that. He said it calmly enough, though, as though it wasn't for the first time, by any means, but the bottom of my own stomach fell out. My God, I thought, *eleven thousand dollars.* And nothing to show for it.

"David said even so he'd probably gotten more enjoyment out of spending his evening getting his wallet beaten up like that than we'd gotten from ours, without spending a dime. 'What we did was invest our time at the piano recital in the theater. He was the very worst so-called "professional concert pianist" I have ever heard. I don't claim to be a connoisseur of music, but you don't have to be to tell when a musician's nonchalanting it, phoning it in, any more'n you have to've played with Ted Williams to know when a ballplayer's dogging it. It really pisses me off when any kind of a performer does that. Means he's so contemptuous of his audience he doesn't think the stupid bastards'll be able to tell when he's doing shoddy work.' I didn't say so—since going to the concert had been *my* bright idea—but I thought David was right.

"Burt said that made him feel at least a little better. 'And if I seem to've been complaining, I didn't mean it that way. You always bet against the house, anywhere you gamble, no matter what you gamble on. And what the hell, huh? That's what it's all about. As Amy always said: "Hell, *life's* six-to-five against. You've got to know that in the long run, we're all going to lose."'

"I guess I'm sorry to say that I've begun to think those odds are better than the ones I'm facing now, speaking of Points of No Return. I'm fairly sure that David's been with that little harlot now three mornings in a row, and that he's planning to be with her tomorrow morning, too. Burt and I ran into her on our way to meet David for lunch, all dolled up in her Ralph Lauren camel's hair suit—she was just *so* sweet, the ultimate-Southern-belle act, but then of course she ought to be: she's been practicing so long. 'Oh, *Frances,*' she said, 'I feel so guilty, but I've just been *so* busy. . . . Still, I really should've *made* time to see you.'

"I thought, 'You've been making quite enough time for me, you little tramp.' But like the captain this morning, I bit my tongue and didn't say it. It would've given her too much satisfaction. I just said we've been enjoying the trip very much, and introduced her to Burt. From the way she looked him over, I think maybe Burt's safe from her grasp. Maybe once your husband passes seventy, you don't have to worry about young tarts like Melissa anymore." She had intended to continue, "just the widows of his friends seeking their second husbands at the funerals of their wives." But she reckoned Kitty might take that the wrong way. "That's something at least to look forward to. She said she hoped David's been having a good time too, and I really wanted to say, 'Well, you'd be the best judge of that,' but once again, I held my tongue.

"After we'd left her, all apologies because she had to go work, Burt said he assumed that was the shameless hussy in the flesh, so to speak, and I said Yes, it was. And he said maybe he shouldn't say it, but if that was what my enemy looked like, he thought I'd been in a tough fight. 'And one I've lost again, I guess,' I said. But then I told Burt that thanks to him and how he's taken care of me I think I might be making some progress. Maybe even growing up at last. I'm really very grateful to him; I really owe him a lot. I must think of some way to thank him before our shipboard friendship comes to an end. This voyage—'crossing,' they call it—it's so long when you start and so short at the end. I really don't have that much time left.

"But I'm finally realizing, resigning myself to the fact, that there's nothing I can do if David's going to cat around. He always used to, whenever he saw a woman who attracted him, after I got sick. And then he stopped for a few years, for what reason I don't know—no honey who appealed to him? Or maybe he was tired. But now apparently he's back at it, up to his old tricks. And so he'll cat around again now, if he sees another one. Or an old one he still likes. Well, at least I know.

"In fact, after talking to Burt, I've decided maybe that's one of the big reasons that I made David come on this trip (which with all the worries he's got at the bank, he really didn't want to take): I knew that little whore would be aboard. Partly I wanted him to get away, but partly also, I think now, to find out what he would do. To see if he'd succumb again, as of course he did, at once. So, to make the best I can of it, at least now that's settled, and perhaps now I can move on.

"At lunch Burt and I didn't mention meeting Melissa. Burt just picked up where'd he left off on his Vivaldi lecture, and said he'd meant no offense against Vivaldi. He said he couldn't: 'I like all eight hundred of his one songs myself, no matter how many times he repeats it. And anyway, there's no shame in it; Monet did the same thing with his lilies and his haystacks a long time after that, and nobody complained very much. Most people applauded in fact. As far as I know, nobody else except my old friend Eldred'd found old Antonio out either, even three hundred fifty years later. At least far as I'd ever heard at the time, when Eldred first said it to me.' "

"I really envied Eldred," he said to the Carrolls at lunch. They had all ordered coq au vin, and Rutledge had specified a Château Palmer. "I don't think he knew it but I'm sure Amy did, and she knew the reason as well. It must've hurt her to know what it was, that I knew how come she'd decided to pursue him. And not me. And she must've known as well, although we never discussed it, that over the years she'd spent with him I gradually came to resent it—after all, she knew as well as I did that I'd developed a yen for her. But I *did* know, and I *did* resent it, and there wasn't one damned thing I could say to protest it. I knew what the reason was.

"He had more money than I did. Or, a greater net worth, 'd be closer to it, I suppose. It was as simple as that. She'd been in what they used to call 'straitened circumstances' all of her life, and she was utterly sick of it. I was a working stiff, myself. I didn't have enough money to get her what she was looking for: security, and no worries.

"When Eldred died, which was eleven years after Henry Neville'd died, those circumstances'd changed. *Her* circumstances by then were all in very fine shape. I'd warned her how Eldred felt about money, and that he'd spend hers too, if he could. So before the two of them got married, she and I'd tied all hers up. Yes, I was protecting, and preferring, one client at the expense of another and that's a clear conflict of interest. What I should've done was tell each of them that I wanted to stay on good terms with both of them, and therefore as far as this particular matter was concerned, acting in the best interest of each of them in planning the merger of their estates, I couldn't represent either one of them.

"But I didn't, tell them that. What I knew about Eldred's estate was that while it was substantial, it was all in nonliquid assets. There were no bank accounts, that he knew about at least, and the trusts were all depleted. Eldred's idea of estate planning was: Spend it. As he'd told me numerous times, when I tried to make him behave.

"But the value of those nonliquid assets was very considerable. She had his house and his cars; what she'd gotten from the sale of her house and still had, and what Eldred'd bought over the course of the years and carried home, to squirrel away in that house and the barn: the booty and plunder of all his campaigns, and there'd been many of them. I told her, after he was dead and I'd had the appraiser go through it all and so forth, that I figured that what he'd left her was worth close to one and a quarter million dollars. Plus a little over seventy-five thousand dollars in a joint bank account his father'd opened back in the late forties and then'd apparently forgotten about. Otherwise Eldred would've poached it.

"So it wasn't that Eldred'd *meant* to leave her that well-fixed—which he probably hadn't. If he'd ever thought about it at all, he would've *meant* to make sure to leave her safe and secure financially when he went out of the picture, but then'd just never gotten around to doing a damned thing about it. But that was the result, just the same: He'd left her safe and secure. He'd run out of time before he'd planned to, so there was still some money left of his, and almost all of hers. She'd given him a portion of it, 'just to tide him over when he saw something that he really liked, but had no cash available at the time.' But if he'd been reckless—and he had been—time'd proved that he'd been *right*, to trust his luck. The things he'd bought and kept, in his extravagance, were worth a lot of money—lots more than he'd paid for them.

"She said: '*No.*' I said: '*Yes.*' She said: 'I can't believe what you've just said.' I said: 'Fine by me. Believe what you want. But it's still going to remain the Lord's truth. Two of those four cars—the Caddy and the T-bird—are worth about sixty thousand dollars. The stuff in the wine cellar's worth another bundle, hundred, hundred-fifty. The furnishings: That's not drugstore aluminum lawn-furniture you've been sitting on, as anyone could tell. Those are valuable antiques'; even I knew that. But I had no idea until I got the appraisal how valuable they really are. Eldred bought lots more than he should've, living in the grand style, and he spent like a rajah, every damned dollar he had. Keeping up his collections, his *interests.* That was all we saw. But there was something else, that we *didn't* see: That while he was spending far more than he should've, he was spending it wisely.

So he wasn't living stupidly, and *that* was what I refused to see, regardless of how many times he told me it was so.

"The chinoiserie and the coin collection; the firearms and stamps and currency: Those were all very sound investments. Or turned out to be, at least. I had no idea, for instance, what Confederate money's worth now. I scoffed when he told me—he was a bit strapped for cash and needed to sell something to buy what he had his eye on then: 'Genuine, uncirculated, mint-condition, Confederate States of America one-thousand-dollar bills're going for three times face value. And I've got twenty of them.' He did, too. He showed them to me, and they were still in what appeared to this untrained eye to be the original straps.

" 'That's preposterous,' I said, but I was wrong and he was right. He wasn't as right as he believed he was, nor for the reason he thought or wanted to believe, but still, by accident or dumb luck, far closer to the actual truth than *I* was prepared to believe. When Eldred tried to peddle them, back then, the expert said he was a little off the mark. The bills were genuine, all right, but those were *not* the original straps. The serial numbers *weren't* consecutive. The bills *had* been circulated. 'And while mint CSA one-thousand-dollar notes can be worth several thousand dollars each now, they're the ones that are extremely rare. You don't have any of those.' He said Eldred'd be lucky to get an offer of ten percent face value for the lot of them. And that'd come only from someone who was hoarding them, betting the market'd go up some more, and therefore trying to get a corner on it. Someone like he was, the expert said. 'I deal in this stuff, and bet on it. I'll give you two thousand bucks for the lot, take it off of your hands.' Said if Eldred couldn't find a speculator like that, who wouldn't pay him any more, or even quite as much, he'd probably get a good deal less if he sold them off in small lots.

"Eldred was *very* disappointed. He insisted the figure was too low—chiefly because he'd had his eye on a valuable violin that he needed to raise a good deal more money than that to buy. The expert assured him that if anything his appraisal was a little on the high side. He suggested that the person—the tone of his voice and his facial expression implied he thought it'd probably been Eldred, though he didn't actually come right out and say that—who'd assembled the collection had done so because he'd become vaguely aware that 'Save your Confederate money' over the years had become fairly decent advice, but hadn't bothered to make sure what he'd heard was completely accurate, or 'd made sure he had it completely right. So he'd started picking up bills, catch-as-catch-can. At flea markets, auctions, estate sales, and so forth. 'Hoping to palm them off later on someone who'd heard the same thing, but hadn't checked it out either.'

"That expert was a shrewd one. That description fitted Eldred's habits to a T. He always had several acquisition programs underway at any given time, and he went to those sales like good Catholics go to Mass. No matter what kind of stuff was being offered, the odds were it included something that interested him. So he'd bid on those old notes, brought home by Union veterans as curiosities, war souvenirs, and'd put them back into old straps. To a casual buyer they'd look like what they were not: an uncirculated set in mint condition. Eldred liked to think of himself as a pretty crafty fellow. He wouldn't go so far as to tell a bald-faced lie, but he was not above a bit of subterfuge if he thought it would improve his bargaining position. This collector just happened to be too smart for him; he knew those bills weren't quite what they seemed to be.

"Eldred'd been indignant at the mere suggestion that he'd tried to pull a fast one. He'd turned the offer down flat, and the bills went back in the safe. He'd found the rest of the money somewhere else, that he needed to buy his old fiddle, and when he died *that* was worth maybe eight grand more'n he'd paid for it. So on that sad day, Amy still had not only the high-priced violin but also the bills Eldred'd intended to sell, to raise the money to buy it. In the intervening years that money'd gotten scarcer. The market in them'd gone up. Man in Montgomery, Alabama, paid us twelve thousand dollars for them. Represented some society of Confederate descendants, he said, so he'd compiled their mailing list. What he was going to do was resell the bills as priceless rarities, every last one, which of course they weren't, but set a price on them nonetheless—for forty-five hundred apiece. Said he wished we had a million of them. 'I'd take the whole bunch off your hands.'

" 'People will pay that for something like that?' I said to him. I really didn't believe him. 'Oh, you betcha,' he said, 'you betcha they will. How many people buy those memorial Elvis collectors' plates, a hundred or two hundred bucks? China moppets; naked little boys baked out of clay, peeing into little pools you hitch up to a hose in your back yard; hand-painted models of Heidi's whole Swiss village; replicas of the forty-five automatic John Wayne used as Sergeant Stryker in *The Sands of Iwo Jima;* copies of old baseball uniforms;

reproductions of antique whiskey bottles and old beer cans: people'll buy *anything*, and pay hundreds of dollars to do it.

" 'The mailing list is the key to it, though. That's how you make the big money. Knowing who can't help themselves, who's almost a sure thing to bite and to buy what you've got to offer. That way you avoid the big-overhead ticket: the four-color magazine ads to reach people who couldn't give less of a damn. And that's why you're selling these bills to me: I've got the list, and you don't. We'll net us about, oh, say, seventy-five grand, the advertising and all, the time we get through sellin' these. Small potatoes, I know, but hey, after all, you take whatever God gives to you. Never turn no blessin' down; tell Him, "Nope, it's not big enough." Might not see Him again for a while. Haven't got any other old Civil War stuff around by any chance, would you here now? Don't matter which side, Union, Johnny Reb, one's as good's the other one is, gettin' people to part with their money. You got any swords, now, those're really worth really big money. The real things're like diamonds and jewels. And old *flags* from the war, well, you could retire, on what you'd get from selling just one.' I was sorry to say we had no swords or flags, but if any turned up as we went along, taking our inventory of Eldred's pack-ratted hoard, I'd be sure to have him in mind. 'But as full partners this time,' I said, and he laughed. He was surely a rascal, no doubt about that, but he wasn't a bad guy at all.

" 'And then there's the house and what the barn's worth,' I said to her at the time," Rutledge said, disposing of the last of his chicken. " 'The appraiser says: three-quarters of a million. They usually come in under the number it finally goes for. Protecting themselves in the market.'

" 'My god,' she said. 'Nuts,' I said. 'Spare me the posturing here. You had a purpose when you married him, and you knew very well what it was. I didn't, until you declared it, that you'd always wanted to be well-off. And then it dawned on me, over the years, that that wasn't quite all of it. What you really wanted was to be a rich widow—if you had to be one at all, as most women in time have to be. And while I truly wished it had been otherwise, I couldn't help but approve. Your problem'd always been cash flow. It flowed *out* at a steady rate, but not much'd ever flowed in. So when your father died you decided what you needed was a man who had a lot of cash on hand already, even if he didn't have that much flowing in. And that wasn't Carl, still hitched to Eleanor. Or me, either, still plodding along in my small-town law practice. It was Eldred, the world traveler and boulevardier. Who could retroactively undo the damage Hitler's dream'd done to you. Make the whole land new again, and bright.'

" 'But where will I live, if I sell it all off?' she said winsomely, and I said: 'Come on. Cut it out. You'll live here with me, as you probably planned to do all along. Once Eldred predeceased you, as the actuarial tables said he almost certainly would, and you got his money. There's plenty of room in this place for us, and we can spend most of what I take in, with all Eldred's money behind us. You can hang onto your own. We'll have a hell of a time.'

"And we did," Rutledge had said. "My deceased client'd taught her a lot, things that I'd never dreamed of. He'd *told* me about them—*Normandie, France, Andrea Doria* and *Queen Mary,* a whole bunch of other big boats; the best hotels in London and Paris; where to eat when in Rome and so forth. But that stuff was way out of my league in those days, so I'd never paid much attention. With Amy it'd been different. He not only *told* her the same stuff; he'd brought her into that world with him, and she'd been smarter than I was. She knew what was being handed to her, and by God, she'd paid attention. She took me to La Scala and the Gallery of the Uffizi; the cathedral at Cologne and the Wallace Collection and Stratford-upon-Avon, and we did exactly what I'd said we'd do: Oh, we had a hell of a time."

"He said: 'She died too soon,' " Frances wrote to Kitty. "Like David and I've said so many times about Sam. Even though it was his own choice, he did it far too soon. 'She was only 68. Barely past the middle of the journey.' It was really quite affecting, the true feeling in his voice.

"He said: 'The day after tomorrow we're going to pass too far south of where you live, the state where I've been for most of my life, so we won't be able to see any of it. And then the next day—always a hectic day, the last day of the crossing—we'll have to get up around dawn, if we want to see what our ancestors saw, if they came into New York in this century. If they too got up early—if they didn't, they didn't. Well, there's nothing we can do about that. But at least we can look at our own lives as they go by us, and ponder what they mean.'

"I don't think we've done that," she wrote to Kitty. "At least I don't think *I* have. The days go by so fast, and we're all so busy doing other things, whatever it is that we do, we overlook most of the fun.

"There is nothing I can do about what I know David's done and what he's doing, and what he'll always do. It makes me *sad* to know this, but that's the way it is. So what I have to decide now is what I want to do, whether I want the sad or happy ending to the story. I guess I want the happy one. I'm too old now to be sad."

She had long since finished the letter, addressed it and sealed it, and was working on the postcards when David came back to the cabin. "Seventeen-thirty hours," he said, opening the refrigerator and taking out the wine. "Cocktail hour, my sweet. Late, as a matter of fact. Sun's well over the yardarm."

She faced him in the mirror without turning. "I thought we said at lunch we'd meet Burt for cocktails at seven," she said.

"And so we did," he said, pouring a glass of the wine. "But we can be a little late, if we have to," he said. "Or at least *I* can, if I have to. There's something I want to do here, first, and I can't do it 'til at least six forty-five."

"What?" she said.

"Call the office," he said.

"At six forty-five?" she said. "Why wait 'til then? No one'll be there. Everyone will've gone home."

He came over to the counter and sat down in the other chair. "No, they won't," he said. "Sandy will be there, and so will everybody else, or at least they'd bloody-well better be. Because *there* it'll be around *five* twenty-five—we've still got a time difference here, and while they may be about forty hours ahead of us as the seas rage and the land lies, they're a little more than eighty minutes behind us in time. So if I call from here at six forty-five, it'll be twenty-five minutes after they closed at five today, and they should be still settling up. Unless while this cat's away, his mice're goofing off, in which case all the more reason to call and find out, and read them the Riot Act when I get back to work on Monday."

"But you'll be home the day after tomorrow," she said. "I don't see why you feel you have to call tonight."

"Well," he said, sipping the wine, "I'll tell you exactly why. We're scheduled to dock at the Passenger-Ship Terminal at Pier 94 in New York on Friday at ten-thirty. As we in fact probably will. Everything's been strictly Bristol-fashion on this ship since we left England, and therefore I see no reason whatsoever to expect that we'll be late. This afternoon three of us from the NavStation wangled a tour of the ship's bowels, as it were, from one of her real navigators who'd seen us in there from time to time."

"You didn't tell me that's what you were doing after lunch," she said.

"That was the deal with the officer," David said. "He agreed to our wheedles on condition of strict silence. 'It's not something we can offer to everyone on the boat, you see,' was what he said. 'But there's no way we can possibly explain it to everyone else on the boat if the word gets out that we did it for you three but will not do it for them. Even though what you want to see wouldn't mean a blasted thing to them; they'd only get in the way of everybody who's trying to get a job done, and'd screw everything up to a fare-thee-well. So if it gets out, and that uproar happens, I'll be thrown over the side.' So we gave him our solemn promise in blood, and if you tell anyone, including Burt, what I've just told you now, I'll deny it like Nixon, and then to be safe, I'll put *you* over the side."

She laughed. "Just what was it you saw," she said, "on this magical mystery tour?"

"Well," he said, "we saw the engine room from the catwalk. Very clean, very orderly, people down below in coveralls going about their tasks in a serene and patient fashion. Didn't look a bit like the black-gangs you read about in the histories of steam. And quiet. The ship's forty years old, but those diesels are new and state-of-the-art. Not silent, but not noisy, either: 'Vibration damping's improved quite a lot and that's where the racket mostly came from.' The generators that they drive sort of hum. It's not a choir exactly, you wouldn't call it that, but it isn't deafening—not by any means.

"We didn't ask to see the garage, though they do have one aboard. Gives you an idea of how big this thing is: twenty-four-car garage. But we *did* see," he said, "and I know you're thrilled by this, the wine cellar, very large, and banks of refrigerators for meat and fish and vegetables and so forth. And the lockers, for storing dry food, one of which was labeled Canned Fish. Perfectly enormous thing. And one of the other amateur magellans said, 'What the hell do you need all that for? Keeping a regiment of cats on board or something? Or does the crew subsist on canned tuna?' And the officer said, without missing a beat, 'Caviar, sir, caviar.' We saw the hospital and another refrigerated locker next to it, and this time I'm afraid I was the one who raised the question. 'That freezer there,' I said, 'for passengers and crew who decide to go to meet their Maker before they get to New York?' The officer looked unhappy, but he nodded and said Yes. I couldn't leave well-enough alone. 'Any tenants in it right now?' I said. 'Two,' he said, 'one passenger and one crew. And that's all I'll say about that.'

"The passenger I would've expected, you look at the age of this bunch. But a crew? I suppose so; it would make sense. They spend their whole adult lives out on the ocean, working for one line or another, and in the normal course of things, some of them're bound to die at sea. Before they get to retire. People who work on land do that, of course: die on the job, not at home. And there's no ambulance out here."

"I suppose so," she said.

"Anyway," he said, "with that preamble: When we'd finished our clandestine tour, I asked the officer what time he thought we'd actually be ashore, day after tomorrow. He was very confident. 'We'll dock at ten-thirty,' he said. 'You'll be marshaled in the lounges where you boarded, at least twenty minutes before that. Your luggage, except for what you need for tomorrow evening, will have been collected by the stewards outside your doors during the early morning hours and prepared for unloading. As soon as all lines have been made fast and all ramps secured, you will be debarked. You will be in the terminal at eleven hundred hours.' He got this getting-even little grin on his face. 'We're very glad you've all been with us and we hope you come again. But you see, we'll have another eighteen hundred people excited on the dock, waiting to come aboard *America* themselves. No later than thirteen hundred hours they'll be on their way down the Hudson, en route to Southampton, and we want them to be happy, too. Besides, it costs like the very *devil* to keep this floating island going. She has to turn around in every port as quickly as we can make her, or Hayden Lines will go broke.'

"So anyway, that'll leave us at the West Side Expressway, looking for our limo, somewhere around eleven-thirty, and if we can get around Manhattan without grief, home by three clock. But I learned long ago never to count on getting through Manhattan without grief, especially on a weekday afternoon. Still, if we do, I'll be at the bank by four. If I'm going to have some nasty surprise waiting for me when I get there, I want to be prepared to deal with it. And if we *do* get stuck in New York, or on the New England Thruway, I don't want to have to hang suspended until Wednesday to find out if I do. So, that's why I'm gonna call tonight. To find out what I've got in store, at the store. So I can be prepared."

She stood up. "I'm going to shower and change," she said. "Will you come up to the lounge as soon as you're finished?"

"Indeed I will," he said, "in my best bib and tucker. And if I hear what I hope I will hear—which is 'Nothing'—when I ask what's been going on, we'll be drinking some champagne tonight."

19

It had not been sex that had made David late for lunch. As they had the first time that she had invited him, they'd just gone at each other with such pent-up eagerness that they were finished with that part "of the entertainment," as she called it, and he'd laughed, by 11:45. What had delayed him after that was the quick shower that he insisted upon taking, despite the fact that she reached for him—cooing, "Nooo, what's the hurry?"—as he got out of her bed, trying to keep him in it. "Uh-uh, sorry, my dear," he said, evading her grasp, "your fragrance apparently lingers. I got caught like that once and I paid dearly for it. She won't catch me that way again."

She laughed at that and took the pillow he had used, stuffing it under her own and lifting herself higher in the bedclothes. "She didn't approve, I take it?"

"Let's just say she was miffed," he said from the shower, turning the faucets on.

"Well," Melissa said, "I suppose I would've been too, if I'd been in her position." When he emerged, having hastily rinsed, turned the water off, and begun to scrub himself dry, she said: "Did she know it was me?"

"Oh yeah," he said, "she recognized your cologne. That was the last week that you stayed with us. Then you had to go home. It was also the week that her mother took sick, had a bad heart attack, and she had to go home, down to Richmond. Claudia went with her; both the boys were away; we had the whole house to ourselves."

"Oh *yeah*," she said, growling it, "I *remember* that week. We went at it like wild animals. Four or five nights, and *days*, in a row. *Wonderful* exercise, really. I went home wearing a smile."

"A good time was had by all," he said. "But that was also the week that the cleaning lady got the flu and couldn't come. As she normally would've that Friday morning, the day after you left. So when Fran got back from her mother's the same sheets were on the bed, and I guess she must have some bloodhound in her: she knew at once who those sheets smelled like, and therefore she knew where you'd been. It didn't take long for her to deduce who'd asked you to snuggle in between those sheets, in her absence, or what my motive'd been. She never *accused* me, but, boy, I paid. You got a hair-dryer here? There was one night, a couple years later—by then I'd learned to be careful, and after I'd gotten better acquainted with this lady I'd known for a while I remembered spouse Sherlock and took a quick shower. But then I went home with wet hair, like a fool, and that made me a second offender."

"In the top lefthand drawer," she said. "Plug's in the side of the frame of the mirror. Was the punishment double what you'd gotten for our little fling?"

"No, it was lighter, in fact," David said, finding the dryer and plugging it in. Over the noise that it made while he tousled his hair in hot air, he said in a louder voice: "Fran didn't know this particular woman, so that mitigated the offense. And I hadn't had her where you'd had me, desecrating the conjugal bed. So that I guess reduced it from felony to misdemeanor. The penalty still what a friend of mine calls 'the delicatessen treatment' that the sinner gets after the tears, but that time it was only a month or so's ration of cold shoulder; she didn't serve the hot tongue."

"Does she ever ask you why you do it?" Melissa said, crossing her arms under her breasts, watching him looking at her in the mirror as he dressed, snickering as he drew his shorts up over his penis, erecting again. "Are you quite *sure* you want to rush off?" she said.

He laughed and put on his shirt. "You bitch," he said. "No, I'm quite sure I *don't*, as a matter of fact, but I know what's good for me now. And I am expected at lunch, six decks up"—he picked up his watch from the vanity—"four very short minutes from now. This is a very big boat, to be sure, but we're still three days out of New York, and if Fran suspects I've succumbed to you again, this boat will become very small."

He put on his trousers and went over to the bed, sitting down to put on his socks and shoes. Then he twisted his body around so that he faced her, and leaned over and kissed her. He fondled her left breast as he did it. She reached down and grabbed his crotch. His second erection was complete. Through the kiss she murmured, "Such a terrible, terrible waste."

He pulled away and studied her. She reached up and mussed his hair lightly. "Gray becomes you, David," she said, still with her hand on his crotch. "You're aging well, I must say."

He grinned. "You really like this sex stuff, don't you," he said.

She stretched a little, languorously. "It gives me pleasure," she said. "The first few times I did it, my boyfriend had all the pleasure. But then I went up north and met you, and that's when *I* started getting pleasure, and then I gave more to you."

"I'll say," he said. "There's a noticeable difference between passive acquiescence and enthusiastic participation; you were an apt student."

"And then after I went home again I got a new boyfriend, and by the time I was through school and headed north again, I had him trained so he could give pleasure to me, too. Not just take it from me.

"Look at this job I've got here: What is it I do? I give people pleasure, hundreds of 'em, all at once, for days at a time. I don't go to bed with all of them—I'm choosier than *that*—but what I do for Hayden Lines, how I earn my pay, is making sure that everyone who sails with us has the most fun they ever had, so they'll come back again. So that's what I am, in public and private: I'm a pleasure machine."

"Is your schedule the same tomorrow?" he said.

"Tomorrow," she said, "and every day after that. Until we arrive in New York. Shall we meet for coffee again tomorrow?"

"That would be nice," he said. "I'll be looking forward to it."

He started to get off the bed, but she took his left forearm and held it. The playfulness vanished from her face and her eyes seemed to darken with concern. "Tell me something, David," she said. "Aside from the sex part, which I assume must be okay, if not much more than that, are you ever happy with her? Are you happy with Fran now? You can tell me, if you want, to mind my own damned business, and we'll pretend I never asked, but you're a valuable man and you should be a happy one. You don't look to me like you are."

He pulled gently away from her. "I've had a lot on my mind these past couple of years," he said. "Too much, I guess, from what people tell me. You're not the first one to say that. But it isn't Fran; it's not her fault. It's been at the bank, and it scares me. It scares the hell out of me."

"Do you talk to her about it?" Melissa said. "Does she know what you've been going through, and understand why you're scared?"

He took a deep breath and exhaled. "Do I talk to her about it?" he said. "Yes, I talk to her a lot. Does she understand why it is that I'm so afraid? Yes; Frances ain't dumb. The problem is what she thinks I should do, and what she keeps telling me to."

"What does she tell you?" Melissa said.

"That I should stop being scared."

He had told her as much as he could before he looked at his watch again and saw that it read 12:28. Then he got up from the bed again and put his blazer on and said: "I've really got to go to lunch or she'll never forgive me." Then he bent and kissed her lightly and promised he would finish telling her when they met on the next day.

"And the next day and the next day, and then the day after that," she said, her hands clasped above her head, stretching like a great smooth golden cat.

He said: "Done, and done, and done."

By the time Frances reached the Senator Lounge in the pale light of their next-to-last Atlantic evening aboard, she was feeling particularly pleased with herself. She had always liked the way her dark orange jersey dress moved and felt on her body, and she had thought of a very good way to thank Rutledge for his complicity in bringing her to the new peaceful resignation she felt about how David chose to lead his life. Before entering the lounge she stepped into the powder room and sat down at the mirrored makeup table. She opened her pocketbook and took out her checkbook and pen, and when she had finished writing a check for eleven thousand dollars to Burton Rutledge, put everything back into her bag and went out into the lounge. Six-foot seas carried small whitecaps to the horizon; they were burnished to bronzed blue by the declining sun ahead. She knew from the captain's lecture that by oceanic standards the ship was making headlong progress on its course, but there was no sense of motion but the thrumming deep below to suggest how much way it had on.

She sat down opposite Rutledge, so that she faced the entrance, and told him David would join them when he'd completed a call to his office. "At least I don't think he's sneaked back to Melissa right now, because this's the way that he's always been: never able to vacation completely, just go away and forget about things for a while. His work's always somewhere on his mind." Then she said how odd it felt to know that by the terms of the mean of transportation you had chosen you were proceeding very fast, and yet not really be able to feel it.

"Yes," Rutledge said, "it's not like being in an airplane, or being in a car, or on the French bullet-train, *train à grande vitesse,* that goes tearing through the countryside from Paris to Lyons at a hundred and eighty-five miles an hour—or did, at least, when I took it with Amy; maybe it's even faster now. You know you're going fast when you're in one of those things. Or even, I'd imagine, when you're on a boat like yours and for a sailboat, anyway, it's going very fast."

"Oh, there's no doubt in your mind at all on the boat," she said. "You can hear the water rushing around the hull, feel the wind on your face; the boat is heeling eight degrees off the vertical, and the foam's just three feet down, sounding like the rapids in a fast stream."

"Yes," he said. "But when you deliberately design and build something this big and this heavy to minimize the sensations of motion that make passengers first uncomfortable and uneasy, and then seasick and panicky—up-and-down and side-to-side, not to mention back-and-forth; pitch and roll and yaw, in other words—in the natural course of things you're also going to insulate them from any real sense of forward progress. If you succeed at what you really have to do, which is keep us sissies comfy enough so that we'll come back again and again—the supply of prospective transatlantic-liner passengers out there isn't big enough to insure enough revenue from one-timers to keep the ships in service, which is why for a long time the QE-*Two* was the only one in the business—willy-nilly, like it or not, you're going to succeed at insulating them from any feeling of speed. So that if you're lucky and you don't hit a storm—seas so high they're bashing in the ports on the Quarter Deck, people eating dinners on the floor like they're dogs because the boat's rolling so much they can't stay in their chairs, plates flying off the tables; that's been known to happen on vessels that sailed too late in the season—what you're going to give everyone aboard is a feeling that they've been in a coddled state of suspended animation, very comfortably if not luxuriously immobilized for five days, while giant pulleys towed New York smoothly through the water *to* them and sent Southampton receding behind them."

He said what he was drinking was a Bombay Gin martini on the rocks. It contained a lemon twist. She asked the waiter for a vodka martini straight up, with an olive. "On the other hand," she said, when the waiter had gone away, "I feel as though I've been traveling at the speed of light through my own personal life these past few days. Getting some things straight in my own mind. I really can't thank you enough, you know, for all the help that you've been to me."

"All I really did was listen," he said. "I certainly didn't take out my mortar and pestle and make you a magic potion that would help you to see your own way. You did all that by yourself."

"Sometimes listening can be just the thing to do for someone in the dilemma that I found myself in," she said. "Just listening and nothing more. Sometimes that's the best counseling, legal or any other kind, that anyone could possibly do. You have a remarkable ability to inspire trust. And confidence. You must have been a very good lawyer. I'll bet your clients liked you a lot, and I'll bet they were also sorry when you felt you had to close your office. Regardless of what that one man'd said."

"Oh, I don't know about that," he said, as the waiter returned with her drink. "There's a certain fungibility to the lawyers who do the kind of work I mainly did. I think a lot of the reason people tend to stay with the same one, or the same doctor, the same dentist, plumber, insurance man, electrician, carpenter or cleaner—in your husband's case, the same bank—isn't generally because they don't think there's anybody else around in the same line of work who's as good or even better. About the only personal stamp you can put on conveyancing and estate work is thoroughness, and a reputation for carrying out the client's wishes. Most everyone can do that. So if you asked my clients, *before* I took down my shingle, if they thought there was as good around, most of them probably would've said, 'Yeah, I guess there probably is.' I think they stay with the same lawyer out of static inertia. If the work you've done for them in the past seems to've been good enough, then when they need some more of it done, they'll come back to you for it. They know where your office is, where to park, what you're likely to charge them to do it, and they won't have to repeat their legal or medical history, or have their mouths x-rayed again. So it's *easier* if they stay with you.

"Easiness matters a lot in my business. Nobody looks forward to hiring a lawyer or getting their teeth cleaned, no matter how often they've done it before. Nobody likes to do it. It's something that has to be done, so they do it, but the reason it has to be done is that the situation will get even worse if that something doesn't get done. So they come to me again to have their taxes done, or they go to your husband's bank to borrow money to meet a price that they don't really want to pay, because they have to do it to get something they want. They don't have any real choice. But they seldom enjoy it." He chuckled. "Either that or else the bumper crops of new lawyers that harvested themselves every year that I was in practice just hadn't figured out that Barlow could support a few more lawyers, so my clients didn't have enough choices."

She said she doubted that. "And anyway," she said, "if the people on this ship know your credit's good enough to take your check for what you lost at craps the other night, you must be pretty well off."

He laughed. "Oh, my dear lady," he said, "they're nowhere *near* as trusting as that. You *buy* your chips, whatever amount you want, either with cash or on your credit card. Then, before they give them to you, they check your credit limit at home, electronically, to make sure you're good for it, and if your bank okays it, then you sign the credit slip, and *then* you get your chips. So, no, I didn't empty out my bank account to pay for my little frolic. But I'll have to, when my American Express bill comes."

"No, you won't," she said, opening her pocketbook and taking out the check. She pushed it, folded, across the table to him. "This's your fee for my case."

He made no move to pick it up. "I never took on any case of yours, Frances," he said. "I did nothing whatsoever that a layman couldn't do, or a layman wouldn't do, if he encountered another perfectly nice human woman like yourself in a bad quandary like yours. I can't accept a fee for legal services, not when I've rendered no such services to you. Especially since I'm no longer licensed to practice—that *would* be unprofessional."

She saw David enter the lounge and begin to scan the room for them. She urged the check a little farther toward Rutledge. "Burt," she said, "in the first place, I want you to. To pay you for your wise counsel. That alone should be enough. But even if it isn't, you have to take it anyway. Because David's just come in the door, and if that check's still on the table by the time he gets to us, he'll recognize it as one of mine, from the color of the paper, and want to know what it's for. And I don't want to tell him. So if you don't take the money, you'll be forcing me to give up what I thought I had a right to expect, when I confided in you: my half of the attorney-client privilege. You'll be forcing me to disclose. And *that*, in my opinion, will certainly be unprofessional."

He smiled with his eyes as well as his lips, and nodded very slightly as he pocketed the check. "You're a very clever woman, Frances. David's a fool to risk what he has with you. But surely you realize all I have to do when I get back to my cabin tonight is tear up the check, and that'll be that. Nothing you can do about that."

"Yes," she said, "I do realize that. But I think that when you've thought about it some more, you'll decide not to do that. I'm an adult, Burt. I feel better, paying my way."

David came up to the table, pulled a chair out and sat down. He steepled his fingers over his nose, and then dropped his hands to the table. "Yes," he said, "well, how're we all doing, this lovely evening, since we last got our feet in the trough?"

"You tell us, darling," she said. "Are we having champagne tonight?"

"We can if you'd like," he said, "sure. But myself, I'd prefer," as the waiter came over, "a double vodka martini on the rocks. Little something to settle the nerves."

When the waiter had gone away he allowed sadness to wash into his face. To Rutledge he said, "The FDIC's been into my bank, before we left and now again." To Frances he said, "I don't know how they did it, a spy in on my payroll . . ."

"Oh, I doubt that," she said, "I would doubt that. Surely there's no one who works for the bank who'd want to see it get in trouble."

"Surely there very well *might* be," he said. "I've denied people raises, withheld promotions, refused to hire relatives of theirs. And then there's examiner's power, to make people do things they don't want to do; make them believe that if they don't do what he tells them to do, they'll get into trouble themselves.

"Then there's the other possibility, which is that after my past run-ins with Bettancourt, Bettancourt did something else. Which from my days at Treasury, I know he's got the power to do, and that is institute a notify-on-departure watch at all points of embarkation from the country, so the morning after the night that we flew out of Logan for London, good old Gary knew we were gone. The next day he was back in the bank. So it could've been that way it happened.

To Rutledge he said: "The examiner's name's Gary Bettancourt. We are not a happy pair. For no good reason he came in the first time hating my guts, and because of that I despise him." He sighed. "So it could've been that way it happened.

"Anyway," he said, "he went through some elaborate rigmarole and saber dance for four more days, throwing his weight around, showing off how much power he's got, and then yesterday he gave them the news: By the first of next week we'll be officially notified that Ted Goodall's loans and four others've been classified, and that unless they're secured by additional collateral or reduced by amounts sufficient to make the ratio between debt and the value of the security acceptable, the bank will be placed on the watch-list. And we'll have six months under *his* swaggering supervision to shape up to his satisfaction, or else we'll be seized, and sold off. 'Liquidated.' What a charming thought that is."

Rutledge nodded. "They keep on doing it, don't they now, huh? Despite all the damage it does. I've had three clients who lost everything they had, had to go into Chapter Eleven. They were not young, brash businessmen who overextended themselves starting out and got themselves into the soup. These were established, family firms, in business at least twenty years, just needing some time and a better economy to get back on their feet. Didn't matter at all—they got kicked right into the old filter beds, and their people were put out of work. It's really a terrible thing. You'd think that these government people'd finally see what they're doing, catch on to the damage they've done."

Frances put her left hand on David's arm and patted it as the waiter brought his drink. "Have your drink, kiddo," she said, "and then we'll have a good dinner. By this time tomorrow you'll have thought of something. I'm sure you'll think of something. You always have before this, you know, when you've had what looked like a major setback, and you'll manage it this time, I know."

He looked at her and his eyes were dead. "You think so," he said, his voice flat.

The next morning with a bad hangover he followed her to breakfast, allowing her enough time to caution Rutledge to expect no conversation, but Rutledge was bleary himself, from their long night in the casino lounge, and no threat to be talkative. David had declined his suggestion that he might find some distraction from his problems by shooting craps for a while, saying that a man about to lose his job without another one lined up should not be gambling; Rutledge won four hundred dollars and quit, and out of his winnings had paid for all of what David later that day at lunch would assess as "far, far too many drinks."

At breakfast David treated his condition with two Bloody Marys, and when Rutledge saw him commence to do that, he ordered a mimosa for himself. Except for such communication with the wait-staff as was necessary to select pastries and choose coffee over tea, none of them spoke at all.

David's head had started to clear by the time he arrived at the NavStation, but his calculations took him much longer than they ordinarily did, and he did not have sufficient confidence in their accuracy to enter the daily mileage pool. When he arrived on schedule at Melissa's suite she was in a long white satin décolleté negligee. "You look very nice," he said, "as I'm sure you know. And I of course look like pure hell, and that I'm sure of as well."

"You sure do, old-timer," she said, closing the door behind him. "Rode hard and put away wet." He collapsed into one of the chairs in her sitting room. "Can I get you a fixer-upper? Nice little double shot of ice-cold Stoli, cut down on the throbbing a little?"

"It's probably not a good idea," he said. "I had two Bloodies for breakfast. But what the hell, what more harm can it do? Yeah, bring me the Stoli, and also the pamphlet: I've forgotten eight Steps of the Twelve to recovery, and the way that I'm going I'd better brush up before things get completely out of hand."

"What the hell happened to you last night?" she said, as she gave him the drink. She sat in the chair next to his, and held his left hand with her right. "Did the cow jump over the moon?"

"Feels more like the cow misjudged its altitude some, and jumped right *onto* my head," he said. He told her what had set him off.

"Oh, poor *baby*," she said, so that he glanced at her sharply, but decided she intended it to be dispassionately but realistically sympathetic, not sarcastic, "does this mean you won't have any money? That can be so inconvenient."

"That certainly seems to be a real possibility," he said. "That house on Pilot Hill that you remember," he said, "was a lot more house—"

"A lovely house," she said.

"Indeed a lovely house," he said, "but as I say, a lot more house than we really could afford when we bought it. But after all, we told ourselves, we'd come up there because I'd been practically guaranteed success in a very short time, and that was the time in the market to buy, and as you might expect I had very little trouble with financing. So, a seven-percent, thirty-year mortgage, I'm hardly forty-two years old? Seemed like a bargain to us. But as a result we're still about fourteen years from paying it off—how do we do that, no salary coming in? We don't, that's how we do it.

"This is not how I thought things would turn out. After I'd been president a few years, things were going real good, I traded in my boat on this lovely Hinckley, gave us a reward for being so good. Took out another loan to do that. That one's got eight years to run.

"Don't misunderstand me," he said. "I made good money at the bank, and we weren't by any means wastrels. But it's considered good form in a position like mine to plow back most of your unspent earnings and take all your bonuses in the stock of the bank. Proves you really believe in it. So while I own a lot of it, and've got thousands more in stock options, a hell of a lot of those, too, pretty soon all of it's likely to be worthless. The bank won't exist anymore. Which means there goes the house, and there goes the boat, and here comes the big moving van. We do own the furniture outright, at least, and we've got some equity in the house. But my car belongs to the bank, on a lease, so that leaves us with just Frances's little Bimmer Three-twenty-five coupe, to take us down the rest of the road."

He pulled his left hand from her grasp and stood up, jamming his hands in his pockets. "Jee-*zus*, what a damned mess," he said.

"Does Frances know about it?" Melissa said.

He turned his head and looked at her. "You know something?" he said. "I don't know. I don't know if she really does know. She's aware of the facts; I've explained them to her, all along. What they probably meant in the right-now, back then, as the situation developed, and what they would mean if things came to this, this disaster that they've come to now. And that's the right word for it, too: a genuine, fucking disaster. But: Does she know? I couldn't tell you. She's not an unintelligent woman. In fact she's a very smart one, and a well-educated one, too, who never stopped learning to learn.

"But she believes in the power of positive thinking, or some such 'Don't-Worry, Be-Happy' balderdash. She seems to think, to serenely believe, that I'll get us out of this thing. 'You'll think of something,' she says to me. 'You always have in the past.' Yeah, I tell her, but in the past, there *was* something I *could* think of doing, that would get us out of the corner. This time there's no such thing. It's like it was after Sam shot himself—this friend we had in Washington a long time ago killed himself one day, and none of us really knew why—it's the end-game, that's what this is. This time I'm really trapped. There's no way to get out. There's nothing left *for* me to think of.

"I dunno. Maybe she grasps it. Maybe she doesn't. All *I* know is that I'm not sure. After all of these years, I still don't know how her mind works. I don't know how dear Frances thinks. Except she knows things will turn out for the best." He combed his hair back with his hand.

She stood up and came up to him, putting her arms around his neck and linking her hands behind it. "Well, old-timer, you know what I think. But this one I think is your call. Has your disaster gotten to you? So you're too distracted to play? Or do you want to do something that'll get your mind off your troubles? At least for a little good while. I'll understand, either way. But this will be our last chance, though, you know."

He put his hands on her buttocks and squeezed. He managed a damaged smile, and as he leaned forward to kiss her he said, "Sure, let's give the old boy one last one for the road, the long lonely road, and a big hand for the little lady."

The next morning after they had seen the skyline of New York in the freshly polished by a still-chilly May sunrise, and tried futilely to put themselves in the attitude that immigrants must've taken on seeing the Statue of Liberty, Frances and David and Rutledge had a continental breakfast, exchanging hopes, sincere only on her part (hers was heartfelt), that living so close to each other as they did, they'd soon see each other again. Rutledge dawdled behind them, almost alone in the Grill, saying that he wanted "just one more cup of coffee," and then after they had gone below, took his checkbook out and made two out to Gregor and William for a thousand dollars each. Then he made out a third to Melissa for twenty-five hundred. He got up and went up the stairs to the unattended maitre d's desk; in a little while Gregor appeared. Rutledge handed him the checks. "Your two customary tens and her customary twenty-five percent, my friend. You'll see that she gets it, of course? As always, I appreciate your discretion."

"Of course, Mister Rutledge," Gregor said, bowing and accepting the checks. He smiled. "It's always a pleasure to see you again, sir. And always a pleasure to work with you, too. That charm of *yours* is a wonderful gift. À bientôt. May we see you again soon, in good health."